Dave Hill has been a journ
years, writing on family m
and popular culture. He l
and has six children. This
contacted via his weblog Temperama.

THE ADOPTION

DAVE HILL

headline
review

First published in 2006
by HEADLINE REVIEW

an imprint of HEADLINE BOOK PUBLISHING

1

0 7553 2632 6 (ISBN-10)
9 780 7553 2632 7 (ISBN-13)

Typeset in Baskerville by Avon DataSet Ltd,
Bidford on Avon, Warwickshire

Printed and bound in Great Britain by
Clays Ltd, St Ives plc

HEADLINE BOOK PUBLISHING
A division of Hodder Headline
338 Euston Road
London NW1 3BH

www.reviewbooks.co.uk
www.hodderheadline.com

For my parents, Denis and Rosemary Hill

AUTHOR'S NOTE AND ACKNOWLEDGEMENTS

This novel is mostly set in a particular part of east London. However, the streets, schools, various buildings and public spaces described in it are entirely fictional.

I would like to thank my agent Sara Fisher; my editor Martin Fletcher, his assistant Jo Matthews, my publicist Lucy Ramsey and their colleagues at Headline; copy-editor Hazel Orme; the incomparable Sheila Fitzsimons and Alan Superdad.

PART I ONE WEEKEND

CHAPTER ONE FRIDAY

She felt a bit ashamed about the thing she planned to do. It wasn't a big secret, or even much of a deception, but it still made her feel dishonest – and that was something he had never been.

Where was he anyway?

She'd reached for him with warm toes and found him gone. But now the squeak of a vinyl floor gave him away. So, too, the scrape of a toothglass being returned to its holder. The edges of these sounds were dulled, which told her he had pulled the bathroom door closed behind him to avoid disturbing her. This helped her to believe that he still loved her – which was good because she still loved him. It also reassured her that he was sincere in contradicting her whenever she declared, in moments of wild honesty, that the hallmarks of her life were foolishness and failure, and that he deserved someone better.

More small sounds travelled up to her: planted footsteps and the plunk of the pull-switch putting out the light. She hugged up under the duvet, feigning sleep as he came back into their room. Was he staring at her and, if so, was her hair, the one visible part of her, falling gorgeously across the pillow? She hoped so, then chided herself for hoping so, then chided herself for her self-chiding. This clamour went on beneath the surface silence, which she broke only when she sensed he was about to leave.

'Good morning, Darren,' she whispered.

'Good morning, Jane,' he replied, and there was just a touch of tender mimicry.

'Where's my tea?' she asked.

'Still in its teabag.'

'What's it doing there?'

Darren paused. Jane curled up a little more tightly under the tog fourteen.

'Same things as the rest of us, I expect,' he said. 'Laughing, crying, dreaming, looking for love.'

Jane sat up, blinking. 'You're so *silly*,' she scolded.

'Yeah . . .' He added, with a mock sigh, 'It's my only talent, probably.'

'Please don't,' she begged. 'Please don't make fun of me.'

The central-heating pipes were clanking but the bedroom was still cold. From this Jane knew roughly what time it was, but glanced at the clock-radio anyway. Six eleven, said the red-lettered display. It did not say in addition, Friday, 25 January 2002, but that was OK with Jane because she had worked that out all by herself.

Darren was half-way out of the bedroom door. He smiled at Jane in soft apology and studied her through his glasses – his groovy glasses, Jane had always called them, because they weren't. She called her winter pyjamas groovy too, for the same reason. They were towelling-thick, mauve, and bought from Marks & Spencer, which she still found incredible even though for her, at forty-four, style now outranked discomfort less often. This was mostly a relief although, now and again, she feared there might be hidden costs.

'I'm sorry,' Darren said, 'but when I tell you you're perfect you say I'm just making it up.'

Jane's eyes were adjusting to the gloom. She took in Darren's appearance: his untidy brown hair and his long, bony body, the baggy suit; the loud, unsuitable tie, which hung, unknotted, from the open collar of his shirt. *Very* Darren Grice. '*You* are the perfect one, O husband,' she told him.

'Hmm,' he said. That was all. But Jane had detected clear signs of devotion, so a murmured 'Hmm' would do. Also, she saw distance, imperfectly concealed, and strain. She could tell that in his head Darren was already at his difficult morning meeting and now she felt bad that she had asked him to make tea, even though she'd been teasing – mostly.

Darren spoke again: 'You look lovely,' he said firmly.

'Oh, *do* I?' She snorted, knowing she had overdone the attempt at disbelief.

'And I'm sorry I woke you,' he added.

'That's OK. You didn't, really.'

'Yes, I did.'

They both fell quiet and were still. Together they had reached the understanding each required. It would bind them until they met again that evening.

'Tea, then,' Darren said, and turned to go.

'No, I'll get it.'

'I've got plenty of time.'

'Honestly, Darren, just get going . . .'

He walked back to the bed. She offered him her forehead, which he kissed. They touched cheeks. 'You smell of Aquafresh,' she said, 'you sexy beast.'

Darren waved on his way out; one of the comic-melancholic glove-puppet waves he'd been giving her since the May morning in 1978 when they'd woken up together for the first time. She waved back in the same way, then pictured him in her imagination as he went down the stairs and rooted for his coat and briefcase. Keys rattled as he unlocked and passed through the front door, closed it and headed off into the sludge-light of the Bow dawn.

'Jane looked at the clock again. Six twenty-three. The house was quiet but it wouldn't be for long.

She switched on the bedside lamp with its silken orange shade and bathed in the illusion of sunshine. The glow sustained her as she got up and walked a little stiffly to the chest of drawers she'd bought from a junk shop back in the days before all discarded furniture was rebranded retro or antique. She slid open the third drawer down, reached to the rear of a tangle of underwear and touched the Cellophane-sealed carton it concealed. Momentarily, she dithered: now quickly, or at leisure later? Later, she decided: a more meditative mood was required.

She closed the drawer, pantomime-padded to the landing, paused to listen outside the adjoining bedroom, heard nothing, then descended the short stairs to the bathroom. It was still steamy from Darren's shower. She used the toilet, washed, cleaned her teeth and confronted the misty mirror warily. 'Gorgeous hair!' she gushed, and poked out her tongue. It was a deeper brown than Darren's and infinitely more obedient. Even on bad days it fell straight to her shoulders like dark honey pouring from a jar. Despite the first threads of grey she still considered it her most attractive feature, and cherished it but, being Jane, she felt ambivalent about it too. From the rear she looked lovely, but what did people think when she turned round? It was an old-companion worry: she'd been tormenting herself with it since she was ten.

Back in the bedroom Jane dressed rapidly: comfortable jeans, slipper socks, old green cardigan over old black T-shirt.

Six fifty-two.

She pricked her ears. No waking-up sounds reached her from above, below or next door. She stole back to her underwear drawer. This time she drew out the carton. What a rip-off, she thought – twenty quid for something so flimsy and light! Yet she held it with reverence and read the directions for the thousandth time.

Once you have decided that you would like to have a baby, it's important to know when you are at your most fertile. These days occur around ovulation when an egg is released from the ovaries. Boots ovulation test allows you to identify these days by detecting the sharp rise, or surge, in the level of luteinising hormone that occurs 24–36 hours before ovulation. Making love in the 36-hour period after the surge has been detected should maximise your chance of becoming pregnant.

Jane thought: How I love that word 'surge'.

What had brought on this dire broodiness? There were a few obvious suspects: the reality sinking in that if she wanted a fourth baby after all she'd better get a move on; the gap left in her routine when Clyde began school; the speed with which Lorna and Eliot were growing up. It wasn't as though they didn't have space: there was the small room next door, which had junk and the computer in it. Just because the estate agent had called it a bedroom didn't mean it couldn't be one.

More recently, something else had occurred to her. Jane had begun to imagine catastrophes in which Darren, Lorna, Eliot and Clyde all perished while she was at home baking a cake or Hoovering: a motorway pile-up, maybe, or a plane crash preceded heartrendingly by a mobile phone call that lasted just long enough for everyone to say, 'I love you' and 'goodbye'. Of course, having another baby would not prevent this happening (although, in more melo-dramatic versions she at least had her newborn or maternal bump for comfort after she had listened to her loved ones' voices for the last time). Contemplating the larceny of death brought home to her the preciousness of life. And it helped her to combat the sliding-away feeling that had disabled her too often recently; the damning hindsight judgement she inflicted on herself for never having become whatever she might have been.

Jane was a pianist: a good one. She owed this to her father, Jeffrey, a professor of botany, and her mother, Dorothy, a respected social historian who had encouraged her and her elder sister, Julia, to make music from the earliest age. Their home had been a roomy old place in a village not far from Gravesend. It was the type of liberal intellectual household that played host endlessly to lady vegetarians in cavalry twills and bearded men in mustard ties, where the human condition was pondered, and where creativity was seen as a form of resistance to the tyranny of the machine age. Jeffrey painted landscapes in his spare time; Dorothy sang in a humanist choir. As a baby, Jane had been marched to Aldermaston to protest against the Bomb, and at eight she could sit at the family baby grand and lead gatherings of peaceniks through 'We Shall Overcome'.

A background of this kind, with its stress on liberty, was always going to limit the girls' options. Of the two on offer, the busy, serious Julia took the one that came most naturally to her, which was to bring salvation to the world. After reading history at Oxford she volunteered for a third-world charity and now ran an HIV clinic in Angola from which she dispatched upbeat monthly emails and returned twice a year to say how glad she was still to be a spinster. Jane had taken the other route to righteousness: artistic penury.

Not that she had ever failed to make some sort of living from the piano. It was just that it had never delivered quite the life she had, every so often, had in mind. There'd been an absence of direction, it now seemed, although for a long time that had seemed a virtue. After moving to London, where she completed a degree in music and English, she'd done session work, live work, from classical to pop, and she'd hung out a lot, especially when she'd been young and in the first flush of her relationship with Darren or else when drifting through those three footloose years when they had gone their separate ways with the idea of growing up, which was what they'd since settled on calling it when describing it to other people.

And then? Well, she'd got older. She'd stayed at home more. She'd depended increasingly on being a piano tutor, initially in schools teaching pupils ranging from half-feral to sweet, then more and more at home where she gave private lessons now to, among others, Maurice Pinder, a bumptious, semi-retired bachelor accountant who lived with his mother in Spitalfields. He had a lesson every Tuesday and Friday morning, except not this Friday for 'medical reasons' he had not disclosed. He was her longest-serving student and so stubbornly an oddball that Jane felt well balanced by comparison.

'Be grateful, Jane Ransome,' she would sometimes say, after Maurice had gone. As if what she had wasn't enough:

a good, good man like Darren, three healthy children and a nice, if rather shabby, home in east London near a tube station and Victoria Park. Occasionally, though, through the mists of rumination, Jane saw something that scared her: the longing for a fourth child represented her last chance to have wild wishes and beautiful dreams.

There was a small disturbance nearby. On Roadrunner legs it travelled to her side.

'Hello, Clyde.'

'Hello, Mummy.'

'How are you?'

'What day is it?'

'Friday.'

'Is it snowing?'

'No.'

'Why not?'

He was jogging on the spot. 'Do you need the toilet, Clyde?'

'Yes.'

'Then why don't you go?'

'*Why* isn't it snowing?'

'Because it doesn't always snow on Fridays.'

A debate took place behind Clyde's wide blue eyes. He needed to know something. He needed to wee. Which, though, did he need more urgently?

'Is January winter, though?' he asked.

'Yes. But it doesn't always snow in January either. Some winters it doesn't snow at all.'

There was an interlude while Clyde, six years old, took this on board. What his mother had just said went against all that he believed but, then, she was his mother. He did a cartoon spin and whizzed away. The creak of floorboards reached Jane from above: she watched the ceiling grimly.

Then she heard Clyde again, this time scampering to the ground floor. 'Clyde?' she called. 'Did you flush?'

No reply.

Jane set off after him, selecting the pace of her descent with care. Her footfall had to send the right message: I am resolute yet I am calm. 'Clyde? Clyde Grice! I want you to pull the flush!'

She shielded her eyes from the staircase walls. Ten years had passed since she and Darren had stripped them of layer upon layer of old wallpaper until they struck flaking plaster. They'd had to hire decorators to finish the job properly. Since then white-with-a-hint-of-green had morphed into off-white-with-a-smear-of-grey. The display of family photos she'd hung there had deteriorated too. The glass in two of the frames was cracked and there was a gap where another had been knocked down. Clyde had explained that Sonic the Hedgehog was to blame.

Jane reached the hall. Despite the slipper socks, cracked Victorian tilework chilled the soles of her feet. 'Clyde, I'm coming to tickle you!' She listened for a snigger, but no joy. Shivering, she moved to the front room. The light switch was a dimmer and she turned it on half-way.

'Clyde?'

Disorder greeted her reproachfully: miniature cars everywhere; the lid of a board game inverted on the floor with two corners trodden down; a rash of spots on the rug from spilled drinks. She scanned this landscape for boy pests, but her shortcomings were all that she could see. Next she went through to the kitchen – still no Clyde. She peered into the downstairs toilet – no Clyde. That left only the sitting room. He'd be wedged behind the piano, oozing glee.

'I wish you'd come out, Clyde,' she wailed theatrically,

and went into the room braced for Clyde's 'Boo!' It didn't come. Instead, before woodwormed french windows stood a taller boy wearing a long, blue dressing-gown – an image from a ghost story, thought Jane. He had one eye to the crack in the curtains.

'Eliot! You made me jump!'

He didn't acknowledge her.

She softened her voice. 'What are you looking at?'

His back remained to her.

'What is it, El?' She stepped closer, riskily. Pallid daylight had limped into the kitchen by now but this was a more shadowy space. She still couldn't see Clyde. He wasn't tucked behind the piano, after all, and she was anxious to prevent him breaking the bell-jar of tranquillity in which his older brother was encased.

'A fox,' said Eliot, quietly.

'What? In our garden?' Jane exclaimed, and took herself to task immediately. As if the fox could have been anywhere else.

'Hello, Mummy!' said Clyde. His face popped out from behind the edge of the curtain, the nearest to the party wall.

'Shut up, Clyde!' hissed Eliot.

'*You* shut up!'

Eliot let out a sad sigh. 'It's gone now! Why can't you keep quiet?'

'Mummy,' said Clyde, emerging. 'Mummy, have you ever seen a fox before?'

'Yes.'

'They're all crusty, aren't they?'

'Well, yes. They're wild, so they would be.'

'Are people wild?'

'Oh, I can think of one or two who are.'

'Because *we*'re animals, aren't we?'

'*You* might be,' said Eliot.

'No! No! We *all* are!' insisted Clyde. 'Fatima told me.'

Fatima was his teacher; young enough to be my daughter, thought Jane. 'We are in a way,' she said.

'In *what* way, Mummy?'

'We're part of the animal kingdom. Now, Eliot, you need to get ready for school.'

'The animal *kingdom*?' said Clyde, wonderingly.

'Yes, Clyde. I'll explain later. Do you want breakfast, Eliot? Or will you get dressed first?'

Eliot's secondary school was a tube ride and a walk away. He'd need to be going soon.

'Can I have *my* breakfast, Mum?' asked Clyde.

'Just hold on, Clyde. Eliot?'

For the first time since she'd walked in Eliot raised his face to Jane's. He was quite tall for eleven and Jane was five foot three so he didn't have to raise it far. His grey-blue eyes were wide and his cheeks were pale peaches, easily bruised. Here was the boy-child Jane was hassling to ride with hard-bitten users of the Central Line.

'Do you want to get dressed or have breakfast first?' Jane asked gently.

'I'll get dressed,' he said, and left.

'Mummy, what do foxes eat?' asked Clyde.

'Small boys,' Jane replied.

She headed back to the kitchen, Clyde pressed to her side.

'Do they eat cats?'

'I hope not, for Simba's sake.'

'Oh, yeah! Do they eat birds?'

'Clyde, will you please stop quizzing me?' She gave a private laugh. A fanciful snap-image had formed in her

13

mind, in which her insistent youngest was a door-stepping reporter and she a hunted celebrity. Where were her minders when she needed them?

She poured out his Coco Pops guiltily – rubbish cereal again. There were red grapes in the fridge. Maybe she could get him to eat some of those too. She passed him a bottle of milk, which he was now entrusted with pouring for himself. He did so without spilling it, then plunged his spoon into the bowl. Jane switched on Radio Three discreetly, a new habit whose significance she'd yet to settle on. Was it a sobering confirmation of her advancing age or a sign of flowering maturity?

She knew the music well: Johann Strauss. As she put a teabag into the pot she remembered Darren's daft remark: 'Laughing, crying, dreaming, looking for love.' He'd be half-way to work by now, spray-lashed on the M25 *en route* to the ragged inter-war Essex estate whose tenant-led renewal he was steering. Jane took waltzing steps to the bread-bin and took out two slices of Best of Both. As she put them in the toaster, Eliot came down in his uniform. It still retained a little of the cardboard stiffness it had had when it was new in September and he'd started at the clandestinely selective co-ed school he'd got into thanks to his keyboard skills – he preferred his Yamaha to the piano – and his parents' sweet-talking of the head. Eliot's clean white shirt was buttoned at the neck and his tie knotted in the regulation way. He was clean, handsome and fair. Protectiveness disarmed Jane like a swoon Would he really soon be all grime and bum fluff?

'How are you getting on, Clyde?' she asked.

'Finished!' he announced, letting his spoon clang into the empty bowl.

'Are you going to get dressed now?'

'Maybe.' Clyde scarpered.

Jane huffed, but in truth she didn't mind. She could now scrutinise Eliot properly. What was rippling under that bland passivity? Fear? Misery? Some deep-seated maternal-deficit need? Or maybe nothing, and all she was seeing was a projection of her insecurity.

'Marmalade on the toast?'

'Yes, please.'

His rucksack dangled from his hand. As he sat down at the table he lowered it to the floor, where it sagged sideways before settling.

'Have you got your PE kit?'

'It's in my bag.'

Jane considered asking him to prove it. In his far-away state it seemed only too possible that Eliot thought he'd packed it but had not. With a view to checking later, she played for time. 'Have you seen a fox out there before?'

'Oh, yeah! From my bedroom window. Lots of times!'

Jane knew that foxes had roamed their garden for years; their games and copulation had frequently caused disturbances in the night. But her pleasure in Eliot's animation made her forget she'd asked the question as a ploy. His joy drove his PE kit from her mind. 'I wonder where they go to in the day,' she said.

'They hide,' said Eliot. 'I found out on the Internet.'

The daytime doings of foxes kept them talking till the toast popped up. Jane spread it and gave it to him wrapped in a sheet of kitchen roll. 'You'd better get going,' she said.

He accepted the toast as he rose, hoisting his rucksack on to his shoulder. ''Bye, then,' he said.

Jane followed him as he tramped to the front door, becoming vigilant as she passed the stairs. Clyde and Lorna didn't seem to be fighting up there. Maybe they'd killed each other already.

Eliot had the front door open and was waiting patiently for his mother.

'Goodbye, good-looking,' said Jane, and kissed his temple. 'Have a good day,' she added.

'You too.'

She watched him walk to the end of the road, then give his usual farewell wave before disappearing from her view maybe, as Jane reflexively speculated each day, for the last time ever. She drew a fortifying breath and closed the door.

Now for Lorna. Lorna, who went to the local girls' school, a good school according to Ofsted, a 'crap school' according to someone who knew someone who knew someone Lorna knew, at least according to Lorna; Lorna who had already seized the initiative in her and her mother's now regular undeclared tussles for control of the morning mood. She had come downstairs and slipped into the kitchen while Jane's back had been turned and was already at the breadboard, buttering ostentatiously, parading her self-sufficiency. Similar recent manoeuvres reran through Jane's mind, rather as a person's whole life is said to race before their eyes when they know they're about to die. Her thirteen-year-old daughter had invaded her space. How could it be retaken peacefully, especially now that it had been planted with mines?

Contriving cheerfulness, Jane walked back loudly down the hall.

'Hello, Lorna,' she said. Well, it was a start.

'Hi-ya!' The returned greeting was light, one of the properties of artifice. It gave Jane two bad feelings: one arose from the knowledge that her own airiness was equally phoney, which made it harder to disapprove of Lorna's; the other came from her recognition that Lorna was really saying, 'Go away.'

'Have you got everything you need?' asked Jane, noticing that the radio was no longer on.

'Yes, thanks.'

'Are you sure?'

'Yes, thanks . . .'

Ah, that loaded brittleness – go away, *go away*, GO AWAY!

'What about your saxophone?'

'Oh. I don't need it.'

'But it's Friday.'

'I know.'

'And that's when your lesson is.'

'I know.'

Lorna was chopping cheese into shape now – meat-eating had lately been consigned to the realm of unspeakable savagery. Her tunnel task-immersion was as total as it was contrived. Nettled, Jane raised the stakes. 'But you need your saxophone on Fridays.'

'Mr Bell was ill yesterday.'

Mr Bell was the music teacher, who gave Lorna personal tuition after school – a big commitment on his part, given the fervour with which his colleagues fled the premises at the end of the week.

'Does that mean,' essayed Jane, 'that Mr Bell will still be ill today?'

'Yes. No. They told us he would be.'

'Who did?'

'The other teachers.'

Jane saw her dilemma in stark terms: was it better to force the issue or withdraw? She opted for cowardice, which in the heat of battle she was able to dignify as subtlety.

'Why don't you take it just in case?'

Lorna's Nickelodeon voice came into play. 'Mum, I don't *need* my saxophone. OK?' Like, this conversation is so over!

Wounded, Jane sighed and backed away. How best to hit back? How best to restore Radio Three? 'There are grapes in the fridge,' she remarked bitterly, and looked round for something she could do: something that was not a transparent, screamingly obvious excuse for staying in the room. There was a dried gravy splash on one of the sink-unit doors. She took a cloth, sank to her knees and began to rub. Lorna took a box of clingfilm from a drawer and tore off a generous piece. Let it stick to itself, prayed Jane. To no avail: Lorna wrapped her sandwich with a supercilious flourish.

Then she went for the grapes and took a fat fistful from the fridge. She moved quickly, haughtily, one of those look-at-me-I'm-busy modern girls of the type Jane recalled appearing in a TV documentary proselytising for the 'child-free'. She stood upright. 'Have you left any of those?' she asked.

Lorna swivelled, wrists limp with contrived surprise. 'No. Why?'

'Because Clyde wants some.'

'Oh?'

'Just a few, if you don't mind. He needs to eat more healthily.'

'So does he *actually* want some?' I mean, does *he* want some or do you just want him to want some?'

'What difference does it make?' asked Jane, who knew exactly what difference Lorna thought it made.

'Well, like, what's the point of leaving them if he isn't going to eat them?'

'Because I want to encourage him.'

'But he won't eat them, will he?'

'He might.' Jane felt the earth splitting beneath her. Lorna was doing it: sparks were jagging from her fingertips.

'Yeah, right,' replied the teenage witch. She looked at the bunch of grapes and thought about it. Disdainfully, she detached a modest sprig. 'Where shall I put them?'

'On the table, please. He'll be back down in a minute.'

Jane watched as the fruit was relinquished. Did this qualify as victory? Lorna stuffed her lunchbox into her rucksack, a cheap, canvas affair with a picture of Tinkerbell on it she had bought at a street market. Her long mousy hair had acquired purple streaks, which she'd put in at her friend Kazea's house the previous week. She'd seemed eager to hear Jane's opinion of them but, as Jane had noticed, this was not the same as seeking her blessing. She wore the sleeves of her school cardigan way down below her wrists so that even her fingers couldn't be seen. She yawned and said, 'He didn't flush the toilet, by the way.'

'OK,' said Jane, frantic for her to leave.

Lorna advanced upon her and looked down. ''Bye-ee!' she said.

''Bye-ee.'

'See you tomorrow, probably.'

'Tomorrow?'

'I'm staying at Kazea's tonight, remember?'

'Oh, yes. Silly me.'

'Don't worry,' Lorna breezed. 'I'll be going straight there after school.' She patted Tinkerbell. 'I've got everything I need.'

'Good for you,' said Jane, drily, as Lorna tossed her regal mane and left, leaving her mother to hunt for Clyde again.

* * *

19

The school run took thirty minutes. Clyde had hopped, skipped and prattled all the way there, requiring Jane to say, 'Oh, really?' and 'Amazing!' several times. She hadn't lingered in the playground because her near neighbour Maggie was there with her new baby, Nadine, in a pram.

When she got home Jane went upstairs and was just about to reach for the third drawer down again when the bedside phone rang. It's Maurice, she thought, to say he's coming this morning, after all. Or one of those automated telesales calls that reward your 'hello' with nothing. Yet she couldn't just ignore it – she was too hopeless an optimist.

'Hello.'

'Hello.' It was Darren.

'Hello. Is everything all right?'

'Yes. They were worried about "them ethnics".' He'd been chairing a tenants' forum, listening to 'local concerns'.

'Oh, no. How many of them?'

'The usual master-race intellectuals.'

'Was it difficult?'

'A bit. But now they've made a smell in public they'll calm down. What are you up to?'

'Nothing much.'

'Isn't Maurice coming soon?'

'He cancelled,' said Jane. 'I've a feeling he has a hospital appointment.'

'How much of him are they removing?'

'That's not very nice.'

'True.'

'My guess is it's piles.'

'That would explain a lot.' Darren had met Maurice only once. That had been more than enough. 'How did the kids go off?' he asked.

'OK. Lorna was a bit sniffy – as usual.'

'Oh dear . . .' He left it there.

'Well,' said Jane, 'I'd better be a housewife, I suppose.'

'I can count, you know,' said Darren.

'Pardon?'

'I can count. I have a calendar on my desk. I have a diary. Day fifteen, I make it. Am I close?'

'Close to what?'

'Oh, come on, Jane!'

'I expect so.'

'Don't you *know* so?'

'No, I don't.'

'What about those kits?'

'Kits?' She made her face all innocent, as if he could see as well as hear her.

'Yes,' Darren said. 'Remember? You have to wee on a stick.'

'Oh, *those*! I've given up on *those*!'

'Have you? Why?'

'Oh, I don't know. It makes it all too . . . clinical, somehow. If it happens, it happens.'

There was a moment's silence. Then Darren said, 'All right, then.'

Jane panicked: he sounded *far* too relaxed about it. 'Mind you,' she resumed, 'it is your birthday on Sunday. You wouldn't want the weekend to be a disappointment, would you?'

'You mean we wouldn't want all that sex to be for nothing.'

'Goodbye, Darren.'

'Goodbye.'

She hung up, smirking, then tore at the carton's Cellophane membrane. It crackled as it came away, making her feel rebellious, like a child eating crisps in a library. In the bathroom she did what Darren had described. Then she placed the testing stick on the floor under a towel so that she couldn't sit and stare at it. She consulted her watch, then removed it, washed her hands, dried them, looked at her watch again. Two and a half minutes to go. She took a long, deliberate walk all the way downstairs telling herself that, yes, she was still completely serious about doing this mad thing, then walked all the way up again.

The three minutes had now passed. The towel gave up its secret: identical thin red lines bisected both of the square white panels of the testing stick's rectangular window. Jane was surging and needed Darren urgently.

At twenty past seven that evening, Darren had given up the losing battle against his breath misting up the car windscreen. The view wasn't great anyway. He was at one end of an industrial side-street in Battersea, marvelling at how the redevelopers of London could squeeze a chi-chi residential conversion into virtually anywhere. Brute brickwork and shadows loomed on all sides and yet the tropical-plant-lined, security-guarded reception hall of the building where his old friend Ian had washed up was only fifty yards away. What lay in wait beyond this portal was a mystery, which Jane had not been eager to explore.

'Can't we get out of it?' she'd begged him when, a fortnight earlier, he'd told her about Ian's surprise email, the phone call that had followed and his acceptance of the dinner invitation.

'That might be tricky,' he'd replied.

'Do I *have* to come with you?'

'Jane, it'll be fine . . .'

'Why don't you just have a drink with him, like normal blokes do?'

'Because he wants to show us his new place and because he invited you too.'

They'd been sitting in the kitchen. It was after ten at night, but Darren had only just got home. His briefcase had lain flat on the table where he'd dumped it. Fixing his upward gaze on a convenient cornice cobweb he'd gently presented his defence: Ian might have mellowed; turning him down would have been rude; 'You're always saying we should go out more'; and the clincher, 'You might really like his girlfriend. You always said a good woman would sort him out.' Jane had listened tetchily, but by the end she'd given in. It was so awful, she'd complained: everything Darren had said had been so reasonable and true. Why couldn't she be that way too?

In the cold old family car Darren pulled his overcoat around him and balanced his mobile on his knee. On arriving he'd called Jane and learned that she was on her way. They'd planned this little rendezvous late in the afternoon during their second phone conversation of the day. Being explicit about it had been their way of tacitly agreeing that the night would end in deeper intimacy. That hunger. It stirred him. Yet the demands it would make worried him too. Sleep, he told himself – just drift off for a bit until she's here.

And he did drift. But only for a minute or two. The passenger door opened without warning. In jumped Jane. 'Hello, Darren!'

'Hello, Jane. I'm sorry.'

'Why?'

'I was asleep.'

'I'm not surprised! You must be *so* tired.' She leaned across the gearstick and kissed his cheek.

'Cold lips,' he said.

'Cold nose too!' She rubbed it with a gloved hand. 'Where's this place, then?' she asked.

'Further down on this side.'

'Have you had a look?'

'Just a quick one.'

'A quick one, eh? And?' She was all lit up. Darren hoped the next few hours wouldn't snuff her out.

'And?'

'Is it posh?' she asked.

'It is on the outside.'

Jane rubbed mist from the windscreen and squinted through the smeary space she'd made.

'You can't see it from here.' Darren felt groggy and touched his brow. Jane's smell revived him, though: Chanel, if he wasn't mistaken. She looked nice too, even though he could barely see her: black fake-fur coat, matching gloves and hat . . . the things he'd bought her for Christmas. 'Are you OK?' he asked.

'Yes. Thank you for making me take a cab.'

'Daft not to, really.' He'd urged her to treat herself. It had been a coded plea. Only four months had passed since 9/11 and edgy talk of dirty bombs exploding on the tube had only just begun to bore the media. Jane, though, had yet to become bored by her own fear.

'The driver asked me if I had a boyfriend,' she said.

'Did he, now?'

'And I said no.'

She kissed Darren again, this time on the mouth. He saw her pearl earrings and smelt the perfume more strongly. He saw, too, that she was wearing the bright red top he liked, the one that sat wide on her shoulders in a style whose name he'd forgotten.

'Shall we do it here?' she whispered, snaking an arm around his waist.

Darren looked at her soberly. 'I think he may have gone.'

'Who?' Jane was puzzled.

'The cab driver.'

'You *idiot*!' she told him warmly.

'Thanks.'

'Come on,' she said, jumping away from him again. 'Let's go!'

Two hours later dessert was on its way. Jane emptied another glass of wine. In her opinion – still a private one for the time being – stepping into Ian's new place had been like entering one of those snob glossies you killed time with while awaiting dentistry. It was a luxury apartment. The term itself had not been used, but Jane knew it was more than just a nice new flat because it had been constructed – or 'created', probably – within the reconditioned frame of a century-old former factory and because it felt as though no one lived there.

It had hardwood flooring throughout and you could see every square inch of it. In the stark naked living room a glass-topped coffee-table bore the weight of nothing save a *nouvelle*-ish bowl of blown-glass flowers. In Jane's increasingly tipsy and volatile imagination the blooms emitted the fragrance of fresh Styrofoam chips. That would be in keeping with the rest of the furnishings, which gave the same impression of having only just burst from their bubble wrap. Since the moment she'd walked in she'd had mixed feelings about this: she wished that her own home was as orderly and clean and she was also rather proud that it was not. The contradiction was troubling her, the company too. And now the conversation turned to sperm.

25

'You can sell anything online these days,' Ian was saying. 'You can sell your own semen if you want.'

'Can you?' said Darren, equably.

'Certainly can,' Kath confirmed.

'To a sperm bank, you mean?' Darren asked.

'No, no,' said Ian. 'You can do it through an online agency. A woman who wants to get pregnant can pick a potential father from the vendors on the agency's files. She pays her money and takes her choice. She doesn't meet him or anything. All he has to do is fill the flask.'

'Flask?' Darren asked.

'To keep it fresh,' said Ian.

'Courier delivery,' said Kath.

'How efficient,' observed Darren.

'It's only in the States at the moment,' said Ian, 'but you know what they say.'

He and Kath swapped a satisfied glance.

'It's heading this way,' Kath chimed in.

Ian smacked his lips, Mr Ironic Relish. 'Yep. Sure is.'

'A kind of cyber stud-farm service,' said Kath.

'Spunk-u-like,' Ian confirmed.

It had been an evening of surprises, none of which had done a lot for Jane. The first had been Kath. Jane hadn't known what to expect – someone thin and beaky, maybe, just like Ian.

Instead a booming blonde had greeted her. 'Lovely to meet you!' she'd announced, and engulfed both Jane and Darren in bear-hugs. She was tall, fairly fleshy, looked five years younger than Jane and was a vision of executive couture. Ian had stood behind her smugly.

'I used to know you, Jane Ransome,' he'd said slyly. 'I wonder if you've changed?'

'Hello, Ian,' Jane had replied, knowing that something

smarter was required. She'd felt mugged by Ian's greeting. He'd robbed her of a consoling certainty. For a long time, as Darren had reminded her, she had reasoned that he was only prickly and unnerving because he hadn't got a girlfriend. She'd buoyed herself with this view since the first time he'd nettled her when she'd stomped off to hide in Darren's student bed, leaving him and Ian to scavenge their own dog ends and carry on their trippy bickering about synapses and genes, and play their Burning Spear albums till dawn. 'He never *will* get a girlfriend either,' she'd told herself vindictively, hugging a greying pillow to her rage.

She'd held fast to this theory for the next twenty-five years. OK, during that time Ian had had relationships of sorts but never a *proper* one, never a *partnership* until Kath. And so, in her fecund, frisky optimism, Jane had arrived expecting the porcupine's quills to be shorn. How galling – how complete a failure of character reading – to grasp as the evening had progressed that Kath's loud, social embrace came with a set of sharp claws and, if anything, she had made Ian worse.

The second surprise had been the presence of a third couple, Ronald and Sophie. Ronald was stern, Dutch and in his mid-thirties, with lychee-coloured skin, tufty blond hair and a chubby physique that somehow added to his pomposity. In precision-built English he'd explained that he was an academic and an environmental activist. He was visiting London to 'make contacts' and 'exchange ideas'.

Sophie was one of his PhD students. This information had emerged during the aperitifs and mostly from Ronald who, as Jane had quickly noticed, spoke a great deal on Sophie's behalf. This was despite Sophie's accent conveying – in a low-key but unmistakable way – the ingrained sense of entitlement from which the smart parts of the home counties are made. She was pale, poised, petite and probably no more than twenty-three. Her reticence had left a vacuum in the small-talk ecosystem, which Jane had struggled not to fill with babble.

Seeking relief from sudden nerves and irritation, she had sipped her gin and tonic too quickly and become conscious of Ian and Kath retreating to their bloodless kitchen, whispering. She'd assumed they were fretting over the dinner. In fact, the food arrived a few minutes later, provided by hired caterers. Ian had complained that the rice hadn't been washed properly.

'Oh, Ronald, you're so *worthy*,' Kath was saying. 'So *what* if it's a sort of shopping? Isn't everything, these days?'

'That is what disturbs me,' Ronald said.

The connection between Kath and Ronald had come into focus for Jane just before everything else had blurred. Kath, she had gleaned, had recently moved on from whatever job she'd had with an advertising agency to specialise in the promotion of 'ethical' products for a marketing consultancy. As such she was one of the contacts Ronald had made. During a main course of hybrid Pacific Rim titbits, friction had grown between them. Environmentally friendly products were of interest to both but made them cynical in different ways: Ronald doubted their value; Kath did too, but didn't care.

'If it makes people feel virtuous to buy an oven cleaner that won't get their oven clean and won't save the planet, why should I spoil their fantasy? We all live in a fantasy world, don't we? We all want to feel good about ourselves even if we're not being good. Even you, Ronald, probably.'

'As a rule I try not to live in a fantasy world,' he had replied defensively, and glanced at Sophie for support. She had said nothing, her muteness glamorised by candlelight.

Kath had laughed, given Ronald a 'face it' shrug, then checked that her shirt cuffs were still neatly folded back.

From this point Jane had longed to go home. The tensions round the table were unsettling, even though they hadn't touched her directly. Her seating position made it worse. Kath had commandeered the table head to her left and Sophie was sitting to her right. She had worn the scarlet top to please Darren but the proximity of the two younger women made her neck feel exposed.

Ronald was at the far end of the table. Ian was sitting opposite her. Despite this, he'd hardly said anything to her so far: no change there, Jane had grumbled inwardly. He'd said plenty to Darren, though, who was to his left and diagonally opposite Jane. She'd noted that they were the only couple unable to hold hands or play footsie under the table, and doubted that this had occurred to him too.

She'd mouthed, 'Traitor,' at him. He'd mouthed, 'Sorry,' in reply but there was nothing he could do. A sense of isolation had encompassed Jane; that, and simmering fury.

Now the waitress cleared some debris from the table.

'It stinks, though, doesn't it?' said Jane.

Everyone looked at her. All but Darren appeared surprised to find her there, as though she had just materialised in an empty chair. It wasn't such an odd thing, really. Jane had been feeling much the same.

'Does it?' said Ian, sharply. 'Why?'

The spotlight had never really suited Jane. Her love of singing and playing, her adolescent singer-songwriter fantasies, had never made a true performer of her. She was fine in an ensemble, parked at the rear of a small stage. She could get a little kick from setting the evening mood in the corner of a bar and enjoy enigmatic anonymity. But that was quite enough limelight for her. Working a crowd was beyond her, and what held for music held for after-dinner argument too.

'It just stinks, Ian,' she said, sounding more angry than she'd meant to; more angry than she'd realised she felt.

'But why?' repeated Ian. 'Why does it stink?'

'Why?' she replied, as if the answer was obvious. In the way of panic measures, this time-buying riposte only made her situation worse.

'Yes – why, Jane? Why does it stink?' asked Kath.

'Yes, why?' repeated Ian.

Ian waited. Jane felt his eye – sights pin her down. He'd always had this way of speaking when he'd decided you were talking rubbish. It was a tone pretending to break it to you gently that you were dim and uninformed, and at the same time was overtly insincere. Jane had never been quite sure if Ian did it deliberately to patronise you, to make you feel more stupid still, or because he didn't have any social skills. Whichever, when he did it he acquired a slight lisp.

'*Yeth, why? Why doeth it thtink?*'

The lisp was a distraction. It made answering his question harder still.

'Well, it just seems wrong, that's all. Making money out of . . . well, creating life.'

'Why is that wrong?' persisted Ian.

'Because,' said Jane, 'there should be something *natural* about it.'

'But it is natural,' said Ian, 'because it's human beings co-operating in a transaction where one human needs something, another wants to provide it and someone else functions as the go-between. It's a trading arrangement driven by compatible self-interests. Surely it's merely a new form of the sort of co-operation that humans are programmed to engage in. What's not natural about that?'

He waited. Jane tried to stop thinking about the lisp. She said, 'I don't know, I . . .' The word 'love' rushed to her but she flinched from it: it would only make her look girlish and weak. 'It all seems so cold and emotionless,' she said, and glanced quickly around the table in the forlorn hope that someone would help her disappear again. She knew it couldn't be Darren: the chemistry of the occasion had somehow rendered their potential solidarity a liability – vulnerable to others' derision. Sophie? She was a cut-glass ornament, merciless in her passivity. Ronald? Jane saw only a waxwork frown.

Kath simply weighed in behind Ian. 'But there's nothing *emotional* about conventional sperm donation, is there?' she said, smiling hard to hang a veil before her scorn. 'It is, in fact, completely functional.'

'Is it?' said Jane. She was drowning.

'I suppose the difference is that donation is giving.' This came from Darren. He was throwing her a lifebelt.

'But is it?' countered Kath. 'Isn't it mostly male students making a bit of easy money? *They* get paid for it, you know – twenty pounds a shot or something, isn't it?'

'I'm afraid I don't know the going rate,' Darren replied.

'You haven't given of yourself, then?' Kath asked, lowering her lashes blatantly.

'Not even when I was a poor undergraduate in Peckham, I'm afraid.'

'What about you, Ian?'

'Me neither.'

'Well, well,' said Kath, shaking her head. 'I am *so* disappointed in you, boys!'

Her switch from browbeater to flirt had been effortless. It filled Jane with profound sickness and pain.

31

'What about IVF?' cried Ronald, suddenly. 'What about surrogate pregnancy? What is one to think about these things?'

The lines were loud and delivered much too late: a clumsy actor didn't know he'd missed his cue.

'I don't know, Ronald,' said Ian. 'Let's ask Jane.'

Ronald looked puzzled.

'She's the one who's had all the babies,' Ian explained.

Think of it as a lioness thing. That was Jane's usual way of making sense of the torrents of protective, defensive, visceral bloody rage that had carried her away with them every now and then. In that diner, for example, when some prissy-arsed proprietor had complained about the little Lorna putting her feet on the seats when just three tables away a gaggle of pissed singletons were free to flick hot fag ash everywhere. Again, she repeated Ian's words back to him, but this time as the prowling aggressor: '"*She's the one who's had all the babies.*" What the *fuck* is that supposed to mean?'

Her vehemence took her completely by surprise; it gave Ian a jolt too. 'No offence,' he muttered snottily.

'What do you mean, "no offence"?'

'He means "no offence",' said Kath. 'There's no need to get upset.'

'How many children do you have?' Ronald enquired, oblivious to the drama developing. He had his nose in his own script.

'Three,' said Jane, distractedly. Again, the glare of unwanted attention. Again, the heat of it melting her composure.

'That's enough for you, I expect,' Ronald said.

'Not necessarily, no.'

'Oh?'

'Four would be wonderful,' said Jane.

'Wonderful?' said Kath. 'I have to say it sounds like a nightmare to me.'

'Why do you have to?' asked Jane.

'I'm sorry?' Kath pushed back her hair and turned Jane's way.

'Why did you *have* to say that thing?'

Kath shrugged. 'I'm just making an observation.'

'Don't you think it might have been a bit insulting?'

'Well, no, actually . . .'

Even Ronald was feeling the *froideur* now – the caterers too: they delivered a sextet of pert fruit tartlets, then darted away. But the chilling atmosphere had quite the opposite effect on Sophie. As Jane would put it later, it proved there was life in the Ice Queen.

'But don't you think,' she observed, 'that people who have too many children are being quite selfish?'

Jane didn't know where to begin. Too many? How many was too many? What exactly did this ornament, this sugar-daddy-chaser, know about being unselfish? She was aware that her mouth had fallen open.

Darren came to her rescue. 'What do you mean by selfish?' he asked Sophie, tolerantly.

'Well, it's obvious, isn't it?' Sophie replied. 'There are too many people on the planet already. Even in this rich country they're a drain on resources. I mean, when you see some of these big families it's as if people haven't heard of contraception.' She shrugged and said no more, an eloquent device to convey her opinion that anybody present who required elaboration must be a fool.

Nobody spoke – except Ian.

'Are you insulted, Jane?' he asked.

'Of course I am, you – fucking sadist,' she replied.

'What?'

'Don't you patronise me, Ian.'

'Hey, whoa, come on everyone . . .' Darren brought his hands down firmly on the table. 'This is silly. Let's calm down.'

But it was already far too late for Jane. Tears were welling now, dissolving the lioness ire and betraying her wretched fragility. She looked across at Darren. 'I'm sorry,' she said, 'I can't take any more of this.' She pushed back her chair and left.

'Let's go, then,' Darren said.

He'd followed her down after ten minutes and was heading for the driver's side of the car, sorting through his keys with more absorption than he required.

'I'm sorry,' said Jane.

'It's OK.'

Darren climbed in behind the wheel and fired the ignition, closing communication. The engine started with a stammer. Darren revved and Jane saw in the wing-mirror a spectral plume of fumes pumping from the exhaust. Darren indicated and pulled out from the kerb, wiping the new mist from the windscreen at the same time. Jane logged the incongruities: he was impatient; he was too quiet; he was annoyed. Then she cowered in alarm as another car flew past them from the rear, hooter blaring.

'Shit!' breathed Darren. He wound down his window and stuck out his head, craning his neck for a clearer view.

Jane said nothing; this awfulness was all her fault. She said nothing for almost the whole journey, except when she phoned Melba, the babysitter, to ask if everything had been OK. Melba was the grown-up daughter of a schoolteacher friend. Yes, yes, Melba said, no probs at all. Clyde had watched *Toy Story* and fallen asleep in bed while she had read him a story. After that, she'd played cards with Eliot. 'I taught him poker,' she said. 'I hope that's all right.'

'Of course it is!' said Jane, although it wasn't. Why hadn't *she* thought of teaching Eliot poker? Not that she knew how to play.

Then Jane rang Kazea's mother. 'They're upstairs,' she was told. 'They're fine!' Upstairs was where they'd been when Jane had called at four thirty. She pictured Lorna and Kazea bunkered in some chat room, all flushed cheeks and online eyes.

She put away her phone. They were crossing Tower Bridge. 'Crap, isn't it?' she said.

'What is?'

'Everything.'

'No, it isn't.'

'Yes, it is.'

The Thames slunk by beneath them – that was how it looked to Jane, anyway. Soon they were moving through Whitechapel, with its mosque, its market bays and the London Hospital, home to the bones of the Elephant Man. This brought back a perturbing memory. She and Darren had been to see the film version of the Elephant Man's life just months before they'd decided to split up, with very different consequences for each. Darren had spent his three years as a volunteer aid worker in Guatemala. Jane had spent hers drifting, embarrassingly.

'Darren, let me out.'

'Why? What's up?'

'Please just let me out.'

'Are you going to be sick?'

'No . . .'

'OK, no offence.'

'Don't *you* start.'

'That wasn't . . . Look, I can't let you out here. It's too busy.'

They were through Whitechapel now. Soon they would turn off and into the matrix of their neighbourhood.

'Can't you just pull over here?'

'OK, OK!'

He swung the steering-wheel hard left and halted at the end of a bus stop. Jane took off her seatbelt.

'Jane, please. This is mad.'

His words had an imploring tone. It plucked at Jane's conscience: yes, this was mad, and the madness was mostly her own work. She couldn't yet admit it, though.

'I want to walk for a while, that's all.'

A bus drew up behind them, very close; the driver might have been making a point.

'I'm going,' said Jane, and released the door.

Darren, squinting, scanned the pavement ahead. A bunch of lads swaggered past, swearing. 'For God's sake, Jane . . .'

'Darren, just let me do this! Leave me alone!'

When Jane got out she walked off quickly. There was a turning to the left and she went down it, then right, fleeing the eyes-down making-up scene she knew she would share with Darren some time soon.

Off you go, then, till you're feeling better.

That was her mother talking, her words reverberating down tunnels of memory as they often did when Jane performed a walk-off. (It was always her mother who triggered them, never her father.) Her adolescent exits had been not from a car but from a room – her bedroom, the living room, the kitchen-dining room – and then from the house, and after that . . . well, a fast flounce down the road to her friend Olivia's, where she'd sit sniffing and railing and vowing not to go home ever again, or not for ages anyway, or, well, maybe in half an hour now that Olivia's mum had had a phone call and was making her way up the stairs.

She was heading along a street she didn't know. Strange, she thought, how you could live in a place for ten years and still stumble into somewhere completely unfamiliar only minutes from your own front door. It was a murky, grubby, narrow way: a mishmash of short terraces, shops and other small commercial premises. There was a cab office ahead. As she approached it, Jane saw it was that of the company she'd used to take her to Battersea. Spotting it cheered her a little. It fostered an illusion of belonging in a strip of foreign territory.

A firestorm of flashbacks had speeded and emboldened her when she'd first left the car. But now, beneath the swirl of her emotions, her homing signal was strengthening steadily.

She had two options: one was to admit she'd become ludicrously lost and go to the cab office; the other was to wander hopefully. Which type of fool would she rather feel?

There was a late-night minimarket by the cab office. Jane went in, needing a sheltered space in which to think. The shop was tiny, its stock lining three shadowy aisles. The lone assistant, a young man with Balkan cheekbones, was slumped behind his till, reading a foreign newspaper. From a corner-mounted TV, game-show hysteria seeped from his homeland, thanks to the satellite miracle. There were no other customers. Jane posed as a shopper, conscious of a security camera. Like an aesthete in an art gallery she stepped back to peruse jars of unfamiliar pickles, eager to convince the monitor.

She hadn't heard the door open again, but the voice got her attention.

'Hello.'

'Hello, boss.'

There was a pause for thought. Coins clinked in the customer's hand. 'I'll take these, please,' said the male voice. Till buttons bleeped and Jane kept mum in her dingy corridor.

'One twenty, please.'

'There you go.'

A new indecision seized Jane. Should she wait to be discovered or was she meant to jump out and cry, 'Boo'?

'See you, then.'

'OK, boss.'

The customer left. Jane emerged uncertainly like a kid who'd played hide and seek too successfully, causing the others to give up and go home. The shop assistant was standing up. Jane smiled at him without meeting his eyes.

'Back in a minute!' she trilled unconvincingly. She stepped outside and began to flap. Where was the car? She looked in panic to left and right. Only when Darren switched on the engine did she see that it was right in front of her. She opened the passenger door and got in. 'What did you buy?' she asked.

'Three Yorkies.'

'Who for?'

'The kids.'

'You didn't get one for me, then?'

'Or for me.'

He drove home wearily. Jane sat hunched with her coat wrapped chastely round her knees. 'I'll see you upstairs,' she said, when they got in. She was still hopeful that her luteinising surge would prevail over everything. But while

Darren was paying Melba and saying goodnight to her, washing up a few pieces of crockery, locking and bolting the doors, then checking that Clyde and Eliot were peacefully asleep, she vomited so violently and so despairingly that even if her raddled body had been willing to make love her saddened soul might not have stood for it.

CHAPTER TWO SATURDAY

'What's that on your T-shirt, Clyde?' asked Darren.

'I don't know,' said Clyde.

'You haven't even looked.'

'I have!'

Darren rolled with this reflex fib. 'Look,' he said. 'On the front – a big dark splodge.'

'Oh, yeah!' said Clyde.

'Jam,' said Darren. 'It must have fallen off your toast.'

'Oh, yeah!' Clyde said again, even more happily than the first time. The blob was at the bottom, near the hem. With a finger Clyde rubbed it lovingly.

'Come on,' said Darren. 'Let's get you changed.'

He was relieved to be locked into a cubicle. Although he was on easy chatting terms with several fellow parents who did swimming-lesson duty on Saturday mornings, he wasn't feeling sociable today. Clyde was pleased to be concealed by the cubicle too, although for different reasons. Standing on the bench seat, he kicked off his trainers, then held each foot aloft, inviting Darren to tug off his socks. The T-shirt followed then, more watchfully, his joggers and pants. 'Is the door locked, Daddy?'

'Yes. Here's your trunks.'

Darren had had only four hours' sleep. He'd been too wound up about Jane – *by* Jane, if he was honest – and the dinner-party débâcle to get his head down before one and work worries had disturbed him around five. He'd woken to Jane's soft snoring with his entire body clenched. Now pressure was building in his head. The poolside changing area had the fuggy, murky smell that no disinfectant seemed to purge. He felt hot in there, too. The contrast between the cold damp outside and the warmer damp within was working on the fault lines in his carefully constructed mood. A day of slow repair work lay before him. To complete it required him to sustain a steely serenity.

'Come on, Clyde, which leg first?'

Leading with the right, Clyde stepped quickly into one side of his bright red knee-length trunks, then the other. He hoisted his waistband high. Darren double-knotted the cord. 'Well done, Clyde.' He glanced at his watch. It was nine twenty-seven. Clyde's lesson began at half past. Darren reached down and lifted Clyde up. He closed his eyes as he hugged him, the better to feel those skinny arms round his shoulders and that whiffy morning breath on his neck. Earlier, in the quiet of the kitchen, with the others still asleep, Clyde had insisted there was time for jam-on-toast and, once it was eaten, no time for cleaning teeth. Darren, brain giddy and fatigued, had taken the path of least resistance.

'Ready now?' he murmured, in Clyde's ear.

'Yes, Daddee!' Clyde replied, robot-style.

'OK, let's go.'

He lowered his child to the ground and led him by the hand to the pool. Youngsters from the first lesson of the day shivered up to parents holding open towels. The instructor hailed her next group with a heartiness that made Darren feel cowed. He released Clyde's shoulders and watched him pit-patter towards the learning pool, goosebumps already forming on his skin. Darren marvelled at the readiness of young children to accept the cards life dealt them, then reflected that it should come as no surprise.

Darren was an orphan. His father, Norman Grice, had been the first of his parents to die, taken by a mystery illness on 4 December 1960, less than two months before Darren's third birthday. His mother Lillian Grice, *née* Coates, had followed Norman to their maker thirty years later, and eleven days after holding the newborn Eliot for the first and final time. At Clyde's age Darren had yet to grasp that most South Yorkshire families were not the lone-parent kind. The questioning had soon begun, though, and Darren learned from his mother that Norman had been a steel-mill worker's son, who'd risen to become a quantity surveyor. But though she answered all his questions she never encouraged him to ask more. Lillian was of a class and generation that saw no virtue in dragging out pain for inspection when, with a bit of effort, it could be concealed. Having no memory of his father had not disturbed Darren at the time or for many years after. What you've forgotten you don't miss, he'd long assumed.

Clyde edged into the lapping water. Darren was aware of two other men, about his age, looking on as their own children submerged. Both were regulars. A feature of these leisure-centre mornings was the number of fathers there. A New Dad love-in, Jane called it, Saturday *Guardians* wall to wall.

Every week Darren recalled this characterisation and usually it made him smile.

Keeping his head down, he returned to the changing cubicle and locked the door behind him. He sat and began to fold Clyde's clothes. There was no need to do this yet he felt he should appear, if only to himself, to be doing something legitimate in there. His *real* reason for being there was to ponder his wife's dear little deceits. That line she'd given him yesterday morning: 'Kits? Oh, *those*! I've given up on *those*.'

How sweet! Several times Darren had considered revealing to Jane that he knew how closely she was monitoring her cycle, and every time he had decided against. It wasn't that he feared her finding out. He didn't even feel bad for poking around in her underwear drawers because they'd always made a virtue of invading each other's privacy. Aha, so *that*'s what you're up to, is it? Oh, so *that*'s what you really think! And he knew what she'd be thinking now. She'd be beating herself up. Tears, loss of temper, throwing up: this was her customary build-up to a big bout of self-doubt. Knowing it was helping Darren to forgive her for last night's fury, yet he was not proud of it. He shouldn't need her to be weak before he could be magnanimous. For him, it polluted the sentiment.

Clyde's clothes were neat and tidy in the swimming bag now. Darren had hardly noticed himself do it. Chin in hands, he dug down a little deeper. He unearthed guilt but also true compassion. Ian had been an arsehole. Kath had, too. That other pair, Ronald and Sophie, had been as perceptive as pig iron. Should he have challenged them more forcefully? Should he have done more to rescue Jane? He took off his glasses, breathed on them and cleaned the lenses with his cuff. He should have found a way to save her. That was what she'd always needed him for.

They'd met at a punk night in a Clapham pub. As was the custom at the time the headline band – an art-school outfit called Pollock's Scab with a four-track DIY EP to its name – were supported by anyone eager to make a din. Among them had been a poet known as Gobb, whose free-form anti-verse on themes of psychosis, impotence and rusks had been augmented by an electronic keyboard backing, played by a small female wearing a flying cap and fingerless gloves. At one point Gobb attracted a hail of the substance from which he took his name and not all of it found its mark. His sputum-flecked accompanist had completed her contribution from beneath her instrument, picking out dole-queue death chords blind. Darren had felt strongly drawn to her, and when Gobb's set was over he'd slipped away from the group of fellow students he was with and sidled over to her at the bar. 'You were very good,' he'd said.

She was sipping a glass of Guinness miserably. 'Very stupid,' she'd replied.

'Oh, do you think so?'

'He's mad, isn't he?' she said.

'Who is?'

'The poet.' She'd nodded across the smoke-fugged bar. Gobb had been leaning against the cigarette machine doing an interview with a fanzine. Judging by his volume and animation it might have been a reprise of his show. 'I only did it as a favour. He's on my English course. Hello, by the way.'

'Hello. I'm Darren.'

'Darren. That's a groovy name.'

'Oh, do you think so?'

'That's twice you've said that.'

She'd removed the flying cap and looked up at him with kohl-blacked eyes. Her hair was tied back with a big bow. Darren had liked that, and her cute nose. She was quite good-looking, he'd thought. Better-looking than he was. Still, he knew how to nurture fondness in a girl.

'Does it make me a bad person?'

'No. On the whole I don't think so.'

'That's very nice of you,' he'd said.

'Groovy glasses too,' she'd replied.

'Compulsory for neuroscientists,' he'd said.

'I'll bet you say that to all the girls.'

They still reminisced about this scene, sometimes as an aspect of foreplay.

'What was it you liked about me first?'

'You were so sweet and sexy.'

'But I was all covered with spit!'

'Details, details . . .'

Darren, though, had long since speculated that some corner of his subconscious had spotted and, even then, been drawn to the stuff her quirky prettiness and sense of humour belied: neediness and fragility – the weaknesses that made him feel strong.

He sighed. Someone tried the cubicle door. He glimpsed a child's trainer in the gap at the bottom. He heard the adjoining door open and the child go in. Feeling furtive now, Darren stood up, slung the coats over an arm, the swimming-bag over a shoulder and walked rapidly towards the exit. Stepping outside, preoccupied, he was caught napping by the alarm calls of the street. A bus dragged itself from the kerb in a rage of vibration and exhaust. Two women with buggies, whose path he was obstructing, pushed past him, giving him wake-up looks he failed to spot until it was too late to act on them. He shook himself and walked off in the direction he was facing. At the end of the block he turned into a quieter street, stopped, checked for potential muggers and took out his phone. He called home.

'Hello?' It was Eliot.

'Hello, Eliot.'

'Hello, Dad.'

'Sleep well?'

'Yeah, fine.'

Darren disliked his older son's use of the word 'fine'. It always sounded like some kind of cover-up.

'Good. I'm outside the swimming-pool. Is Mum awake?'

'Yeah. I think so.'

'Don't you know so?'

'Yeah . . . yeah, she's up.'

'Do you know what time it is?'

'Yeah.'

Darren's first impulse was to put this to the test – 'So, what time *is* it, then?' – but he resisted. 'Have you caught Simba?' he said instead.

'No.'

'Have you got his basket out?'

'Uh, not yet.'

'When is the appointment?'

'Ten thirty, I think.'

'You think?'

Silence. Wind whipped round the corner. Darren closed his eyes and tried to relocate his plain of Zen. Then Jane came on the line. 'Hello?'

'Hello.'

'Did you need me?'

Darren thought that one over. 'I'll always need you,' he said.

'I doubt it,' Jane replied.

'I see.'

'Has something happened?'

'No.'

46

'Why are you calling?'

'To see how you are.'

'I'm pretty crap. I've caught Simba, though.'

'Uh-huh. And his vaccination card?'

'And his vaccination card. I can be quite grown-up, actually.'

She's in her dressing-gown, thought Darren. Eliot's been sent for the basket. The cat is nowhere to be seen.

He said, 'Can you tell Eliot I'm sorry for sounding cross?'

'Oh. OK. *Are* you cross?'

'No. Just a bit frayed around the edges. How are you?'

'I'm all right, apart from my ruined marriage,' said Jane.

Darren found that he was heading back towards the leisure centre. It was a bad spot for reception. This meant that if he wanted he could curtail the conversation and let the network take the blame. Ignoring Jane's last remark he said, 'Are we still on for tonight?'

'On for what?'

'Going out.'

'Oh, I see. I expect so.'

'It's in the sideboard, by the way.'

'What is?'

'The vaccination card.'

'Thanks.'

'But you've already got it, haven't you?'

'Goodbye, Darren.'

'Goodbye.'

Darren put his phone back into his pocket. Ten minutes of Clyde's lesson remained. Next to the leisure centre was a café in which he sometimes killed time. He went in. As usual, most of his fellow patrons were elderly: grey-powered women who parked plastic shopping trolleys and sat in pairs, picking at cakes and sipping tea; lone whiskery males who looked up from unresponsive meat pies in the slim hope of finding better company. Darren paid at the counter for coffee and a cheese roll and took them to a corner table where he strove to salvage meaning from his gloom.

The café took him back in time. The waitresses were perky. The wooden furniture wasn't bolted down. These things recalled a place where his mother had sometimes taken him and his two older brothers, Graham and Scott, when they were boys. He recalled chips and skinless sausages with two slices of bread and margarine; a fancy glass bowl of raspberry ripple ice-cream with a wafer wedged rakishly on the top. Lillian's sister, Auntie Joyce, and her electrician husband, Uncle Bill, were frequently there too, with their children Kevin and Tina. At the end there'd be a polite wrangle over the bill, which Auntie Joyce always insisted that Uncle Bill should pay.

The hidden meanings of these exchanges, their well-meant exposure of his mother's diminished means, had been lost on Darren at the time. He had concluded in long hindsight that he'd gone through his whole childhood and early adult life with little or no awareness of being deprived in any way. Materially, the family had got by. Norman had made reasonable life-insurance provision and Lillian, a butcher's daughter with typing skills and a tidy mind, had taken a job as secretary to the headteacher at the primary school her sons went to. Even at secondary school, where he, with all his peers, learned by social osmosis that economic status could be divined in the shininess of a blazer's elbow or the frayed collar of a shirt, he'd never felt he wanted for anything. And he was the bright spark of the family. He'd thrived in the science subjects and his cheeky wit had kept bullies at bay. University had followed – a big adventure down south such as his brothers had never contemplated. They had his mother to take care of, anyway.

Not until his parents were reunited beneath the earth of Doncaster did Darren begin to dwell on his upbringing and brood about how much had passed him by. In fact, he thought about it more and more. Sometimes he obsessed about what might be revealed if memories of his infant past could be recovered like lost computer files. Would they give form and animation to a phantom dad who had lived obscurely in his subconscious for decades, or was that just a psychobabble fantasy? Mostly, though, he thought about Lillian.

'Well, this is a weepie scene,' she had observed to her latest grandchild, as she'd cradled him in her nursing-home bed, giving a closing demonstration of the jokey fatalism in which she'd specialised. It hadn't missed her notice that her impending demise was nicely timed. Darren and Jane had just bought their house. With Eliot on the way they'd needed more space than was available in their rented flat and the end of the eighties heralded good times for first-time buyers. Darren's inheritance wouldn't be huge – a one-third share of the value of the old family home – but knowing it was coming had enabled him and Jane to raise their sights to a shabby old property with scope for a loft conversion and french windows containing the original stained glass, or a half-decent facsimile. They and Lorna had taken residence in April 1990. Eliot had joined them in early May, with half of the tea chests yet to be unpacked. Lillian had left them at the end of June.

It was nearly ten o'clock. Darren got up and left the café with his coffee barely supped and most of the cheese roll in his hand. He had to get his act together and be strong. There was Clyde to towel down and a night of romance to be had with Jane. Making a fourth baby together: he knew all the reasons why it was a bad idea but none had yet doused Jane's desire. Darren was pretty scared: scared for Jane and scared for any potential infant. But the thought of Jane's unhappiness scared him most.

They left the house together shortly after five. The winter dusk enclosed them, recalling for Jane a childhood sense of injustice that this should happen when it was still afternoon. She struggled to shake this off, and a scarier feeling too. 'Happy birthday,' she said to Darren.

'Thank you.'

'For tomorrow.'

'Thanks again.'

Jane removed a glove and pushed her bare right hand into Darren's coat pocket. There, his fingers made a warm purse round hers.

'I'm terrified,' she said.

'I know.'

Jane hadn't ventured once on to the underground system since the twin towers were attacked and she was horrified by her cowardice. Every weekday she sent Eliot to the place where she envisaged her own suffocating end, yet didn't dare go there herself. This evening, though, she'd vowed to overcome the drag effect of fear. She owed Darren for the night before, and one way to pay the debt was to be brave.

They walked quietly for a while, through puffs of their own vapourising breath. Jane tried to put some streetwise spring into her stride. It did not come easily. Her mid-winter Saturdays had usually drifted into snoozy domesticity by the time the light had gone. 'I haven't dressed up much,' she remarked pre-emptively.

'Neither have I.'

'It doesn't matter, does it?'

'Of course not.'

There hadn't been much time for grooming anyway. Jane had returned home from the vet with Eliot, her helper, and an inoculated Simba. Her mother, Dorothy, had arrived soon after, having made her way up from Kent by train and bus as usual. She was bearing baggage of two kinds: one was her weekend holdall; the other appeared to be a prepared statement. 'I'm sorry about your father, Jane,' she'd said.

'That's all right.' Jane was surprised. She'd already known he wasn't coming. Like her, he sometimes wanted to be alone.

'He's got things to do in the garden.'

'In January?' said Jane. She hoped this comment hadn't revealed her ignorance. Her own garden was a source of perennial mystery to her. What was she supposed to cut back when? How could she turn it into an enclave of delight?

'He says he's got to patch the summerhouse.'

'Patch it?'

'Fix the roof. It's leaking. So he says.'

The doubting caveats weren't laboured but Jane noticed them anyway. She was primed for danger signs. Her father, Jeffrey, had had a stroke back in the spring. It wasn't catastrophic but it had hit him hard enough to lay him up for a few weeks and force him, for the first time in his life, to submit to a pharmaceutical regime. At first, this had furnished him with a rewarding new obsession: as a scientist, he'd researched all the drugs he'd been put on; as an anti-corporatist, he'd researched the companies that made them and been gratifyingly appalled. More recently, though, Jane had detected a longer-term impact on the dynamics of her parents' relationship. Jeffrey had become a man in need of care who disliked being cared for. Dorothy had had to become his carer. Something was bound to give, and Jane sensed she would be told soon what it was. Not until Sunday, though, she had decided, taking the holdall from Dorothy and changing the subject to Julia and her latest email, the usual hearty missive about landmines, corruption and poverty.

This had kept them going while Eliot had comforted the cat. Then Darren and Clyde had returned from swimming and everyone had eaten something on toast. After that, Jane and Darren had felt their way towards reconciliation under the cover of muddled multi-tasking: eye-contact beside the tumble-dryer; swapped civilities about bank balances and baked beans. She'd stuck out her tongue at him when they'd met by chance on the landing. He'd grinned. After that, Jane had briefed Dorothy about the evening: a chicken casserole was defrosting for dinner; Eliot would be happy on the computer; Clyde ought to be tired but that wouldn't mean he'd fall asleep; Lorna had promised to be back by four.

In the event, of course, Lorna had been late. She'd let herself into the hall at four forty-eight with shoulders slumped and skin like whey. 'Hi-ya!' she'd said to Jane.

'How are you?'

'Yeah, fine. Sorry I'm late.'

'Never mind. How was Kazea's?'

'Yeah, fine too.'

Going out: what an effort it required.

As she walked with Darren, Jane became immersed in reliving this exchange with Lorna. Darren whispered, 'You're talking to yourself.'

'I'm a madwoman. I've always told you so.'

Mile End tube station was coming into view.

'I'll get the tickets,' Darren said.

Jane nodded, gearing up to face the void. Standing like a frightened fawn at her husband's side she was reminded of what boys had required from girls when she'd first tried the dating game: decorative passivity – until, that was, the lights went down. This recollection reacted with her nerves and the compound bubbled up as mirth.

'What's so funny?' Darren asked, as he ushered her through the barrier.

'Nothing. Just hysteria.'

The escalator plunged them to the platform. Jane's heart drummed. When the gas hit, would she know? Would they be crushed in the frenzy to escape? Would Darren wait for her even though she'd scream to him to save himself? A westbound train arrived. Darren helped her aboard, and she clung on gladly to his gallantry. They found a pair of seats together and the doors slid shut, leaving an old man beached upon the platform. Jane signalled sympathy to him with her eyes. The train, indifferent, burrowed towards Bethnal Green.

'Talk to me,' said Jane.

Darren pulled a rolled-up *Time Out* from his inside pocket and folded back the film-reviews page. 'How about *Iris*?' he said.

Jane made big eyes at him. 'A film about a woman getting Alzheimer's! Oh, Darren! You sure know how to please a lady!'

Darren made eyes back. 'All the reviews suggest it's a mature and moving film about a love that endures through everything.'

'Are you trying to tell me something?'

'Yes.'

'I see.'

She sank back into her seat and waited. At least they'd die together, which was nice. They talked films a little more as the stations came and went: Mile End, Bethnal Green, Liverpool Street, Bank, St Paul's, Chancery Lane, Holborn. When the train clattered into Tottenham Court Road, Darren rose. 'That's settled, then,' he said. '*Iris* it is.'

It wasn't settled but Jane didn't care. She rode up to Oxford Street elated at still being alive. The West End was at its least alluring: the New Year sales were flagging and the Christmas lights were gone. Yet heading into Soho still gave them a thrill. They linked arms, close and tight, and walked into the big picture of the night.

During the trailers they played a making-up game. It began when Darren confiscated the Maltesers they'd bought on the way in, telling Jane she didn't deserve any. It continued with her snatching them back just as the film began and popping one in a lewd manner whenever Kate Winslet was in the nude.

Afterwards they found a bar and sat at a tiny corner table. They looked past each other at their fellow patrons, an agglomeration of fun-seekers. Neither Jane nor Darren felt quite right in this setting, but they kept working hard at being on the town. Their knees touched and they hung on to their bottled beers.

'So, what did you think?' asked Jane.

'I liked it,' Darren replied.

'Why?'

'Hmm. Well, it was tender. It was touching. The acting was very good.'

'Which acting?'

'Judi Dench. Jim Broadbent, isn't it? All of them were excellent.'

Jane sipped her beer and said, 'She's gorgeous, isn't she?'

'Who is?' Darren looked round.

'You know who I mean. Kate Winslet.'

'Is she?'

'Of *course* she is. She's stunning.'

Darren knitted his brow. 'Doesn't everyone say she's too fat?'

'Only crap blokes say that.'

'Yes, yes . . .' Darren nodded. 'You're right, she's very beautiful.'

'How beautiful?'

Darren pursed his lips. 'Not quite as beautiful as you.'

And Jane was feeling a bit beautiful. Darren had forgiven her and slowly she was forgiving herself. 'Thank you,' she said. 'That's very nice.'

They went quiet, both pleased to have arrived at a shared destination and happy to leave space for the other to lead the way to wherever they would go next. Darren took the lead. 'How did your mum seem?' he asked.

'Oh, working up to telling me something.'

'About your dad?'

'Yes. He's getting on Dodie's nerves I think.'

Dodie was her father's favoured diminutive of her mother's name. No one else had used it until Lorna became old enough to talk, whereupon Dorothy encouraged her to use it too. 'He rechristened me Dodie,' Dorothy had reminisced, one afternoon in April 1995, pressing Jeffrey's hand where it had rested, unresisting, on the table of a family-friendly restaurant in Clerkenwell. Two hours earlier Jane and Darren had got married – a simple register-office affair with Lorna, then six, as the sole bridesmaid, Eliot, approaching five, in a smart waistcoat at her side. The future Clyde was due in late October. Julia had been too busy to come. Her mother's story of her father laying claim to her had caused Jane to revise her view of her mum and dad. They might be exhausting eccentrics but they were also valiant allies.

For the first time, she'd felt like a grown-up in their presence. What had it meant that she had been in her mid-thirties yet the sensation had been such a novelty?

In the Soho watering-hole, Jane dwelt on this memory for what seemed like an hour. Then her attention strayed to her surroundings. It was loud in the pub. Every other accent seemed foreign. A young woman was wearing floral wellingtons.

Darren, speaking low, was saying, 'You're all far away again.'

'Yes,' said Jane, hurrying back to him. 'Yes, I was.'

'What's it like, this place you've been to?'

'Oh. Ridiculous.'

'Come on, don't say that.'

'Sorry.'

'And don't be sorry!'

'Sorry, I mean, you're right. I haven't done anything wrong.'

What she was thinking, though, as she had often thought lately, was that this was her problem: she was so sorry about such a lot of things. The apology she had been making implicitly about the previous night's rages ever since she had picked up the phone and lied about Simba's where-abouts had simply jumped to the head of a long queue.

'Shall we go?' said Darren. Once again his voice seemed to reach her from a distant cloud.

'Yes,' she said. 'I'd quite like a walk.'

'Are you hungry?'

'Not really,' she replied, then added, realising that he might want to eat, 'but I might be in a minute.

They were on their feet already and were soon pushing their way back on to the street. The pavement teemed with people going nowhere and everywhere, but it was still a release to breathe the outdoor air.

'Where are we going?' Darren asked.

'Oh, anywhere.'

He linked his arm through hers and she was glad to have him steer her, although she knew he wasn't sure where he was going. He stuck to the wider streets, pausing now and then to calculate, then pushing on, and soon enough they were away from all the thronging and into a square she vaguely knew but couldn't name and which was almost quiet. Their walking pace slowed accordingly.

'I told a lie,' she said.

Darren looked down at her. 'Oh, yeah?'

'About ovulating,' said Jane.

Darren affected puzzlement. 'I can't remember what you said.'

'I lied about doing a test,' Jane said. 'I did do one. I was about to do it when you rang yesterday morning – after your difficult meeting.'

'Oh, I *see*,' cooed Darren, and nodded to show he recalled.

'I'm as ripe as a fig,' Jane said flatly. 'At least, I was yesterday.'

'Yes, well,' Darren replied, 'as you'll remember I'd worked that out. And what about tonight?'

'Still might be.'

'Good.'

'Is it?'

He brought them both to a halt. 'Yes. Isn't it?'

She fashioned an expression to show hopeless indecision. 'I must be mad,' she said.

'Why do you say that?'

'Oh, come on, Darren! I'm forty-four years old. I ought to face the facts and get a dog instead.' Darren laughed and the change in his expression emphasised to Jane how tired it looked in repose. That was her fault too, of course. 'A sweet little puppy,' she went on. 'Something silly like a poodle or a Pekinese. I could dress it up in pink.'

'Nice little fluffy collar,' said Darren.

'White lace bootees.'

'Call it Fifi.'

'Or Trixie.'

'So it's definitely going to be a girl, then,' Darren said. 'And a nightclub entertainer, obviously.'

Jane withdrew from him a little. 'I gave myself away then, didn't I?'

And not for the first time. She'd done it straight after they'd begun trying nine cycles ago. It had been a hot July night, and when it was over they'd stayed entangled, savouring their slipperiness. She'd wedged his knee between her legs, making a joke of sealing herself up. 'We don't want her draining away, do we?' she'd whispered.

'Her?'

'Oh, I can always tell.'

'Already?'

'Trust me, I always know.'

The time that had passed since then had been characterised for Jane by rigid date-watching and regular patterns of lubricious highs and bloody lows. With each of the latter Jane had become more despairing and correspondingly more secretive about the intensity of her hunger. The white-lying had begun in the autumn: first, the fabrication of a dismissive attitude towards the ovulation kits ('They're so expensive'; 'If it happens, it happens'; 'It's not an exact science'), then the outright lying ('Oh, I've given up on them'), each stage accompanied by her heaping a bit more lingerie in front of the box, which, as a consequence, moved further to the rear.

Jane pulled her phone from her pocket, studied it and put it back again.

'Should we call Dodie?' Darren asked.

'I suppose one of us should.'

'Shall I do it?'

'Do you mind?'

Darren shook his head to show he was content and stopped walking to pat his pockets one by one. Jane waited, shivering a little, and blew on her interlaced fingers to warm them. She allowed her surroundings to make her pine: Charing Cross Road where, beneath the contemporary mainstream veneer, Jane saw the ghosts of a lost Bohemia she had never really got to know.

Darren had found his phone now and was speaking: 'Good . . . good . . . If you could check on him in a while, you know how restless he gets . . . And Eliot? . . . Yes . . . and how's your grandmother?'

So Lorna had answered.

'Oh, right! . . . No, no need to disturb her, not for something important like that . . .' He laughed, listened some more, then said, 'We're fine, thank you. Just talking and wandering . . . We're feeling very old indeed, thanks, Lorna . . .'

Jane searched for clues in Darren's face as he said goodbye and put away the phone. He was smiling privately.

'What's happening?' she asked.

'Well, Clyde's asleep. And Dodie's playing Sims with Eliot.'

'Sims! They haven't played that for a while.'

They linked arms and walked on again, still hazily, and unconsciously north. Jane found she was rather nostalgic for the first family of cyber-interactivity. She recalled buying the first ever Sims game for Lorna soon after it was released – can't have been more than two years ago. The fun the pair of them had had with it! Such dramas! Such catastrophes! Barely had you finished doing up your lounge when your kitchen burned down. No sooner had you got the baby to sleep than a burglar made off with the TV. And when the social workers or the bailiffs came to call, as they always did eventually, the Real Life mother and daughter would laugh, give in and sit discussing ear-piercing and high-heeled shoes.

'And what was Lorna doing?' she asked Darren.

'Supervising, I expect.'

'Being superior, you mean.'

'Let's just say knowing best.'

'It's so annoying, isn't it?'

'Oh, well. It's only temporary, I expect.'

'God, I hope so,' said Jane, and wondered if that was her problem: as her children's lives had moved on, hers had stood still. Instead she'd found Maurice Pinder and a supporting cast of shorter-term tutees and gradually the nest became the centre of her world without her having planned it. Now she was restless there but had no idea where to travel to instead.

'Last night was pretty awful, wasn't it?' she said.

'Well . . . ye-es.'

'Was it all my fault?'

'No. It was mine.'

'You aren't the one who threw a tantrum and stomped off.'

'No, but it was my idea to go in the first place.'

'Stomped off twice, in fact.'

'Oh, Jane, come *on* . . .'

His tone had been pleading, not irritated. It made his exhaustion clearer to her. She felt bad and said, 'Shall I do guilt tomorrow instead?'

'If you insist on doing it at all.' He rubbed the side of his face and yawned.

'What shall I do now, then?'

'How about letting me put my hands inside your coat?'

'Oh, well. I suppose.'

There was a small office doorway with no lights on behind the glass. Darren backed into it and Jane allowed him to pull her after him, holding her gently by the wrists. She unbuttoned her coat and pressed up to him as his arms encircled her. His hands settled on her shoulder blades, fingers spread. He held her very tight.

'We might get arrested,' she said.

'Why? Are you hoping I might do something indecent?'

'Yes.'

'Ripe as a fig, you said?'

'Yes.'

She buried her face in his chest. They turned the heads of passers-by as their sniggers grew into snorts and shakes. Jane fished for a tissue and wiped her nose. 'Sorry about this, darling,' she said, and dabbed a little at her eyes as well. 'Oh, fish,' she said. 'I knew this was going to happen.'

'Come on, come on,' Darren soothed.

'That bloody, snotty little Sophie cow.'

'Not the big blonde one, then?'

'Her too.'

'And my oldest friend.'

'Oh, I'm not selfish, am I? Wanting one more? Why is that selfish?'

'It isn't, it isn't.'

'It's so hard to explain,' said Jane. 'Sometimes I forget all about it. Then sometimes it's terrible. It *really* hurts. It's a physical pain.'

Darren produced another tissue. Jane accepted it, blew her nose, sniffed, blew it again and said, 'I'm so attractive when I'm like this, aren't I?'

'Yes,' said Darren, wondering if she'd noticed he meant it.

'I've been hiding from Maggie, you know.'

'What? Because of . . . I've forgotten her name.'

'Nadine. Yes, I've been avoiding her. It makes me so jealous.'

'Jane, Jane, Jane . . .'

'I'm so pathetic. I'm *forty-four* years old,' she repeated. 'Why can't I just be pleased with what I've got?'

'Because . . .' Darren began.

'You don't have to answer that,' said Jane. She knew what he would say: that babies are little packages of pure human potential, or something along those lines, which meant that not to want one was almost absurd. This had been his line from the very beginning, going right back to when they'd shared a housing co-op flat in Hackney and discussed having a child for the first time. It was, Jane had thought, a rather intellectual way of looking at something she felt entirely in her heart, body and soul, but she welcomed it for that. It anchored her, somehow.

The consequence was Lorna, arriving a few days late after a model pregnancy. As a newborn she'd been co-operative and complication-free, apart from a touch of jaundice early on. She'd slept in a Moses basket next to her parents' bed. Jane had liked that, and just as well, because they'd lacked the space to do anything else. They'd carried on being dissenting spirits until then in their close-coupled way, unimpressed by the *Zeitgeist* lust for conspicuous wealth and property. Jane was playing pub gigs and mini-festivals with a Latin jazz combo, wearing a flowered shirt and cruising with the burgeoning World Music scene. Darren was making a small post-graduate living in the foothills of academia and beginning to want to move on.

It couldn't last. The pleasant temporariness of an alternative lifestyle became an inconvenience and then a worry as Lorna's arrival had obliged them to stop living for a succession of moments and start imagining their future. They had also imagined Eliot, and before long he was on his way. Darren applied successfully for a job as an environmental regeneration officer with a local authority. His PhD had been on the effects of urban pollution on the functions of the brain. This, in combination with his time in Guatemala, had made him an oddly irresistible candidate, even though he had no experience in the field.

He bought a suit and got used to the alien concept of getting up and going to work at the same time every morning. Later he would joke that the day he and Jane sold out was 31 March 1990, when the London Poll Tax riot took place. Had the demonstration happened even a year earlier he was sure they'd have been there, joining the marchers as they rallied in Trafalgar Square, then hiding when the violence began. He'd been as keen to chant down Thatcher as almost anyone, even though he was a nerd biologist. Instead, though, come the day, he and the heavily pregnant Jane had weighed their options and gone to Allied Carpets, pushing Lorna in her buggy.

'Are we bourgeois now, then, boyfriend?' Jane had asked him, as they'd meandered round the showroom, visualising twist pile on the stairs.

'Is that the royal "we"?' he'd enquired.

She'd buffeted him with her belly: 'That's the last time I'll be having sex with *you*.'

They'd moved a few days later. When Eliot had arrived so soon after the removal men had gone away, sweet bedlam had ensued. Home-visiting midwives had had to pick their way past carpet-fitters and tea-chests. The house was a dear old musty dump, vacated by a pair of pensioners who were fleeing the big bad city for the sea. But to Jane it felt beautiful and huge: three proper bedrooms – four, if you counted the small room, as the estate agent had – two receptions, a kitchen you could move around in. Jane still felt lucky about it. But had she made the best of it? Of anything?

In the darkness of the doorway, Darren yawned.

'Don't yawn when I'm baring my soul!' scolded Jane, and pinched his chest, right next to a nipple.

'Ouch!' he said. 'I'm really sorry. I'm just so knackered. I can't help it.'

'You know,' Jane said, stuffing the soggy tissues into her pocket, 'after we finally had Clyde I really thought that would be it. I really, really thought that was enough children for me. I felt my breeding mission was accomplished.'

'Was that because he took so long to make?'

'I think that had something to do with it. My body seemed to be telling us something. Why has that changed?'

Darren yawned again.

'Come on, sexpot,' Jane said, heaving him back on to the pavement. 'I think I'd better get you home.'

It was half past eleven when they got in. The house was dark and quiet. Jane found her mother dozing on the sofa in the front room with a pillow behind her head and her knees tucked under her like a child. She wore a jumper over a pair of striped men's pyjamas and bedsocks that had a home-knitted look. A copy of Jung Chang's *Wild Swans* lay open, face down, next to them. On the floor stood a mug of cold herbal tea.

'Mummy? Mum?'

Dorothy spoke without opening her eyes. 'Hello, darling.'

'Is everything all right?'

'Yes. They went up a while ago.'

'I meant with you.'

'Oh, yes. No problems at all.'

Jane was uncertain if this reassurance encompassed her father. Had Dorothy rung him? she wondered. Yes, probably. And if there'd been something really wrong she would say so, surely. Jane watched her mother struggling to sit up. Yes, discussing Jeffrey would wait until the next day.

'Shall I sort the bed out for you, Mummy?'

'If you wouldn't mind, Jane, yes.'

Jane had expected a brisk declaration of independence in the form of a refusal: that would have been the usual thing. 'Just give me a minute, then.' She hastened upstairs. Fetching the spare bedding gave her an excuse to flee while her mother recovered her dignity. She'd looked so worn and weak.

On the main landing, Darren was listening at Clyde's door.

'Is he all right?' whispered Jane.

'A bit restless.'

'We don't want him waking.'

'No.'

Their collusion drew them into a small kiss. Jane went into their bedroom and lifted the spare bedding from the floor of their wardrobe. Before she took it downstairs she turned back her own bedcovers and smoothed the sheet beneath it, wishing it was cleaner but deciding they'd get over it. She clicked on the orange bedside light and, with Dorothy's duvet, sheet and pillow bundled in her arms, assessed the comfort of the love nest from the doorway. As she switched off the main light she saw that Darren had left his listening post. His voice, though, reached her from Clyde's bedside, not as words but as soothing ambience. He's dead on his feet, thought Jane. She would draw out of him the last gasps of his energy and with it all the anguish she'd caused him.

She went back down to Dorothy, who had pulled out the sofa-bed and sat perched on its edge like a tethered bird. She rose to help Jane spread the sheet, but stood back while her daughter bent to tuck it in.

'Will you be all right, Mummy?' whispered Jane, conscious of caring roles being reversed.

'Darling, I'll be fine.'

'Goodnight, then.'

'Goodnight.'

Jane faltered before departing. She was unsure if she and her mother should embrace. But Dorothy had already turned away, looking for a surface where she could place her spectacles, and the decision did not need to be made. Relieved, Jane climbed back up the stairs and, after checking that Eliot was sleeping peacefully, went to the bathroom to prepare. Maybe Darren would join her there and they would clean their teeth together, as they used to in their early days. She listened for him and when he didn't come the focus of her anticipation moved to the far side of their bedroom door. Maybe she would add a dab of perfume. Maybe she would leave some jewellery on.

This picture set her trembling pleasantly. But the sensation did not last for very long, only for the time it took her to walk the distance from the bathroom to Clyde's door. Darren's shoes were lying on the carpet by Clyde's bed. His body, fully clothed, was curled in a ball at Clyde's feet. She could have prodded and shaken him. He would have woken and said sorry, meant it very sincerely, then performed. But Jane wasn't looking for a performance. She was looking for omens about her destiny and wondering if she had just found one.

CHAPTER THREE SUNDAY

Lorna woke at ten to eight hoping, deliciously hoping, that at last she had found a best friend. How they had talked, Kazea and she! How they had walked, too! Up and down Oxford Street, in and out of H&M, Top Shop, Gap, trying on all sorts of things, even though the sales assistants looked down their noses at them, and even though Kazea said she could spot the store detectives a mile off, and they were *definitely* being watched. Kazea was looking for jeans but she didn't buy any. She'd said it was more fun helping Lorna choose her T-shirt, which they'd eventually bought from a big bazaar-type shop where they had Goth stuff and surf stuff and loads of really freaky shoes. The T-shirt was tight and pink and had a kitten on the front, and Lorna was wearing it now, all curled up in her bed, and thinking about the stuff that Kazea had said and the stuff she had said to Kazea.

The real talking and walking had begun after the shops. Kazea had led the way down Regent Street, which Lorna knew only from Monopoly but hadn't said so, and then through Piccadilly Circus, though Lorna hadn't realised this until Kazea had mentioned it later. Trafalgar Square was next and they'd both climbed up on the lions, then chased the pigeons, flapping their arms and screaming, making the tourists stare.

Tourists: sad or what?

It was in a nearby McDonald's, where they'd had milkshakes and fries and looked on in a superior fashion from their high-stool counter seats at everybody else eating death-burgers and heading, Kazea said, for only, like, *guaranteed bowel disease*, that Lorna had asked Kazea about her dad.

'He's a bastard,' Kazea had said.

'Oh. Why? What happened?'

'He was, like, really, really nasty to my mum.'

This had begged so many more questions that Lorna hadn't known where to begin or, more worryingly, how. She'd only known Kazea since September when Kazea had started at Lorna's school. As all new girls must, she'd had to feel her way at first, working out which peer group she belonged to. Lorna had observed the process uneasily. Kazea had all the marks of potential high popularity: thinness, a desirable, caramel-coloured prettiness and just the right kind of humorous self-effacement to ensure that her unusual name was judged interesting rather than pretentious. By comparison Lorna Grice felt rather plain.

Then Fate drew them together. A humanities project about sustainable farming led each to discover the other's firm belief that vegetarianism could save the world. This common moral platform broadened rapidly. Lorna and Kazea agreed, among other things, that PE, RE and PSHCE were completely pointless subjects, that school uniform was quite a sensible thing because without it certain people would 'go over the top' and that smoking was a 'stupid' thing to do. They moved on to agreeing that tattoos were only cool if they were small and discreet and, in a hot flush of confession over their meat-free packed lunches, that it was better to wait to Do It until you found someone you loved.

The first sleepover took place in December, offering Lorna ample time to worship Kazea's mum. Her name was Sinead and, to Lorna, she seemed shockingly young. Sinead was a jewellery designer who wore her blonde hair in ribbons and braids. She had a stud in her nose and a tummy as flat as her daughter's, which she showed to the world with the same confidence. She said, 'Hi-yah!' and 'Yeah, fine!' She was a Cool Mum, unlike some mums Lorna could mention. But where was Kazea's dad? It seemed clear that he didn't live in their neat, clean second-floor flat – a flat! Wow! – yet his absence was not remarked on. As such it became a Great Unanswered Question in Lorna's mind, and there was only so long it could be ignored.

'So,' Lorna had said, looking tentatively at Kazea across the globalised fast-food products both so thoroughly despised, 'don't you ever see him, then? Your dad?'

'No. Not any more.'

Kazea's brown eyes became quite hard.

'I don't mean to be nosy . . .' Lorna began, suddenly fearful.

'Oh, it's OK. He left my mum when I was ten. I used to see him a bit at first, but not any more. No way.'

'What happened?'

'He was just a bastard to my mum. I don't know too much about it. He's gone back to France now and good riddance.' That seemed to close the subject. But Kazea opened up another front. 'Anyway, what are your parents like?' she asked.

'God, I don't know,' Lorna had said reflexively. 'They're

just a bit boring, really.' She knew this wasn't nearly good enough. She was intimidated by Kazea's vitriol towards her father and the sheer *glamour* of her lone-parent plight. She needed a grievance, a wound, something to maintain the precious empathy, which seemed fragile now. She'd reached for the first thing that came to hand. 'They're just desperate to have another baby,' she'd said, working a little moan into her tone. 'God knows why.'

'Well, yeah. How old is your little brother?'

'Six.'

'And how old are your parents?'

'Forty-four. Well, my mum is already and my dad is on Sunday.'

'*Forty-four?* That's *really* pushing it!'

'Tell me about it,' Lorna had agreed, surprising herself with the phrase, which she had never used before, only heard from the mouths of harder girls. Not until later, as they'd sashayed together across Hungerford Bridge, had it dawned on Lorna that she'd dug herself into a hole.

'So do they, like, talk about having another baby?' Kazea had asked, returning to the theme out of the blue.

'Well, yeah.'

This was totally untrue. The subject had never been mentioned in Lorna's presence. Her insight into her parents' procreation ambitions had been gained by wholly ignoble means.

Once you have decided that you would like to have a baby, it's important to know when you are at your most fertile ... Making love in the 36-hour period after the surge has been detected should maximise your chance of becoming pregnant.

'The surge' – really gross! And that underwear the box was tucked behind – all red and lacy. Tacky, or what?

These were the sentiments Lorna had coached herself to express in the pious privacy of her own head. They were fig-leaf feelings, though, and no real protection against her true emotions, a keening blend of sorrow and shame.

Still, she'd bought Darren a birthday present: a Superman stress ball. Which reminded her – she hadn't wrapped it yet.

Forgetting Kazea for five minutes, Lorna got out of bed and retrieved the present from her Tinkerbell rucksack. Opening a desk drawer she took out a sheet of silvery striped paper and a roll of tape. She was about to get to work when she paused. Footsteps were coming very softly up the stairs. On her door Lorna had a homemade sign, saying, 'WARNING!; BRAT-FREE ZONE!', but compliance with the ordinance was patchy.

'Who is it?' she called sharply, although the delicate tread of her would-be visitor gave her a fair idea. There was no reply to her question, only a meek knock at the door.

'Eliot, is it you?'

The door opened and Eliot stepped through, wearing his dressing-gown over his pyjamas. His fair hair was sticking up and the corners of his mouth were half turned down. He said nothing, simply looked at his sister like an attractive puppy needing a good home.

'Hello, handsome,' she said.

'Hello.'

'What are you after?'

He shrugged. 'Nothing.'

Lorna had a mental list of people she liked. It had begun to shorten lately, but Eliot's name was still there.

'I'm just about to wrap Dad's present,' she said, very businesslike.

'Oh.'

'Have you done yours?'

'No.' The word emerged slightly on the back foot,

'You have got him something, haven't you?'

'Yeah,' said Eliot, defensively. 'Oh, yeah.'

'You can come up here and wrap it, if you like.'

'Uh. OK. Yeah.'

'Uh. OK. Yeah.'

'Shut up!' said Eliot, with a smile.

'You boys, I don't know,' tutted Lorna. 'You're not very communicative, are you?'

Eliot didn't speak.

'See what I mean?' Lorna said.

Eliot declined to rise to this. He watched his sister cut the paper to fit the cube-shaped box the Superman stressball was packed in, then looked round her room, intrigued. A poster on the wall said, 'Meat Is Murder'. There were clothes strewn everywhere, including underclothes, which other older sisters might have concealed from younger brothers, and other younger brothers would have felt awkward to see. Her saxophone stood in its stand. Her shelves held a stack of CDs and a compact music system from which, at low volume, seeped winsome female warbling. Eliot did not know the name of the singer but he liked the sound. He also liked it that Lorna's collection of nail paints was too big to fit into the drawer of the Ikea storage box she kept them in so the little bottles stuck out of the top. He liked it that Lorna sometimes let him look at her young women's magazines, with their lifestyle quizzes and problem pages. They were boring, but it was nice when Lorna teased him for reading them.

'Do you think he'll like it?' Lorna asked him.

Eliot shrugged. 'Yeah.'

'It's a thing you squeeze to relieve stress,' Lorna explained, adding knowledgeably, 'He's been under a lot of stress lately.'

Eliot hadn't noticed this, but he nodded in agreement and kept listening as Lorna carried on.

'I got it yesterday in town, when I was out with Kazea. It's *so* cool,' she declared, though actually she was thinking *Kazea* is so cool, and *I*'m so cool for being friends with Kazea!

'I'll bring her round some time so you can meet her,' Lorna went on. 'She hasn't got a little brother, or any brothers *or* sisters. In fact, she's only got her mum . . .'

She'd almost finished wrapping Darren's present. She fixed the final piece of Sellotape and admired the results for longer than she really thought they justified. She was, in fact, leaving a space for Eliot to ask her about Kazea's dad. But he didn't. He just stood there. So Lorna said, 'She doesn't see her dad any more.'

Eliot still said nothing, so Lorna looked up at him. He was frowning very hard and shook his head as if trying to dislodge something wedged in it.

'Are you all right?' Lorna asked him.

'Oh, yeah, yeah. Just thinking about something.'

'Like what?'

'Nothing much. Don't worry.'

'Strange boy,' said Lorna, fondly. 'Are you going to get your present for Dad, then?'

'OK.'

Eliot made his way back down the narrow stairs. These were uncarpeted and he took pride in being able to negotiate them almost silently. On the main landing he stopped and listened. Still no sounds came from the two half-open doors: those to his parents' bedroom and to Clyde's. He knew his mother was awake. He had already eavesdropped on her talking with Dodie in the kitchen, but he'd been unable to make out what they were saying: they'd been speaking in the hushed, agitated way that meant the subject matter was unsuitable for children and that Darren probably wasn't with them.

Now Eliot peeped round his parents' bedroom door, expecting to find his father sleeping there. Instead, sprawled sideways across the bed, lay Clyde, fast asleep. Eliot eyed his brother critically for a moment, then withdrew and stepped into Clyde's room where he found Darren sleeping on Clyde's bed in a tucked-up sort of shape that reminded Eliot of a stranded prawn. It was a shock to see his father like that. He was dressed for the daytime except for his shoes, which lay kicked off on the floor. His glasses were on the bedside table next to a Science Museum safe. He had Clyde's duvet, with its space-rocket cover, half twisted round him. Eliot edged closer. There was a pallid stillness about the body on the bed that concerned him until at last he detected the shallow rise and fall of Darren's ribcage. Then he returned to his own room and closed the door.

He had already forgotten why he'd gone back there; forgotten totally about his birthday present for Darren, which was concealed beneath his bed. It was a mug with a picture of a man wearing a fedora and a pencil moustache and clutching the steering-wheel of something that had probably just rolled off a Detroit production line. 'FATHERS!' it said in big letters. Then, underneath: 'Providing A Personal Taxi Service Since 1934!' Eliot had bought the mug while he was out with Jane the previous day, at the gift shop round the corner from the vet. He couldn't see what was so clever about it, but Jane had told him that Darren would love it so he'd shelled out his pocket money without resistance, glad to have the decision made for him.

'Will you wrap it up?' his mother had asked, when they'd got home.

'Yes.'

She'd found him some wrapping-paper.

'You won't forget to do it, darling, will you?'

'No.'

Eliot's room was a small, cluttered square with a blocked-up fireplace, a well-stocked bookcase full of fantasy fiction 'for older readers', a large poster of wild horses galloping through an open field and a Yamaha keyboard on which he practised every day, enjoying the warmth of his mother's praise. Right now, though, he needed instant distraction. He got down on his knees, took up the gyroscope he'd been given for Christmas and set it spinning at an angle on its little plastic plinth. He stared at it, hoping to become so absorbed that his mind would wander from the terrible place where it had become trapped yet again.

For some months now, especially when he was alone, Eliot had fallen prey to dreadful imaginings. Sometimes these were reveries of physical revulsion, such as the one in which he put a fat slug in his mouth, the one that had made him jump when he'd found it in the kitchen in October. In the fantasy he didn't want to put the slug into his mouth and no one was making him do it, but somehow he had to anyway. Another vision was darker still, and this one had taken hold of him. From a helicopter's hatchway he would be staring down helplessly at the swirling ocean waters into which Simba had just fallen. There was rescue equipment

– a harness, rope and winch – but sharks were already circling. He could see poor Simba, drenched and flailing with his little paws, but being lowered by the winch would take too long. He'd have to dive into the sea and maybe die, but it was the only way that Simba might survive. Eliot was a good swimmer: level eleven, and doing advanced coaching sessions every Tuesday and Thursday evening. But did he have the courage to leap? Could he find the plucky boy hero inside?

These questions were never answered. The horror-thought narrative always jammed at this juncture, as if someone had paused a video.

The gyroscope fell off its plinth to the carpet. Eliot's head, though, kept buzzing. He slapped it with his hand to make it stop.

'Are you all right in there?' called Lorna. She was right outside his door.

'Yeah, yeah,' Eliot replied.

Lorna barged in, looked back over her shoulder and lowered her voice. 'I thought you were coming up to wrap Dad's present.'

'I was, yeah. It's just that I haven't found it yet.'

'What do you *mean*, you haven't found it? Where is it?'

'Under my bed.'

'So if you know where it is, how come you can't find it?' Eliot looked at her, befuddled.

'God, Eliot, I worry about you sometimes.' Eliot quite liked this because it meant he could be rueful and shy.

'Anyway,' Lorna went on, 'I'm going to have a shower so, handsome boy, if you still want my help you'll have to wait.'

She bustled off, wrists limp, forearms cocked, her kitten T-shirt fitting like a skin. Eliot watched her disappear into the bathroom – she was like an actress on the telly, he thought – and listened to the bolt slam into place. Her interruption had rescued him: it had caused him to forget about slugs and drowning cats. And after Lorna had gone he left his room once more and eased himself down the main staircase again, hoping that this time he'd be able to hear what his mother was saying.

Half an hour earlier, when Jane had come downstairs having checked that her husband wasn't dead, she'd found that Dorothy had already laid the table for Darren's birthday breakfast, presenting her with the first problem of the day. This was the job Clyde always liked to do. The sight of the six white plates arranged on the table, each with a matching bowl placed on top and a knife, fork and spoon positioned as correctly as heraldic bearers at the sides had sent her into a spin of diplomatic calculation behind a mask of astonished gratitude.

'Oh, Mum,' she had exclaimed. 'Look what you've done!' She'd heard her words' vying meanings as she'd spoken them. Which had her mother heard? The phoney acclaim or the consternation it concealed? Dorothy, though, might not have heard her at all.

'I'll put the kettle on now you're here.'

Now you're here.

It was only eight o'clock. Jane had wondered how long Dorothy had been awake. She was already dressed and pressed in smart blue jeans, a man's white shirt tucked into a broad belt and a peach-coloured felt waistcoat that further advertised her continuing possession of a waist. Her glasses swung from her neck on a plaited cord in African earth colours. Her silvery hair was pulled to the back of her head and clasped in place. She filled the grubby plastic kettle with the forgiving circumspection of a liberal baroness touring below stairs.

Jane had tightened the knot of her dressing-gown. 'Did you sleep well, Mummy?' she'd asked.

'Beautifully, darling,' Dorothy had replied.

The orderliness of the table had stirred nostalgia in Jane and, with it, memories of teenage irritation: if the Ransome family is so alternative, she'd once carped, why are our mealtimes so formal? Her parents had laughed that away, declining to acknowledge the slightest inconsistency. Thirty years on, it still vexed Jane that marching on Aldermaston had not lessened her mother's reverence for crockery.

'Are the others coming?' Dorothy had asked.

'I don't think they're even awake yet,' Jane had said. She'd thought this was mostly true. Clyde had climbed in with her at some point in the night, complaining about Darren's snoring, and he'd still been sound asleep when she'd come down – just like Darren, the mighty Casanova. There had been no sign of Lorna; nor was there likely to be for at least an hour, especially if she annexed the bathroom with her customary opportunism. Eliot might have stirred by now, but if so he would probably be reading – or listening at the top of the stairs.

Jane had hoped they'd all stay away for a bit longer. If Clyde was going to be fed up about the table being set she'd like to fortify herself with tea beforehand. And, of course, there was something else: something on her mother's mind that it would be better to get out of her while it was just the two of them together.

'So, how's Daddy?' she'd said.

'Not terribly good, I'm afraid.'

'Oh dear.'

'Quite frankly, he's driving me mad.'

Dorothy had said this while reaching three matching mugs down from their hooks: grey-blue earthenware ones decorated with old gold Aztec suns. She'd spoken with a note of mannered wonderment as if spinning a yarn for a small child. Jane had not found this as patronising as she might have: it was how her mother covered up distress.

'How's he doing that?' Jane had asked.

'Oh, you know . . .' Dorothy had placed the last of the three heavy mugs next to the teapot as carefully as if it were an egg. Jane had waited. 'He's grumpy and forgetful,' Dorothy had gone on. 'He's not himself.' She had not elaborated but instead offered Jane a look of morbid resignation. Behind her, the kettle had begun to work up its head of steam.

'What does the doctor say?'

'That he has to keep taking his tablets and doing his physiotherapy.'

'Is that all?'

'There's not much else he can say, darling. Your father has had a stroke. He's seventy-three years old.'

Dorothy had broken off and poured a little water into the teapot to warm it. Her body language had been as blunt as the doctor's advice. Jane had noticed that a white china toast rack she hadn't seen – let alone used – for several years had emerged from the back of whichever cupboard it had been buried in and placed beside the toaster. She had felt rebuked and colonised by her mother's re-employment of this forgotten article. 'Mummy,' she'd said, 'is there something I can do?'

'No, no, I don't think so. I can manage.'

'I didn't mean about the tea.'

'I know what you meant, dear.'

Dorothy had dropped two teabags into the pot just as the kettle had come to the boil. Jane, silenced, had watched her mother pour the water, put the lid on painstakingly, then look around for the tea cosy. Jane had seen where it was – on the drainer where, presumably, Dorothy had left it after removing it to empty the pot before Jane came downstairs. Jane had permitted herself the momentary pleasure of watching her mother's perplexity before revealing to her where the cosy was. Fortified, she had probed about her father's health again.

'But, Mummy, if he's getting worse shouldn't you be thinking about, I don't know, getting someone in to help?'

'What sort of someone, darling?'

'I don't know. Someone to help with the housework? Or do the garden?'

'Ah!' Dorothy had laughed. 'Do you really think he'd let anyone touch that garden except me?'

'Yes, well,' Jane had admitted. 'I know what you mean.' The further her father had travelled into his retirement years, the more concentrated his attention had become on the garden's flowerbeds and trees. For the first time it had occurred to Jane that this might be some sort of literal return to his botanical roots as he anticipated his own planting in the ground.

'Best just to let him struggle on,' Dorothy had said. 'He's happy out in the summerhouse. He finds it therapeutic, actually.'

Once more Jane had felt her mother closing off any avenue that might lead to the conclusion that she could not cope alone with Jeffrey. It had seemed that Dorothy wanted her frustrations to be acknowledged but to place off bounds the idea that someone else might help to alleviate them. As she'd watched her mother fumbling a pint of milk out of the fridge, Jane had felt impotence enfold her. It hadn't passed her notice that her question about housework had yet to receive a reply, but pressing the point had appeared futile. She'd decided to confront the table-laying matter again.

'Mummy, I hate to say this . . .'

'Oh dear. Perhaps you shouldn't, then.'

'No, no. It's just that you've laid the table so nicely, but I think Clyde was hoping to do it – as part of wishing Darren a happy birthday. I'm sorry,' she'd added. 'I should have told you yesterday. Then you would have known.'

Dorothy had not turned round. She'd been removing the cosy from the teapot again and had commenced to fill two of the three mugs. 'The trouble is that he's stopped listening,' she'd said.

'Has he?'

'Of course, he's always been that way at certain times, when he's been terribly absorbed in a particular project or some special piece of research, but that wasn't ever a worry because one accepted that a professor is sometimes going to be like that. In fact it was rather lovable in a way, because he always felt rather bad about it. You see, Daddy didn't want to be one of those men who don't hear what women say. That was the radical in him.'

She had delivered this speech more to the tea-making paraphernalia than to Jane, who'd only half taken it in, distracted by her urge to interfere. Dorothy had kept underestimating the speed of the flow from the teapot's spout, resulting in pools of ill-directed PG Tips gathering round the bases of the mugs. There had been a cloth on the worktop, barely a foot from her right hand. Jane had willed her to see it, seize it and mop up before the tormenting impulse to do the job herself became too fierce. At the same time, her equilibrium had been discomposed: Dorothy had spoken of Jeffrey in the past tense.

'There's a cloth next to you, Mummy, if you need it,' she'd said finally.

'Thank you, darling.' Dorothy had found it, used it, and placed one of the mugs of tea in front of Jane. 'The children were *very* good last night,' she had observed.

'Oh, great,' Jane had said, as warmly as she could.

That had been the moment when Lorna went into the bathroom – Jane heard the door slam above – and Eliot had resumed his eavesdropping. He wouldn't have been able to make out anything, though, partly because Clyde had just emerged from the grown-ups' bedroom and trotted across to his own. Noisy pest.

Dorothy was saying, 'That Sims game is really quite compelling.' She said it as though she were making a brave admission. 'Eliot in particular found it fascinating.'

'So Lorna told me on the phone,' said Jane.

'I suppose it is quite creative,' Dorothy went on, 'and basically non-violent, which, sadly, seems rather unusual these days.'

Now the whoosh of the bathroom multipoint reached Jane's ears. She hoped Lorna wouldn't set up camp in there.

'Oh, it's ridiculous, of course,' continued Dorothy, 'the idea that so many disasters could happen. But it does go to show that the suburban ideal doesn't quite work out in practice. It's American, I presume?'

'Sorry, Mum,' said Jane. She'd heard more movement above and then a yell. Small footsteps were thundering down the stairs. Then Clyde burst into the kitchen, wearing the jolted look of a woodland creature torn from hibernation by ECT.

'Boo!' Jane observed, by way of welcome. 'You've slept very late.'

Clyde's pupils were adjusting to the light. He scratched the top of his head, making his hair stick up even more than before. 'I had a nightmare,' he said. 'And Eliot kicked me.'

'Eliot kicked you? When?'

'Just now. Ow!'

Delayed agony seized Clyde's imagination. His features contorted. He fell to the floor and rolled around on it, clutching his right shin.

Jane said, 'Are you *sure* he kicked you?'

'Ow! Ow! Ow!'

'Actually *kicked* you?'

'Ow! Yes, Mummy! Ow!'

'Good morning, Clyde,' said Dorothy. She had switched to the benign and slightly barmy schoolmarm tone she took with all her daughter's children, as if to demonstrate that her interest in them was exacting and substantial, not some fluffy, sentimental thing.

Clyde executed a few more death throes, then sat up. 'Good morning, Dodie,' he replied weakly.

'Is Daddy awake?' Dorothy asked.

'No.'

'Well, good for him,' replied Dorothy, stagily. 'He deserves a lie-in on his birthday.' She had her glasses on by now. She looked over their rims along her nose at Clyde and smiled.

Jane thought of Darren in his foetal throwback position on Clyde's bed. Maybe Clyde was thinking of this too; perhaps of mentioning it loudly. For some reason she couldn't really put her finger on she didn't want him to do that. She stepped into the conversation smartly. 'Clyde,' she said, 'in case you were wondering, Dodie didn't know how much you like to lay the table on birthday mornings. I should have told her. Sorry. But I'm sure you can help with other things.'

Clyde looked at her, faintly bemused. Then he looked at Dorothy, who said, 'Aha! We've got a little plan, haven't we, Clyde?'

Clyde nodded. He climbed back on to his feet. No need for surgery, then, thought Jane. She said, 'Oooh, a plan!' with rising dread. 'What plan?'

'You'll see, Mummy,' said Dorothy, addressing Clyde. 'All in good time! Perhaps you should go and find out what Lorna and Eliot are up to. If they don't hurry up, half the day will be gone.'

'Who? Me?' said Jane.

Dorothy was rooting in the fridge again, and this time emerged with three packets of bacon Jane hadn't known were there. Invasion of the alien rashers – as if being colonised by Lorna every weekday morning wasn't enough. 'Did you go shopping yesterday, Mummy?' she asked, beginning not to care that her synthetic equability was sounding strained.

'I sent the children to the corner shop,' Dorothy replied. She was squinting at the bacon's vacuum packaging.

'What? You sent all three?'

'All three together.'

'In the dark?'

'That's why I sent them together, darling. They were very good about it. I said they could choose whatever they wanted for breakfast, as long as they agreed to respect each other's differences of view. I told them that was how democracy works. Didn't I, Clyde?'

Clyde nodded enthusiastically. Jane contained an explosion of outrage. Democracy? What about muggers, madmen and dangerous roads? There was a more subterranean sentiment too: envy. What response would she, Jane, have got had she asked Lorna, Eliot and Clyde to co-operate in that way? 'Are they going to cook it too?' she asked, knowing the answer already.

'They're looking forward to it,' Dorothy said, her attention shifting to a frying-pan. She placed it over one of the gas rings at the front of the cooker. Jane would have put it on one at the back.

'I'll just put some clothes on,' said Jane, getting up, 'and I'll be with you.'

'Very good, darling,' said Dorothy, who now reached for the third Aztec mug. 'Here's Darren's tea. Don't worry, you can leave everything to me.'

Jane took it. But before she resigned herself to temporary exile there was one thing she badly wanted to know. 'Did you phone Daddy yesterday?'

'Yes, darling, I did,' said Dorothy. The glasses were off again. She was reading the label on the cooking oil.

'How was he?'

'Absolutely fine, darling. Absolutely fine.'

Jane had bought Darren a bird box for his birthday. She presented it to him in the front room, where the family traditionally gathered for present-opening rituals.

'Is it time for breakfast yet?' Darren enquired. He'd just polished off four rashers of bacon, three fried eggs, two grilled tomatoes and a slice of toast.

'I'll make you some!' said Clyde.

Jane groaned inwardly. The debris of the first meal of the day was uncleared in the kitchen. Clyde had had a fine time with the grill-pan, poking and turning the streaky strands and repeatedly triggering the smoke alarm while

Dorothy had kept watch, wearing a satisfied expression that said, 'Jane, darling, this is how they learn'. Lorna had spooned organic yoghurt and, in the same spirit of conspicuous sanctimony, poured lentils into a pan of water, leaving them to soak for use in the veggie loaf she planned to bake later. Dorothy had promised to help her. Eliot had sat, waiting his turn at the cooker. Jane had made sure he got it.

'I'd love you to, Clyde,' Darren said. 'But first I want to unwrap my new toys.'

'Toys?' cried Clyde. 'But you're a grown-up!'

'I can still have toys!' Darren replied indignantly. Dressed and refreshed, he was ready to play the role demanded of him by the day. He sat in the middle of the sofa, the one Dorothy had slept on in its folded-out form and, part mindful of her dependence on Jane the previous night, packed away efficiently at dawn. Clyde, clutching his own present for Darren, sat pressed up against him, eyeing the one from Jane covetously.

'I wonder what it is,' said Darren. He doubted this feigned innocence fooled anyone in the room, but that was not the point. The pretending was everything.

'I *wonder*,' echoed Lorna, sarcastically. The Superman stressball, still wrapped, was right next to Darren on the sofa cushion where he'd placed it after she'd given it to him. She, by contrast, was positioned as far as possible from him, leaning against the doorframe, determined to keep her excitement concealed. Darren could see this just as clearly as he could feel Clyde's glee. Eliot was the one he couldn't read.

'Oh, just get on with it, Darren!' said Jane, impatiently. 'It's supposed to be ripped open, not dissected like somebody's brain!'

'Yes, come on, Darren!' said Dorothy.

'I have dissected people's brains, you know,' Darren retorted warningly.

'Euuugh!' said Clyde.

'God, Dad, you're disgusting!' said Lorna.

'No, he isn't,' corrected Jane.

'It's a *joke*, Mum,' retorted Lorna.

Eliot, meanwhile, continued sitting on the floor, holding the packaged Dad mug quietly. He had grinned at Darren's brains remark but part of his own brain was occupied with more serious things. All the gift-giving protocol had started him thinking about Father Christmas. In spite of being inducted into the ranks of Claus-denyers he had been having problems not believing. The formal breaking of the news of Santa's non-existence had not surprised him greatly, what with all the glaring contradictions in the myth, and he'd sworn to feign keeping the faith for Clyde's sake. But all the doubts only intensified. Could it ever be definitively proved that no flying reindeer had ever landed on the roof? Eliot thought not. Now and again, this bothered him.

'Can I open it, Daddy?' asked Clyde.

'Too late!' said Darren, all of a sudden. He ripped off the paper like a man possessed, then stared in rapture at what it revealed. 'Oh, wow!' he exclaimed, swapping a secret look with Jane. 'Let's get out there and fix it up!'

An hour or so later Jane smuggled a leg of lamb out of the fridge, blessedly free from maternal advisers and other unwanted company. A bird-box-installation team had been assembled: Eliot to hold the ladder; Clyde to pass up drill bits, Rawlplugs and screws; Dorothy to reminisce about blue-tits pecking off milk-bottle tops. It was now congregated outside at the back of the house next to the section of wall containing Eliot's bedroom window and every bit as absorbed in its task as Jane had hoped it would be. Only Lorna had opted out. She had sneaked back to her room to have a textfest with Kazea.

Jane patted rosemary into the leg of lamb and peeled twenty potatoes at high speed, putting the skin into the compost bin in the frail hope that one day it would enrich the garden soil. She placed the lamb under foil in a ceramic roasting dish and put the potatoes into a large pan of cold water. She left both on top of the cooker, the most conspicuous place she could think of – look, Mummy, I'm cleverer than you think – and then, as a hammer drill began puncturing external brickwork, she slipped away to find a space where she could figure out why she was in such turmoil that she could barely breathe.

She went into the sitting room, but didn't sit. Her record collection was shelved in one of the two alcoves formed by the now redundant chimney-breast. She put her head on one side to read the spines of the old vinyl albums' cardboard sleeves. A song had popped into her head at some point in the night and had been there ever since. The spines were furred from use and age but she could still make out the artists' names: Joni Mitchell, Cat Stevens, old, old Elton John . . . the dead giveaway soundtrack to her teens. The song she couldn't shake, though, was by Carole King: 'It's Too Late' from the album *Tapestry*. The copy Jane hoped she still had had first belonged to Julia and, strictly speaking, it still did. Julia had liked the album too, but not in the same way as Jane – not with her intense identification. This had provided Jane with just enough moral justification for her gradual relocation of the album from Julia's bedroom to hers. Maybe Julia had noticed, maybe not. Whatever, possessing it, listening to it, moping to it with friends had stirred and vindicated Jane at that time in her life when she'd been all wrapped up in noticing herself. Maybe there *was* a way, she had decided at fourteen, for her to play the piano *and* be fantastically interesting. It was a clothes and an attitude thing too. Long hair. Tie-dye vests. Exquisite existential misery.

Jane found the sleeve she sought and slid it out. She had remembered its cover quite clearly: the Brooklyn girl reclining in shadow against a wickerwork bedhead. No more evidence had been required back in 1971 that life was made of melancholy.

She laid the album on the top of the piano: maybe she'd indulge the masochism of playing it later. Someone had left the cordless phone extension on the easy chair in the corner – Lorna, probably. Jane went to it and picked it up. She punched in some numbers from memory, then listened to far-off ringing down the line. 'Come on, Daddy,' she whispered.

As she waited she wondered if she'd been dim. Daddy hadn't been so bad at Christmas – had he? A little slower, certainly, but he was bound to be only three months after the event. In fact, she'd been relieved to find him so bright and welcoming. He and Dorothy had insisted on hosting Christmas dinner as usual, and Jeffrey had made his traditional contribution: stirring the gravy, carving the bird, ladling brandy on to the pudding and setting it on fire. Jane had seen no sign of the cantankerous and maddening old man her mother was now describing. Had Darren noticed any change in Jeffrey's personality? He hadn't said so. Had Julia? She hadn't said so either and, being Julia, she surely would have done.

Still Jeffrey didn't answer. And Jane heard footsteps heading her way from the kitchen. She replaced the handset and moved just fast enough to intercept her mother in the hall. 'Hello, Mummy, how's it going out there?' She'd placed her body in the hall so as to block her mother's way, although quite why she didn't know.

'Darling,' Dorothy said. 'It's gone twelve. Should I put the oven on?'

'I'll see to it, Mummy, if that's OK.'

'I'm just thinking about the time . . .'

'I know, Mummy, I know.' Jane closed her eyes and raised a hand, appealing for peace. 'Please, just let me make the dinner. Why don't you sit down with the paper?'

Straight away, she saw hurt in Dorothy's face. 'I was just thinking about doing the potatoes . . .'

'I've already done them. Please, Mummy. I'll be fine.'

Shame festered around Jane's heart as she watched her mother disappear back out to the garden, looking somehow smaller than before. Her immaculate appearance, which had made Jane feel so dowdy first thing in the morning, now filled her with pity, bringing home as it did an unwelcome reminder of the futility of façades against old age. Bad daughter, thought Jane. Bad girl.

One of the things Darren loved most about his wife was her over-evolved sense of the absurd. He'd noticed it when he had first laid eyes on her – in that pub, wearing that hat, taking cover from all that sputum aimed Gobb's way – and their first ever conversation had confirmed it ('Darren – that's a groovy name'). Only later had he grasped that her talent for finding ridiculousness in almost anything, and for offering these perceptions to him like a bag of sweets, was the brave-faced up-side to the wishfulness that lurked in her constantly.

He sometimes tried to recall when he'd first had this insight. The older he got, the more important it became to pinpoint the time in question. Was it before or after they had gone their separate ways for those three years at the start of the eighties? Had it, perhaps, occurred to him earlier than that but he'd preferred to hide from it because the implications were too onerous? And was the underlying reason why he had sought Jane out again, after he returned from Guatemala, that he yearned to take care of a woman like her, such was the sort of man he'd started to be?

From his birthday seat of honour at the head of the kitchen table, Darren drank tea out of his mug from Eliot and watched Jane secretly as she scraped uneaten food from the plates into the bin and smiled painfully and privately. And Lorna was saying, 'So were you and Grandad, like, serious rebels, then?'

'Well, people said that about us, of course,' answered Dorothy, 'but we believed we spoke for the majority.'

Darren shifted his attention back to the conversation. Lorna's fork hovered over the last bite of her lentil loaf as she said, 'What? Most people didn't want a bomb?'

'Not in their hearts,' replied Dorothy. 'Like most of us, they wanted peace and that was what we were campaigning for.'

'Peace, man,' said Clyde, in a dozy hippie voice, and raised two fingers in a droopy V.

'Where did you learn *that*?' Darren asked him.

Clyde giggled. 'Peace, man,' he repeated dreamily.

'At school, I expect,' sniffed Lorna.

'At school, I expect,' mimicked Clyde.

Eliot observed this silently: his sister was so stroppy; his brother was such a pain.

'Shut up, idiot,' said Lorna to Clyde.

'Shut up, idiot,' said Clyde in return.

'Whoa, whoa,' urged Darren, gently. 'I don't want to wear out my stressball.'

He had it next to him beside the mug and gave Superman's midriff a little squeeze. Lorna offered him a tight smile of affectionate insincerity. 'You're quite a lot like Clark Kent to look at, aren't you, Dad?' she said.

He returned her smile in kind, then checked on Jane again. She was approaching the table with a cloth.

'Everything's coming back these days, isn't it?' said Dorothy, sagely. 'Now, vegetarianism. That was very big in the sixties, wasn't it, Jane?'

'I don't know, Mummy. I'm *far* too young.'

'Me too,' said Darren, and tried catching Jane's eye. He failed and caught Eliot's by accident instead.

'Julia went in for it,' said Jane. 'She was always the serious one.'

Leaning over Clyde, Jane dragged the cloth across the tabletop towards her, gathering stray peas and cold, spilled gravy into her waiting spare hand. Darren thought, I ought to be doing that for her.

'There are quite a few vegetarians at my school,' said Lorna, selecting an informative tone.

'Are there really?' said Dorothy.

'Yes, but not all of them take it as seriously as me and my friend Kazea. They, like, think a few bacon sandwiches don't matter.'

'The vegetarian cause has come a long way,' said Dorothy. 'There are vegetarian meals available in supermarkets and vegetarian options in restaurants. That was unheard of years ago. And some of them are jolly tasty too. Have you tried them, Jane?'

'Oh, yes,' said Jane. 'Believe me, we've tried them all.' She did not elaborate. The muck in her hand joined the rest in the bin. Then she opened a cupboard and reached in.

'What other issues do you and your friends care about?' asked Dorothy. 'What about Africa, for example?'

'Where Auntie Julia's working?'

'In Angola, yes.'

Jane returned to the table, holding a large chocolate cake. On top of it were stuck two candles, each in the shape of the number four.

'Yum!' said Clyde, licking his lips like the Big Bad Wolf.

'What a fantastic cake!' Darren enthused, sensing that Jane was feeling more and more invisible, the longer the conversation went on.

'Yum! *Yum!*' said Clyde, as if his position needed further clarity.

'What do you think, Eliot?' asked Darren.

'It's good,' Eliot affirmed, in a matter-of-fact way. He was waiting for his mother to make a joke.

'I suppose,' said Jane, sitting down with an eight-inch-bladed knife in her hand, 'that this is where I say it took me hours and hours to make.' She raised an eyebrow at Eliot. He raised one in return.

'Has it got gelatine in it?' asked Lorna, darkly.

'I don't know,' replied Jane. 'Could you fetch some side plates, please?'

'Have you got the box it came in?' persisted Lorna.

'It's in the bin.'

'Oh, fine . . .'

'Come on, come on,' urged Darren, softly.

'She's working entirely with Aids victims now,' said Dorothy, 'particularly children.'

'She was telling me about it at Christmas,' Lorna said – so, *so* interestedly.

'It's *very* important work,' said Dorothy. 'There's such an enormous job to do there. Such a tragedy for so many, this terrible disease.'

'Yes, yes,' Lorna agreed, sighing tenderly. 'It's so *awful* what's happening there.'

'Shall I get the side plates, then?' said Jane.

'Oh, sorry!' Lorna sang unconvincingly. She got up, went to the bin and began to poke around for cake packaging.

'Who wants the first piece?' asked Darren, as Jane pushed the cake and knife across the table towards him.

'Me!' shouted Clyde.

'Hold on, hold on,' said Darren. As he received the cake and knife his eyes met Jane's with questioning concern.

She made a puking face at him, then said quietly to Clyde, 'Why don't you get the side plates for me?'

'OK.' He scampered off

'Would you like the first piece, Dorothy?' asked Darren, preparing to submerge the point of the knife into the cake's dark coating of butter cream. He was uneasy about what Jane had just done: a bust-up between Lorna and Clyde was the last thing they needed. But Clyde was back with the plates and Lorna hadn't noticed.

'Wait!' cried Clyde, on his return. 'You haven't lit the candles!'

'Oh, no!' said Darren, and his dismay was genuine. There was too much going on. 'Must be old age,' he said, covering up. 'Do we have any matches, Jane?'

'We have a better attitude to Africa now,' Dorothy said. 'When Jane and Julia were young they used to pick a black baby from a catalogue.'

Jane looked up. 'Did we?'

'Oh, yes, oh, yes,' said Dorothy. 'People would come to your door, they were Christians probably, and they would show you this little booklet full of pictures of black babies. And you chose the one you liked best and they tore it out for you to keep and you gave them a shilling. Don't you remember, Jane?'

'I don't think so,' said Jane.

'Well, it was something like that anyway,' said Dorothy. 'That was how we thought about Africa in those days. Of course, people meant well. But we didn't understand the wider picture – why children were starving in the first place.'

'We've been learning about that in humanities,' said Lorna, returning to the table, all thoughts of side plates long banished, her fears over gelatine assuaged. She was loving being treated as a grown-up by her grandmother – loving it so much that she'd overlooked Dorothy's earlier consumption of dead sheep pieces alongside the non-meat dish they'd created together once her mother had got the roast potatoes on.

'But then,' Dorothy continued, 'in some ways things have got worse as well. These days almost everyone has a bomb.'

'Yes,' said Lorna, regretfully. 'They really do, don't they?'

The telephone rang. To Darren, this came as something of a relief, like the end-of-round bell in a boxing match. It was Jane, though, who jumped to take the call. There was a lull around the table, brought about by the usual blend of politeness and nosiness.

'Hello Daddy,' said Jane. 'Yes, yes, it was. Are you all right there on your own? . . . Oh, good . . .'

Darren got up from the table. The matches were usually kept on a high shelf behind where Jane was standing. He went over to reach for them.

'Darren's very well,' Jane was saying. 'Yes, he's very old

now, isn't he? . . . Oh, no, he understands. We'll be coming down to see you soon anyway . . .'

The box of matches was wedged beneath a dust-covered lemon-squeezer. Fittingly, Darren squeezed Jane's free hand as he located them.

'And I'm fine too, thank you, Daddy . . .' Jane said, and squeezed Darren's hand in return.

The lift this gave him was almost palpable; his rejuvenation was absolute. 'Pull that curtain shut behind you, Eliot,' he said cheerily. 'Let's make it good and dark in here.'

'Can I light the candles?' piped up Clyde.

'I don't mind who lights them,' said Darren, 'as long as I'm the one who blows them out.'

That night, before getting undressed, Jane had a quick look inside the small room, the one next to hers and Darren's. She measured it mentally and found that, yes, it could be very nice for a small child. Often, in catalogues or in other people's homes, she'd seen those clever bed-and-storage-space combinations that made the most of a limited area and helped create a cosy, play-den feel. As for the stuff that was in there now, well, the computer could be moved to her bedroom and . . . Oh, well, she could dream.

She went to join Darren, who was waiting.

'What have you been doing?' he asked. He lay flat out on the duvet in his glasses, T-shirt and boxer shorts.

'You know what I've been doing,' she replied.

'That's true,' he said, taking off his glasses. 'Why don't you lie down next to me?'

She obliged, making him laugh by collapsing her legs beneath her as though she were a newborn giraffe. 'So how's your bird box, birthday boy?' she asked.

'Is that slang?'

'What do you mean?' Jane said, to the bedroom ceiling. She would have rolled over to look at him as she spoke, but the effort this would have required seemed too great.

'Well,' said Darren, earnestly, 'I thought it might be some kind of sexual reference. Like "lunch box".'

'No. *Not* like "lunch box". Like "bird box" – my lovely present to you.'

'It's still there,' said Darren. 'I checked. A few weeks from now a family of blue-tits will have moved into it and will be taunting Simba from the safety of their perch.'

'I'm very proud of you, husband,' said Jane.

'It's nice to be appreciated for my nurturing side.'

'I wish I could say the same.'

'Oh, come on now.'

'I'm sorry,' said Jane, feeling for his hand and taking it. Then she said, 'Oh, God,' in reference to nothing in particular and just about everything in general. The room was dark, save for what light seeped in from the landing through the half-closed door. It was late. Even Lorna was asleep, or so Jane judged from the lack of ceiling-creak.

'Was your dad all right?' asked Darren.

'He sounded absolutely fine.'

'But your mum says he isn't.'

'Yes, she does. She says he's driving her mad.'

'Maybe he has good days and bad ones.'

'Maybe that's it, I don't know . . .'

She didn't know if that was it and she didn't know what else to think either. Lorna was so pious, Eliot was so distant and Clyde was so in love with his dad. And her mother was shrinking, and her father was ill. Jane blew a raspberry; she aimed it directly at life.

'What was that for?' Darren asked quietly.

Jane ignored the question. 'I've got all my clothes on, haven't I?' she said.

'Yes.'

'And we're in bed.'

'Yes.'

'That doesn't make any sense.'

She got up and took off almost everything, throwing each garment into the corner of the room in a daft parody of a striptease. Then she jumped back on to the bed, and lay on her back as before.

'I thought I'd keep a few things on for the time being. Do you mind?'

'Not at all,' said Darren, softly. 'Red is my favourite colour.'

'You don't think I'm too old for this, do you?'

Darren let his hand fall on her thigh. 'Sssh,' he breathed.

Jane ssshed. She did this for a while until it came to pass that making certain noises and saying certain words became a good idea once more. She locked her legs round Darren so that her ankles crossed. She didn't cross her fingers, though.

CHAPTER FOUR MONDAY

Monday morning. Twenty to nine. Eliot and Lorna had left for school on time stewarded by Darren, who had decided that, for once, he'd be a little late for work. Dorothy had gone too, declining Darren's offer of a lift to London Bridge station and instead walking out with Lorna. Finally Darren had departed, though not before planting a deep kiss on her unsuspecting mouth. Then he'd said, 'Elvis is leaving the building.'

'Come back soon, Elvis,' Jane had said.

Now only Clyde remained in the house with her. She assumed he had gone into hiding as usual but she decided not to let that fluster her. She pulled on her black fake-fur coat, the matching hat and gloves, thinking, Why the hell not dress up a bit? In keeping with her unfamiliar state of calm, she allowed herself some preening time in front of the hall mirror, concluding that she would make a truly marvellous widow and reviewing the reasons for her strange tranquillity. These included not having been in the kitchen at the same time as Lorna, saying goodbye to her mother with more warmth than relief, and the centring effect of she and Darren making love with the same licence and longing as they had twenty years earlier when they'd found out they couldn't bear to be apart. But Jane knew there was another reason too.

'Now, where can Clyde be?' she said loudly, walking into the front room. An interesting sight awaited her. A crude monument had been erected in the middle of the floor using every cushion available. The soft-furnishing construction was two feet high, vaguely pyramid-shaped and did not seem very stable because when Jane spoke again it vibrated. 'What a marvellous bit of sculpture! I wonder what would happen if I poked it?'

As she reached out a hand the pyramid exploded and a pink-faced Clyde emerged.

'Come on, nitwit,' said Jane. 'Put on your coat and let's go.'

Clyde did not put on his coat but Jane was philosophical: if he felt cold she would be the first to know. Instead, she slung the coat over her arm and followed Clyde outside. She saw her neighbour Maggie up ahead, accompanied by all four of her children: the long-suffering George, aged nine; the censorious Lily, five; three year-old Poppy, who had lately entered her pink phase; baby Nadine in a silver, coach-built pram. It was like following some royal procession. Clyde, who was considering making George his hero, raced after them. Jane picked up her own pace. She wasn't going to hide from Maggie any more.

'Hello, Jane!' Maggie called, looking round as Clyde overhauled her. 'Lovely outfit.'

'Hello, Maggie. Thank you.'

'Lovely day, too!'

It was cold and drizzling unpleasantly.

'Lovely, yes.'

Communal sarcasm: the bedrock of school-run empathy, along with tales of personal inadequacy.

'I'm in trouble this morning,' Maggie announced.

'Oh dear. Why's that?'

'I have offended the Pink One,' Maggie said.

Poppy's socks were pink. Her suede ankle boots were pink. Her cardigan was pink. Beneath it, her pink summer frock had a pattern of pink hearts. The temperature was barely ten degrees.

'Why is she cross?' asked Jane.

'I told her she looked gorgeous,' said Maggie. 'I was supposed to tell her she looked beautiful.'

'Well, who wouldn't be cross?' said Jane, watching the Pink One pleasurably.

Poppy was slight and lightweight, even for her age. Her fine, fair hair had had a brush with sandiness and it framed an elfin face. Deaf to their discussion, she skipped ahead of the two women, both hands held in front of her in fists.

'Are the horses with us?' Maggie asked her.

'I've only got *one* horse today,' Poppy replied, sounding like the infant Joyce Grenfell.

'How *wonderful*!' Maggie exclaimed.

'It's pink,' said Poppy.

'Oh! And what's its name?'

'Pinky.'

'Of course,' said Maggie. 'Silly me.' Shoving the pram forward, she rolled her eyes Jane's way.

'How's Nadine?' asked Jane. She peered into the pram quickly, before her new-found bravery could ebb away. In sharp contrast to Poppy, Nadine wore a polar-explorer snowsuit and lay fast asleep on her back, blissed-out and bulbous from her morning feed.

'She's poo-ing a lot,' said Maggie. 'Big exploding ones all up her back. Remember those?'

'Vividly,' said Jane.

'And my nipples are just *raw* – like some builder's been at them with a rasp. You probably remember that too.'

'Who could forget?'

Jane was happy to engage in this repartee. But, in fact, she *had* forgotten. And now that she'd remembered, she couldn't place which child it had happened to her with. Not Clyde, she thought – too recent to have slipped into the backwaters of her memory. So had it been with Lorna or Eliot? Maybe Darren would remember. Whichever, it seemed long ago. Jane trawled for a pearl of experience. She was about to say that the worst thing about breast-feeding was when they first got their front teeth, but by the time she had resurfaced Maggie had moved the conversation on.

'Anyway,' she was saying, 'the *look* on Nigel's face! But, let me tell you, I was *dying*. I *had* to undo my bra.'

'Did you?'

'Yes! And do my crisis-breathing thing. Nigel was *horrified*.'

It didn't matter that Jane's mind had been elsewhere when the telling of this anecdote began. The point was to join the teller in relishing the moment when it all became *so* embarrassing. Her neighbour had built a big, blowsy persona out of weaknesses and grand calamities. Jane recognised this as a social performance: elderly clergymen and maiden aunts appeared in Maggie's tales of dropped clangers too frequently to be believed, as did affronted filthy-rich clients of her husband Nigel, a bone-dry financial adviser half her size. Maggie's whole persona was founded on exaggeration for effect, which, paradoxically, confirmed her as completely genuine. She was over-tall, too blonde and thoroughly bell-bottomed with a face made for bawdy comedy. The only problem Jane had with her was that behind the front of hopeless self-mortification Maggie's life seemed free of even dulling disappointments, let alone authentic catastrophes.

'Your crisis-breathing thing?' Jane asked.

'Don't you know about my crisis-breathing thing?'

'I don't *think* so, no . . .' Jane did, though, know about Maggie's liking for depicting herself as the helpless slave of mind-and-body fads. She always claimed to have discovered them while 'slobbing out' in front of day-time TV, though her spotless kitchen, clutter-free living room, the website she ran, offering investment and lifestyle tips to fellow home-based businesswomen, and the glorious blooms that cascaded from her window boxes every summer suggested that she didn't spend all *that* many hours lounging with Phillip and Fern.

'You go like this,' said Maggie, coming to a dead halt. 'George!' she called. 'Watch Lily and Poppy, please.' She lowered her eyelids, lifted her chin, inhaled regally and let out a steady, high-pitched hum. George made an attempt at chasing his sisters' hands but Poppy kept hers on her imaginary reins, and Lily snatched hers behind her back. Clyde looked on, enthralled. After five grand inhalations, Maggie's soaring spirit rejoined her flesh upon the pavement.

'That's *much* better.' She smiled. 'The only trouble is it makes your thong go up your bum. Doesn't it, Lily?'

Lily frowned.

'Doesn't it, George?' said Maggie, more loudly. George looked skywards, perhaps wishing his mother was still up there. Clyde stood boggle-eyed. 'I don't wear thongs, by the way,' Maggie confided to Jane, 'in case anyone asks you – as I'm sure they're doing constant-lee!' Her voice went up at the end, like an Avon lady's. Then she said, 'Uh-oh, there's the bell!'

Jane hadn't heard it, though. As Maggie forged ahead she was remembering more things she hadn't thought about for a while. Lorna, Elliot *and* Clyde: she'd kept them all on the breast for well over a year. There were, of course, sound health reasons for this but they had been only supplementary. The main reason she'd done it was that she hadn't had the heart to stop.

'Earth calling Jane!'

'Oh, I'm sorry, Maggie. I was miles away.'

'Yes, well, I know the feeling.'

Maggie had accelerated. Jane had to scurry to keep up and as she scurried an impulse seized her. 'Are you planning any more, then?' she asked.

'Oh, no. My gigantic social gaffes are never planned. They're always spontaneous.'

'I didn't mean that.'

'Oh! Sorry! What did you mean?'

'Nothing.' Jane was staggered by her own nosiness. Had she really been that crass?

'Ah, you meant babies, didn't you?'

'I did. Sorry. Yes.'

'No need to be sorry! And, no, I won't be having any more. Nigel's had his tubes done – the poppet, just for me! It's supposed to be painless, but they looked like a couple of boiled plums for a week.'

Jane was so relieved, not least because her companion had been even less discreet than she had. 'Should you be telling me this, Maggie?'

'Don't worry. They went down eventually.'

There was no answer to that, except to laugh – she'd never be able to think of Nigel in quite the same way again.

But there was a sad finality about the story too. How old was Maggie? Possibly not yet forty, if her skin was any guide.

They were within sight of the school gates now. Clyde, up ahead, called, 'Mummy, can I go in with George?'

The request mildly unbalanced Jane. There was no compelling reason to say no. George was wry and rather Zen, much as his father had to be to survive being married to his mother. The problem lay with Jane. How ridiculous, she thought, not wanting to let Clyde go.

'I'll keep an eye on them,' Maggie said. 'I'm going in too – parent-governor business, for my sins.'

''Bye, Mummy,' called Clyde.

''Bye, Clyde.'

Then Maggie and her daughters were gone too. Jane watched them sail through the playground gates, before lowering her head for the walk home.

The emptiness of the house soothed Jane like a balm. She sat for a while at the bottom of the stairs and listened to the sound of solitude. It was welcome, but she knew it could become an addiction. In the kitchen she cleared away the few vestiges of breakfast mess that Darren hadn't dealt with and, after some deliberation, decided to leave the toast rack in circulation at least until its lack of use made it a nuisance to her again. It was the compromise she found between acting on her own wishes and respecting those of Dorothy. What a bittersweet thing a family could be. What a long, exhausting weekend it had been.

Jane went through to the sitting room. She sat down at her piano and picked out a nostalgic chord or two. Then she stopped and looked down at the backs of her hands as they rested on the silent keys. Her fingernails were short, unpainted and as clean as she ever expected them to be. What was different, she concluded, was that she'd ceased being surprised by the way her skin rucked up round her knuckles and, when she plucked at it, didn't spring back quickly into place.

She got up from the piano stool and wandered reflectively to the sitting-room phone, which she'd reinstalled in its plinth the day before. Up the staircase she went, carrying the phone and singing little snatches of old songs. In the small room, she switched on the computer. For a good hour she sought and sifted through reams of real-life stories, comparing and contrasting them with Darren's and her own. As much as anything, it was a ritual; a necessary process preparatory to a more human interaction she'd already decided to instigate. Once more taking up the phone, she punched in a number, reading it straight off the screen. Her call was answered promptly.

'Hello,' said Jane. 'I'm hoping you can help me. I'd like to know if I'd be able to adopt.'

Later, mired in forward-edging traffic in the opaque late afternoon, Darren thought about the word 'expecting'. It was no coincidence, he thought, that the most popular euphemism for pregnancy also alluded to all the wishing and hoping that parents feel about a child-to-be and served as a reminder of such optimism's lurking nemeses: a miscarriage, a stillbirth or the awful, guilty disappointment of a live birth marred by the discovery of a disability. The power and purchase of the word could even be felt before conception. Darren was aware of that capacity right now as, once more, he engaged first gear, released the clutch and crept a few more feet towards home. He saw how much he'd been expecting and that he had stopped doing so now.

Last night's lovemaking had been close and fulfilling yet also consoling. He had known what Jane had not needed to say, which was that they had missed the latest in her ever-diminishing fertility peaks and Darren's retrospective instinct was that some aspect of their closeness had contained a shared admission of defeat: no sperm and egg would meet, no embryo would be formed. Darren had the distinct sense that somebody had been removed from his future, an enthralling small person who might have been, and he wondered how Jane was feeling.

He could not be certain about this. All logic argued that if he could sit in a London snarl-up and locate loss in his soul then Jane, the prime mover behind their failed mission to conceive, would surely be desolate. But maybe he was wrong and she didn't share his certainty that they had reached the end of the road. Maybe she had taken last night's deep intimacy as a sign of some kind, as symbolising the inevitable, impending triumph of her procreative will. He felt he knew Jane body and soul. And yet there was no telling with her.

He revved the idling engine, crawled past a green light and thought of his old friend Ian. He recalled that, for a time, his smartass student time, Ian had been the kindred spirit he had never really found in Doncaster, but the events of Friday night had brought to an end a process of separation that had begun way, way back when Darren had first found Jane. There had been an instant tension between his fascination for her and his friendship with Ian, which was built on something Jane disliked and feared – a sort of boffin clever-cleverness that far too frequently excluded her. But what she figured out, and forced Darren to admit eventually, was that behind the comradeship of dope, dub reggae and cocky egghead repartee, his relationship with

Ian was really a dependency. There lay between them a concealed inequality, arising from the different ways in which their clever-cleverness had been acquired. Ian's was inherited: he came from a clever-clever West London family. By contrast, Darren had had to work at it. He didn't want for intellect but clever-cleverness was something else, the style in which your intellect was worn. Darren had had to work at putting on this style. It was a garb that he dressed up in. And so, within his skin, he'd always felt like a learner compared with Ian.

With Jane, though, he'd never felt inferior; never felt any need to strive to prove that he was otherwise. Instead there was discovery: mutual discovery of the other. For his part it was an ongoing process and sometimes it was as though he was forever searching in a darkened room. He never tired of it, though, or of the joy of finding her. He bent his head over the steering-wheel and pressed on.

After completing her momentous phone call in the morning Jane had roamed the house testing the strength of an exultant fantasy. She inspected from all angles everything that had been said to her and decided that, yes, she had what it would take and that her resulting resurgent happiness, her rekindled self-worth would carry all before her, including the rest of the family. Fortified by this conclusion and in need of a different bit of territory to pace, she'd put on her black coat, hat and gloves again, decided they lent her the deadly sexpot allure of a glamorous Russian spy and taken a brisk walk to the newsagent. There she'd bought a Fry's Chocolate Cream. She'd been seduced by her childhood memory of a TV ad for the confectionery classic in which a woman eating a bar had attained such ineffable *sangfroid* that when her cat took a stroll across the mantelpiece she knew where to stand to catch the vase it dislodged. Just held out her hand and waited for it to fall. Didn't even need to look.

Then Jane's day got better still. The newsagent had a radio playing quietly on a shelf behind him and from it had come a song that Jane had forgotten she loved. The lift she got was the greater for not having heard it in years. It was Gladys Knight singing 'Take Me In Your Arms And Love Me', and for the following three hours, Jane had rediscovered the thrill of it, then invested it with meanings she'd been too young to project when it had been in the charts. Preparing a Lancashire hotpot, her heart had swelled and her body ached as she recalled the way that Gladys sang 'boy', 'need' and 'adore'. Soon she'd begun rehearsing what she would say to Darren that evening after the hotpot had gone.

That sustained her through the most intensive hours of her day, those between three thirty and eight. They began as always with fetching Clyde from school, and, on this occasion, settling him with a sandwich in front of the television while in the sitting room she gave a half-hour lesson to a boy called Sajid. He was the same age as Clyde, and maybe that was why Jane found his reticence unnerving. Shouldn't six-year-olds talk you to death? On the other hand if Clyde was less voluble maybe he'd show more interest in the piano. He was tone-deaf, though: his daddy's boy.

Sajid and his mother left two minutes before Lorna arrived.

'Hi-ya!' she said to Jane, without quite looking at her.

'Hello, Lorna,' Jane replied neutrally. It was gone five o'clock – nearly two hours after Lorna's school's home time and the journey back took only half an hour. That made ninety minutes of hanging out and ninety minutes less to do homework. 'How's Kazea?' she enquired.

'She's fine,' came Lorna's breezy reply. She was already in the kitchen inhaling the meaty aroma with the disdain of a princess in a navvy's lavatory.

Jane might have taken exception but for her Gladys vibe, and at that moment Eliot came in. 'Hey, good looking,' his mother said.

'Hey, Mum,' replied Eliot, dreamily. He smiled and wafted up to his room. Lorna swept past Jane and followed him, saying in passing, 'Will there be plenty of vegetables, Mum?'

'Yes.'

'Vegetables, yuk,' said Clyde, emerging from the front room. 'Where's Daddy?'

'He'll be back soon,' said Jane although, come to think of it, she didn't know if that was true, only that he'd said he'd try to. She had confidence in him, though. She had her charm-offensive tactics worked out too. ('Darren, I know you think I'm mad. But I also know you love me so much that you'll think about adopting anyway . . .')

'How long is "soon"?' demanded Clyde.

'Not very,' Jane replied.

Clyde frowned up at her, clearly dissatisfied. 'Is it more than a minute?'

'Probably.'

'More than ten minutes?'

Jane knelt down before him and took his little shoulders in her hands. 'Clyde,' she said, in a low voice, '*I* have a question for *you*.'

'Oh,' said Clyde, drawn instantly into the conspiracy.

'If another child lived here, would you mind? A little child, I mean. Smaller than you.'

Clyde's eyes narrowed suspiciously. 'Would it have to share my bedroom?'

'I don't think so, no.'

'OK, then!' Clyde said brightly, and, on hearing the theme tune to *Scooby-Doo*, shot straight back into the front room.

'That's that settled, then,' murmured Jane. And at that moment a key slotted into the lock of the front door, causing her to check her face in the mirror and prepare to welcome her husband.

Five hours later Jane sat at her piano as she often did at the end of the day. Usually she would play something sad or schmaltzy: 'Cry Me A River'; 'I Only Have Eyes For You'. This time she picked out the motif of the Gladys Knight song – *da dadada dada dah*. Then, after messing around with it for a while, she got down from the stool and joined Darren on the sofa. She told him she had something to own up to. Darren saw the tension in her and suppressed all thoughts of flirtatious replies. The confession, when it came, did not appal or even surprise him very much – after all, as he revealed, he had thought about adopting too. He had a larger problem with it, though.

'Jane,' he'd asked, 'are you happy?'

She didn't answer straight away. Instead, she slipped down from her place beside him and knelt between his parted knees. 'With you, yes,' she said, 'but not really with me. Do you see?'

Their eyes levelled. She looked at him almost defiantly. He reached for her hips and told her, 'Yes, I see,' then added, 'Jane, please don't take this the wrong way, but are you sure you understand what this could mean?'

He thought he had a pretty good idea. In his job he was

required to deal with the sorts of people and places that produced most of the children in need of fostering or adoption. Once at an office party, Salina Mackay, a colleague in Social Services, had described the matching of them with new families as 'a nightmare' for everyone involved. 'You're trying to find a happy ending to stories that have been filled with misery and often end up making things worse.'

Well, Salina could get gloomy after a few drinks. But she was a grounded professional too. How grounded, Darren wondered, was Jane?

'I know that nothing about it would be easy,' she said.

The comment struck Darren as self-consciously severe. It made him watchful, yet more protective too. 'You know you wouldn't get a baby,' he continued carefully, adding, 'Both of us are probably too old.'

'Unless it was disabled, probably.' She was showing him that she had done her homework.

'I think that's how it goes.'

'We could look abroad,' Jane said knowledgeably, 'although that sounds even trickier.'

'Yep.' Darren nodded, sensing he should seem impressed. 'From what I've heard it would be.'

'Still worth thinking about, though.'

And that was all Jane asked him for: to think about it, then talk to her. 'You don't have to say anything now,' she said, taking his hands and squeezing them.

'OK,' Darren said. 'I have one question though. What sex do you think it will be?'

'A girl, I should imagine,' Jane replied.

'Why?'

'Oh,' she said, 'don't ask me to explain. You ought to know I'm always right about these things.'

PART 2 THE PLACEMENT

CHAPTER FIVE MAY

The little girl sat in the niche between the end of the piano and the wall. In her arms she held the doll she had brought with her. On the floor beside her lay a book Jane had retrieved from the fluffy wilderness beneath Clyde's bed. It was called *Grandpa's Handkerchief* and Jane was perturbed at being unable to recall if she had bought it for Eliot or Lorna. She knew for certain, though, that she had read it aloud at bedtimes scores of times to both and also to Clyde to instil knowledge of colours and days of the week and, most of all, to be close to them in that special reading-together way.

So there lay the book, unopened.

There sat the quiet little girl.

Her name was Jody: Jody Jones. The surname was her mother's, thanks to her father, apparently one Kirk Lovell, having disappeared without even knowing she was on the way. That, at least, was the story Jane and Darren had heard from the social worker assigned to Jody's case. The social worker's feeling was that it was probably true although, as she put it, 'You can't really be sure about anything with Ashleigh because she has so many problems.' Chief among these 'problems' was alcohol abuse, and with

117

it incompetence, depression and penury. She'd had Jody
when she was just seventeen. Professional loyalty to neutral
terminology prevented the social worker, a young French-
woman called Giselle, to whom Jody's file had been passed
only recently, from confirming Darren's suggestion that
Ashleigh was, in fact, 'a bloody mess'. But Jody's foster-
mother, a cheerful gossipmonger called Anne, was not
bound by such inhibitions. 'Always on the piss,' she'd said,
the first time Jane and Darren went to her home. 'Stank of
it, she did.' As she'd fished down the side of her armchair
for the TV remote, she'd added, 'Forgive my language, by
the way.'

That was the day they'd met Jody for the first time. She
was the first possible match put forward by the agency and
the only one they would ever consider. Jane shuddered
often at the memory: as she and Darren accepted Anne's
milky tea and chocolate-chip cookies, she'd battled to
suppress the bilious sensation that they were being soft-sold
the pallid infant sitting with her back to them on the carpet,
taking in Cartoon Network all but intravenously; or else
being plied to pick the child to take part in some reality TV
show. 'Offer them a biscuit, Jody,' chivvied Anne. 'This
might be your new mum and dad!'

It was the dumb compliance that did it for Jane; the
cookies expressionlessly offered on a cardboard party plate.
She had to get that child out of there. She had to get her
out of those back-of-a-lorry, market-stall clothes; drive the
ennui out of her wary blue eyes and put some bounce into
her flat brown hair. Anne wasn't going to do it. Jane bit into
the biscuit, knowing she couldn't rest until Jody was saved.
And now, here she was, fifteen months after starting out on
the adoption trail, finding out what becoming an unknown
child's mother could ask of you.

'Jody,' she said gently, coaxingly, as if she was trying to tempt a kitten to come out from under a parked car.

Jody looked up from her doll.

'Shall we go now, Jody? Shall I hold your hand?'

Jody wasn't saying. She had said just about nothing since she'd arrived at six o'clock the previous evening, delivered by Anne's husband Don to the front door with all her possessions stuffed into a couple of bin bags. Anne had given Jane and Darren two hours' warning by phone, short-cutting official procedure, cheerily presenting them with a *fait accompli*. They'd been expecting her two days later. They hadn't even finished constructing her bed.

''Bye, Jody!' Don had said, turning speedily to leave as if fearful of being asked to stay – a misjudgement on his part. With each successive visit to Jody at her foster-home Jane's longing to wrench her from it had grown fiercer. On the way home from those encounters, a twenty-minute drive from a tired old street on the twilight fringe of Docklands, she would sit quietly in the passenger seat at Darren's side and interrogate herself about why she had so taken against Anne. Snobbery, she knew, was some of it; a taste reflex instilled by her upbringing despite its earnest concern for the less well-off. But her zeal was fortified by her firm conclusion that, to Anne, Jody was first and foremost a commission, a job of work, one that she was fulfilling for a tax-free fee and had become a little bored with; she wanted to move on and replace it with some more amusing scrap of damaged humanity.

'What did you think of her?' she'd asked Darren, as he'd nosed through the traffic after that first time.

'She seems competent enough.'

'Would you describe her as caring?'

119

He'd paused before replying, 'I'd say so. Not sentimental, though. I suppose she can't afford to be.'

'Fair enough,' Jane had said, which let him know that in her head she agreed but that her heart dissented furiously. Anne's was the third foster-home Jody had had since she had been taken into care at eight months old. Ashleigh had opposed it, but in vain.

'She's very quiet,' Darren had said. 'Jody, I mean.'

'We're going to take her, aren't we?'

'It sounds like it,' he'd answered softly.

Jane had embarked on her rescue mission that first evening, trawling her bookshelves and the Internet for insights into impaired development, foetal alcohol spectrum disorder, malnutrition, emotional dysfunction, the whole panoply of infant neglect. In addition, she'd refamiliarised herself with texts she'd consulted routinely when Lorna, Eliot and Clyde were younger. From these, she'd compiled a picture of a typical three-year-old that daunted and sobered her when she contrasted it with the numbed creature at Anne's.

At that age, she read, remembering as she went, three-year-olds are leaving babyhood behind. They may still get scared by strange noises or imaginary beasts, and may still cling to comfort blankets. But mostly they are becoming sociable. They begin to enjoy the company of other children; they like to laugh and act daft; they start to grasp the shocking truth that grown-ups cannot read their minds and sometimes need to have things explained. This, Jane learned, should not be beyond the average three-year-old, who knows over a thousand words and constructs short sentences. Time's passage, too, begins to have meaning for children at this age. They start to talk about the future and the past.

The past: Jody's past; the mental space from which it was Jane's mission to retrieve her.

'Jody?' she said. 'Shall I carry you?'

Jody got slowly to her feet. She'd woken four hours earlier – too early – at ten to six. Jane, so primed to react to any sound or movement from the small room, as it would no longer be called, that she had barely slept a wink, had been up and beside her instantly. She'd found her peering up from her brand new bed wearing a vaguely stranded look yet one that, it seemed to Jane, had long ago discounted hope of being retrieved. After accompanying her to the toilet in her bobbled pink nightie, Jane had persuaded her to put on some of the new clothes she had been half secretly buying for her: a blue denim skirt with a Spanish frill, an orange T-shirt with a picture of a daisy on the front. To Jane's eye she looked less woebegone in them. At the same time she worried that they added to her disorientation.

'Come on, Jody. Let me give you a hug.' Jane held out her arms. Jody stepped into them, keeping hold of the doll and leaving *Grandpa's Handkerchief* behind. Jane lifted her up, shocked by her lightness yet almost breathless with the weight of responsibility. 'Let's find the others, shall we?' she said.

She knew that they were all waiting to go, kicking their heels on the front step, or loafing in the hall or, in Darren's case, out on the street refixing Clyde's old child seat in their new and larger car: an old eight-seater MPV; a minibus, virtually. It was the last Friday in May, also the last day of the last week before half-term. Jane and Darren had awarded Lorna, Eliot and Clyde the day off school. The decision had been taken amid the drama and confusion of the previous evening, when Jane and Darren had concluded that a family day out at Legoland, in Jody's honour, would be more pleasurable for all if taken when most kids were still confined to their classrooms. It had occurred to Jane that the day would have been calmer still, had it been education as normal for Lorna, Eliot and Clyde allowing Jody time alone with her prospective new parents, yet that option had barely been considered. Why not? wondered Jane, as she carried Jody into the sunlit hall. Why the desire for her first full day with them to be an action-packed excursion? Was there something about the house they wished to flee?

Eliot was waiting by the door. Jane smiled at him and, as always when she looked at him these days, swallowed a sigh of loss and dismay. The puppy-fleshed angel who'd watched foxes from the window had stretched upwards and contracted inwards. He'd become all awkward edge and sinew. His hipbones seemed to act as hooks in holding up his jeans, which was just as well because no other part of his physique was doing it. The bottoms swamped his blue suede trainers. The seat sagged almost to the backs of his knees.

'All right, Mum?' Eliot said. His voice was still unbroken but his tone was pitched low.

'Yes, thank you, Eliot. We're all right, aren't we, Jody?' Answering as if on Jody's behalf gave Jane a way to avoid being transfixed by the fuzz on Eliot's top lip. She shuffled past him, feeling like a mouse in the shadow of an unexpected giant.

'Shall I shut the door, then?' Eliot asked, once she and Jody were outside.

'Thank you, El, that would be helpful. And could you lock it for me, please?'

Still carrying Jody, she handed her key to him and

watched him use it to be sure the job was done properly. Looking down the street she saw that the car was a good twenty yards away, as was frequently the case with so many houses turned over to multi-occupancy and no spaces reserved for residents. The rest of the family was moving untidily towards it. Jane began to follow cautiously. Her sense of Jody's vulnerability became more acute outside, as if her charge were a prisoner freed from a dungeon and struggling to breathe above ground.

'When did you last go on an outing, Jody?' Jane asked, shifting the child's position so that eye-contact could be made.

Eliot, compulsively twirling the door keys on his middle finger, bounded past them.

'Do you remember?' coaxed Jane.

Jody shook her head. She was half watching Eliot, who had slowed to a slouch five yards ahead.

'I think *I* can remember,' said Jane, and how she loathed her chirruping timbre. It did nothing to loosen Jody's tongue either. The car seemed even further off, though she could clearly see Darren loading the cool-bag into the boot. Lorna stood beside him, possibly half watching him from behind her sunglasses but possibly not. She wore a lemon sun-frock, which made a statement so glaringly at odds with its wearer's mood of late that Jane had had to look away when she had come downstairs in it. To add to the incongruity a little straw basket swung from Lorna's right hand. Jane wanted to save her from herself – so much she could almost have strangled her.

A little further from the car Clyde trudged in circles swinging a stick. Only Eliot had waited for Jane and Jody to emerge, and now matched his pace to Jane's, keeping just far enough ahead of her to think she wouldn't know he was eavesdropping. But when Jane spoke again to Jody, she was accutely aware that Eliot was half her audience.

'You came with me to the seaside, didn't you? Me and Darren.' It was impossible to refer him as 'Daddy' yet or to even *think* of herself as Jody's mummy – too presumptuous by far.

They'd been to Brighton in April, just the three of them, for the day. An outing was the next big step towards placement, after all the visiting at Anne's. For Jane, it had been truly liberating. It was the first time that the context had been more hers than someone else's to control. There had been pebbles, chips and paddling, even some smiles and nearly a chat or two.

'Do you like the seaside, Jody?'

A slow nod. Then: 'Yeah.'

'Have you been to the seaside before?'

A shake of the head. 'No.'

Jane had believed her – by then she'd heard more than enough about Ashleigh to doubt that healthy outdoor trips were her thing. But it had occurred to her, too, that if Jody had, in fact, been to the seaside many times, perhaps with some concerned relative or community group, she, Jane, might never know. What else might she never know? A million things: nearly three and a half years' worth of things had gone missing, just about all beyond recovery. And maybe that wasn't such a bad thing. She and Darren had been shown Jody's life-story book, the collection of photographs and biographical details compiled for her benefit and those of her carers so that Jody's history would be known to all. Now that Jody had been placed with them, the book had passed into Jane and Darren's possession. It was a paltry thing, far from the lovingly maintained journal it should have been. Such writing as it contained had clearly been done at the last minute by each of those through whose custody Jody had passed. There were a few undistinguished snapshots, none of which included Ashleigh, let alone Kirk Lovell. Although she'd had limited contact with Jody at her various foster-homes Ashleigh, apparently, had consistently failed to provide a photo of herself and claimed not to possess one of Kirk. Jane had dwelled upon this frequently. Having been parted from her child, it was almost as though Ashleigh was readying herself to be erased. Or maybe she just didn't like the way she looked in photos.

At Brighton Jane and Darren had bought Jody an ice-cream and forayed with her to the water's edge. A bold seagull had landed nearby.

'Leave me!' Jody had screamed. 'Leave me!'

'It's all right, Jody,' Jane had said. 'It's only a big, silly bird.'

'Leave me!' She'd picked up a pebble and thrown it at the gull.

'No, darling, no.'

'Leave!'

The pebble had landed nowhere near its target. The fury of the attempt, though, had left Jane alarmed. And then Jody had run off and kept running, still holding the ice-cream, floating and skittering across the shifting surface like a feather in the breeze. Darren and Jane had given chase, and when they'd overhauled her Jody's response to capture was to make her carapace impermeable. When restrained, she'd struggled, smearing melting Cornetto up Darren's arm. When released, she'd fled once more. In the end they'd stopped chasing her. They had calculated that she would be scared to stray far. The gamble had paid off: having settled to pick at a tangle of beach detritus fifty yards off, Jody had checked surreptitiously every now and then that the latest grown-ups she was obliged to rely on were still there.

To rely, though, is not the same as to trust. And now, six weeks later, the distinction loomed large in Jane's mind as she edged Jody down the east London street towards the family and its car. A long road lay ahead.

To get to Legoland meant heading south of the river via the Blackwall Tunnel, then threading through the suburbs and beyond to the westbound lanes of the M25. For this, the first and most exacting part of the journey, the confinement of the car interior, the air of concentration spreading from Darren behind the wheel, and the unknowable presence of Jody had an emollient effect on the travellers. None the less, a shared and pensive sense of occasion endured.

'So is Jody, like, ours to keep now?' Clyde asked Jane, without warning.

'Don't say things like that!' snapped Lorna, who was reluctantly beside him in the rearmost of the car's three rows of seats. She added sarcastically, 'She can hear, you know.'

'All right, Lorna,' warned Jane, who was beside Jody in the middle row.

'I'm only *saying* . . .' Lorna complained.

'I know what you're saying and please don't say it again.'

Jane closed her eyes as if in prayer. It conveyed to Lorna more eloquently than words how badly she wanted this day to run smoothly. And it seemed to work: no umbraged explosion ensued, and when Jane opened her eyes again Lorna was looking blankly out of her window, watching the road slip by as remorselessly as the sands of time. For all her touchiness she had seemed more subdued lately, as if her strop-hormone level had run low. Jane wondered in passing why this might be but opted to let the small mercy go unexplained. She was, in any case, more worried about Jody who was sucking the neck of her T-shirt. It could only be anxiety, thought Jane. Oh, God, this had been a bad idea: a tense car journey lasting well over an hour, surrounded by people the poor child barely knew.

'Yes, Clyde,' Jane said at last, for everyone to hear, including Eliot in the front passenger seat. 'Jody has joined our family now.' She eyeballed Clyde, and, with a prompting nod, provided him with a mandatory right answer to the question she then asked: 'Do you understand?'

'Yes, Mummy,' said Clyde. 'But what if she doesn't like us?'

'Oh, I think she will.'

'But what if she doesn't?'

'Clyde!' Jane checked herself: she'd been about to say the same thing she'd ticked off Lorna for saying. Instead she said, 'If we make today a lovely one for Jody, she'll know that we want her to stay. And if she knows we want her, she'll want to stay, won't she?'

Clyde shrugged. 'I suppose so.'

The soggy patch Jody had made on her T-shirt neck had now grown to the size of a satsuma. Jane tried to read her face but her impassivity was absolute. Whatever internal realm she was inhabiting seemed to comfort her. Perhaps this was her response to stress and insecurity. Jane felt as if she was standing on a high ledge. Below her were spread the many things that could go wrong. She tried not to think about them; tried not to look down.

Darren was engaging in a little private driving therapy, keeping to an even sixty miles per hour and counting off the junctions patiently: five . . . six . . . seven . . . There'd be another full-house outing before long to visit Dorothy and Jeffrey and show Jody to them for the first time. He hoped it would provide Jane with the triumph he knew she yearned for, the clinching confirmation of the vigorous approval they had already expressed for her rescuing a child from misery. He anticipated Dorothy's busy welcome and Jeffrey's small relapses into vacancy, which had become more noticeable and filled those who witnessed them with apprehension they still barely dared express. Darren anticipated the private speculation all this would stir in him. How would his own parents have received this co-opted new grandchild, this refugee? He'd yet to tell Jane how it pained him that he'd never know.

'How are you doing, Eliot?' he asked.

'Yeah, fine.'

Why do they do that, Darren thought, say 'yeah' before answering a question that hadn't asked for a simple 'yes' or 'no'? And why do they then say 'fine', a fobbing-off non-word for all occasions?

He said, 'What do you think of the new car?'

'Yeah, fine.'

Eliot had got the front berth, thanks to the toss of a coin. Lorna had had the bad luck to call 'tails'. She'd taken it in good heart because she still liked Eliot (although she'd stopped calling him 'handsome boy') but her attitude had failed her when she'd learned it meant she had to sit by Clyde. Eliot had sympathised because he'd have to swap with her for the journey home. He still liked Lorna, and he could tell she wasn't too happy. His father's irritation with him, though, had passed him by. His head was travelling elsewhere: to the edge of the swimming-pool the previous

Tuesday evening with Ivanka, his willowy, olive-skinned Bulgarian instructor, showing him how to execute a swallow dive; Ivanka, wrestling with her imperfect English and for once not wearing a baggy T-shirt over her black Speedo costume. He saw this and then some things he hadn't seen: Ivanka showering in her private cubicle, tugging the tight Lycra down and then her beckoning him to her, pulling his head against her chest and, with her spare hand, loosening his swimming-trunks cord. After that, the images got cloudier. What would he be meant to do? Ivanka would have to show him; he wouldn't mind doing as he was told.

Eliot curled up more in his seat, shifting his weight on to his left side.

'How far now, Darren?' Jane enquired, mustering every last ounce of levity.

'About ten miles to the turn-off, then it's some wiggly little roads towards Windsor. Half an hour should do it. How's everyone back there?'

'Fine. They're doing fine.'

'Only "fine"?'

'More than fine, I'd say.'

Yeah, right, Lorna thought. She was reliving the moment when it really hit her that it was over – 're-dying' would put it more accurately. She'd walked into her tutor-group room first thing on a Monday morning and seen the huddle, heard the hot chatter and shrieks, then the closed-ranks silence when they saw her. Five year-ten girls from the peer group she no longer belonged to: Lisa Raine, Nicky Browne, Daisy Carmichael, Lindsay Small and . . . Kazea; Kazea Massie, her ex-best friend.

Later she'd pieced together the background, walking home alone, almost bent double in agony. They had been

out at the weekend, to some club or something in the West
End, and Lorna had not been told of the plan. It was their
cruel, cowardly secret from her. She was, she supposed, not
that surprised. For some weeks she'd been accumulating the
small wounds of exclusion, half the time flinching from
them, the other half pretending they weren't there. She'd
been consigned to the margins of conversations. A school
rock band had been formed, the Sindie Killers, that didn't
need anyone to play saxophone. At break times she often
found she was alone.

'Are you all right, Lorna?' her mother had started asking,
on learning she no plans for weekends.

'Yeah, fine.'

'Are you all right, Lorna?' she asked now.

'Fine, Mum, yeah. Just tired.'

The landscape seemed to rotate past her window like a
carousel. She stared absently down through the windows of
smaller, lower, overtaking cars. Fuck you, bitches – that's
what she should have said to them. She'd said nothing,
though. Instead, she'd shuffled off to bleed. A few days later
she'd stayed at home pretending to be ill and, while Jane
was out, phoned Kazea's mum but lost her nerve and hung
up when she answered. What exactly had she thought she
was going to say? 'Please, please, Sinead, tell your daughter
to love me again'? 'Please make her see I'm nicer than those
other girls'? For four weeks now she'd been bereft.

By the time they reached the M3, everyone but Jane and
Darren was sleeping. It was the first time since she'd arrived
that Jane had been able to interrogate Jody's face without
having to fear its replies. The sun fell hot across her cheek,
rendering it almost translucent. The soggy spot on the T-
shirt was drying. Jane licked the suction cups on a movable

sunshade and stuck it on the window beside her head. She hoped, none the less, that colour would enliven the poor child's features soon.

She leaned forward to be closer to Darren's ear. 'We've got her, then,' she said.

'We've got her,' he replied.

'How do you feel?' she asked.

'I feel OK. How does she feel, I wonder?'

'I wish I knew.'

He offered no reply to this, making some play of watching an overtaking car in the wing mirror.

In a lower voice Jane said, 'Do we still love each other, Darren?'

He couldn't turn to look at her so she couldn't see his eyes when he replied, 'Of course we do.'

The first thing that had become clear to Darren when, as they'd agreed, he and Jane had begun thinking and talking about adopting was that Jane's mind was made up, even if she'd not realised it herself. And this put him in an unfamiliar place. Their love had long drawn strength from their unravelling of Jane's complexities. Her passionate unguardedness had never ceased to enthral Darren from the first time he'd detected it just beneath the surface of her wit. To her he rapidly became the man she hadn't known she'd been looking for.

Previous boyfriends had been unreliable artists and affable young fools. Darren was more solid and more sweet. As her student lover he'd been ready to sit up and listen to her talk for hours – to her total rubbish, as she'd called it. Then, come the dawn, he'd make love to her with the wonder of a plain man exploring a casket of jewels. Now, suddenly, their positions were reversed: she became the rock, he the ferment of uncertainties. The difference was that he, unlike she, felt compelled to keep his weaknesses concealed.

They had agreed to take things a step at a time. The first was simple and congenial. After finding an agency that welcomed and encouraged them – a small children's charity with an honourable history – they were invited to a meeting where they and two other pairs of hopefuls received further information about what might lie in store. They heard the first-hand accounts of a couple who had adopted three biologically unconnected children in seven years. It was a warts-and-all account: there had been bad times and phases of terrible self-doubt before the rewards outweighed the difficulties. The couple looked to be in their mid-to-late thirties. They alluded to infertility, but their rosy, sweaterish appearance and the crucifix with which the woman fiddled suggested Christian principles put to good work too. Near the end of the meeting, the agency facilitator invited the newcomers to say why adopting interested them.

'I've been lucky in my life,' Jane had said, 'and rather spoiled. I had an easy upbringing, I have a nice life now and three healthy children of my own. Now that I'm forty-four, I think it's time I did something for someone who hasn't had things as easy as me.'

Her sincerity was utterly unvarnished. Others nodded their approval. Darren, though, was unnerved. He couldn't echo her convictions, yet that was the whole point of his being there.

In the following weeks their induction began in earnest. Forms were filled in, police checks were made, and then came the home-study phase, which they were warned would be exacting and go on for several months. They were assigned to a social worker called Lucy. She was in her late twenties, soft-spoken, serious and bespectacled. She made eight home visits in all, each lasting for at least two hours, sometimes with one or more of the children present, sometimes with one or other of the parents on their own, but most often with just the pair of them alone together. From the start she was every bit as gently yet insistently intrusive as her job required her to be.

'When did your relationship begin?'

They'd looked at each other, uncertain who should speak first. The one thing that had become clear to them already was their need to display unity. They laughed nervously at their shared indecision before Darren, keen to show willing, took the lead.

'It was when we were at university. We were both in our second year.'

'So you've been together for a long time.'

'We don't look that old, do we?'

Lucy had smiled, but nothing more.

'Since 1978,' said Darren. 'Twenty-five years almost to the day.' He'd smiled at Jane.

'And you've been together since?'

Her tone was confirmatory. Darren's instinct was not to disabuse her. But Jane said, 'Except for a short time.'

'For a short time, yes,' said Darren, quickly.

Lucky looked up over her glasses. 'All right, and when was that?'

Jane had the answer ready: 'Between 'eighty-one and 'eighty-four.'

But the timeline question was the easy part.

'So,' said Lucy, after she'd written down the dates, 'why did you split up at that time?'

Darren thought he'd always remember what happened next: how they'd looked quickly at each other to touch base, then just as quickly looked away. When he'd reviewed those few seconds the next morning, as he'd lain awake at dawn, he'd felt forlorn.

'I think it was the usual thing about university relationships,' he'd volunteered.

'We were both very young,' Jane had put in. 'After we graduated we wanted to do different things. We decided to split up for a while and see how we got on.'

'OK,' Lucy had said, putting her pen to work again. 'And how *did* you both get on, would you say?'

When they got to Legoland Darren and Jane were not surprised that Lorna, *angst* and irritation clogging every pore, would want to break away and have Eliot gangling at her side for company. They gave the teens permission on the sole condition that before they disappeared they sampled some of the park's attractions with Jody, to help her learn that she could trust them. They had already made Jody's acquaintance: at Anne's place on a couple of occasions and once more at their home when she, Giselle, Lucy and a too-eager Anne had come to Bow to look them over, or so Lorna and Eliot characterised the visits when they'd discussed them later. This cynicism, though, was the garb in which they draped themselves when huddled in adolescent solidarity. When the encounters were taking place they'd conducted themselves charmingly, just as they had when Lucy had asked each of them alone how they would feel about a younger child coming into their home. Both had been quite clear it would be 'fine'.

They made a similar effort now. Uncertainly (in Eliot's case) and rather bossily (in Lorna's) but willingly enough, they had accompanied Jody on the Sky Rider, a kind of kiddie roller-coaster without the dips. Then each had taken a hand and led her to the Imagination Centre where together they built for her a Duplo menagerie and pretended the giraffes could speak Chinese. Jody watched them at their work, sometimes smiling tentatively, before moving off a short distance to some other pieces and attempting to assemble them herself.

This was the point at which Clyde became involved. Until then he'd kept his distance, but sensed this was his moment to connect with Jody on terms of his choosing. He'd abandoned the robot he'd been constructing and scampered across to her. 'Would you like to make a robot, Jody, like I did?'

She looked up at him cautiously. Lorna called, 'Clyde, don't hassle her.'

'Would you like to Jody?' Clyde insisted. 'Shall I show you?'

Before Jody could have answered, had she been going to, Clyde seized the bricks out of her hand. 'See, Jody, like this! You put them together like this!'

From a parental distance, Jane and Darren looked on nervously. They watched Jody step away, as Clyde slammed pieces together, providing a commentary on what he was doing, then walk off and half skip towards the exit door. Jane intercepted her before she slipped into the drifting crowd outside and Darren went to Clyde to say, comfortingly, 'I think by accident you might have frightened her.'

The shepherds reconvened their flock with soothing sounds: there now, no one's cross, shall we go on to the next thing? They went outside and entered the flow of families, walked down a long, staggered slope to the sprawling Lego-modelled world called Miniland. Here were boats and cars and village scenes, and the prime tourist sights of London re-created in interlocking miniature.

The parents were watchful, Jane in particular. Jody seemed absorbed, though, watching tiny trains rush by, staring at boxy little plastic citizens with fixed-on smiles. Clyde, at her side, was drawn in too, or maybe just drawn to Jody, pointing details out to her and bending down to speak into her ear. Lorna and Eliot, meanwhile, scuffed along, nodding at things now and again and chuckling to show that they were well above all this until, after half an hour, Lorna announced that they were striking out on their own now. Could they, like, have some money, please?

With a ten-pound note to last them, they disappeared. Darren and Jane exchanged modest admissions of relief, then took the two little ones by their hands. It hammered at Jane's heart to see that Jody was so small, her hair straight and bunched into a plain ponytail, her skin, ghostly. Clyde threw action poses and stole glances at her from the far side of Darren.

For two hours, they meandered from balloon carousel to battery racing car to twister slides. A lot of queuing was required, which, for the grown-ups, had the up-side of keeping the little ones corralled. Both passed their waiting time in fantasy worlds. With Clyde, this involved the slaying of imaginary foes, valorous tasks he accomplished by emitting slashing and swishing noises and by mentally transforming any object that came to hand into a sword. Jody's place of escape was quieter and impenetrable to outsiders. All that was clear was that her doll had gone there with her. Her name was simply 'Dolly' and her lot was to be poked a bit, shaken a bit and to live with it.

Jane observed this apprehensively. It was all a far cry from the landscapes of adventure that Poppy down the road galloped across. 'What do you think she's thinking?' she asked Darren.

'I'd love to know,' he replied

He shrugged and put his arm round Jane, pulling her close. He kissed her on the temple too. It was his way of saying sorry for not wanting to play guessing games. Faced by the unknown – the unknowable, maybe – he found speculating unhelpful. Developmental tests had already confirmed that Jody was off the pace compared with most three-year-olds but no one could be sure why. With lots of love and stimulation she might make up lost ground. But if Ashleigh's drinking had been as heavy during the pregnancy as it had been after the birth the damage might be permanent. Sometimes a child showed physical signs of having being hurt by its mother's boozing while in her womb: a small chin, a short, upturned nose, drooping eyelids, a lack of ridges between nose and mouth. But the more Jane and Darren looked for these in Jody, the less clear they were about what they were or were not seeing. And with no photo of Ashleigh to compare her with, there was no way to tell how much of her appearance she had inherited.

The scientist in Darren craved clarity, of course, yet also urged caution. Nothing about Jody's facial features offered clear-cut evidence – even the doctors had said so. Only time, trial and error would tell. Moreover, the process of adopting had involved enough delving in the dark to last him a lifetime.

Lucy had asked him about his time in Guatemala. 'Did you have any relationships?'

'Yes, well . . . yes, you could say I did. While I was there.'

'Was it, I have to ask, a sexual relationship?'

'Yes.'

It had been very sexual – purely so, if that was the right word. Geraldine Dowling had been his project field director or something Darren could not recall – her job title wasn't his strongest memory of her – and, at thirty-four, twelve years his senior. She had split from her partner before Darren had arrived in the village where he would work and most of the volunteers were girls. Geraldine had taught him a few things: about taking it more slowly; about thighs, shoulders and earlobes; about himself and the rewards of letting the lady be in charge.

'It wasn't love,' he'd explained to Lucy, wondering if Jane, sitting beside him, could smell his nerve ends burning.

'How did being away change you?' Lucy had asked.

'It helped me grow up,' he'd replied.

Lucy had written all this down, then cleaned her glasses and asked Jane, 'And how did you spend those three years?'

'Oh, my God,' Jane had begun.

At Legoland it was nearly two o'clock. The cool-bag wouldn't be cool for much longer. Lorna and Eliot had agreed to rendezvous with their parents beside a small play area for younger children with slides, seesaws and climbing frames. Darren and Jane found a bench and settled down while Clyde and Jody ran off together towards a slide that wound round a spotted fibreglass dinosaur. Dolly the doll was left behind, which Jane took as a good sign: other mothers were clucking and fussing over their children; her charges were looking after themselves. Jody and Clyde took the slide a dozen times, then chased each other about, Clyde pretending to be slower than he was. Jody let out squeals of delight, the most expressive she'd yet been.

'This is good,' Darren said then looked at his watch. 'I wonder where the floppies are.' He was referring to the teenagers.

'Being floppy, I expect,' rejoined Jane. She wasn't anxious about them. In fact, she hoped they wouldn't roll up too soon. Jody was doing so well, she feared that any change in the chemistry would break the spell. Jody wore her scruffy trainers from her previous life, which Jane hadn't wanted to risk changing in case a new pair turned out to be uncomfortable. But her new T-shirt suited her and the skirt bobbed and twirled as she ran.

'Sandwich?' offered Darren, fishing one out of the bag.

'Sweet talker,' she replied, accepting.

'They look happy, don't they?' said Darren.

Jane said, 'Darren, do you think I'm mad?'

'No. Why?'

'Oh, I don't know.' She was thinking compulsively of the men she'd slept with while Darren had been on his learning curve with Geraldine. She'd thought of them as boys, but they'd all been adults and she a young woman – hardly a grown-up, though. Not that she'd put it quite this way to Lucy.

'What I mean,' she'd explained, after the 'Oh, my God,' had escaped, 'is that I made a few mistakes during that time. I learned a few lessons.'

'Can I ask what sort of lessons?'

'Oh, about relationships, you know.'

There had been five men altogether: four musicians and someone she'd known at school. Jane had told Lucy there'd been three and in so doing remained true to the fib she'd told Darren when they'd taken up again after he came home from Guatemala, and which she had maintained ever since. Of the five, she'd only really cared for one, a guitar-player called Sean, and that had been because she was gullible enough to believe he had cared for her. Until, that was, the Monday evening she'd returned to her housing-co-op basement flat in Haggerston to find that all the possessions he had moved in over the months had now gone; the yukka palm, the stereo, everything. He'd bolted, leaving no physical trace except a sink full of plates and a frying-pan.

The sheer efficiency of Sean's self-removal and her failure to spot the signs had shaken Jane. It was as though he was trying to fool her into thinking he'd never been there at all, that his presence in her life had been an illusion: the sex fiercer than with Darren, the shopping for old records, the intermittent free lines of cocaine, *everything*. To Lucy, the nod-nodding social worker of not much more than half her age, Jane said only of Sean that it had 'ended badly'. To Darren, she'd said much more some twenty years earlier, lazing and contemplating up on Parliament Hill during the bitter summer of the miners' strike. He'd had the last, pinkish layer of his Central American tan on his face and the backs of his hands; she'd fiddled with the mock-Gothic earrings Sean had chosen for her (but not bought) at Camden market. Darren, lying on his front, had removed his glasses, placed them folded on the grass and said, 'He was pretty exciting, though, wasn't he?'

'Don't make me talk about him,' Jane had begged.

'Admit it and I'll stop.'

Jane had stared morosely at the panoramic view of London, wishing she could simply leap into it and disappear. 'I suppose he was fun while he lasted,' she confessed painfully. Darren had looked so vulnerable without his specs. 'The shit,' Jane had added supportively.

As Darren rooted in the cool-bag, Jane, remembered they had gone on to find a cheap hotel in Bloomsbury and how Darren had been. Yes, it had mattered to her that some of his new tricks had been learned from the libertine

Geraldine but this failed to prevent her feeling like Aphrodite succumbing on a silver cloud. He had remained her constant worshipper.

'Do you think they're hungry?' she asked, as Jody ran shrieking from Clyde, who was pretending to be a wolf.

'I expect they'll tell us when they are. Hello, look who's here.'

Lorna led the way, basket swinging, face ominously set. Eliot walked behind her, a young lion yet to grow into his paws.

'Mum, there's a café over there,' Lorna said, dispensing with all preliminaries and nodding in the direction she'd come from.

'I know,' Jane replied.

'Can we go there?'

'We've brought a picnic.'

'Yeah, I know but—' She broke off, welcoming the chance to look peevish.

'But what?' asked Jane, sharply.

'Oh, never mind.'

Jane bit her tongue.

'They're quite exciting sandwiches,' said Darren, drily. 'For vegetarians we have cheese and, er, cheese and, er . . .'

'Very funny, Dad,' said Lorna.

Darren smiled at his daughter hopefully, appealing to her not to cause a row. With half an eye on Jane he said, 'And what about you, Eliot? Do you want some of the magnificent spread I've prepared?'

'I'm not hungry, thanks.'

Jane said, 'Are you sure, Eliot?' But her attention was being pulled elsewhere. Jody had abandoned chasing Clyde, who'd re-entered his own small world and was annihilating some unseen assailant with a sequence of cartoon martial-arts moves. Jody had acquired a new toy: a stuffed animal of some kind – a rabbit, maybe? Jane squinted to see.

'Oh, Daddy, please, can't we go to the café?' Lorna wheedled.

'Oh, shut up, will you, Lorna?' snapped Jane.

'Haw?' Lorna's expression moved to the next stage in its repertoire of wrongedness, from pained supplicant to blameless victim.

'Just shut up!' repeated Jane, jumping to her feet.

A woman was walking fast towards Jody, dragging a small girl wearing a blue cotton frock. Jane recognised the woman's body language. She'd spoken it often enough herself. The girl in the frock was crying.

'Hello!' Jane called, breaking into a half-run. 'Hello!'

The other woman didn't hear her – too intent on what she was doing, too deafened by the howls of her daughter. When she reached Jody, the woman bent down to her, pointing and speaking. Reaching out she took a slow grip of the soft toy – it was indeed a rabbit, blue like the girl's frock, with button princess eyes and floppy ears – at the moment when Jane joined the scene. Jody hugged the rabbit and pulled away.

'That isn't very nice, is it?' the other woman was saying, steely-sweet.

'Hello,' said Jane, loudly.

The face that turned to her was harder than she'd expected: more plucked and pencilled than the shorts, trainers and T-shirt had suggested.

'She's taken my little girl's toy,' the other woman said. The look, the accent, the words: raw data that compiled themselves into a warning sign.

'I'm sorry,' said Jane, then turned to Jody. Softly, she said,

'Jody, could you give the little girl her rabbit back? I think she's feeling sad.'

This appeased the other mother for the moment. She comforted her daughter, whose frock, Jane had observed, had a lace panel on the bodice, and whose eyes were smeared with makeup. She had quietened down, though, perhaps smelling victory.

'Jody,' Jane continued, 'can you give me the rabbit, please?' She held out her hands, fingers spread wide to emphasise the sincerity of her appeal. Jody hugged the rabbit to her throat and shook her head dolefully. 'Jody, please . . .'

'Can't you just take it off her?' the other woman said. 'I'm in a hurry, actually.'

'I will, I will,' said Jane, quickly. 'I'd just sooner she understood what she's done wrong.'

'Yeah, well . . .' The other mother trailed off, but her implication was brutally plain. She breathed out, impatiently.

'All right, all right,' said Jane. 'Jody, please give the rabbit to me.' She reached for it as she spoke, began to prise Jody's fingers off it.

Jody screamed. She screamed louder as Jane took hold of her, wrenching the rabbit and the clawed hands asunder. The rabbit fell to the ground, and the other girl seized it, Jody twisted half free and landed hard on her bare knees. Already, the other mother and her daughter were away. Under her breath, Jane spat daggers at their backs.

Darren appeared beside her. 'Shall I take her?' he asked, as Jody continued to scream.

'Am I complete crap, then?' Jane asked him. 'Come on, darling,' she said to Jody. 'Where does it hurt?'

'Jane, I didn't mean—'

'Oh, take her, then!' said Jane.

She lifted Jody and handed her over. Her legs were flailing, her eyes were closed. Darren hoisted her to his shoulder and pinioned her feet against his chest. Then he whisked her away, talking any old drivel to distract her from her pains. Jane, standing alone, pushed her hair off her forehead, pretending to be unaware of the audience of other parents who were pretending not to watch her. The social pressure helped in the fight for composure. She was stung by the other mother's contempt. How bitterly unjust that even had she been able to explain about Jody and why she wasn't to blame, why she, Jane, wasn't to blame either, the other woman wouldn't have wanted to know.

Lorna and Eliot had been joined by Clyde. All three stood helplessly. Jane was thankful for their helplessness – it gave her something to do. She walked over to them, resolving not to shout or cry. By the time she reached them, she knew what she wanted to say. 'I'm sorry I was cross with you, Lorna,' she said, steadying her voice valiantly.

Lorna shifted noncommittally. Eliot stood behind her, chewing the cord of his hoodie. Meanwhile, at Jane's elbow, Clyde resumed laying waste to invisible assailants, hordes of them non-appearing everywhere. It struck Jane, as such thoughts did, that this surrealistic sideshow would have worked well as a comedy-sketch. She wasn't laughing, though. Instead, a jagged sadness rose.

'OK, Lorna.' She sighed. 'The problem is, you're bloody miserable. Everyone can see it. Everyone knows.'

'I'm *not* miserable,' Lorna protested, scowling.

'Yes, you *are* miserable,' seethed Jane, furious and tearful now, 'so don't make it even more bloody unbearable by lying about it and turning nasty when somebody points it out.'

144

Lorna straightened and took half a step away. 'Why not, Mum?' she said, cowering and yet defiant. 'That's what you're doing, isn't it?'

Jane's face fell. Clyde broke off from his exertions to stare. Eliot stood back and kept quiet, chewing. And by then Lorna was tacking off and away, head lolling on one side, straw basket swinging absurdly from her hand. Her mother sat in dismay amid the wreckage of the day, left to pick it up and take it home.

CHAPTER SIX JUNE

On the way back from Legoland it had occurred to Jane that having Jody might wreck everything. This belated epiphany had the same seizure-like effect as when she'd just got settled on a cross-Channel ferry and become paralysed by the fear that she'd shut Simba in Clyde's bedroom; and the numerous occasions when, driving the kids somewhere, she'd succumbed to a panicky urge to check she hadn't left one on the pavement. What if, after all the analysis and heart-searching, all those squeamish explorations of motives and memories, it turned out that adding a neglected three-year-old to her family would turn out to be a catalyst for the destruction of her marriage, a trigger for her birth children to slump into dysfunction?

All these threatening questions had reared up around Jane as she'd brooded beside the baby seat in which Jody had dozed off inscrutably. Behind her, Eliot had plugged into his CD Walkman beside a grubby, snoring Clyde. Lorna, now in the front, had kept her lemon-face turned away. After some consideration of the back view of Darren's head Jane had concluded that he had taken on the classic male role of stoic motorist, the first stage on the journey to divorce. By the time they'd got home and she'd tucked Jody into bed, the future had looked so unavoidably bleak that Jane could see no other course than to sail blithely into it and pray.

Yet the half-term holiday, which straddled the transition from May to June, was negotiated peacefully. Perhaps this was an indirect consequence of the Legoland trauma, with each established member of the Grice-Ransome household entering a separate and distinctive state of distance, denial or delayed shock. Darren quietly took command of the domestic basics – the shopping, the cooking, the laundry. Eliot went off to see friends, dragging himself and his enormous Vans trainers to the home of a boy called Alex from his school, who lived in a middle-class enclave bordering the Hackney side of Victoria Park. Alex, by contrast, did not visit Eliot, which might have made Jane and Darren pause for thought had there been any time to pause. All they knew about Alex was what little Darren had gleaned when he fetched Eliot in the car and drove him home amid the slumped silence and vaunting height increase of his early adolescence. Alex seemed a polite if possibly boisterous boy, whose father had moved out a few months earlier and whose mother's dress sense and demeanour whispered, 'How about it?'

Lorna, meanwhile, did nothing much around the house with an air of profound philosophical detachment. She noted Eliot's nascent social life with a resentment she felt bad about, but somehow couldn't shake. For all that she despised it she needed the sanctuary of home and dreaded going back to school. Kazea and the others weren't being horrible to her, but their laboured civility offered no hope. One day on her way home she'd seen Kazea sashay down the street amid a shrieking crowd with a fried-chicken box in her hand, tearing the flesh from a hot wing with her teeth. This was the final betrayal. Every night Lorna went quietly to her room, often taking her Quorn bake or bean salad with her. Her one consolation was that her mother and father were too preoccupied with Jody to force the torture of their sympathy on her.

Of Jody's three potential siblings, only Clyde engaged closely with the household's small newcomer. As his parents guided and encouraged her, he tagged along eagerly, echoing their enthusiasm, keen to participate and shine. 'This is a nice book, isn't it?' he'd baby-talk, elbowing in on Jody's bedtime stories. 'This is your sponge, isn't it, Jody?' he'd demand, during her bathtime, looking her up and down as she sat bare among the bubbles. She would stare mutely at him as he waved it beneath her nose.

'Do you like breakfast, Jody?' he'd nag relentlessly.

'Do you like your dinner?'

'Do you like drawing pictures?'

'Do you like this kind of sweet?'

Within two or three days Jane and Darren were taking subtle steps to separate them: they feared Jody feeling crowded and that Clyde's fascination with her was acquiring on a manic quality. An informal division of childcare emerged. When Darren went out to the shops, he encouraged Clyde to slip away with him, proffering money bribes and sweets. There were father-and-son PlayStation sessions, an outing to the Natural History Museum and spun-out bike rides in the park. In the male pair's absence, Jane worked hard at finding out who was the stranger in the house. She probed and cajoled, often conscious of how much she sounded like Clyde.

'Do you like your bedroom, Jody?'

'Do you like this book?'

'Do you like this picture?'

'Do you like this toy?'

She didn't yet dare ask the bigger questions in her mind: do you like it here, Jody?; do you like me?; do you wish you were back with Anne?; with Mummy Ashleigh?

'Mummy Ashleigh' was the formula, the standard one, recommended by Lucy for use in talking to Jody about her birth-mother. Such conversation was to be encouraged, Jane and Darren were told. Well, they tried. They spoke to Jody of Ashleigh as her 'tummy-mummy', and they experimented with referring to each other as 'Daddy Darren' and 'Mummy Jane'. None of these devices, though, caught on. Mention of 'Mummy Ashleigh' triggered no visible interest or recognition on Jody's part, and the absence of any photograph in the meagre life-story book doomed any attempt at conversation to a lifeless, faceless end. 'Daddy Darren' and 'Mummy Jane' felt contrived and pushy and like tempting Fate – the loveless, rootless fate of which Jody had tasted too much in her short life.

This was a child who needed room to breathe. Often, Jane would grow sick of the sound of her own cajoling and leave Jody alone, only to sneak back a few minutes later to spy on her. Sometimes she would return to find that Jody, having previously blanked her, shaken her head or said, 'No', had begun to show some interest in whatever item or activity Jane had brought to her elusive attention. Yet she never became convincingly absorbed. There was no fantasy-world babble, no showing off what she was imagining or what she'd learned. Give her time, Jane told herself. Let her get used to us. She'll blossom once she gets into our routine.

At first, this routine meant she and Jody being alone. Darren had arranged to take off half-term anyway but his sabbatical was not intended to begin for three more weeks. Secretly Jane was quite pleased.

On Monday they stayed in and no one called. But Tuesday was a Maurice Pinder day. When he knocked, Jane took Jody with her to the door. She made formal introductions in the hall. 'Jody, this is Maurice. He comes here to play the piano. Maurice, this is Jody.'

Maurice knew about Jody, or should have – Jane had rung him at the weekend to explain. But she waited in vain for him to contribute to the civilities. He simply acted as though Jody wasn't there. 'I will *attempt* to play the piano,' was all he said.

Jane wasn't sure if that was terse self-deprecation or an implied complaint that Jody's presence would disturb him. If the latter was the case, she didn't care. Let Maurice find another piano tutor who would tolerate his personality. Maybe there was one on Jupiter.

Maurice wore a cream-coloured, sweat-soiled linen jacket, a pair of beige summer slacks, an open-neck checked shirt and white socks inside his buckle-up sandals. He marched, uninvited, into the sitting room. Jane picked up Jody and followed him.

'I am appalled by our royal family,' he observed, removing the jacket and dropping it irritably on to the sofa, like some colonial bureaucrat who'd been out in the sun too long.

'What have they done now?' asked Jane, who didn't give a damn. She could have said, 'Maurice, I'd like to boil your testicles,' for all the notice he'd have taken of her.

'Charles – the buffoon!'

Ah, *now* Jane was beginning to catch on. The previous day, she now recalled, had been the Queen's Golden Jubilee. She'd barely given it a second thought. Twenty-five years earlier the Silver Jubilee had been a huge national occasion and the catalyst for fierce debate about the value of British royalty. She had attended an alternative celebration, a Bash the Monarchy street party in Brixton. These days, by contrast, the royals seemed to excite very little passion, especially with Diana dead. Trust Maurice to be the exception.

'Camilla Parker Bowles!' he bristled, standing beside the piano as if on guard. 'She was sitting in Westminster Abbey next to bloody Shirley Williams as if she had some proper business being there, when she's nothing but the heir's bit on the side! She's been the *ruin* of his reputation. And he wants her to be accepted! Accepted! It's madness!'

'Shall I fetch you a glass of water?' offered Jane. She hugged Jody tight in the face of the tirade, binding her into an imagined confederacy just as Jody was binding in Dolly.

'Water would be very welcome,' Maurice replied, calming himself reluctantly, and spreading his bottom across the piano stool. Jane wished she found his rump less suggestive. Every time she found her attention drawn to it she thought of haemorrhoids. Not that she had any evidence that Maurice suffered with them. It was just that when he cancelled a lesson for 'medical reasons', he was so mysterious about it she couldn't help but suspect.

She led Jody out to the kitchen and bent down to her ear. 'He's a bit mad, isn't he?' she whispered.

Jody nodded and sucked Dolly's ear. Jane filled a glass, recalling her first contact with Maurice nearly two years earlier.

'Why *not* learn the piano?' he had enquired forcefully down the telephone line, when answering Jane's advert on an Internet directory. 'There's nothing *wrong* with it, is there?'

'Well, no,' Jane had replied, suddenly worried that perhaps there was. 'No, no. Nothing at all.'

'Nothing *strange* about wanting to at my age?'

'Definitely not, no. Um, I don't actually know what age you are.'

'Well, quite!' Maurice had snapped. 'At least we can agree on that!'

Jane had grown accustomed to his affronted con-frontations with non-existent opposition. He was such a *complete* outsider, a man at odds with all that was modern in the world. He was a fully rounded misfit and this inspired a certain sympathy in her.

She and Jody went back to the sitting room.

'Shall we begin?' Maurice said, when they arrived, looking at his watch with his usual absence of diplomacy.

'When you're ready, Maurice.'

'I'm not the teacher!' retorted Maurice, starchily.

Jane giggled. '"On Cat-like Tread"?' she suggested.

Without a word, Maurice launched into this highlight from *The Pirates of Penzance*, his hands high-stepping across the keys like haughty chorus girls. Jane settled on the arm of the sofa beside him, holding Jody firmly on her knee. She remembered being taught the song in music lessons at school and how other girls had corrupted its lyrics.

> *When we're in bed,*
> *Our filthy way we feel . . .*

Was Maurice a virgin, wondered Jane. She knew nothing at all about him, except that he always paid her the exact amount in cash and could be a terrific pain in the arse.

'How was that?' he demanded, on completing the tune.

'Excellent!' said Jane. 'Bravo!' She clapped enthusiastic-ally, mostly for the benefit of Jody who failed to join in.

'She seems bemused,' Maurice observed.

'She's shy, I expect,' said Jane, defensively. First Maurice had failed even to acknowledge the child, and now he did so only by speaking about her as though she wasn't there.

'She is patron of Dr Barnardo's, you know,' said Maurice.

'Who is?' asked Jane.

'The Queen,' said Maurice. 'How embarrassed by her foolish son she must be.'

Jane noticed that as he barked his non-sequiturs Maurice was not looking at her but at Jody, who had slipped off Jane's lap and taken cover behind her.

'They used to stand for something you know, the royal family,' Maurice went on, though with diminishing brio and a puzzled look in his eyes, which were focusing beyond Jane's shoulder.

Seeing this, Jane looked round. Jody was sucking the neck of her T-shirt again.

'Is she all right?' Maurice enquired.

'Oh, yes,' said Jane, caught unawares by Maurice's sudden interest and slightly found-out too. 'She's still settling in, you see. It's been difficult for her.'

'Not disordered in some way?' said Maurice.

Jane said, 'Shall we move on now?'

'Mmm, yes, yes . . .'

Maurice turned back to the piano and Jane was about to suggest he try something by Flanders and Swann when the telephone rang. It was a call from Rose, the secretary at Clyde's school.

'I'm sorry to disturb you, Jane,' she said, 'but could you come in? Clyde isn't feeling very well.'

Clyde had some dried glue on his fingers that had got there during art. He picked at it as he sat waiting outside Rose's office, watching the goldfish swim around their murky tank.

Mummy was taking a long time to come and he was bored. The foyer area was empty and quiet, except for Rose's voice on the phone. He jumped up and did a forward roll along the blue carpet, bouncing back up to his feet just short of the opposite wall. Then he did some karate moves, but suppressed the sound effects. The villains he despatched were even more brutal than the ones who'd messed with him at Legoland but his own skills had improved, so bring it on, bad guys, impress me – *if you can*!

'Hello, Clyde,' said Rita, the cheery dinner lady, bustling by.

Clyde dived back to his chair.

'Are you feeling better?' Rita called, over her shoulder, with a smile.

Clyde looked straight ahead, pretending to be deaf, until she'd gone, then listened to see if Rose was coming. No, he was safe, although a new thing called his conscience was troubling him. The best way to deal with this, he was discovering, was to pretend really hard that a lie he'd told was true and then he'd start believing it, especially if, at the same time, he tried just as hard to forget he was pretending. Also, by concentrating like mad, he could begin feeling not very well, although not so much that he was actually ill. He hoped Mummy would believe him, and if she didn't that she'd understand. He was pretty sure she would. He still didn't like lying to Mummy, though.

'Hello, Rose!' came a familiar voice.

Here she was at last. Clyde arranged his features into a grimace.

'He's round the corner, Jane,' he heard Rose say. 'And who's this *lovely* little girl with you today?'

'This is Jody.' People at school had been told about Jody, so there was no need to explain who she was.

'Oh! How exciting! And how old is Jody, I wonder?'

'Jody?' Clyde heard his mother say. 'How old are you?'

He couldn't make out Jody's reply.

'Three!' exclaimed his mother. 'That's *right*, Jody! You are three!'

'Ready for nursery soon, I expect,' said Rose.

'Well, yes, we'll have to see. Now, Jody, shall we find poor Clyde?'

'Oh dear, yes,' said Rose. 'He's just round the corner on the chair.'

'Poor Clyde', she'd called him! This was encouraging. He intensified his grimace and as Jane came into view presented it to her like a charity appeal: please, please, help this little boy.

'Hello, my *darling*,' Jane said, when she saw him.

'Hello, Mummy,' said Clyde feebly.

'Clyde is feeling poorly,' said Jane to Jody.

'Hello, Jody,' said Clyde, but Jody was looking at the fish. She put her nose up to the glass. 'You're not allowed to do that, Jody,' said Clyde. 'It says, "Do Not Touch".'

'I don't think she can read it, Clyde,' said Jane.

'But it says it, Mummy,' said Clyde.

'I know it does, darling.' She peered at him as though he were the one in an aquarium. 'Are you feeling *very* ill?' she asked.

Clyde's grimace had slipped. Keeping one eye trained on Jody, he hastily put it back in place. 'Yes, Mummy.'

'Oh dear,' said Jane. 'Let's take you home.'

He was exultant to be leaving. Yet his demeanour during the short walk home was subdued. The need to maintain his fiction of being ill accounted for only part of this.

'Don't step on the cracks, Jody!' Jane said, when they reached a slabbed section of pavement. She turned to

Clyde and explained, 'Jody and I have been playing this game when we go for walks. We used to play it, didn't we, Clyde?'

'No, we didn't,' said Clyde, as his mother chopped and lengthened her stride to avoid the moss-lined joins. Jody followed tentatively, looking up for reassurance.

'That's right, Jody!' Jane exclaimed.

'No, it isn't right,' said Clyde, stepping on the cracks deliberately.

Once back at the house Jane asked to take his temperature. He complied, mournfully, hoping for bad news.

'Not *too* bad,' said Jane. 'Shall I tuck you up in bed?'

Oh, well. At least the tucking-up part sounded good. Clyde accepted Jane's outstretched hand. He saw Jody watching his progress from the doorway and let out a little moan.

'Oh, *poor* Clyde,' said Jane. 'Maybe you'd like just a *little* bit of Calpol. What do you think?'

A surge of triumph bore Clyde up the stairs and then it was the medicine, the glass of juice, the patting and stroking. But after that Mummy explained that she had to go and make sure, you know, that Jody wasn't doing anything she shouldn't. And after a while he was fidgeting and tuning in to noises from the kitchen: sheets of newspaper being shaken out, objects being lifted down from shelves, Mummy's voice, solicitous and sweet. He knew whom she was talking to.

By the time he'd crept back down Jody was already spreading glue. All the art materials were out: paint, scissors, dried pasta and sparkly shapes for sticking to card.

'Oh, hello, Clyde!' said Mummy, all surprise. 'Are you better now, darling?'

'A little bit,' Clyde said quietly.

She was acting all kind and forgiving, but he knew she was making fun of him. It was hurtful to discover such a thing.

He climbed on to the seat next to Jody's and pulled a piece of blue card towards him. His eyes, though, were on the tube of PVA. He'd just been doing art so he knew how to use glue properly. He *knew*. 'No, Jody, you don't put glue on like that.'

'I do.'

He watched her as she smeared, ignoring him. 'No, Jody! No, you don't!'

His raised voice had the opposite effect to what he'd wanted. An argument was meant to happen next, and Mummy would come and sort it out. But Jody did not engage. Instead, she did the opposite. She laid her right arm, the one nearest Clyde, across the table in front of her so that it made a barrier and she rested the side of her head on it, facing away from him. It was the perfect position from which she could watch her left hand close into a fist round the tube of glue and see it languorously splurge.

'No, Jody! No!' Clyde made a grab but couldn't reach her left hand. His body, though, fell across Jody's back. Her reflex was to clutch the glue into her chest and curl up like a squirrel with a nut. Clyde punched her arm. Jody screamed.

Jane came running down the stairs. 'What happened, Clyde? Clyde?'

Jody was already quiet again, her defensive wall rebuilt. But her wounded eyes gave Clyde away. He looked at his mother hopefully. Even her wrath would be OK.

'What happened, Clyde?'

'Nothing.'

'I don't believe you. Jody?'

'She was messing up the glue, Mummy,' said Clyde.

'Why did she scream?'

'I don't know.'

The bad feeling was with him again: shame. It was mixed with hope, though, and a degree of calculation – she couldn't *prove* anything, could she? He tried looking pitiful.

'I don't believe you, Clyde. You must know why she screamed.'

'I don't!'

'You were sitting next to her.'

'No, I *wasn't*!' Clyde made a growly noise, folded his arms and dug his chin into his chest. Mummy would be the sorry one, not him.

But then he heard her saying, 'Jody, Jody, it's all right. This is some *wonderful* sticking you're doing. Can I see?'

Clyde made the growly noise again and looked away. His mother coaxed and murmured, giving comfort to the wrongdoer. He wanted to be nice to Jody, and he couldn't stand Jody, and nothing was fair any more.

'Yeah . . . don't worry . . . OK . . . 'Bye.'

Eliot let Jane say ''bye' in return, then put his phone away, satisfied that the others hadn't overheard. They were far too busy on Alex's PlayStation, killing themselves over Tony Hawk's Pro Skater 3. Yan had managed to balance his virtual skateboarder on a high catwalk railing in the virtual airport lounge, so he was racking up a score by doing absolutely nothing, just like Eliot had taught him to. He'd slung the console over his shoulder and was standing there, arms folded in a parody of some badass rapper's bodyguard, while Alex rolled on the battered old settee, laughing and howling, 'Get him offa dere, boy! Get him offa dere! This poor sinner wants to play too!'

Eliot, smiling, rejoined them in the fray.

'This is so *nang*!' Yan said.

'Jump, boy! Jump!' bawled Alex, going up to the screen on his hands and knees and pawing at it like a soft dog left outdoors. 'I beg of you, please jump!' He made a blubbery face and clamped his hands together in mock-prayer. As he did so, the skateboarder plunged and hit the floor. The three boys guffawed as the figure lay there for a second, spurting blood, then got up, remounted and carried on.

Yan bowed and tossed the console to Alex, who grabbed his moment in the limelight greedily.

'And ah-now,' he boomed, switching to wrestling MC mode, 'lay-deez and gentlemen, I present on his *bear wicked* skateboard, the very, very big idiot . . . Mr Wilson!'

Eliot and Yan capsized, clutching their sides as a new skateboarder appeared, petite with yellow hair and dressed entirely in mauve. Under Alex's command he – or was it a she? – slammed directly into the nearest wall, fell over, bled a bit, got up, slammed into the wall again, fell over, got up, bled a bit . . .

Mr Wilson was the boys' English teacher, a married man with three young children, as they knew. But this wasn't going to stop him being gay. 'I'm sit wiv 'im legs cross, innit?' Alex had guffawed the other day. He'd even once touched Yan on the arm. Well, how much more gay could you be?

They were in Alex's basement, a low cave of bare brickwork and exposed timbers, which, as well as the PlayStation and the settee, contained a fridge, a musty rug, two disembowelled bicycles and a grimy early iMac connected to the web on which guests could Google 'big boobs' undisturbed. Upstairs, Alex's barrister mother was sitting on her polished floorboards hoisting her left leg up behind her neck and wondering if Sandesh, her lean, brown-eyed, lightly bearded, twenty-five-year-old yoga teacher had noticed the way this tightened her leotard over her crotch. Alex's father, Henry, was ten miles away in his Greenwich bachelor flat, marking the wretched essays of his second-year psychology students, dreading Alex's next weekend visit and wondering why middle-class white boys such as his son all talked like black boys from sink estates.

'Go there, Mr Wilson!' yelled Yan.

'Now, pipe down, Yannick, please,' said Alex, impersonating Mr Wilson's voice extremely badly but capturing perfectly the mannerism that condemned him utterly – a delicate hand that flapped ineffectually.

'Yes, Yannick, pipe down *immediately*!' said Yan, not one to miss a cue. His parents were at church this evening, preparing his little sister for her first holy communion. He hoped they wouldn't stay when they came round to fetch him later. He especially hoped Alex's mother had put some more clothes on by then. She'd never get away with going around like that in Nigeria.

'ET, mon! You tek it now!' said Alex, lobbing the console Eliot's way.

Eliot caught it neatly and sat down. He immediately filed away 'Mr Wilson'. The others would claim that the gay thing was just cussin' but Eliot felt sorry for Mr Wilson. He covered himself by saying, 'Mr Wilson has gone to paint his toenails,' and while Alex and Yan guffawed he called up another skater, dressed him in basic blue and sent him careering, making mayhem, through a multi-decked shopping mall as Motorhead growled 'Ace Of Spades'.

'Go, the extra terrestrial!' boomed Alex, admiringly, and Eliot felt secure, respected for his gaming mastery.

'Cool, mon!' said Alex, admiringly.

'What's your new little sister like, ET?' Yan asked him suddenly.

'Little,' Eliot replied, keeping both eyes firmly on the screen. He'd introduced the subject of Jody to his male classmates circumspectly. He'd wanted them to know about her, yet their indifference had come as a relief. So Yan's question tensed him a little.

'Is she messin' up your room yet?' Yan asked, alluding to a wealth of cruel experience.

'Nah. She ain't allowed in.'

'Nah, mon,' said Alex, gravely, shaking his head. 'You got it wrong, innit? She prob'ly in dere now, playin' wid yo' stuff and pullin' out all them *naaase* Bench T-shirts in yo' drawers.'

'Yeah, right,' Eliot said.

'Doin' *naaase* big smelly pee-pees in yo' bed!'

There was a thud. Yan, powerfully affected by the picture Alex had painted, had collapsed in a thousand sniggers to the floor. Alex himself made a trio of demented inhalation sounds, like some vast sub-aquatic beast surfacing in need of air. Eliot laughed too, loud and genuinely, because Alex was such an insane comedian you *had* to laugh at him and Yan's helplessness was infectious. United in hilarity, they forsook the PlayStation briefly and play-wrestled on the rug instead, until Yan banged his head on a stray set of handlebars and had to curl up in cod agony. From the fridge, Alex fetched him a can of Coke. Eliot's mind wandered clandestinely. Jody had never wet his bed, but she'd got caught short in her own bed once or twice. She had been terribly distressed. And there was something else on Eliot's mind too.

161

'Gotta go, bruvs,' he said, dragging himself upright and pursing his mouth to show regret.

'It's early, mon!' cried Alex, going back to the PlayStation and slipping Grand Theft Auto into the machine.

'I got stuff to do,' Eliot said.

'Laters, then,' said Yan.

'Laters, bruv,' said Alex, not turning round.

Eliot tramped up the stairs from the basement, emerging in the still-sunlit kitchen. He wondered if he should say goodbye to Alex's mum, whose voice he could hear faintly coming from the knocked-through living room. She was talking in that slightly breathless, so, so *interested* way she employed when speaking to his dad. Who was in there with her? he wondered.

He soft-trod down the hall.

'Oh, I can feel *that*,' said Alex's mum.

'Now hold the tummy in,' said a male voice. 'Two . . . three . . . four . . . five. And relax.'

Eliot accessorised his sag-arsed jeans with a grey webbing Billabong belt. The metal tip of the spare end, swinging promiscuously, cracked hard against the frame of the living-room door.

'Hello!' called Alex's mum. 'Is someone leaving us?'

Eliot leaned into the room self-consciously. 'Um, hi. I'm going home now.'

Alex's mum was lying on her back. Her leggings and leotard were of matching olive green. With arms outspread she smiled up at him beatifically from the polished floor. 'Isn't your dad fetching you today, Eliot?' she asked.

'No. I'm going home by bus.'

'Will that be your first time?'

'Yes.'

'You know where the stops are, do you?'

'Yes.' Eliot saw that her nipples were poking through. 'Er, thank you for having me.'

'Any time, Eliot. Take care.'

''Bye then.'

''Bye.'

Eliot raised a paw to Alex's mum and then, more briefly, to Sandesh, whose eyes he had been avoiding.

''Bye then,' said Sandesh, coolly.

Eliot let himself out and headed towards the bus stops on Grove Road, which bisected Victoria Park and linked Hackney to Tower Hamlets. It was after seven but still warm. He tugged his cuffs down, pulled up his hood and touched the back pocket of his jeans. He touched it a few more times, doing his dear little version of a gangsta rolling walk. Once out of sight of Alex's house, he eschewed the bus stops for the park. Just inside the main entrance there was a wide path lined with seats. He came to a vacant one and planted himself there, as a monk might settle into a pew. Behind him, younger children ran and squeaked among the same seesaws and mini slides he'd watched Jody and Clyde play on the previous Sunday and had often played on himself in the old days. He'd had a quick go on the swings for old times' sake until Jane had asked him to get off: he'd been holding up a queue of five-year-olds.

Eliot's hand went to his back pocket again. This time it fished out a crumpled envelope. Eliot opened it, extracted a piece of pink notepaper and read.

> *You don't know me but I know you,*
> *You don't see me but I see you,*
> *You don't dig me but I dig you,*
> *Maybe one day you'll dig me too.*

It was signed off with a kiss and the swollen imprint of red lips.

Eliot's stomach lurched deliciously, exactly like those of the heroines in the teenage fiction paperbacks he'd sometimes pored over in Lorna's room. He had no idea whom the letter was from. He'd found it in his rucksack two days ago, a Thursday, on his way home from the jazz club at school. At first he'd suspected a joke played by Alex or Yan, but he'd just spent an afternoon with them and they weren't capable of keeping up the innocent act for so long. In any case, even if it was a joke, he doubted any boys were responsible. It had to be from a girl, or girls. Which, though? Eliot thought it would be OK if it turned out to be a bunch of them having a bit of fun with him, because he got on with lots of girls so they wouldn't have done it to be nasty. But it would only be OK because Eliot hoped – badly, badly hoped – that the letter was for real.

He put it away again and looked out warily from under his hood, aware that he'd become lost in his thoughts. All the talk at school lately was of the mugging or knifing of some kid that some other kid knew, and it had hammered into him the iron imperative to be on guard against bad boys seeking victims. The immediate vicinity seemed safe: it was mostly old people and families, and what older kids there were seemed safe enough and uninterested in him. With every corpuscle pumping and every nerve end jingling, Eliot got back to his feet and prepared to meet the challenge of being a wanted man alone on the bus journey home.

Sitting on her bedroom floor beneath her open window and listening very hard, Lorna was getting a good idea of what was happening below. She could hear Eliot poking idly at the dying embers of the barbecue with a blackened pair of tongs – he was going through his pyromaniac phase. From further away, close to the end-of-garden wall, she could sense an impromptu parental strategy confab taking place. Darren and Jane were barely audible but she knew they were discussing her, Lorna, and her 'moods' and her 'moping' and how worrying she was and how maddening, and also the latest tiff between Jody and Clyde.

It had happened when she'd been down there half an hour ago, just after she'd snapped at Clyde that, no, pest, she didn't want a delicious sausage so would he, like, *please* stop waving them under her nose? She'd been sitting with her parents on a little garden chair, making an edgy attempt at family togetherness while Eliot burned things to a crisp, when it had all gone off in the paddling-pool.

She'd watched with vindictive foreboding as Clyde had shown Jody how if you sat down really hard on the inflated wobbly wall the water gushed over it and flooded the grass. In this small patch of instant marsh he then showed her his impersonation of Tigger, first springing dementedly up and down, sending shallow splashes everywhere, then becoming more ambitious, leaping from the boggy grass into the pool, then from the pool back on to the boggy grass and shouting, 'Boing', at the top of his voice.

'Boing!'

'Boing!'

Then, splat!

'Ow! Ow! Ow! Ow!'

Jane had jumped to her feet. 'Clyde, are you all right?'

Lorna had noticed that Darren had simply put his face into his hands.

'Jody tripped me!' Clyde had howled.

'Darling, I don't think she did. It was an accident.'

'She *did* trip me! She *did*!'

She hadn't, and everyone knew it. She'd been trying to clamber back into the pool at the same moment as Tigger had bounced out. He'd tripped over her ankle in mid-air and landed face down in his own murk. Jody had absorbed the force of Clyde's wild accusations, unprotesting, almost unaware, as if she'd become mummified standing there. Then she'd wandered off to hide while Jane had wrapped Clyde in a towel and begged him to calm down. Darren had gone to Jody to hug and comfort her, and pointed at the bird box to try to distract her, but she'd cowered and chewed her thumb and sort of stared nowhere and everywhere.

Lorna had savoured the spectacle of her parents at their wit's end. Then she'd slipped away before one asked her to be helpful in some way. Now, from her loft eyrie, she'd gleaned that they'd bought Clyde's silence with an ice-cream from the freezer and given one to Jody and Eliot too. Not to her, though. Not fair. And now Clyde was inside being numbed by something on TV and Jody was wrapped in a dressing-gown, hanging off Darren's shoulder and declining to let Jane take her instead: she preferred Dad, and it was definitely getting to Mum, anyone could see it, and it had all been her idea, this adopting. How typical, thought Lorna. Mum makes a calamity of everything. And after all that trying to make their own baby.

She peeked out of the window again. Jane was now supervising Eliot and she couldn't see Darren or Jody. From within the house she heard rising footsteps coming up to her door. Cunning and fleet, she went and sat on her bed where she composed herself to receive her visitor.

'Hello, beautiful,' said Darren, after she'd told him it was OK to come in.

'Hello, Dad.' He'd offloaded Jody somewhere. Must be serious, then.

'I need to talk to you.'

'OK.'

And, yes, it was OK, though only up to some point that Lorna was unable to define.

Darren sat down next to her and said, 'What's the matter, Lorna? Please tell me if you can. I can't rest for worrying about you.'

Oh, no, she thought, oh, no. 'It isn't really anything,' she said. 'It's just . . . everything.'

'Everything?'

'Yeah, everything.'

It came out crossly. She screwed up her eyes. This achieved exactly what she didn't want, which was to compress the dammed-up tears so that they overflowed and trickled down. She hid her face. Darren tried to take her hand, but she pressed the heels of both hard against her cheekbones and wouldn't yield.

'What do you mean by everything?' he asked.

'Nothing.'

'Oh, Lorna . . .'

Darren dithered. Should he put an arm round her? Her shoulders were hunched and rigid. He thought not. Instead, leaning precariously closer, he said, 'Have you fallen out with someone?'

'No.'

But Darren saw the bind she was in: the very people – her parents – who most wanted to take away her pain were the last ones she wanted to disclose it to. And this put him in a bind too. Should he leave her alone or persevere? All he was sure of was that he couldn't do nothing, so he left the decision to his heart. It would feel worse if he abandoned her so soon. He continued with his pressure, her cruel-to-be-kind inquisitor. 'You haven't mentioned Kazea lately . . .'

Lorna sniffed and drew her wrist across her nose.

'Have you fallen out with her?'

Lorna shook her head slowly. 'Not exactly.'

'Has she been horrible to you?'

'No.'

'Has anyone been horrible? Has something horrible happened? There must be something or you wouldn't be this way.'

Lorna's shoulders began to shake.

Now Darren did put an arm round them but when they kept shaking he took it away. 'Should I speak to your school?'

'No, no, don't do that.'

'OK, I won't,' said Darren, resolving to do so first thing in the morning. 'But if I don't do that,' he said, 'what can I do?'

'Nothing.'

'Oh, come on now . . .' He shut up in case his frustration showed. To cool down, he took a wander round her room. The loft conversion had been for Lorna's benefit after she'd grown out of sharing with Eliot and it had seemed mean to move either of them into the small room (which they'd convinced themselves was a compact dream now that Jody was ensconced in it). As he drifted to the window and watched Jane and Eliot carry the last of the barbecue stuff in, he explained to himself that to expect a teenager to be grateful for anything was to be on a hiding to nothing. It rankled that she allowed the room to be so dusty and untidy, that mucky, crinkled tissues were littered on the floor and that her saxophone, gathering cobwebs in a corner, had gone for months unblown. But there it was: you had to keep on loving them; and how grateful to his mother had he ever been?

'Can I asked you something?' he said.

She nodded and went 'Uh-huh,' meaning 'yes'.

'Has it upset you, Jody coming here?'

'No. Of course it hasn't. She's so cute.'

'Demanding, though,' Darren said, flinching at his daughter's insincerity.

'I suppose so. Not as demanding as Clyde.'

'Well, yes and no.'

'Well, *yes*.' She scowled, red-eyed. 'He's so *annoying*.'

'I know, I know,' Darren said. 'But he's struggling at the moment. He's finding it very hard adjusting to Jody and I think that's why he's so volatile. But they're sitting together quite happily now.'

'He's so *noisy*,' Lorna said, unappeased.

'Yes, yes, I know. He'll change, though.'

'I hope so.'

'We're all trying our hardest, you know. It's bound to be a bumpy ride at least some of the time for a while.'

Her hands were away from her face now. She felt for tissues under her pillow.

'I was a bit like him when I was little,' Darren said, trying to ease the conversation on to softer ground. He took off his glasses, vaguely imagining that this would help.

'Were you? What – rude and attention-seeking?'

'Cheeky, I'd prefer to say. A live wire. Always asking questions and jumping around. I used to drive my brothers mad. That's what they tell me, anyway.'

Lorna blew her nose. She nodded, smiled. Was Daddy handsome? Not really. She looked quickly at his legs, which stuck out of a pair of khaki shorts. They were a bit gross and hairy, she thought, although it probably showed up more cos he was dark. She asked him, 'Do you remember being little?'

'As little as Clyde is now, you mean? Yes, I remember some things.'

'Life in Doncaster in t' olden days,' she said, harking back to a favourite teasing theme.

'Oh, yes,' said Darren, seizing the opportunity. 'I was thinking earlier about the coal we kept in our bath.'

Lorna let her mouth hang slack, then curled one side of her top lip. 'Like, you actually kept *coal* in your *bath*?'

'Oh, yeah. Sometimes we ate it too.'

She threw her sodden tissue at him. 'Liar!'

Darren laughed, but checked himself in case he laughed too hard; he didn't want to betray how relieved he felt. 'I don't suppose you even know what coal is.'

'Yes, I do!'

'And if you do, you think it's made in coal factories in China.'

'Ha. Ha.'

Sarcasm – that was a good sign. 'But no, seriously,' Darren said. 'I do remember being about Clyde's age. I think you start to understand things better when you're seven or eight. You start to figure out where you belong with regard to other kids, you see, and I think that's why he's so obsessed about Jody. Especially as she's at home all day and he isn't.'

'What do you remember, though?'

She was giving him her full-beam treatment. This, too, was encouraging, eye-contact having lately been with-drawn. It was also a bit embarrassing. 'Well, I'm not sure if I was seven. I might have been eight, you know. It was well before I went to secondary school. It was when I began thinking about space.'

'Space?'

'Yeah, space. The final frontier. The planets. The Milky Way. I used to think about it all the time.'

'Aww! Sweet Daddy. Did you want to grow up to be an astronaut?'

'No, Lorna, I don't think so,' Darren replied. Perhaps he preferred her mopey. 'I do remember lying in bed, though,' he continued, 'unable to sleep and giving myself a headache thinking about the edge of the universe. I had this general-knowledge book with lots of interesting facts and pictures about science. It showed you the solar system, and where all the planets were in relation to Earth, and how big they were and everything. And I discovered that the sun was a star, and that there were millions and millions of stars that were millions and millions of miles away, and probably millions more that even the most powerful telescope can't see. And I thought, But at some point there has to be an end. The universe can't just go on for ever. It has to stop somewhere. But where? And if you could get there, what would it be like? Did you just bump into a wall or something – an invisible wall? And if you did, then that meant the whole universe was contained by this invisible wall, which had to enclose the universe totally – I mean it did, didn't it, otherwise it wouldn't be a proper edge? And *then*, of course, the next question was, what's on the other side?'

At the conclusion of this rather lengthy speech, Darren offered Lorna a single raised eyebrow. She studied it with interest and said, 'You were obviously a total weirdo, Dad.'

'Thanks a lot. Haven't you ever had those kinds of thoughts?'

'No-wuh!'

'Don't say it like that! I'm not dangerous, or anything!'

Lorna giggled. Darren said, 'Maybe it was just part of being interested in science.'

'Oh, yeah. You did science at university, didn't you?'

'I did neuroscience and molecular biology.'

Lorna made a retard face. 'What's *that*?'

'It's finding out about the tiny bits of us that make us what we are, how we look, and other things we inherit from our parents, such as talents or being vulnerable to certain illnesses.'

'And our personalities?'

'Maybe. But that's more controversial. It's much harder to say.'

Lorna wedged a fingernail between two of her bottom teeth. Then she removed it and said, 'I think I used to wonder about God.'

'Yes. Yes, you did. You had a religious phase – kept wanting to go to church.'

'Did you take me?'

'No.'

'Why not!'

Darren shrugged. 'We don't know anything about churches. I suppose it's because we're atheists. We took you to some graveyards, though.'

'How lovely.'

'Well, you thought so. Couldn't stop staring at the head-stones. You were fascinated. That's something else about being seven – you start to realise that one day you'll die and so will everyone else.'

This insight was fresh in Darren's mind because he had been reading about these things, researching seven-year-olds on the Net. One passage from a website had stuck fast:

Although he makes a lot of noise, there is a strong theme of withdrawal and self-protection. He spends a lot of time alone, thinking and planning. He is concerned about what his mother thinks of him and his place in the family and worries that he may have been adopted.

'But why take me to a graveyard?' Lorna asked incredulously. 'Wasn't it spooky for a little girl?'

'It didn't seem to bother you.'

Lorna paused, sniffed and said, 'What was I like when I was little?'

Darren bit his bottom lip, looked at her and said, 'Very sweet, imaginative, a bit cross.'

'Cross?'

'Yes. Now and again.'

She said, 'Did your dad die when you were little?'

'Yes,' said Darren. 'Yes, he did.'

'That must have been horrible.'

Darren wasn't enjoying Lorna's sympathy. 'I don't remember,' he said. 'I was too young.'

'Don't you remember him at all?' She had her knees pulled up now, her arms folded across them and her head resting sideways on her hands. From this position, mouth hidden, she fixed on him unblinkingly.

'No, no, I don't. Sometimes I think I might be able to, just a . . . a tiny fragment of a memory that has a man in it who might be him. But I can't be sure. So, no, I don't remember him. I was younger than Jody when he died. No one remembers much about anything that happened to them at that age.' As he said this, he wondered how far it was true.

'So do you wonder about him?' Lorna asked.

'My dad?' Darren flinched at his own dissembling. To his surprise he now wanted to tell Lorna about his father but also to let her think that she would have to push him into it.

'Yeah. I mean,' she said, 'do you think about him much? Like, what it would have been like if you'd known him.'

'Yeah, now and again.'

'Do Uncle Scott and Uncle Graham talk about him?'

'I don't know.' And he really didn't, although he had learned recently, during one of their infrequent telephone conversations, that Graham was compiling a family archive. 'They remember bits and pieces about him,' Darren went on. 'They're that much older than me, you see. I was the baby of the family.'

'Like Clyde is.'

'Well, yes.'

'But not any more.'

Darren was puzzled: 'Who, me?'

'No, Clyde.'

'Oh, because of Jody? That's a good point, actually.'

He acted like it was the first time he'd heard it made, though of course he and Jane had discussed it endlessly with Lucy and each other. Not that he wasn't impressed that Lorna had thought about it too; and maybe a little threatened.

He continued: 'Actually, that's something me and Jody have in common – not knowing our dads.'

'Oh, yeah,' Lorna said, recovering steadily. '*Poor* Daddy!'

Manfully, Darren refrained from throwing up. 'It's "poor Jody", isn't it, really?'

'Well, at least she's got you now.'

Darren opted against reminding Lorna that this wasn't quite true. Jody would not be confirmed as joining the family until the agency was content that she'd settled in happily and the adoption was sanctioned legally. Before that, there would be meetings and case consultations, Ashleigh's consent would have to be sought and, they hoped, readily secured. It was all weeks away.

'Yes, she's got me now,' Darren said. 'The big difference is she'll always know she's got another daddy somewhere and there's a good chance she'll never meet him.'

'I shouldn't think she'll want to meet him, will she?'

'It's quite possible that she will.'

'Is that what usually happens?'

'I think they always wonder about them. Wouldn't you?'

'I suppose so.'

'Thanks.'

'You know what I mean.'

'It might be tricky in Jody's case, though.'

'Oh?'

'Because nobody knows where her father is. Or even who he is, for certain.'

'Doesn't her mother know?'

'She says she does. She also says he didn't even know she was pregnant.'

'Oh. Oh, I see.'

They were slipping into uncharted territory. The Grice-Ransome household was not a prudish place: its children were taught the facts of life and sensible discussion of sexual matters was allowed. Something had been invoked, though, that made both father and daughter a little nervy. The mystery of Jody's former life had become part of their lives now, bringing with it innuendoes from a world in which different mores held sway. Darren had felt its influence already. Now Lorna was feeling it too.

Darren said, 'So, you know, Jody is an unknown quantity – far more so, really, than most children who need adopting are. And that's the challenge with a neglected and possibly quite badly damaged child. It takes a lot of guts, you know.'

This was Darren's last coded defence of Jane before he left Lorna in her room, taking with him her insincere promise that the two of them would talk about 'everything' again soon.

Down in the sitting room Jane sat on the sofa watching nothing in particular on television with a gin and tonic in her hand. When Darren walked in she moved over to make room for him. He sat down, not touching her.

'What did she say?' asked Jane.

Darren sighed, but kept it light. 'Nothing much. But it's what we thought it was – some sort of falling-out with friends.'

'Including Kazea?'

'I think so. I'm *sure* so. We've been sure for ages, haven't we? But Lorna still won't exactly say so, or say anything about it, and I suppose that worries me.'

'What do you think we should do?'

'Oh, God, I don't know. Check with the school, see if they can tell us anything. Try not to get too cross with her – which is difficult,' he added hastily, 'I know.'

'Just about bloody impossible,' said Jane. She sipped her drink and rolled her eyeballs up. 'I'm such a bad mother, aren't I?'

The piano lid was closed. 'Aren't you playing tonight?' Darren asked.

'Not tonight. Too tired.'

'Yeah, yeah,' said Darren, empathising earnestly. 'How did the others go off?'

'Fine,' Jane said.

'Just fine?'

'Sorry. Eliot's reading, Clyde's asleep and Jody dropped off on the sofa next door. All I had to do was carry her up.'

'So they got over it,' Darren said, 'the little ones?' He wanted to cheer Jane up, but her profile showed deeper lines than usual.

'They got over it. You know, I think it'll get better between them. And there's a little spark of happiness in Jody, I'm sure. Every so often I see it there. We just have to nurture it.'

'I think so too,' Darren said. 'It's early days.'

'Do you really?'

'Yes, I really do. You're being brilliant with her.'

'Hmm. I hope you're right.'

'Of course I am.'

'Then you're my hero.'

Jane emptied her glass and sank lower into the upholstery. 'I wish she'd call us something, though. Am I Mummy, Jane or both? I mean, even I don't know, so I suppose it's not surprising if she doesn't.'

'She'll work it out,' Darren said, for whom Jody didn't have a name either. He added, 'I really love you,' and laid his head on Jane's shoulder to enjoy the sweet smell of her neck and to keep his uncertainties well concealed.

CHAPTER SEVEN JULY

In the summerhouse Jane sat in an upright leather chair that had been there almost for ever. She breathed in the smell of peat, let her eyes wander over old books and boxes, curious tins and tools on cobwebbed shelves. She let her emotions work on her as they were bound to far more hurtfully some day. She was making preparations, albeit for something that might not happen for several years. And while she was waiting she tried to savour each second of sweetness that came her way.

At the scrubbed trestle table Jeffrey said to Jody, 'Now a blue one. Can you find a blue one for me?'

Jody said, 'Yes,' and placed an index finger on a brick of the right colour. She wore a baseball cap and a candy-striped cotton dress, and her bare arms and face were drenched in sunlight.

'Very good!' Jeffrey said. 'And who is going to put it on the tower?'

'You are!' shouted Jody, and pointed at him.

'*I* am?' said Jeffrey. He tapped his breastbone, which was exposed by the neckline of his faded Hawaiian shirt. 'Who – *me?*'

'Yes, *you!*' Jody said. '*You* have to!'

'Can't *you* do it?' asked Jeffrey.

'No,' said Jody, firmly. '*You* do it, Jeffrey.'

'Jeffrey? Is that me?'

'Yes, silly!'

'Oh, all right, then . . .'

The wooden tower piled up between them was already seven bricks high, and wobbling. Jane watched Jody hand the blue brick, the putative eighth, across the table to Jeffrey. He took it, inspected it gravely and reached forward to place it. He was using his left hand. It shook. Jane hadn't seen it shake like that before.

'This is *very* difficult,' he said.

Oh, God, thought Jane.

'Oh, *no!*' Jeffrey exclaimed as, slowly, slowly, the blue brick undid the others' equilibrium.

'Aaah!' squealed Jody, thrilled to bits, as the tower collapsed and the bricks thudded and bumped, green, yellow, blue and red.

'Oh, Jeffrey!' Jane scolded, picking her moment to join the game.

'I couldn't do it,' said Jeffrey, sadly, and may have meant it.

'Oh, Jeffrey!' Jody said.

It was the first Sunday in July, and also the day of the Grice-Ransomes' first visit to Jane's parents since Jody had been placed with them. They had arrived at lunchtime, with Jane at the mercy of an ambivalence encompassing extreme hope, and profound uncertainty. The timing of the trip resulted from a compromise that she, in consultation with Darren, had struck between urgency and caution. There had been no overt pressure from Dorothy for them to come down or for her, with or without Jeffrey, to be invited to London. But her desire to meet the household's newest member as soon as possible had been clear in every phone call – 'Our names rhyme: Dodie and Jody! And "Jeffrey" is yet another "J"!'

Excitement fuelled Jane's anticipation too. Yet she'd put off the excursion, the first ambitious one since the Legoland ordeal, until she'd judged that Jody was ready. The sentiments behind this reasoning were mostly laudable: Jane wanted Jody to have settled into the rhythms and daily expectations of her latest home before exposing her, however briefly, to someone else's. By the same logic she'd yet to take Jody to any homes of other children of similar age she knew or invited any round. Oh, she'd made some introductions, when Jody had accompanied her to school with Clyde. Inevitably this had entailed her first encounters with Maggie's dazzling daughter Poppy, who had just turned four and was now attending the school nursery.

'I'd love to,' Jane had said, when Maggie had suggested the two girls get together. 'But Jody needs to take things slowly.'

'Very sensible,' Maggie had said. 'The Pink One can be overpowering.'

With Dorothy and Jeffrey, though, there was a little more behind Jane's caution. She needed time to put the mark of her virtue on Jody before exposing her to them. In the dark corner of her heart where she concealed her selfishness, Jane *so* craved her parents' praise. Darling, she's a delight! You're doing such a *marvellous* job with her! Here was the self-interested part of Jane's eager introducing of Jody to the pleasures of books, to restricting her TV consumption to short, improving bursts of *CBeebies – Tweenies, Storymakers, Balamory* – and to schooling her patiently in her table manners, her colours, her letters and her conversation skills, playing and pretending and working with simple construction games. There was still a long way to go. But Jane's efforts so far seemed to be paying dividends out in the summerhouse with Jeffrey.

'Well, well, Jody,' he said, 'you are a *lot* of fun to play with!'

Jane wanted to hug her father. 'She did well, didn't she, Daddy?' she chimed in.

Jeffrey smiled and said, 'Now, would either of you mind if I went in for a while?'

He was too stoical to say that it would soon be time for his afternoon nap, but Jane knew it was in his mind. He made a start on standing up. He was tall and wobbled like the brick tower had. Jane was already on her feet. 'Shall I help you, Daddy?' she asked, already half reaching for his arm.

'I don't need help,' he said. His walking-stick leaned against the edge of the table. His hand went for it; the same hand he'd used for the bricks. He grabbed at the stick and knocked it down. 'Oh, bugger.' It was the strongest oath in his vocabulary – the strongest he'd ever let Jane hear, anyway.

'I'll get it for you, Daddy.'

'Oh, OK.'

His acceptance of her offer was mildly irate and this hurt Jane's feelings, for all that she knew it wasn't personal. She slipped past him and bent to retrieve the walking-stick. As she stood up she saw that Jody, still sitting, was watching them closely. 'Here you are, Daddy,' Jane said, acting up for the child's benefit.

Jeffrey took the stick – 'Thank you, Jane. Sorry' – and kissed her forehead. Jody was all meditative stare.

'Shall we *all* go in?' suggested Jane, starting to clear away the bricks. Jody followed Jeffrey out through the open summerhouse door.

It was a beautiful day. On the large, rambling lawn, Lorna and Eliot lay on a blanket conversing in low voices, refining their teen moral overviews. Jane was not exulting yet but the day so far had gone smoothly. The roast dinner had been served and eaten without mishap, and afterwards, when Darren had shooed her outside to be with her dad and Jody while he helped Dorothy clear and prepare the puddings, which they would eat later on. Jane had planted on him a secret, sexy kiss.

She swept the last few bricks into their plastic bucket and was soon alongside Jeffrey and Jody as they made their halting way back to the house, the smaller one sticking close to the larger. Jody seemed comfortable with Jeffrey, almost carefree. Jane could understand why, and it was beautiful to see. French windows gave access to a small conservatory and the wide kitchen-dining room beyond. Jeffrey stepped through them first, deferred to by Jane who was stiffening mentally as she re-entered an orbit of domestic industry. As her father edged past tropical blooms and ragged palms, she felt Jody take her hand lightly and wordlessly, as though she, too, were preparing for a change in atmosphere, and allowed herself to hope that this must surely be a small sign of growing trust and empathy. Perhaps Jeffrey had sown that seed.

They arrived in the kitchen. Clyde was sitting at the table, watching Darren wipe its surface and puzzling aloud about a light year being a distance and not some special sort of time. Dorothy wielded a tea-towel, removing dust deposits from a stack of frosted-glass dessert bowls. Jane took some encouragement from this: she'd been assessing her mother's housekeeping competence like a detective on a stakeout, largely with her father's well-being in mind. There was no missing his decline now. Jane was grateful, though, that it appeared gentle.

The room was dominated by a vast oak dresser, in which the best dinner service was kept. It featured in all Jane's strongest memories of being in that room, at that table: art and craft, doing homework and, perhaps most of all, listening to her parents and that ever-changing cast of visiting egg-heads planning and debating and, unlike Julia, feeling too shy to join in. Décor-wise, little had changed. These days, though, there was a small, wall-mounted TV in the corner. It was on as she walked in and showing the men's singles final, coming live from Wimbledon.

'Who's winning?' Jeffrey asked.

Dorothy broke off from her task, wedged her glasses on her nose and stood to watch the picture properly. 'Federer,' she answered, hand on hip, 'the Swiss.'

'Who's he playing?' Jeffrey asked.

'Philippoussis.'

'He's a Greek fellow, is he?'

'Australian. I *told* you that,' said Dorothy, shortly. 'He's very powerful, but Federer's an artist.' She resumed dusting the bowls. 'He's quite attractive in a rather feminine way. Or perhaps I mean feline.'

Jane wanted to move the subject on – a reflex rooted in adolescent TV-viewing experiences of being in her parents' company when a snogging scene came on. She said, 'It's really lovely out there, you know. The summerhouse was baking.'

'And Federer's winning?' Jeffrey said.

'Yes, Jeffrey,' said Dorothy. 'He is.'

Jeffrey frowned at the TV, cleared his throat noncommittally and limped over to sit next to Clyde. Dorothy's lips were vacuum-sealed. She shook her head slowly, then asked, with dogged social brightness, 'So, how was it out there?'

'It was lovely,' repeated Jane. 'Daddy and Jody played a building game. They made great big tall towers with the bricks.'

Darren, wringing out the cloth, said, 'She's a very clever girl, you know, Jeffrey.'

'I know she is,' Jeffrey replied. 'I've seen.'

'And was it lovely out there, Jody?' Dorothy asked.

Jody and Jane were still standing, Jody still loosely holding Jane's hand. She had slipped back into her shell.

Jane bent nearer to her ear. 'Was it lovely in the summer-house, Jody?' she asked encouragingly. This was a stage-fright moment; she cursed herself for not having seen it coming. Jody was sinking incognito into the aged earthenware floor tiles.

'Was it lovely in the summerhouse?' she said again.

'No, it wasn't lovely, it was poo,' announced Clyde. Every adult head turned to be confronted by a defiant, stuck-out jaw.

'Pardon, Clyde?' said Jane, warningly.

'No, it wasn't lovely, it was poo.'

'Clyde!' said Darren. 'Don't be so rude.'

'It was poo,' repeated Clyde, and then he was off his chair and out of the kitchen, on his way to the garden before anyone could say another thing.

'Oh. That's a pity,' said Dorothy.

'More than a pity,' said Jane, with feeling.

'Well, now,' Dorothy said, 'never mind. I'm sure he'll be back for his pudding. It's bound to be a difficult time for him.'

She broke off to admire Roger Federer again and Jane

silently contrasted her mother's familiar unconcern over the touchiness of children with her own lifelong proclivity for letting sanguinity collapse into despair. A glass that had been half full less than ten minutes ago was now more than half empty and its remaining contents fast evaporating.

'It's not as difficult for him as it is for someone else, Mummy,' she commented sharply. Her mother seemed not to be listening though. This wasn't true of Darren whom she pretended not to notice peering at her over the rims of his spectacles, metaphorically patting the back of her hand and saying 'there now, don't take on so, it's OK.'

But it wasn't OK. 'Jody,' she said, 'would you like to sit with Daddy, er Darren, er, him.' She pointed at Darren. Names were impossible. Everything seemed impossible suddenly. 'What *is* for pudding, Dodie?' she asked. Just to confuse matters still more she tended to abandon daughterly nomenclature when feeling sore.

'Strawberry sundaes,' Dorothy replied.

'Right, then,' said Jane. 'I'll go and tell the others. And if they don't sound happy about it I'll make them go without.'

She stalked off, already regretting what she had said and positively loathing herself for it by the time she was outside in the glorious weather again, spotting Clyde lingering just far enough away from his lounging older siblings to be able to get away with saying grumpy things to them, having correctly judged that they couldn't grab him without making the massive effort even a small movement required.

'Difficult time,' she snorted, under her breath.

The sky may have been blue but that didn't mean there wouldn't be a storm at anytime.

'Let's make this the last one, Clyde,' called Darren.

'Aw-oh!' complained Clyde.

They were doing circuits on their bikes round the pond near the adventure playground in Victoria Park. On the other side, Jane and Jody were feeding the ducks.

'Lorna will be back home soon,' Darren persevered, 'and it is her birthday.'

'I know.' Clyde groaned. His bicycle was sturdy and red and he was bent over the handlebars, pedalling furiously. Darren was cruising on his shabby old bike, far enough behind for Clyde to maintain the illusion that he was out all on his own, but near enough to save him should any bigger boys decide to scrag him. Clyde was wearing a safety helmet, which was a bit of a joke because in this cultural landscape it might as well have been a sign saying, 'Middle-class victim, mug with complete impunity'. Back in the spring, home-printed posters had appeared in their neighbourhood, pinned on trees:

TO THE BOY WHO STOLE MY BIKE
On Friday 11 April, a boy pushed me off my
bike and stole it. He was a white boy with
brown hair about 15 years old in baggy jeans
and Nike trainers.

My bike is a silver and yellow Falcon bike.

I have a message for this boy – the police are
looking for you and my bike.

The poignancy and futile rage of this appeal had affected Darren strongly. He had never forgotten the day his bike was stolen when he'd been about Clyde's age. Playing unsupervised at the rec, as children did in those days, he'd allowed a ten-year-old to have a go on the second-hand Raleigh Chopper his mum had seen in the local advertiser. The ten-year-old had headed off behind the toilets and Darren had never seen him or the Raleigh Chopper again. As the reality of this calamity had sunk in, he'd found he was so stunned that he was unable to speak. He wondered occasionally if this failure to mourn had damaged him.

'Slow down, Clyde! Slow down!'.

Jane and Jody had come back into view. Again Darren reconnoitred for passing psychopaths. For the hundredth time lately he wondered why neurotic protectiveness had become so big in his life. Were public spaces really so much more dangerous than they used to be or was it mostly the fear of danger that had grown? And how much of that fear in him was a product of his age, of fatherhood, of some brewing existential overload? Or was he just being ridiculous?

Well, he was trying not to be. He was working hard at making a success of this work-free summer, for Jody, for Jane, for everyone. God knows, adopting a delicate three-year-old concentrated the parental mind wonderfully. There was no end to the late-night talking, the endless reassessing, the debates about tactics and diplomacy.

And how were they all doing?

How should he know?

Jane was wonderfully alive for about half of the time and consumed with confusion for the rest. Eliot was aloof and self-contained, but then he always had been and perhaps it was good policy to carry on doing what came naturally. Lorna? Deeply worrying. He'd rung her school, of course, and been told they'd try to keep on eye on her. Great. In the two weeks that had passed since the visit to Dorothy and Jeffrey, he and Jane had bought her a laptop for her birthday, a gift of such extravagance that it could only signify their shared desperation for their firstborn to spend her whole time surfing and blogging instead of communicating with them. This had been their little in-joke. It hadn't made them laugh.

The day before they made this rash purchase they had attended a case conference. The two events might have been connected, for the biggest single thing that the conference did was remind them that their established family must under no circumstances fall apart. To a full cast of social workers, they had reported that Jody was slowly but surely settling in, eating better, playing better, no longer wetting the bed, becoming more sociable and getting on well with the other three children. Of this list of triumphs the last was untrue, but only in the case of one child. Hence, the latest innovation in the Jody-integration strategy: taking her and Clyde to the park together where, if nothing else, they had more physical space in which to fascinate each other and fall out. As for him and Jane, it was a blessing that they were getting on so well. Adversity didn't always bring couples together, so he'd heard.

At the pond, Clyde was slowing down. Darren closed in on him and said, 'Shall we feed the ducks too?'

'Yeah, wicked!'

'I hope there's some bread left,' said Darren, deciding on reflection to prepare Clyde to be disappointed.

They drew closer. A good twenty ducks had gathered before Jane and Jody, a feathered food-aid congregation. Jane was doing the feeding and Jody was hiding behind her leg. Darren could see that Jane was preoccupied with treating each duck fairly, but that some were quicker and more ruthless than others, making equality of distribution difficult if not impossible. He saw her struggle and his heart ached.

'Go away, greedy thing!' shouted Jane, at one especially voracious bird.

'They don't speak English, you know,' Darren said.

'What a helpful comment.'

'Just joking,' said Darren.

'Well, stop joking, will you?' Jane snapped.

'Sorry.' Dormant dread stirred in Darren's gut: what have I done to upset her? It took him back to the earliest days of their partnership, after their time apart, when he'd begun to see what she would always need from him and how hard to provide it would sometimes be. To Clyde, he said, 'Go on, it's OK, Mummy will give you some.'

Clyde dismounted, letting his bike fall to the ground. He trotted over but stopped a full six feet away from his mother and slightly further back from the water. He did not speak either to Jane or Jody, who continued taking cover. Jane wore a long, green, oversized T-shirt outside her jeans, and Jody's head was half beneath it. Darren could tell where Clyde was looking: from the ducks to Jody then back to the ducks, then to the little girl.

'Jane,' Darren called, still mounted on his bike, 'I think Clyde would like to feed the ducks too.'

'I know *that*,' she replied, though not directly to him and he swallowed the riposte that formed sharply in his mouth which was, 'So why don't you give him some bread?' A row was to be avoided. Lorna's birthday evening was likely to be exacting and he did not need the further burden of an impending reconciliation at the dog end of the day. Knowing this made what happened next seem worse.

Face scrunched and shoulders hunched with umbrage, Clyde was heading back to him.

'I know, Clyde, I know,' Darren said, wearily.

He laid his own bike on the ground and took Clyde's

hand. He had failed already to avoid what he wished most to avoid – his son's pain of exclusion becoming his pain too.

'Jane, can you give Clyde some bread? He wants to feed the ducks too, and there won't be any left in a minute. And we've got to get back for Lorna.'

'For *fuck's sake*, Darren!'

The effect was like being hurled back in time – back to their student days when they had yet to learn they were in love.

'Jane, what's the matter?'

Clyde had run back to him. Now they both had a child clamped to a hip.

'Of course I'll give him some bloody bread! But can't you see? She's *scared*!'

Jody's face was still hidden. Darren scrutinised more closely what remained visible of her. Her back was bent, her shoulders clenched. What he'd taken for playful wriggling was now revealed to him as a nervous contortion. 'What is it?' he asked.

'It's the ducks.'

'The ducks.'

'The ducks! Yes!' Jane reached down and took Jody into her arms. 'Here, Clyde,' she said stepping away from the ravening birds and holding out the plastic bag with what was left of the stale loaf. Clyde skipped across and took it. Soon he was hurling lumps across the water. The feathery diners scavenged for them.

'They really frightened her,' said Jane. 'I don't know why.'

'OK, I'm sorry, I didn't know.'

'Well, you were off on your bikes, weren't you?'

Darren noted her use of the plural: so he and Clyde were both at fault – and in league against her, he supposed. He steadied himself and said, 'I thought we'd agreed on that. I'd take Clyde on a bike ride so that Jody could feed the ducks for a while without being pestered by him.'

'You're right, yes, we did.'

But she'd conceded the point too readily. Darren, feeling dismissed, wasn't ready for the subject to be closed. 'I'm sorry I misunderstood,' he said.

'I'm sorry I was so cross. OK?'

Jody was calmer now and had clambered into her more customary carrying position, her head hanging over Jane's shoulder.

Darren turned his attention to her: she would be his little stepping-stone. 'Were you frightened, Sweetheart?' he asked, and reached behind Jane's back to stroke Jody's hair.

'They really bothered her,' said Jane. 'I suppose there were such a lot of them and they came out in such a swarm.'

'Or a flock, maybe.'

'Or a flock. You know what I mean.'

'Sorry. She didn't like that seagull either, did she? On Brighton beach?'

'Yeah . . . You know, it's definitely time we were leaving.'

Clyde flung the final bits of the bread and they all headed home, Darren and Jane pretending not to be observing an undeclared truce that had ended an un-acknowledged argument – an argument that hadn't really been about ducks. The truce, though, did its job. It enabled a display of phoney cheeriness for the two young children's benefit, which included a number of out-loud banalities, as much to break their silence as anything.

'Is anyone home, I wonder?' said Jane, as they walked through the front door.

'I don't know,' said Darren, adhering firmly to the script. 'Let's find out, shall we?'

No one was. In Eliot's case this was expected. He was still at school, rehearsing for the end-of-term summer concert. Lorna's absence, though, caused a niggling mix of annoyance and concern. Both Jane and Darren could feel it; both chose not to admit it.

'I'll do the sandwiches,' said Darren.

'I'll dig out the candles.'

In fact, Lorna had forgotten that she'd become fifteen today: forgotten opening cards that morning, being greeted with kisses by Jane and Darren, amiably grunted at by Eliot, studied wonderingly by Jody and ignored by Clyde. She was walking home from school by the meandering route she had adopted recently, one that avoided fellow pupils and took her past a small public garden. She rarely went into it because it attracted drunks, and in the past they had been known to shout remarks.

On this occasion, though, the garden seemed to be down-and-out-free. The day was fine and flowers were blooming in the beds. Ordinarily, Lorna was immune to horticulture's charms but her isolation made her susceptible. The garden looked fresh, calm and clean; she went in.

'All right, Lorna?' came a voice from low down to her right.

Lorna looked round, alarmed. On a wooden bench, overhung by a small tree, sat Bernice Carroll and Deanne Paige. Bernice was smoking a cigarette and both were drinking from dainty coloured bottles. 'Hi,' said Lorna.

Bernice and Deanne were in her year at school but very far from being friends. She hadn't had run-ins with them exactly, just avoided contact so far as was possible within the constraints of the school's buildings. This was sometimes easy because Bernice and Deanne were often not in school, either because they'd been suspended or because they were truanting. They were outlaws of a type Lorna could never emulate, the self-excluded with nothing to lose. She feared them accordingly.

They stared up at her, dead-eyed. Lorna felt pinned like an unlucky butterfly. She could not simply walk on because that would reveal her fear, yet staying put required her to engage. Only their display of hostility would set her free. She braced herself for it. Bernice held up her alcopop. 'Want some?'

'No, thanks.' Lorna managed a strained smile.

'Wanna sit with us?'

Lorna didn't. But without their scorn to release her she had no choice. 'Yeah, OK,' she said.

She approached the bench warily. Bernice wriggled over to make room, keeping her knees clamped together to prevent onlookers seeing up her skirt. The contrast between this concern for modesty and the slag connotations of boozing on a park bench would have roused mockery in Lorna when she'd been close with Kazea, but her old superiority complex was long gone. She sat down next to Bernice, who said nothing. Deanne said nothing either, and picked at her nail-paint instead.

'We're a sight, ain't we?' Bernice offered eventually. 'I bet that's what you think.'

'No.'

'Well, you should do. Just look at it: two slappers getting pissed in the park.'

Deanne smirked, but didn't raise her eyes from her task.

'You going home?' Bernice asked.

'Yes.'

'Where do you live, then?'

Lorna became still more unnerved. What might Bernice do if she revealed this information? Tell some yob or burglar that Missy Prissy's place was bound to be full of valuables? Suggest that Lorna invite her round for tea? 'It's over that way,' she said vaguely, nodding in slightly the wrong direction.

'What's your house like?'

'It's all right.'

'I bet it's nice.'

'It's quite nice, yeah.' It seemed impossible to locate the right note: negativity was needed if she was going to fit in, yet she was being prevailed on to be positive.

'Not like my house,' said Bernice. 'My house is shit.' She giggled bitterly, and flicked her dog end across the path. It alighted on the fringe of the cut grass and lay there, smouldering.

'Where do you live, then?' asked Lorna, using the only line available to her.

'Babbage Estate.'

Lorna didn't know exactly where that was. She'd heard of it often, though: its reputation was large and forbidding. Perhaps Bernice took this as read and that was why she did not elaborate. Lorna considered asking Deanne the same question but decided against it, doubting that her reply would open up any more promising avenues of conversation.

'They ought to knock it down, really,' said Bernice. 'It's full of drug addicts these days.' She spoke as if recalling a lost golden age when everybody scrubbed their front step and stood up for the National Anthem. She swigged the dregs of her drink. As she lifted her arm the sleeve of her blazer rode up to reveal more of her wrist. Lorna saw three straight scabs running in parallel widthways across it.

THE ADOPTION

Bernice saw her looking. She put the bottle down, held the blazer cuff in place and presented her forearm to Lorna. 'Scary, ain't they?' she said matter-of-factly.

Lorna didn't grasp immediately what they were. It must have shown.

'We cut ourselves sometimes,' said Bernice.

'Oh, yeah?' said Lorna, lightly, not daring to show the shock she felt.

'With a Stanley knife.'

'Or a scalpel,' put in Deanne, at last raising her eyes from her nails.

'Yeah, you nicked one from science, innit?' said Bernice.

'Yeah,' confirmed Deanne.

The more she comprehended what she was being told, the more tongue-tied Lorna became. Cutting. Self-harming. She'd read about these things, she'd known they went on, but that hadn't prepared her for the shock of meeting people who actually did them – people in her own year at school.

Bernice put away her scabs but Lorna would see them for days.

'You oughta try it,' said Deanne. 'It's a buzz.'

'It is,' agreed Bernice, gravely. 'But it's bad, ain't it? I mean, it can't be good. It's stupid, really. Don't you think so, Lorna?' Like Lorna was her new best friend.

She was too scared of Bernice to agree that it was stupid. And she was still scared that she was being wound up. 'Does it really hurt?' she asked tentatively, blending innocence with sympathy.

'Yeah, a bit.' This was said casually, almost dis-interestedly, as though the discussion were about socks or sweets. Then Bernice laughed and said, 'I expect you think we're mad.'

'Well, I wouldn't say that.'

'I bet you don't do daft stuff like that.'

'Well, no, I don't.'

She sensed Bernice's attention wandering. She didn't feel insulted by this, only somehow overawed. Their stupefaction made them powerful. Unlike Lorna, they seemed inoculated against disillusion.

'I've got to go now,' said Lorna, but didn't get up straight away. She still required the others' permission.

'See you, then,' said Bernice.

'Yeah, see you,' said Deanne.

'See you.' Lorna left, self-conscious to her toenails, not daring to look back.

She kept walking, head down. Nothing about the encounter added up: the cuts, the boozy breath, Deanne's picked-at nail-paint and Bernice's spots were all trademarks of non-achievement, yet both girls seemed so . . . so triumphant somehow. Lorna had found this alluring; not in *that* way, but in the way that wild-child types drew your attention, like they might do something reckless at any moment and you wouldn't be able to stop watching them. They had charisma, especially Bernice, a slutty, mucky, bad-for-you charisma, and – Lorna couldn't help it – she was envious. Bernice, she guessed, had almost certainly Done It. Lorna did not want to Do It (could not imagine Doing It) but she kind of wished she had because it brought a sort of status and it had been a long time since any of that had come her way.

A group of boys in the uniform of another local school appeared on the opposite side of the road, shoving, loafing, shouting, working hard at being seen and loathed. Lorna shrank into a doorway and was grateful that they didn't notice her. During the hour after school, the hot days and the approaching end of term put craziness in the streets, with water fights, screaming and rumours of confrontation that charged the air with savagery. She was glad when she made it to the front door of her home.

She groped in her rucksack for her key. Before she found it, though, the door opened to reveal her mother. 'Happy birthday again, Lorna!' Jane said, smiling nervously.

Lorna blushed madly. 'Oh, my God. Oh, yeah, right.'

The birthday spread told different stories depending on who was doing the reading.

The person in whose honour it had been assembled saw a metaphor for life's vexations, a dietary narrative of continuing child-status (sandwiches with the crusts cut off), shallow, self-destructive pleasures (crisps) and outright moral failure (sausage rolls from a supermarket chain). It also spoke to Lorna of her bewildered loneliness. Why had she no friends to be out with instead of sitting here? The episode with Bernice and Deanne was the nearest she had come for weeks to feeling she was of interest to someone of her own age.

Darren's interpretation of the food, which he had prepared with 'help' from Clyde and Jody, was more ambiguous: on the one hand it pleased him that it looked appetising and that there was lots of it; on the other, he was already aware of its potential for causing quarrels and generating grievances among those preparing to eat and of the demands this would place on him to arbitrate without blowing his top.

Clyde's take on the food was simpler: he wanted to skip the sandwiches and salad-vegetable sticks and get on to the biscuits and cake.

Jody's view was different again. To her, such gatherings

were still strange and confusing. But, she had a pretty dress on and Darren had said, 'Aren't you beautiful?' to her when she'd come down wearing it. There didn't seem to be any monsters in the room, though she did sometimes worry about the dark, fluffy space behind the fridge. She reached out to a nearby bowl and took a crisp.

'Jody, you're not allowed to start yet!' complained Clyde, who was sitting next to her. He just *knew* she wasn't going to stick to the rules.

'It's all right, Clyde,' said Darren, 'you can start too. Let's relax and enjoy ourselves, shall we?'

'Where's Mum?' asked Lorna. She'd taken a stick of celery and was poking it into a tub of cream cheese. Darren was mildly revolted, but wasn't sure why.

'She's upstairs, changing,' he said.

'Why?' Lorna asked, with a kind of uncomprehending, in-passing disdain: like, is she having a *breakdown*?; like, God, how *predictable*.

'Lorna, you know why. It's so she looks nice for your party.'

It was something about the way Lorna held the celery at its topmost tip, as though she could barely bring herself to touch it, or for its other end to touch the cheese.

'*I* haven't changed,' said Lorna.

And the elbows on the table, Darren thought. 'You look beautiful, anyway,' he said, and placed a mushroom vol-au-vent in his mouth to avoid having to speak again.

Lorna smiled prettily. She ought to cheer up a bit, she knew. 'Jody looks beautiful too,' she said, in a talking-to-small-children voice. 'Is that a new dress?'

Jody nodded.

Clyde, feeling upstaged, said, 'And she helped me and Daddy lay the table, didn't you, Jody?'

Jody nodded again. It was better to stay quiet for the time being. She chewed another crisp.

Jane came into the room, hurrying, saying, 'Sorry,' and wearing a sparkly top. 'Do you like my party clothes, children?' she asked, sitting down.

This isn't really *my* birthday tea at all, Lorna thought. 'Very nice, Mum,' she enthused.

'*Very* nice,' added Darren, and had a small sexual stirring. Good Lord, he thought, it's been *weeks*. Ah, well, time flies when you're having fun.

'Nothing from Eliot?' Jane asked Darren, as she spread a napkin on her lap.

'No.' He was puzzled: surely she'd have heard the phone if he'd rung.

'I just wondered if he'd sent you a text or anything,' Jane explained, reading his mind.

'I don't have my mobile on me,' said Darren.

'Here he is,' said Lorna. From where she sat she could see down the hall to the front door. 'Hi, ET!' she called.

'Don't call him that, darling,' pleaded Jane.

'He doesn't mind.'

'Are you sure?'

'Actually, the spelling's different,' said Darren.

'What spelling?' asked Jane.

'In *ET*, the boy is E-*double* l-i-o-*double* t.'

'I know that,' said Jane, 'we discussed it endlessly.'

'I was telling Lorna,' said Darren.

'Hi,' said Eliot, lurching in.

When did he stop being beautiful? thought Jane, as she did a dozen times a day. She asked him, 'How was rehearsal?'

'Fine.' He sat down next to Jody, on the other side of her from Clyde. Jody put her finger up her nose, took it out and sucked it. Eliot saw her do it. He smiled down at her. She smiled back.

'Are you nervous about it?' Lorna asked him. She badly wanted her oldest brother, the only fellow teenager she seemed able to relate to, to have a few insecurities too.

'About the show?' he said. 'No.'

'Are you looking forward to it?' Lorna tried.

'Yeah, I suppose,' said Eliot, shrugging. 'Should be cool.'

Eliot's school summer concert was a major occasion, an annual showcase for its performing-arts stars. Practice and rehearsals had been going on since Easter and, in view of his masterly grasp of insouciance, Jane was heartened by any sign of commitment to the show on his part. He was in a jazz quartet and would be performing Dave Brubeck's 'Take Five'. She wished he would practise at home more. They could practise it together.

'Daddy,' said Clyde.

'Yes.'

'Where are Jody's mummy and daddy?'

'*Clyde!*' hissed his mother.

'Will they come and get her?' Clyde asked, still addressing Darren.

Darren hesitated. 'Well . . .' His stomach walls contracted and he sensed Jane's doing the same. 'We've talked about this, Clyde . . .'

Clyde looked puzzled. 'She's adopted, isn't she?' he said.

'Well, yes . . .' said Darren. 'Nearly.'

'Does that mean she could go back?'

'I don't think so, Clyde. Please—'

'Am I adopted?' Clyde asked.

'You know you're not,' snapped Lorna. 'So shut up.'

Jane stepped in: 'Lorna, please, let us do the telling off.'

'But he's being horrible!'

'Lorna, he's only seven.'

'How do you think Jody feels?'

'She'll feel worse if there's a row,' Jane answered, the words emerging bone-hard through her teeth.

'Hey, hey, hey,' said Darren. 'Maybe we should do presents now.'

There was an uneasy lull and a psychological shuffle back into celebration formation. Jane fetched the presents from her and Darren's bedroom, flirting briefly with the thought of dropping the laptop down the stairs. There were only two other parcels: a charm bracelet from Jody, which Jane had picked on her behalf and hoped would not be taken the wrong way; a gaudy plaster model of a beagle puppy from Clyde, which he had chosen himself and with himself in mind.

Lorna lightened her demeanour: the laptop was her parents' way of begging her, please, please, Lorna, to cheer up and do well. She forgave Eliot for forgetting to buy her anything. 'You can tidy my room for me,' she said.

'Yeah, right,' said Eliot, unperturbed. He was so pleased to have stopped thinking compulsively about really horrible things that he doubted anything could seriously bother him ever again. Where had they gone, those terrible waking nightmares about slugs and saving Simba from sharks? He didn't know. Now he was just, like, fine. Really fine.

A carrot cake was produced and fifteen candles lit. After Lorna had blown them out Clyde was allowed to too, once he'd made a solemn promise about spit. When Jody had her turn she sat on Eliot's lap to improve her elevation. She stayed there as the grown-ups cleared away the food, Lorna inspected her star gift, and Clyde broke off from scoffing Fox's party-ring biscuits to drum the fingers of his left hand upon the tabletop, then do the same with those of his right, again and again and again. He wanted the sensation in the right-hand fingertips to match exactly that in the left, and his inability to bring this about was starting to hurt his brain.

Only Jody and Eliot noticed what he was doing and only Eliot thought he might know why.

'Hello,' said a girl's voice. Eliot looked round. There stood Harriet Morley, a spindly, gamine year-nine girl who played the cello with a strikingly straight back and didn't seem to fit in anywhere. She had small, neat features and wore her thick brown hair in tight, rather bendy pigtails.

'Your piece went well,' she said. 'Cool, man, and all that.'

'Yeah, thanks,' Eliot replied. 'Was yours OK?'

'Yes, thank you. Didn't you hear?'

'Well, yeah.'

They were standing at the far end of the refectory. None of Eliot's bruvs did music so being in the summer show had meant his moving in different company. He hadn't really spoken to Harriet before and now he noticed that her voice had an amused quality that took him slightly by surprise – still, that was OK. Before them a hot clamour of parents and fellow pupils was edging back and forth from the refreshments table, balancing small cakes on paper plates and spilling their drinks on the floor. Man, he was glad he wouldn't have to clear up after *this*. Nearby stood Mr Bell, whose baby the show had been, looking flushed and garrulous with sheer relief. It was the same Mr Bell who had taught Lorna the saxophone at her school and who had, by strange coincidence, moved to Eliot's to become the dynamic new head of music. He caught Eliot's eye and gave him the thumbs-up. Eliot nodded in return.

Harriet scrutinised him closely. 'Are your parents here?' she asked.

Eliot nodded vaguely in their direction. 'They're over there.'

He could see Darren holding Jody, Lorna standing awkwardly, Clyde hassling Jane. Best avoided at the moment, he felt.

'Why aren't you talking to them?' asked Harriet.

Eliot shrugged. 'I'll talk to them later.'

'In that case you can talk to me instead.'

'All right, then,' said Eliot.

'There's something I've always wanted to ask you,' continued Harriet, then paused.

Eliot waited until he blinked under her concentrated gaze. 'Go on, then,' he said.

'It's about your friends,' she said. 'The ones I see you with in school. I can't imagine why you hang around with that Alex and whoever the other one is.' She grimaced impressively. Alex's name alone seemed to offend against her idea of good taste. 'All this talking like . . . gangsters. It's so ridiculous. You strike me as being more mature.' She finished the plastic cup of orange juice she was holding and lowered her lashes challengingly. 'What do *you* think?' she asked.

'Well,' he replied, 'that's not for me to say, is it?'

'Oh? Really?'

'It might sound conceited.'

'It seems to me you've just proved my point.'

'Well, thanks.'

She nodded towards on open set of sliding glass doors. Beyond them lay darkness and shrubbery. 'Shall we go for a walk?'

Eliot glanced towards his family. No one was looking his way. 'Yeah, all right,' he said.

They slipped through the doors and she took his hand. 'Come on,' she said briskly, and led him down a crazy-paving path that progressed through the foliage in a series of right-angled turns. Eliot was as familiar with the path and the route as Harriet was, yet he felt momentarily like a daft and eager puppy in a maze. The chatter from the refectory receded, as did the bangs of expensive equipment being dropped by inept stagehands in the adjacent performance hall. Harriet stopped, checked that they were alone and backed Eliot into a gap between clumps of hardy bushes. They emerged into an unexpected patch of dead space; a secret space. The ground felt dry and crumbly underfoot.

Harriet undid the top two buttons of her blouse. To Eliot, she was no longer a cellist. 'Put your hand here,' she whispered and planted Eliot's left paw on her small right breast, which was cupped in a gauzy brassière. Eliot held it politely and wondered what was meant to happen next. Oh, yes, he thought, as Harriet's open mouth began rolling over his – that would be it. He had a tumble-dryer sensation, only wetter, and was surprised at how agreeable he found the darting incursions of her tongue. She took hold of his bottom, prompting a rush of fabulous alarm. He put his spare hand up her skirt almost as a form of self-defence. His knuckles brushed against her regulation black school tights. Eliot knew that two layers below lay one of those startling, gaping flowers of mystery he'd studied in amazement in Alex's basement, beamed in from red light cyberspace. How, though, could he reach it? His hand was the wrong way round and the top of Harriet's tights seemed to be some distance above her solar plexus. He was flummoxed and losing the whirlpool rhythm of the snog.

'Stop now,' murmured Harriet, in his ear.

Eliot snatched back his hand. 'Sorry,' he whispered.

'Unfortunately,' she breathed, 'we *are* in the middle of a bush.' Eliot's first thought was that he was being rebuked – unjustly, since she'd dragged him there in the first place. But Harriet added, 'Otherwise . . .' and squeezed his bottom again. 'Come on,' she said, 'let's go back.'

'OK.' Now he was disappointed.

'You ought to come round to my house,' she said. 'I have a lot of other instruments.'

He was cheered up again.

They re-entered the refectory separately. Soon Eliot was watching the back of Harriet as she conversed in an adult way with some posh-looking grown-ups – her mum and dad, maybe? – and he stood and munched through a bowl of Hula Hoops. He didn't seek out his own family: they were all so weird and touchy – he'd be amazed if Jody wanted to stay. Still, that was their problem. His mind was on what he was going to do in the holidays: he would go to Harriet's house at the first opportunity and he would tell no one about it – not a soul.

By the end of the summer term Jane had taken to walking Clyde to school more often than Darren did and leaving Jody at home. She believed that Clyde needed more time in her exclusive company. The reverse perspective on this – that her escorting him from the premises might make Clyde even more conscious of Jody having the run of the place all day – routinely crossed Jane's mind as she mother-henned him out of the door and cluck-clucked about glow-worms or light sabres or anything else that might take her precious, impetuous younger son's mind off his jealousy. But she managed to dismiss it, along with her unease over Eliot's ever-deepening enigma and her guilt about leaving Darren to contemplate the mess left by Lorna's sandwich-making, the daily detritus of hummus and cress. Clyde had to go to school, and that was that. And at least it meant she got ten minutes to herself when she was walking home again; ten minutes in which to tell herself that Clyde would get used to Jody, that Eliot had always been elusive, that Lorna was at a difficult age, that Darren still loved her even though he'd seemed a bit bleak and preoccupied lately and that, in any case, if she didn't make a success of adopting Jody she would never like herself again.

How ironic that in her long-skirted mid-teens Jane had dreamed so hard of becoming a bed-sitter melancholic, confessing lyrically from her piano stool. These were strictly private pep talks, which helped her to keep things bottled up at home. With the treacherous emotional cross-currents of others to navigate it seemed the wisest policy. For reasons more to do with pride she took the same approach in conversations with Maggie, although she knew she couldn't go on like this for much longer without appearing rude. One day, while Jody napped, and no one else was in, Jane engaged with her neighbour in an imaginary conversation.

Jane: 'Maggie, can I be frank?'

Maggie: 'Let me guess – you think you've got your knickers on too tight.'

Jane: 'Yes. All the time. But I'm terrified that if I take them off my entire body will fall apart – in fact, it's doing it anyway.'

Maggie: 'And how are things going with Jody?'

Jane: 'Well, now, let me see. Eliot seems quite fond of her but Lorna only pretends to be. Clyde is being impossible – he can't stop drumming his fingers on things – and I can't help thinking that Darren is secretly wondering what on Earth I've got him into. I wouldn't blame him if he cut short his sabbatical and went back to work. As for Jody, she's made real progress, and when she shows signs of being happy I could cry all day with joy. But she's still desperately withdrawn and I don't know how I'm ever going to solve her mysteries, let alone put right whatever has gone wrong. She likes me but doesn't quite trust me. She seems happier in male company, even though she makes Clyde wild. I suppose that must be down to whatever dreadful things her mother did to her, but I can't change those now. I'll never even find out what they were.'

Maggie: 'We really must get her and Poppy together. She is so excited about this new little girl in your family. She's simply dying to make a great big fuss of her!'

Jane: 'Poppy is the girl-child of every mother's fantasies. She's pretty, sweet, funny, affectionate, deliciously eccentric and has a rich imagination. My prospective adoptive daughter Jody is a shy, pensive, broken little thing. Oh, I don't always think that. But to be honest, Maggie, I've been avoiding having her play with Poppy. I don't think I could stand the comparison.'

Maggie: 'Are you regretting ever starting this thing?'

Jane: 'It's too late for regrets. I'm committed and that's it. So is Darren, I believe, although his commitment is mostly to me. The most ridiculous thing is that Jody will probably grow up adoring him and dismissing me as a loser and a fool, just like Lorna does.'

Maggie: 'Do you think she'll ever think of you as a mother – her mother?'

Jane: 'No, and it's tearing me apart.'

Maggie: 'Sounds to me as though you ought to eat more sticky buns. Then you could develop a larger-than-life comic persona to hide behind, like me.'

Jane: 'Maybe. But I'll probably be dead soon anyway.'

Maggie: 'What makes you think that?'

Jane: 'Suicide attacks. Dirty bombs on the Underground. I'm convinced they're going to get me – or my family, which would be worse.'

Maggie: 'Oh, come round and have some cake! What have you got to lose?'

Jane: 'It just seems futile, somehow. And your kitchen is so enviably clean.'

She went round to Maggie's the next morning, taking Jody with her. Perched on a high stool in a stainless space-age kitchen, she sipped cappuccino and let slip that on bad days she thought she might be nearing her wit's end.

'Have you considered suicide?' asked Maggie, as she punched the buttons on her BlackBerry.

'No,' said Jane, glad that she could say this truthfully.

'Divorce?' said Maggie, slyly.

'No. Darren and I are getting along fine.' Her stress needle flickered at this, but nothing serious. Maggie handed the BlackBerry to her. 'Put this infernal gizmo up your jumper for me, would you? Stop me playing with the bloody thing?'

Jane slipped it into her jacket pocket, leaving Maggie's hands free to tear off one plump end of a full butter croissant. Before popping it into her mouth, she called, 'How's it going in the café?'

The back door was open. Beyond it was a neat, *faux*-Mediterranean patio. From behind the door, Poppy appeared. She was dressed in a big pink frock and sunglasses with pink frames. In her hand she held a miniature pink teapot. 'I think we might need some more tea, Mummy,' she said, and pinched the tip of her chin to show that she had thought about this very carefully. 'And some biscuits.'

'Who's been drinking all the tea, Poppy?' asked Jane.

'Oh, Dolly has!' said Poppy, and tutted indulgently. 'She's *very* thirsty.'

'And how is Jody getting on?'

'Oh, she's fine,' said Poppy, and added, lowering her voice to a confiding whisper, 'She's quite shy, actually. But I don't mind.'

More biscuits were provided. The teapot was replenished. The hostess tripped pinkly back outdoors.

'It seems to be working,' said Jane. Half an hour had gone by before Jody could be persuaded to let go of her leg, but at last she had consented to be Poppy's captive companion. She seemed almost star-struck by the other child and spellbound by the conviction with which she inhabited her fantasy world. Jane found this reassuring because Poppy affected her in the same way.

'I think Jody's very sweet,' said Maggie, enunciating puffily as croissant continued to clog her mouth. 'And you are doing *wonderfully* with her.'

Of course, Maggie had no way of knowing how Jane was doing but Jane didn't let that bother her.

'She *is* very sweet,' she said, resisting her desire to add a dozen caveats or so. 'It's the others who are giving me grief.'

'Hmm,' said Maggie. 'Maybe you should go to my old parenting-skills class. I expect they're still running. I can't guarantee you'll like their methods but they're ideal for meeting people whose children are much more monstrous than yours, and that's guaranteed to make you feel better.'

'What are their methods?' Jane enquired.

'Well,' said Maggie, 'basically, how to do the opposite of what all normal people do.'

'What do you mean?'

'They tell you to ignore them when they're being very naughty and to go mad with happiness whenever they do even the tiniest little thing that's right – even if it's only smashing one Ming vase instead of the usual two.'

'Oh, positive parenting?' Jane had seen some stuff about this on television.

'Stop bickering with your husband in front of them,' Maggie went on. 'Stop criticising, being sarcastic or yelling

209

at them when they've flooded the bathroom.' She had the
last bit of the croissant poised decadently next to her lips.
'Couldn't be easier, could it?' she said drily, and devoured
the poly-oversaturated morsel.

Jane thought about it. She wanted to know more, but
was thinking of Jody and Darren. 'Have you got their
number?' she asked.

'I'll dig it out for you,' said Maggie. 'They're in Islington.
Why not give them a try? At least it will get you away from
the kids.'

CHAPTER EIGHT AUGUST

In the front room, the living room, the place for toys, games and play, Jody turned the pages of *Grandpa's Handkerchief* and gave sense to them in her own way. The words did not connect with her other than as squiggles Jane pointed to when reading the book aloud to her, not even individual letters – not even 'J'. The pictures, though, were calling to her. The kindly Grandpa was on every page, and although she could not name the different colours of his big hankies, a different one for every day, she could point at him and name him and, if barely consciously, associate him with Jeffrey, the first old man she'd ever spoken to. All the other characters were small children. It was these she was studying as she sat, cross-legged, on the carpet. They were sailing toy boats, chasing a ball and dressing up. They were dancing and skipping. On one page Grandpa was using his orange handkerchief to remember about a birthday. Back in the spring, Jody had known next to nothing of such things. Now she wanted to know more.

She looked up at Jane with an expression that verged on the eagerly questioning, which Jane would have welcomed had she been facing Jody's way. But she was preoccupied with dithering over the sash window, trying to see off paranoia with a blast of self-ridicule.

'Too much Sims, if you ask me,' she said, though not to Jody or even to herself so much as to a desirable, more rational *alter ego*, some grown-up equivalent of an imaginary friend.

The house needed airing and she'd opened the window just a little: six inches at most. In Sims, though, such a gap would be more than big enough to allow a masked larcenist, child thief or, who could tell? a plague of killer bees to burst in and make mayhem. Why not in real life as well?

Jody, still a beginner at speaking up, abandoned trying to catch Jane's attention. She put aside *Grandpa's Handkerchief* and picked up a small wooden mallet instead. She wriggled on her bottom towards a wooden peg frame that had previously been Clyde's and set about bashing the pegs deeper into their holes.

The sound brought Jane's head round. Seeing that Jody was absorbed, she quickly lowered the sash a little, reducing the gap by half, then stepped quickly across the room, hoping Jody hadn't seen her open it – she might be on the small side for three years and eight months, but that didn't mean she couldn't find a way to clamber out, fall on her head and sustain life-threatening injuries.

'Oh, get a grip,' Jane muttered, beneath the cover of Jody's banging.

And finally she did. It helped that she understood why she was so disaster-fixated today. Darren, citing fraternal guilt, had left first thing to visit his eldest brother Graham, taking Clyde with him up the M1 to Yorkshire. They would be away for a couple of days – or longer if they died in a pile-up. Eliot had disappeared on her too – only a few stops further down the Central Line than the one for his school, but his destination, Epping, still seemed a universe away. He'd explained that he was going to the house of a girl called Harriet who'd been in the summer concert with him. 'There's a load of us going,' he'd said. 'It's a sort of party for all the musicians.'

Jane tried to emphasise the positives. It occurred to her that she could try to sell to Lorna the concept of some girls' time together. Now that the holidays were here maybe she could find the pretext and even the will-power to reconnect with Lorna, perhaps to feel as though her firstborn was her daughter once more, although she wasn't holding her breath. It was a quarter past twelve and she hadn't made an appearance yet. Could she *really* still be asleep? Or had buying her that laptop, with its addictive properties, been a mistake?

Jane left the room and went to the kitchen where she opened the back door, then a carton of organic orange juice and a packet of wholemeal pitta bread, and poked around in the fridge for anything else Lorna might want for lunch – a food overture was the best she could think of and even Lorna had to eat eventually.

Meanwhile, Jody put down her mallet, got up and went to the living-room window. She stood on tiptoe and looked out through the three-inch gap Jane had left. It was warm and bright out there, and Jody screwed up her eyes as she scanned the cracked, uneven tiles of the little front yard, the raggedy shrubs and row of pot plants, the metal gate and the low brick wall. She had no words for these things, except 'flower', and none to express her disabling, disorienting, dizzying reaction on seeing the female face partly concealed by dark glasses looking straight at her from the far side of the wall. The face did not smile or speak, simply stared for a few seconds, then disappeared. It was this as much as anything that made it so familiar.

'For a boy you make quite good conversation,' said Harriet, as she led the way out of the sports shop on Epping high street, a carrier-bag swinging from her hand.

'Well,' said Eliot, his mind half on what the carrier-bag contained, 'I like a good discussion. Like, sometimes we have them at school but not as good.'

'I think it probably improves as you get older,' said Harriet, wisely, 'when people become more serious. People say I'm very serious, actually. What do you think?'

'Well, yeah, you're quite serious,' said Eliot, 'but not in a boring way.'

'Thank you,' Harriet replied, flashing a smile. 'I'd hate to be thought boring.'

'Oh, yeah,' nodded Eliot, 'me too.' After two hours in Harriet's company he was still acclimatising. He'd stepped from the tube carriage at Epping station, end of the Central Line, and on to a planet he didn't know. Harriet had been waiting for him on the platform, as she'd promised but Eliot hadn't spotted her at first and she hadn't noticed him. She'd been too engrossed in a Penguin Modern Classic to register the train's arrival. He'd never seen her in anything except school uniform before.

She wore, from the ground up: white canvas daps with elasticated uppers and no socks; a short black skirt, slightly flared, so that its hem swayed a little when it was caught by the breeze and when she walked; a plain white T-shirt, much cleaner than the daps, that revealed her belly button with, to Eliot's eye, delicious intermittence; a jeans jacket large enough to fit a man; a big, blue sixties sort of cap atop hair from which the bendy pigtails emerged. Was this really the oddball girl who had performed the seduction – Eliot had settled on the word after much thumbing through Lorna's magazines – in the bushes after the summer concert? By comparison with her offbeat sophistication Eliot felt rather square in his floppy, post-grunge gear.

Yet although he was far from his natural habitat, he seemed to be adapting. Harriet talked constantly, which saved him from having to make any conversational running. The skirt and lack of socks emphasised that Harriet's legs were long and brown, yet comically skinny too, and she walked with pigeon toes, which meant that her allure stopped short of being intimidating. She'd led him first to a café, where they'd sat at a corner table drinking home-made milkshakes and eating strange, knobbly cakes, and Harriet had read out a passage from her paperback: ' "Great Chicago glowed red before our eyes. We were suddenly on Madison Street among hordes of hobos, some of them sprawled out on the street with their feet on the curb, hundreds of others milling in the doorways of saloons and alleys . . ." Do you know what a hobo is, Eliot?' Harriet had asked.

'Er, no. I don't think so.'

'It's what we call a dosser nowadays.'

'Oh.'

Harriet had scanned the pages for the next bit she really liked and then read on:

'First thing to do was park the Cadillac in a good dark spot and wash up and dress for the night. Across the street from the YMCA we found a redbrick alley between buildings, where we stashed the Cadillac with her snout pointed to the street and ready to go, then followed the college boys up to the Y, where they got a room and allowed us to use their facilities for an hour. Dean and I shaved and showered . . .'

Eliot had felt self-conscious at the mention of shaving. The previous afternoon at home, while everyone else had been out, he'd borrowed Darren's electric razor. His top lip still felt tingly from its first use against his skin: a nice tingliness, which he had only been able to enjoy after leaving the house that morning, so self-conscious had he been about the change in his appearance. He'd hidden in his room all evening and on the few occasions when he'd had to emerge had fiddled with his face to conceal from the others the milestone absence of his facial down. Harriet said nothing about it, though. She was too busy with *On The Road*:

'. . . we headed straight for North Clark Street, after a spin in the Loop, to see the hootchy-kootchy joints and hear the bop. And what a night it was. "Oh, man," said Dean to me as we stood in front of a bar, "dig the street of life, the Chinamen that cut by in Chicago. What a weird town – wow, and that woman in that window up there, just looking down with her big breasts hanging from her nightgown, big wide eyes. Whee. Sal, we gotta go and never stop going till we get there." '

She'd broken off, bright-eyed. 'What do you think?' she'd asked.

'Brilliant,' said Eliot, who had no idea what he thought of it.

'It's Jack Kerouac,' said Harriet, casually. 'He was a Beat poet.'

'Oh, right,' said Eliot, and sucked at his straw till the last of his milkshake disappeared from the bottom of the glass with a bubbling rasp. He knew he'd heard the term 'Beat poet' before. But where? That was it: from Dodie! 'They liked jazz, didn't they?' he'd remarked, surging with sudden authority.

'Yes,' nodded Harriet, and she'd peeped cutely from beneath the peak of her cap. 'They were hep cats. They dug jazz – like you.'

'Cool cats!' Eliot had said, thinking briefly of a scene from *The Aristocats*, then banishing the memory in case he should accidentally mention it. Did he 'dig' jazz? He didn't think so. He'd just have to busk it.

Harriet had snapped her fingers five times rhythmically, twitching her head and shoulders to the beat. She'd laughed at herself. Eliot had laughed too, becoming rather short of breath.

'Let's go now,' Harriet had said, in a hurry suddenly. 'I have to buy something before we go home.'

The thing she'd bought was a sports bra 'for stupid PE', dangling it in front of the spotty lad at the till without showing any trace of embarrassment while Eliot had stood a few yards off and watched his toes. 'Stupid thing,' she'd said. 'It's not like I've got big, bouncy boobs or anything.' And now she had linked her spare arm through his and was telling him about how she and her parents were going to Tuscany 'as usual' in two weeks, which was a pain but at least she'd be able to sit around all day and read while they argued about politics and art with all the other people they knew from London who had villas there.

'Where are you going on holiday?' she asked, as she steered him off the high street and down a leafy residential side road.

'Dunno, actually,' said Eliot, who hadn't even thought about it. 'Don't know if we're going anywhere.'

'Why's that?'

'Well, it's a bit mad at our house at the moment.'

'Goodness!' she exclaimed, stopping and popping her fingers again, then giggling hysterically. 'Lay it on me, Daddio!'

Eliot laid it on her and in quite lavish detail.

'So why did your parents want to adopt?' Harriet asked, after he'd given her the picture.

'Dunno.'

'Stop saying "dunno". Is your mum a kind of earth-mother, then?'

'Mmmm. Not sure,' Eliot said.

'Kind of long hair and nurturing?'

'Long hair. She's got long hair.'

'*Very* earth-mother,' said Harriet.

'She plays the piano.'

'An earth-mother, definitely,' said Harriet, with satisfaction. 'And is she always baking bread and being all calm and serene?'

'No,' said Eliot, with a small snort. '*Not* calm and serene. She gets so mad sometimes.'

'But do you like her?'

'Oh, yeah,' said Eliot, 'She's pretty cool, actually. And weird.'

They walked for twenty minutes until the houses got bigger and thinned out, and they arrived at a large set of wooden gates. Beside these was a small door, set into a high red-brick wall. Harriet fished inside her jeans jacket and produced a key attached to a long, see-through cylindrical fob in which glittery shapes floated in a clear fluid. 'Tacky, eh?' she said, holding it up.

She inserted the key into the door and let them in. As soon as he set foot on the other side Eliot could smell something he'd never before been close to: serious wealth. For a moment, it undid him. 'Man, this is *nang*!' he exclaimed, looking in wonder at a huge, landscaped garden and beyond to the large house that overlooked it.

'You don't say "nang", do you?' Harriet teased.

'I mean, it's so . . . *massive*,' said Eliot.

'Come on,' said Harriet. 'Let's see if anyone's in.'

She led the way up the gentle incline of a stone paved path and went round to the far side of the house where a gravelled drive terminated in a wide, circular courtyard with a triple garage to one side. Two of its three doors were open with no cars visible. 'No one here,' Harriet pronounced.

In the sweeping kitchen she fetched them both a cold drink from a vast fridge – 'Sprite? 7-Up? Coke?' – then she said, 'Let's go up to my room.'

The stone-tiled echo of the kitchen gave way to the carpeted quiet of an impressive hall. The décor was all clean and white and beige, and as he followed Harriet up the stairs Eliot grew nervous again. The house was so large that surely it was possible other people were there but that, as yet, neither Harriet nor he had heard them. He watched Harriet's bare ankles, her calves, the backs of her knees but, being a gentleman, allowing his gaze to rise no further. The landing at the top was bright and wide, with windows down one side of what was really a first-floor corridor. Harriet, still holding the tray, used her bottom to push open the second door on the right. She went in. Eliot followed, feeling vaguely furtive and quite small. 'This is my little den,' she said, looking for a place to set down the tray.

In one sense she was spoiled for choice, in another she was not. It was more like a spacious studio flat or hotel room than a bedroom, with separate niches for study (desk, bookcase, computer), relaxation (a suite of furniture, coffee-table, music system and TV) and sleeping (a small four-poster bed). This meant there were several surfaces on which a tray could be placed. The difficulty was that all were covered with clutter: books, clothes, junk, junk and more junk. Harriet solved the problem by stooping to place the tray on the floor, between a naked black female fashion dummy and a prostrate euphonium.

'It's a mess, isn't it?' said Harriet, proudly, as she straightened.

'It's great,' said Eliot, who now felt surprisingly at home. The messiness was like Lorna's room. The difference was that this mess felt happy.

'Have a look round,' said Harriet, making a space on the coffee-table. 'I can do whatever I like here – as long as it's legal.'

Eliot stepped past the dummy, picked his way round an art portfolio or two and admired the psychedelic pictures pinned to the movable partition wall that hived off the study area. There was a colour printer there and he guessed that Harriet had designed the pictures herself on the computer. Then his eye fell on another piece of paper, this one lying on the desk. It had some words on it that he'd seen before.

> You don't know me but I know you,
> You don't see me but I see you,
> You don't dig me but I dig you,
> Maybe one day you'll dig me too.

And the lips. He'd seen those too. More than seen them, actually.

Harriet put on the TV. 'There might be some crappy old film we could watch,' she said. 'I love those, don't you?'

'Yeah, brilliant,' said Eliot.

She was clearing a space on the sofa now, her bendy pigtails wiggling as she shovelled magazines, a bag, some socks and a pair of shoes out of the way. Then she sat down, tucked her spindly legs underneath her and began channel-flicking intensively.

Eliot thought he might go and sit beside her. Possibilities glowed red before his eyes. Wherever she wanted to take him, he wasn't going to stop till he got there – as long as it was legal.

'What are the satisfactions of it?' Darren asked.

'I can't really explain it,' Graham replied.

He had his back to Darren and was kneeling before the floor-to-ceiling 'shelving system' – as he called it – he'd had it installed in the study three years ago. He was a tall, broad top-heavy man whose torso had evolved to fit the extra large proportions of his Pringle sweater as though honouring destiny. Darren had this sort of thought as he watched his eldest brother locate the particular album of photographs he sought and rotate towards him, still on all fours. As Graham looked up at him, Darren corrected himself: it was ignoble and patronising to think of Graham this way and he had better cut it out immediately.

'This is the one,' Graham said. It was a piece of commentary whose only possible purpose was to vent Graham's satisfaction at finding something where it ought to be. The open collar of his shirt rode stiffly above his lambswool crew-neck, making the universal fashion statement of the suburban middle-class that casual is best when conditional. Holding the album in one hand he pulled himself upright with a small grunt and a crack of a knee. He moved towards the roll-top bureau in the corner of the room. From another part of the house Darren heard Clyde's voice cry, 'Out!' as he defeated his auntie Andrea at Sevens yet again. It was after eight in the evening, the time set aside in this household for men to get together and be men. The study, Darren realised, was Graham's equivalent of an older and hardier generation's garage or garden shed: like the lavatories of his social class and post-war generation, it had moved indoors. The bureau top was open to reveal an inlaid panel of green leather for writing on and, facing him, a right-angled archaeology of small wooden ledges and tiny drawers.

'I used to sit and watch him working at this. He used to do his accounts and correspondence here on Sunday mornings, when respectable people were at church.'

Graham spoke these words, but it was their mother's voice that Darren heard: the mild deadpan, the simple pleasure derived from some solemn. convention being ignored. No matter how dull Graham became as he left fifty behind, maternal influence remained his saving grace. Or maybe he got it from their father too.

Darren walked over to stand at his brother's shoulder. He knew the bureau well. It had remained a fixture at his mother's home until she'd passed away, after which Graham had taken responsibility for it and, in due course, the archiving of the Grice family's history. The changes in Darren's attitude to the piece mirrored the main phases of his life. As a young child he'd been fascinated by its rippled curves and where they went to when the bureau wasn't shut. In his adolescence he'd ceased to notice it, as indeed, he now believed, he'd ceased to notice anything except how much cleverer than everyone else he was. And now he was embarked upon an age of reassessment; dwelling on the past instead of disowning it; finding ways of going back to it that didn't plunge him too deeply into gloom. The bureau had become subject to this different way of seeing. Instead of northern-industrial-town torpor it now spoke to Darren of diligence, care and responsibility.

Graham had placed the album on the leather panel. He squared it up, reverently.

'So, here he is . . .' he said. Using the soft pink index finger of his delicately plump right hand, Graham lifted the cover until it tipped past the perpendicular and fell against his waiting left palm. Repeating the procedure he turned directly to the page he was seeking. 'Here he is,' he repeated, his voice less jovial now. 'This is him, holding you.'

The photograph was square with a white border. Its shades were a murky grey rather than the romantic sepia that Darren had envisaged. Was it partly because of this that he wasn't sure he'd ever seen the photograph before? When they'd discussed it over the phone a few days earlier Graham had been sure he must have done – 'Did Mum never show it to you?' – and that Darren's memory would be jogged the moment he set eyes on it. Instead, though, Darren was reminded of something else he had forgotten: that memory is creative, at least as much the invention of the imagination as the human brain's equivalent of a hard disk.

'What am I wearing?' Darren asked, with the hint of an embarrassed laugh that the moment seemed to require.

'That's the family christening robe,' said Graham. 'We all wore it, even though we were boys. It was passed down from Mum's side. She wore it too, apparently, and her brother Tom. But there's no pictures of either of them, unfortunately.'

Darren asked, 'Where is it now?'

'Top shelf, right-hand side,' Graham replied, not looking round. 'It's an heirloom. You were the last Grice to have it on.'

'Didn't your two wear it, then?'

'No, it were out of style by then – and too old, probably. Here,' he said, getting up from the chair, 'you sit down. Have a good look. Take your time. They're all captioned as you can see.'

He moved aside and Darren took his place.

'Be back in a bit,' said Graham, and left the room.

Darren placed one elbow on either side of the album and let his face rest in his hands. For the first time since he had arrived he had space to size up his state of mind. The drive north had done him good. His younger son had been such vivid company and maybe they both needed a break from the complexities of home. But then had come the strain of dissembling when he'd arrived: of reciprocating his hosts' professed delight at seeing him again and trying to relax in a place that felt more like a guest-house than a home. Of course, Clyde wasn't having any problems. He was the centre of attention and nothing could be more of a treat. As for Darren, well, he supposed he was looking for a fresh perspective and he was fretting about why it should be now.

His mobile went. He plucked it from his shirt pocket where, expecting a certain call, he'd placed it to be close to hand. 'Hello, Jane.'

'What are you doing?'

'Looking at a picture of my dad.'

'Oh . . .' Her voice softened. 'You're speaking very quietly. Are you alone?'

'At the moment – I'm in Graham's cubby-hole.'

'What's Clyde doing?'

'Playing cards with Auntie Andrea.'

'He'll be enjoying that.'

'Sounds like he is . . .' Another whoop of 'Out!' had just reached Darren's ears. Andrea was letting him win again.

'Is it the picture you talked about?'

'Yeah . . .' He was still looking at it and it still wasn't familiar to him. But what was he looking for? Clues? To what? And where did he think they'd lead him?

'How are things with you?' he asked.

'It's been a funny day,' said Jane.

'Funny how?'

'Well, Lorna's been quite charming for one thing.'

'Has she left her room at all?'

'Only four times as far as I know – twice to go to the loo and twice for meals that she prepared herself.'

'But she was charming in the process?'

'Yes.'

'Is this the laptop effect?'

'I think so.'

'So she loves us?'

'For the time being. I suppose she's making lots of cyber-friends.'

'Yes, yes,' Darren agreed. 'What else was funny, then?' He was eager to move things on: he could feel Jane's *angst* about Internet grooming coming on and he didn't want to talk about that now.

Jane said, 'Maybe I'll go up and talk to her after I've got Jody to sleep.'

'That's a good idea,' said Darren, who felt as guilty as

Jane did about finding Lorna a pain but not quite so guilty about Jane being the one who would try to get through to her. 'How's Eliot?' he asked. Now there was a different communication problem.

'He came in an hour ago,' said Jane. 'He smelt of girl.'

'Did he? What sort of smell is that?'

'You *know* what sort of smell.'

'I don't, actually. You may have to help me out when I get home.'

'Shut up, Darren. Anyway, guess what he said to me.'

'Um . . . "I want to be a vicar when I grow up."'

'Do you, Darren?'

'Yes. It's the outfits that appeal.'

'He said we ought to get Lorna into his school. He said Mr Bell would put a word in for her, as long as she went back to playing her saxophone. He said it would mean she could make a fresh start and get away from all that bad stuff with her friends.'

'Innit?' said Darren.

'Innit, doh?' said Jane.

'And he asked if we'd noticed Clyde doing that tapping thing.'

'Oh. So he's noticed it too.'

'He's always been observant,' said Jane, proudly. Actually, she also thought he was starting to be handsome again too.

'What do you think?' asked Darren.

'About Lorna changing schools? It would be difficult to get her in. Parents will lie, cheat, do anything to get their kid in there.'

'Like we did?'

'We didn't cheat. We were just extremely winning.'

'Well, I was,' said Darren.

'Ha, ha.'

'Do they have a sibling rule?' he asked.

'I don't know. Isn't that only for younger brothers and sisters?'

'I don't see why it should be.'

A short lull followed in which both Jane and Darren decided against owning up to feeling bad about finding a fancy secondary school for Eliot because he was so sensitive when they hadn't thought the same about Lorna. And she was so painfully sensitive now. Jane said, 'I'll find out.'

'Yeah. And we'll think about it,' said Darren. He liked the idea already.

'OK, then,' said Jane.

'As for Clyde and the tapping thing,' said Darren, 'it's got to be anxiety.'

'Poor little boy.'

'I know, I know. Do you think it's only about Jody?'

'I don't know.'

'Where is she by the way?'

'In Eliot's room. He's playing his keyboard and she's sitting in there, all quiet and listening. And she's had fun making silly noises on it – you know, he can change the settings so it burps or imitates a waterfall.'

'I know. Sounds encouraging.'

'She's quite taken with him lately, isn't she? I wonder why that is?'

'Might be because he's the least interested in her,' Darren suggested.

'What do you mean?' She'd gone on the defensive.

'Or seems to be. I mean, she might just be curious about him – that whole enigma thing.'

Darren turned to the next page of the photo album. There was his mother holding him, sitting in the same chair as his dad had been, baby Darren wearing the same robe. On the next page, his parents were together with their newborn. Darren thought his mother rather beautiful. His father's look of pride suggested he might have thought it too. Shame only Scott had inherited her looks.

'Anyway,' said Jane, 'she wet herself earlier.'

'Oh. That hasn't happened for a while.'

'I know. I found her in the front room all bunched up behind the sofa, soaked through.'

'Did she talk about it?'

'No. She didn't cry either. She didn't say or do anything for a while.'

'Did you ask if there were monsters?'

'Yes. She didn't say so.'

'Maybe it's the summer holidays – you know, people coming and going at unusual times.'

'I suppose it could be. Anyway, she seems calm enough now. Though I don't think she's been back into the front room.'

Darren paused for consideration then said, 'Is it worrying you?'

'A bit. They can slip back, you know, if something feels wrong.'

'Maybe,' Darren said, 'our parenting guru will have something to say about it.'

'Oh, God,' said Jane. 'Are you sure you still want to do that?'

'Yeah, I'm fine. Let's try it. Let's be honest, they're a handful recently. Especially Lorna and Clyde. Any sort of good advice would be helpful.'

'We haven't failed, have we?'

'No, no . . .'

'Has this been a terrible mistake?'

They were in deep waters now, the ones they'd barely dipped their toes in since May. That was the telephone for you, thought Darren: the physical distance reduced your inhibitions and a disembodied voice lulled you into intimacy.

'No, I don't think it's been a mistake.'

'Do you love her, Darren?'

'Jody?'

Of course she meant Jody.

'Yes, Jody.'

'I couldn't give her up now,' Darren said, and wondered whether that would do.

'Oh, I couldn't either,' said Jane. 'I just couldn't. Is that the same as loving her, though?'

'That's a philosophical question,' said Darren, 'and I'm in Graham's house. Need I go on?'

'I mean,' said Jane, ignoring him, 'isn't that how you know you love someone? When just the thought of them not being there hurts you?'

'That's not a bad definition,' Darren said, and added, 'By the way, I miss you.'

'I miss you too. But do you see what I mean?'

Darren flipped back to the first photo he'd looked at: phantom father and baby son.

'Yes, Jane,' he said, 'I think I do.'

Later that evening Lorna was still upstairs, thinking, breathing and clicking on her mouse, clicking again and again, her door ajar so that potential invaders of her edgy privacy could be detected early and repelled. Reflecting gloomily on becoming fifteen, she thought about Bernice and Deanne. She Googled and selected from the list. The livery of the website she selected was purple and pink and the online agony aunt's face was understanding and cheerful. All of this made Lorna want to puke, but she rose above the girls-together overtures. Content was what she wanted, and so badly that she could ignore the style. And here was the problem of 'Anonymous' from Birmingham, aged sixteen:

> Me and my friends like to cut ourselves. We cut our wrists and ankles and sometimes our bellies. It sounds silly but it makes us feel better when we're feeling crap. I know we shouldn't do it. How can we stop?

The agony aunt's reply followed below:

> If it's any comfort you're not the only teenage girls who do this. And you're not the only ones who say it makes them feel better. Yes, it sounds silly but a lot of girls do it to stop themselves from feeling empty and numb inside when they're upset: in a funny way the physical pain helps them to feel their emotional pain more clearly. Also, it can give you a kind of high.

Lorna finished reading, then clicked away the whole website. She went to her door, listened down the stairs, heard nothing of consequence and returned to her laptop to call up the problem page again. Once more, she read the nameless self-harmer's cry for help and the agony aunt's response. She chewed a finger and mused.

There were knives down in the kitchen drawer. Not all that sharp, though. They were fine for slicing cucumber but chopping an onion could be hard work. Lorna cast around in her mind for recollections of keener edges she had known. She thought there might be a Stanley knife in the house somewhere but only because she'd heard Darren talking about it, and she had no idea where it might be. As for Bernice and Deanne's alternative instrument, well, she too had come into contact with them at school but wouldn't dare steal one. She was too much the Goody Two Shoes. How sickening.

What else? Razors. They were pretty dangerous. She'd once cut herself while shaving in an intimate place. It had bled and hurt like hell and even if she hadn't felt too stupid to mention it to her mum she couldn't have done so because she'd secretly borrowed one of Mum's pink Bic disposables and that had made the whole disastrous episode even more of a secret. A vicious little nick, it was. Lorna shuddered at the memory: half the shudder was due to the relived embarrassment, the other half from a flashback to the pain.

She wouldn't be cutting herself, then.

One thing about the agony aunt's observation kept needling her, though: 'Also, it can give you a kind of high.'

As Lorna was very aware, other fifteen-year-old girls spent a lot of time and money chasing highs. They chased highs on roller-coasters, highs on dope in the park, highs getting screwed at parties and in cars. Oh, their hunger for highs was frightening. How weedy Lorna felt, not being involved. And yet she didn't *want* to be involved. She disapproved. And how she disliked herself for disapproving!

On a despairing impulse, one her mother might have related to, she Googled again: 'I'm so crap.'

The search revealed one exact match. It was a very basic weblog with its name across the top. Its subtitle was: A BLOG DEVOTED TO SELF-LOATHING.

Lorna went straight to the blogger's personal profile:

My name is Lottie Mouse. Well, it's not my real name.
I can't stand my real name, but at least I can say
without fear of contradiction that it is not my fault –
unlike almost everything else I hate about myself, of
which there is a very large amount . . .

This was much more fun than Good Advice. She read
on:

Wednesday 20 August 2003
Today I did a really stupid thing. I was out shopping
and I saw two nasty girls from my school. They were
on their own and I was with my mum, which was dead
embarrassing, so I hid behind this big sun-block
display. Anyway, the next thing I know, the two nasty
girls were right beside me and saw me and said, 'Oh,
look, it's Lottie Mouse. What you doing there Lottie?'
and they could tell I was hiding from them. And then
my mum comes up and says, 'Lottie Mouse, I
wondered where you'd got to and what are you doing
there, you silly thing, and are these friends of yours,
how do you do, and what are your names?' And I
could have DIED! And I'm so cross with myself for being
scared of the nasty girls and feeling so stupid and
thinking it's all my fault even though it was just bad
luck in a way, and, of course, having an embarrassing
mum. And now I'm dreading going back to school cos
they've got such big nasty mouths and they're just
BOUND to tell everyone about it. Oh, well, never mind. I
think I'll just go and shoot myself now (except I'll
probably miss).

Then it said:

PS I'm going to go to sell all my old CDs, well, most of them, and give the money to CND. A suicide bomb blew up the United Nations building in Baghdad yesterday and twenty people died. My mum might be very embarrassing and too friendly and everything but she thinks the war is wrong and won't make anything better and I agree with her.

Under this post, like all the others, was the standard 'comment' button. Lorna clicked on it, filled in her email address – *Lornagrice@hotmail.com* – and wrote: 'Really like your blog. Are you a member of CND? Lorna.'

She waited a while to see if Lottie Mouse would reply, but she didn't. So Lorna Googled CND. They were, their website said, always looking for volunteers but Lorna discovered that if you wanted to apply you had to have a referee.

Hmm.

Mum?

No, she'd be too nosy.

Dad?

No, he'd have to tell Mum.

Who, then?

Dodie! What better referee than an Aldermaston veteran? But would she do it without telling Mum? Difficult one. And, oh, Mum's coming up the stairs. Lorna switched off the laptop and became interested in her cuticles. When Jane knocked she called, 'Hi-ya! Come in!'

Jane did go in, teeth on edge – that 'Hi-ya!' business still grated – and did not display them when she smiled. 'How's cyberspace?' she asked cheerfully.

'Oh. Yeah. It's OK.'

She sat down on Lorna's bed. She saw and strove to

delete her awareness of certain features of the décor – the inside-out odd socks, the dried-out orange peel, the school blouse hung over that beautiful saxophone. 'Lorna, I've been thinking,' she began.

'OK!' Lorna replied, as if she'd just been offered a lollipop.

'How would you feel about changing school?'

Lorna's jaw dropped, which Jane found instantly gratifying.

'Like, wow!' Lorna said.

This gave less pleasure to her mother. None the less, she pressed on: 'I was wondering – Dad and I were wondering – if you'd be happier at Eliot's school. What do you think?'

'Like, wow!' repeated Lorna, beginning to resemble a character in *Friends*.

'You'd have to play your saxophone again,' Jane added quickly. Somewhat belatedly, she'd realised that she'd made the whole thing sound like a done deal. For God's sake, there might not be a place for her! She hadn't even spoken to the bloody school! 'You'd like it there, would you?' she asked anyway.

Lorna's mouth and eyes were wide with sitcom wonder. 'I'd so *love* to go there! At least, I think I would. I mean—'

Jane cut in: 'You're very miserable where you are, aren't you?' She spoke abruptly, purposely so, and with no immediate regrets. She didn't want the bad theatrics, the cloying gratitude, any evidence of her daughter's desperate search for a viable teenage identity. She remembered her own search only too well, and the sheer bliss when it was over. Of course, it hadn't lasted long but something had to be done about Lorna. Jane was so weary of walking on eggshells.

'You're very unhappy, aren't you, Lorna? And we have *got* to make that change.'

With satisfaction, and pain, she watched Lorna disintegrate.

'Yes,' she said – barely said, the word squeezing out through the last vanishing space between sobs. Oh, shit, thought Jane – at last, the real Lorna has emerged. She went to her and held her in her arms. 'Come on now, come on now, it's OK . . .'

'It's not OK,' Lorna howled. 'It's not OK.'

'It's *going* to be OK.'

'I'm so crap.'

'Oh, no, you're not. You're not. You're just so bloody . . . fifteen.' For one moment she had been going to say 'like me'. 'We're going to sort you out. And we're going to sort Clyde out, too. And we're going to take care of Jody, and everything's going to get better.'

'I hope so,' blubbered Lorna.

'Trust me,' said Jane, rashly. 'Starting from now. You wait and see.'

The Family Growth Centre was a converted terraced house in a residential pocket north of Upper Street. This being a location that people in her and Darren's income bracket had been unable to aspire to for at least two decades, Jane felt a bit dog-eared as she pressed the reproduction Victorian doorbell. This, combined with her welling worry about the inadequacies that had brought her there, inspired the tragi-comedian within. Mentally she cast herself as a supplicant at the door of some moral-authority figure, begging for absolution and to be given one last chance: 'Forgive me troubling you, ma'am, but this wretched appearance hides a heart of gold; I can play the piano an' all.'

The doorbell's ring was deep and substantial. Beside

Jane stood Darren, cradling Jody in his arms. Jody cradled Dolly and sucked her ear, which was beginning to wear away. The door opened. A plump, middle-aged woman with big set hair met them with the sort of expression that promised sweets if they were good. 'Welcome,' she said. 'Please come through.'

Her name was Hilary Marsh. She was florid and unhurried and wore a plain black dress with a discreet pearl necklace and high-heeled shoes, which Jane thought must be under enormous strain.

'We'll go straight upstairs,' said Hilary. She had a light Midlands accent. As Jane followed her she noticed that the former ground-floor front room now served as an office in which two or three people were sitting at desks bearing piles of documents and telephones. It all seemed very businesslike. This was reassuring, Jane supposed.

'Come in, come in,' said Hilary.

Her consulting room was at the top of the stairs. It was Spartan, with cheap brown corduroy carpet and white walls and contained only a filing cabinet, a *passé* desk and several chairs in the same mid-seventies style. A framed, blown-up photo of three young children laughing on a set of playground swings was the only humanising feature. However, Hilary's manner was warm.

'So it's Jane and Darren . . . and who is this delightful young lady?'

Jody was sitting on Darren's lap. Hilary gave her an encouraging smile. Jody responded with a blank stare.

'This is Hilary,' said Jane to Jody. 'Would you like to tell her your name?'

Jody shook her head slowly, then turned away from Hilary and rested her chin on Darren's shoulder. She focused on the middle distance.

'Never mind,' said Hilary. She took up a thick black marker pen. 'I'm going to write a name on a sticker I have here and maybe later she'll tell me if I've got it right. And if I *have* got it right, maybe she'd like to put the sticker on her jumper.'

And maybe not, thought Jane.

Hilary took some details from the grown-ups: names, dates of birth, occupations.

'Does she like music?' Hilary asked, on learning that Jane was a pianist.

'It isn't obvious that she does,' said Jane.

'We're encouraging her,' said Darren.

'It's still very early days,' said Jane.

'Yes, yes,' nodded Hilary, making a note. 'As you were saying on the phone.'

Jody hates music and we're rubbish, thought Jane. Go on, write it down.

They moved on to the rest of the family: Lorna, just fifteen; Eliot, thirteen; Clyde seven, eight quite soon, and playing at a friend's house today. 'And, of course,' said Hilary, raising her voice a little, 'this lovely girl who is going to be four in December, so I've heard, and is going to get a sticker and maybe a chocolate biscuit after she's told me her name.' She held up the sticker for Jane and Darren's inspection, so they could check her spelling of 'Jody'.

'And she has been with you how long?' Hilary asked, more quietly.

'Twelve weeks,' they said in unison, and laughed nervously.

'So now,' said Hilary, the formalities complete, 'what are your particular concerns about your children?'

It was Jane who took the lead in summarising their predicament; took it and held it for a full half-hour. Lorna, she explained, 'is quite clever and creative – at least she was until lately and I suppose that's one big reason why I'm here. You see she's been so *miserable*. Unbearably miserable, really. Something's gone wrong between her and her friends, and now she thinks everyone hates her and I can't seem to do a thing with her.' She paused while Darren threw in a few lines about the Kazea affair, and worried that her last remark had made her sound as though she were talking about her hair. They explained that they were hoping to move Lorna to Eliot's school, which brought them nicely on to Eliot.

'He's always been the sweetheart of the family, I suppose, the introverted type with big blue eyes who's interested in wildlife, or was, and you worried about him being too sensitive. You know, will they pull his trousers down at school?' The odd thing was, she explained – 'the daft thing, really' – is that of the three older children he was the one causing the least consternation lately: he was going out, participating in school activities and not being a scrap of trouble at home. 'But, you see,' said Jane, 'that's the worrying thing. You never quite know what's going on with him. I mean,' she concluded, almost beseechingly, 'for all I know, he could be really, really suffering.' She added, 'That sounds ridiculous. I think I'll shut up for a while.'

Hilary, though, was not giving Jane's self-flagellation her full attention. Jody had become bored with hanging over Darren's shoulder and had got down to the floor. She was trying to clamber astride one of his legs and losing her balance ostentatiously. When that failed to secure his undivided interest she threw Dolly violently to the floor.

Hilary said, 'Let me see what I can find for you.'

She got up and went to the filing cabinet. From the

bottom drawer she extracted a plastic storage box full of toys: bricks, cars, animals, dolls. She placed them next to Jody, saying, 'Here you are,' then returned calmly to her seat. 'And then there's Clyde,' she said invitingly.

'Yes,' said Jane. 'Clyde.'

'Tell me about him,' Hilary said, beckoning Jane to continue. 'We won't take too much notice of anything else that might be going on.'

Jane embarked on her fourth résumé: Clyde was bouncy and lively and cheeky and hadn't seemed to have a care in the world until recently, but suddenly he'd started to go off school. Often during the summer term he'd had to be fetched home early because he'd been in trouble or because he *said* he wasn't feeling well, but when he got back home he seemed quite all right. 'And you see, the thing is,' Jane went on, 'I feel a bit of a fraud being here in a way because I *know* what the problem is with Clyde—'

Her flow was interrupted by a loud metallic clang.

'Jody!' cried Darren.

Beside the filing cabinet a London double-decker bus was lying, stricken, on its side.

'Jody!' gasped Jane, embarrassed and horrified. 'You *mustn't* throw things like that!'

'Yes, yes, about Clyde,' said Hilary, insistently. She made a palms-down gesture to Jane and Darren as she said it, then mouthed, 'Ignore, ignore, ignore.'

'He's finding the change in the family dynamics a bit tricky,' said Darren.

'Yes, well,' said Hilary, 'that's only to be expected, I suppose.'

'I suppose,' Jane agreed, then cowered involuntarily as another bang, a louder one this time, came from the filing cabinet. She did, however, manage not to look round.

'What was that?' asked Darren, quietly, showing the same extreme restraint.

'Only a tractor,' said Hilary, *sotto voce*. 'Don't let it distract you. Now let me tell you more about our methods.'

The key concept, as they'd expected, was that of learning to hosanna any good bits of behaviour and to ignore the bad stuff as best you could. 'What they're looking for is your attention,' Hilary explained. 'The trick is to lavish it on them when they're doing things you're pleased about. When you do that you'll start to find that the bad behaviour takes care of itself.'

A bulkier vehicle crashed into the filing cabinet: a jumbo jet, speculated Darren, maybe a tank. He was working hard at listening to Hilary, but the accumulating wreckage to his rear was distracting, as was his rather full bladder and a growing worry that he should have put another pound in the parking meter. With his left hand he began to fidget with his mouth, pinching and pulling at his top lip. His right hand, though, remained still.

'I really like what you're doing with your right hand, Darren,' Hilary said.

Instantly, Darren took his left hand away from his face.

'What a *very* good boy you are!' said Jane, with a great laugh. 'I think I may have to buy you some sweets.'

'Thank you, Mummy,' Darren said ruefully.

Hilary smiled modestly.

Jody, meanwhile, her attention caught by Jane's exclamation of delight, appeared silently at her side.

'Oh, hello,' said Hilary. 'Can you remember what your name is now?'

'Jody,' said Jody, quietly.

'So have I got it right on this sticker?' asked Hilary.

'I don't know,' said Jody, barely looking.

'Never mind,' said Hilary. 'The important thing is I know who you are. So would you like to take your sticker now?'

Jane and Darren turned to stone as Jody's hand moved across Hilary's desk. She picked up the sticker, peeled it from its backing and pressed it on to her jumper, where it stayed.

'Well, *done*, Jody!' said Hilary. 'Isn't that marvellous? You told me what your name is and then you took the sticker and put it on your jumper *all by yourself*! Did you see that, Mummy and Daddy?'

Darren and Jane's affirmation was delayed: did they qualify for those titles yet? Only Jody could confer them and she had a different priority. She patted the sticker, looked down at it, kept on looking down.

'Yes, we *did* see!' enthused Jane, recovering. '*Isn't* she a clever girl?'

'A *very* clever girl,' added Darren.

It was they who sought approval now. Hilary gave it, nodding, conducting their praises with her hands.

There was a scene of destruction behind them: a scaled-down tableau from a bombed city or an earthquake-ravaged freeway. Darren contemplated it: could anyone get out of there alive?

'There's a new parents' group beginning early next month,' Hilary said, 'when the holidays are over.'

'I'll be there,' said Jane.

As Eliot had suspected there was no Grice-Ransome holiday that summer. Jane and Darren found the prospect far too daunting, not least because the teenagers had made it perfectly clear that they'd rather stay at home. Eliot spent more time with Harriet, and when she went to Tuscany he spent it with Yan and Alex, whose mother disconcerted him significantly less than previously. Lorna did not join CND, but she did get an email from Lottie Mouse, which said: 'Thanx for your comment. I feel less crap already. Why don't you start a blog too?'

So Lorna did. She called it 'Leavelornaalone'. Her personal profile began, 'The title of this blog is a joke, actually, but I expect you've guessed that already.' That part went very well, but then it got much harder. She was supposed to post stuff, wasn't she, stuff about herself? But she found she didn't have a lot to say. Well, she did, but it looked silly written down. And then Jane and Darren had good news for her: they'd spoken to the head of Eliot's school; there'd been a nudge and a wink from Mr Bell and on Wednesday, 27 August, she informed the blogosphere:

Hurray, hurray, hurray!
I've changed my school today!

Poetry! Now *that* was an idea! To celebrate, she dusted down her saxophone.

Meanwhile, Darren and Jane had instructed a family solicitor. At their second case conference they had been far more confident than at their first: confident enough to relate Jody's wetting episode and occasional bouts of destructive rage. Giselle was there, and she deferred to their opinions – it was clear they knew Jody better than she did now. Ashleigh's social worker was on holiday but had left word: she hadn't had much luck in getting hold of Ashleigh lately, but the last time she'd mentioned it there'd been no sign of her consent for Jody to be adopted being withdrawn. This hadn't sounded very definite, though. 'There's no guarantee that she won't change her mind,' Lucy had explained. 'She's entitled to do that right up to the last minute, although if she did I'm pretty sure a judge would overrule her.'

It was an unpleasant idea. In the days following the meeting, Jane and Darren had spoken more about their dread of Ashleigh deciding to fight them than any other aspect of their situation. They hadn't forgotten that Ashleigh had fought for Jody before, when she was taken into care. A tug-of-love scenario was the last thing they desired. Knowing that they'd be certain to emerge as the winners was a consolation, but a tainted one. All they could do was hope it wouldn't come to that. Jody had now been in the family long enough for them to make their application to the courts. They went ahead and waited. A reporting officer would be appointed to explain things to Ashleigh and obtain her signature. In the continuing absence of Jody's father, hers alone would be sufficient for Jody Jones to become Jody Grice-Ransome – Jody Grice for short.

The sadness of it all was as much a part of the story as the joy. It troubled Jane. It troubled Darren too as, with August coming to an end and with it his sabbatical, he walked with Jody to his favourite café for the last time before his return to work. They moved along the pavement hand in hand, the man letting the child dictate their pace. As they moved forward, he thought of Graham and his archive and was reminded, as Jody dawdled, that even now his head could be turned by a trace memory: the coat of a middle-aged window shopper, a certain incline of her head. He knew it wasn't her, of course, but still he looked twice at the woman as she came back into view from behind a parked car across the street. The rush of hopeful recognition had felt no less real for being utterly unfounded and he wanted to preserve whatever it was about the stranger that had fleetingly brought Lillian Grice back to life.

While he was looking, a large bird flapped low over their heads. Jody screamed.

'Hey, now,' Darren said, snapping back to the present and lifting Jody to his hip. 'It's gone now – just a big, silly bird.'

Jody, he thought, was getting better at being hugged. There was less rigid tolerance in her body as he held her and greater warmth. The more she opened up, though, the easier it was to see her vulnerability. The more she spoke, the more she gave away. Monsters were everywhere, especially at bedtime and, for some strange reason, in the front room. She called them monsters although Darren couldn't help thinking they might be ghosts.

'Where's Daddy?' he asked her, on impulse.

'You,' she said quietly, her head buried in his neck.

'Just testing.' He didn't ask her the companion question. 'Where's Mummy?' was trickier and maybe risky too if, as Darren did, you suspected that the monsters might be something to do with Ashleigh. Would the monsters ever die? Even if they did, he knew that Ashleigh wouldn't die with them.

By the time they got to the café Jody was walking again. They sat down at a secluded table by the back wall, and Darren was encouraged that Jody reached for a menu unbidden. She couldn't read it, of course, but she wanted to be like him and therein lay the hope and the rewards.

'Mmmm. I like chips! Do you like chips?' asked Darren.

'Yes,' said Jody, blandly.

No good, no good, thought Darren – wrong sort of question. He tried again. 'What else do you like eating, Jody?'

She frowned at him. 'Chips,' she said.

'And what do you like with your chips?'

'Ketchup,' she said.

'Oh, Jody! You are *so brilliant*! You answered my question, didn't you?'

He was whispering, of course: as a man in the company of a small girl he was already the centre of barely concealed attention from some of the café's other regulars. He'd nodded to a couple when he and Jody had come in – a wobbly lady eating a pastry delicately with a fork, an old man in a summer shirt always primed for a voluble exchange about nothing much – returned their smiles of recognition at his having someone small and sweet with him today, and hoped that the low tones in which he spoke to her would demonstrate the delicacy of his situation and ward off unwanted conversation. He glanced up: they were looking. He leaned forward to speak to Jody again.

'And what *else* do you like with your chips?' he enquired, making a game of speaking to her secretively.

'Sausages,' she said.

'Oh *Jody*! You're *absolutely right*! You like sausages with your chips! So can you tell me everything that you would like to eat?'

Jody's top teeth gripped her bottom lip. She laid her head on the table as, from behind her, a waitress approached, pulling a pad and pen from the front pocket of her nylon overall and smiling at Darren expectantly.

Jody said, 'Chips.'

'And?' asked Darren, catching the waitress's eye in a way that said, 'Bear with me here, bear with me.'

'Ketchup,' said Jody.

'Ketchup, yes,' Darren confirmed. 'And the last thing?'

'Sausages!' Jody said, and suddenly sat up straight.

'Chips, ketchup and sausages!' said Darren, so the waitress could hear.

'Chips, ketchup and sausages!' repeated Jody.

'Right, then!' the waitress said. She stood neatly, pen wagging, hair tied back. 'So that's chips, ketchup and sausages for the young lady. And for the gentleman?'

'The *young* gentleman, I think you mean,' said Darren.

'Ooh! Sorry!' The waitress did a little curtsy.

'If only,' laughed Darren. He hadn't thought about what he would eat and made a token scan of the menu. Maybe he'd have the same as Jody, for the sake of simplicity. It would be cosy and he could talk Jody through each forkful. Raising his eyes from the menu, Darren saw the door of the café open as another customer walked in. 'I'll have the same,' Darren told the waitress. But he was watching the new customer – a young woman in sunglasses, not shambling exactly, but labouring.

'Any drinks?'

'Uh, yeah . . .'

She would have put on his warning light anywhere. For all her youth, for all the aspirations to high-street fashion betrayed by her thick belt, tight jeans and tasselled ankle boots, she was still one of those who came to paw at you and beg of you and tell you that sorry tale about their mum being in hospital and how they had to get the bus, or that their gas meter was empty and could you spare them fifty pence? Yes, Darren saw all that.

And yet what else? Something, someone, more.

'What drinks would you like?'

'Oh, sorry. A tea, please, and a Coke.'

Before Darren's order was out of his mouth the waitress, seeing that his attention had strayed, whipped round to locate the cause. 'A tea and a Coke, then,' she said, turning back and jotting. She added, 'Don't worry, Mick will deal with her.'

And already Mick had come out of the kitchen and intercepted the newcomer as she'd stumbled up to the counter. He was asking her what she wanted and if she was sure she could pay and if not, 'Listen, love, I'm sorry, but you can't just come in here and hang about.' To Darren, the speech seemed longer than it needed to be. The unwanted arrival put up no resistance and she hadn't even tried to place an order, let alone shown any desire to sit and stay. Of course, it was hard to know where she was looking with those shades on. It did, though, seem to Darren that she'd seen what she wanted in those few, dragged-out seconds when her thin, tired face pointed Jody's way.

CHAPTER NINE
SEPTEMBER

In the main teaching room at the Family Growth Centre all the parenting-skills pupils were asked to write their name on a sticky label and attach it to themselves. Jane accomplished the latter more speedily than Jody had, though not without a setback on the way.

'These will come in handy if we forget who we are,' she joked to a man standing next to her. He was a morose, bulbous figure wearing sandals and a chinstrap beard. He didn't laugh, just cleared his throat, which made Jane feel foolish and wonder if she should have stayed at home. It was a bad week for her to start the course. Oh, she knew that Darren would feed and shepherd the children capably but there were bound to be extra things, what with Lorna, Eliot and Clyde being back-to-school and him adjusting to his return to work. And then, confirming her unease, she ended up sitting beside the humourless man. His name sticker said, 'Ben', and Jane cheered herself up by imagining he had a twin brother named Bill. She checked the names of the other four members of the class, pretending not to as she did it just as they were pretending not to check hers. There were three more women and one more man: Lesley, Nell, Dinky – *Dinky?* – and Paul. All except Dinky appeared close to Jane in age, if you counted not *that* much younger as being close. Dinky looked about twenty-three. Paul wore jogging bottoms, trainers and an Adidas sweatshirt. He was dark and clean-shaven with an athletic build and a dimple in the middle of his chin. He caught Jane's eye and winked at her. She ignored him.

As the class settled down, Hilary Marsh stood waiting next to a whiteboard. She was perfectly groomed and adorned in a loose-fitting, parchment-coloured silk gown. She resembled a small, hand-painted galleon. 'Good evening, everyone,' she said. 'It's so nice to have you here. Let's begin by going round the room and saying just a little about who we are and our children, and what we hope to gain from these classes.' Hilary paused to assess those seated immediately to either side of her, apparently wondering whom to ask to begin. Jane was to her left, Paul to her right.

'Paul,' she said, 'shall we start with you?'

Paul's diction was decisive, his voice clear. He was 'in the financial sector, or was', and the father of two sons, Calum and Kier, who were eight and ten respectively. He explained that he'd recently been made redundant but that his wife had been promoted and they had made a decision that he would experiment with being a house-husband for a year. 'I've got to say,' he confessed smoothly, 'that the boys can be a handful at times. I could use a few good tricks to keep the little devils in order.'

Social chuckles rippled round the circle. Paul settled back with his legs spread. Jane noticed Lesley sizing up his groin.

It was Dinky's turn to speak next. 'Oi yam Paul's au pair,' she said. 'Paul and Victoria's, actually.'

Dinky's accent was eastern European, though Jane couldn't identify the country. She had a whippy sort of body with small breasts and wide hips. Her clothes were tight, her foundation comprehensive and her eyebrows were plucked into the contours of perpetual surprise. Jane wondered if it were possible that anyone else in the room *wasn't* thinking what she was thinking about her working arrangements with Paul, who looked down at his trainers when she spoke.

'Very good,' said Hilary. 'And now you, Lesley.'

Jane didn't like the look of Lesley: from her high-powered hair to her layered blood-red frock, everything about her said 'man-eater.' She slouched slightly in her seat. Her voice was a little slouchy too. 'Well, I have one child,' she began, 'a three-year-old daughter called Camille . . .'

Surprise, surprise, thought Jane.

'I'm a lone parent,' Lesley continued, 'a widow, actually. My husband died a year ago . . .'

What a bitch I am, thought Jane. What a terrible thing I did, judging this poor woman when I didn't know a thing about her.

'I'm an architect,' Lesley went on, 'which means that I can mostly work from home. And I suppose, well . . . I'm having a few problems with Camille. She'll be starting school quite soon and I just want her to be, well, more manageable, really – I suppose that's what it is.'

She shrugged and smiled at Paul, who responded in a perma-tan manner. Seeing this, Jane's heart sank a little. And that word 'manageable' . . . Oh dear.

'Thank you,' Hilary said. 'And Nell?'

Nell was small, fair and bordering on homely. Jane reckoned they were equals as the least coutured women in the room: T-shirt, big shorts, ankle socks, monkey boots and a consolingly exhausted air. This was good. Nell had two boys, Max and Harry, aged nine and seven, and a baby girl, Bethany, although, as Nell revealed, everyone called her Flea. Flea was asleep in a carrycot on the carpet next to Nell, attracting admiring looks from all the females present. Jane felt a small snag of longing: she wasn't free of those yet but at least their existence proved she wasn't yet so old she didn't get them any more.

'Max has become very aggressive recently,' Nell said, in a sweet, medium-paced voice, 'and Harry won't do anything I say. It's very hard having to keep those two happy and look after a baby.' Nell didn't mention a husband or partner. Jane was intrigued and full of sympathy. Was Nell separated, divorced? Did she have a sad song to sing, one to which Jane might provide a sympathetic accompaniment? What was the story with Flea?

'Ben?' Hilary beamed.

Ben had been breathing a bit too loudly for Jane's liking and she had already edged her chair away from him. He was one of those people – one of those men – who wore their glumness like a heavy aftershave, oppressing all who inhaled it.

'I have a son called Miles,' he said. 'He's twelve. I see him mostly at weekends and on one evening a week.' He hesitated for a moment, building a little tension before disgorging the inevitable bad news. 'I find him grudging, truculent, uncooperative and given to what I can really only describe as dumb insolence. I wish I could see it getting better. But, frankly, I can't at the moment.'

There was a discernible tremor of unspoken non-sympathy before Hilary moved in and said, 'Thank you, Ben. And finally . . .' She smiled benignly down at Jane.

Jane said, 'Gosh, well, after that what can I say?'

Her question broke the dismal spell that Ben had cast. And then Jane, to her surprise, turned out to have a great deal to say. Lorna was a worry because she'd been so miserable and what if she wasn't happy at her new school either? Eliot, well, he wasn't as much of a worry, except that he was so very, *very* self-contained and seemed to have this older girlfriend, which she, Jane, didn't know *what* she thought about. Then there was Clyde. He was so *hyper*! And although he'd always been a bit that way, he'd been more manic since Jody had come along. And Jody? 'She's settling in well, generally. Though I've a feeling she has problems that are very deeply rooted and getting to the bottom of them will be hard. You know, taking on a child like her, there's just so much you don't know.'

Jane broke off: she'd spoken for far longer than any of the others and didn't want to gush about her plight when it was trivial compared to Lesley's. Yet it was Lesley who wanted her to talk on: 'So was she abused in some way, this little girl?' she said. 'If you don't mind me asking.'

'No, no, I don't mind,' said Jane, although she sort of did. 'She wasn't abused,' she said. 'At least, her social worker doesn't think so. But she was certainly neglected. Her mother has a drink problem, you see.'

'You're a very special lady, then,' gleamed Paul.

'Not really,' said Jane. Paul had his headlights on her, full beam. And she was discomfited, too, by having referred to Ashleigh simply as Jody's mother rather than as her natural or birth-mother. Of course, the absence of a qualifying term might signify nothing about her own subconscious and, in any case, Jane had no legal right to call herself

Jody's mother, adoptive or otherwise. Yet her involuntary failure to differentiate between the sort of mother Ashleigh was and the type that she, Jane, was seeking to be had the effect of elevating Ashleigh to a senior maternal status. Was that the way Jane saw her situation? Would it, could it, should it change?

'Does Jody know about her mother?' Nell asked kindly.

'She doesn't talk about her,' said Jane. Now she was pleased to have a question to deal with. It made it easier not to look at Paul. 'Jody may hardly remember her,' she said. 'She's been in care and foster-homes since she was eight months old, although she did have a little contact with her mother – her birth-mother – until fairly recently.'

'And do you tell her about her birth-mother?' asked Lesley, picking up on Jane's revised terminology.

'Not really,' said Jane, and she felt that she was making an admission. 'When we've tried she hasn't seemed to understand. And we have so little background material. What the birth-mother has said may be unreliable, you know. Alcoholics aren't always the best at remembering, are they? Or telling the truth, I suppose. We don't even have a photograph of her. She hasn't provided one so far.'

'What about the father?' asked Ben. There was an umbraged air about him; he was a sociopathic bison nursing a grudge against the herd.

'He's disappeared,' said Jane. 'No one knows where he is. We're not even certain *who* he is, actually. But we may be able to help Jody track him down when she's older. These days, you probably know, adopted children are given every help with finding their birth-parents if they want to. There will probably be what they call "letterbox contact" between the birth-mother and Jody. It means they write to each other using a third party, the adoption agency usually, as an intermediary. But I don't know if that will happen much with Jody. We'll have to wait and see.'

Jane was surprised at the things she was hearing. But yes, no doubt about it, it was definitely her seeming to know what she was going on about – and what a novelty it was to hold her audience in the palm of her hand. She wondered if she might go on, revealing, grippingly, the fears she still harboured of being in denial about her true motivation for wanting Jody, which was to compensate herself for not getting pregnant at forty-four, and whether that was a good enough reason. She wondered, but self-preservation prevailed. Instead, she smiled at Nell and said, 'It's hard to imagine, isn't it?'

'Yes,' said Nell, sadly, looking down at the sleeping Flea. 'What a dreadful state to be in.'

There seemed to be a clear consensus about Ashleigh's desperation and, this being established, Hilary resumed her command of the gathering. Soon Jane was hearing all about the vital importance of praising, of verbally reflecting children's rages back at them instead of minimising or arguing, and how to rehearse them verbally through the right type of behaviour for a forthcoming social situation in a way that made them think *they*'d thought of it. All very interesting, although at one stage she did lose concentration and began contemplating the ridiculous idea that as well as saving Jody she should be saving Ashleigh too.

'What's going on?' said Eliot to Lorna. His voice cracked during the 'going' and his sister laughed at him. 'Shut up!' he said.

'Sorry.' Lorna composed herself. 'I don't *know* what's going on. She's nuttier than ever, if you ask me.'

Well, Eliot didn't think Jane was nutty, just, like, really

stressed. But he and Lorna had discussed their mother's sanity loads of times, so he didn't take it up with her again. Instead, he just listened along. They were camped in a corner of the front room among the toys but they could hear their mother in the kitchen talking to Clyde in that peculiar new way of hers: 'It's *fantastic* that you didn't get very, very cross because all the Jaffa cakes have gone! I'm *so* proud of you, Clyde!'

Lorna rolled her eyes. 'This is the parent-skills classes, right?'

'Right,' said Eliot.

'Can we run away and join the circus now?' asked Lorna.

Eliot wagged a finger at her satirically. 'Now, now, Lorna! Mummy and Daddy have just got you into a lovely new school and *this* is how you show your gratitude!'

'Yeah, yeah, all right,' said Lorna. 'Crap uniform, though.' Neither she nor Eliot had bothered to change during the half-hour or so since they'd got in. She looked down at her skirt, blouse and tie with deep distaste, although her heart wasn't in rebellion. The truth was that she was so much happier: nervous, yes, but happier. Her first few days had gone well. Being Eliot's sister had helped, although she didn't intend to tell him so. She said, 'I think Jody might like her princess crown back now, Eliot.'

'Oh! Not fair!' Eliot whined and stuck out his bottom lip. For no particular reason, just a boy-adolescent thing, he'd put the crown on when they'd come in and Jody, who was hiding and watching them, had really liked it at first. 'Take the hat off!' she'd demanded, getting all excited and giggly as she did more often, these days, although she could still be very, very far away.

'No, *my* hat,' Eliot had said.

'No *my* hat!'

This had gone on for a while until Jody had got bored and burrowed into the fluff and lost Lego behind the sofa to become invisible with Dolly. Once or twice she'd peeped out and stared suspiciously across the room at the window.

'Is there a monster out there, Jody?' Eliot had asked.

'No.'

'Shall I scare it off for you?'

No reply.

'You won't scare anything with that crown on,' Lorna said.

At last, Eliot removed his regal headgear and placed it where Jody could reach it without having to break cover.

'Do you think she's all right?' asked Lorna.

'I don't know,' said Eliot.

'You're the one she likes.'

'Yeah, well, I'm the loveliest in the family.'

'Hmm,' said Lorna, and screwed up her nose at him.

'Is, she like, *ours* yet?' Eliot asked, lifting his forehead meaningfully Jody's way.

'Supposed to be, I think.' Lorna shrugged. 'There's some sort of hold-up, like, before it's all legal and official. I don't know what. I hope we keep her, though.'

'She's pretty cute,' Eliot agreed. 'What if we don't keep her? Where would she go?'

Lorna said, 'To someone else, I suppose. Or into care.'

'Like Tracy Beaker, yeah?'

'Yeah, right, Eliot. She can't go back to her mother.'

Eliot thought a bit and said, 'Why didn't they want their own, you know, if they wanted another kid, why didn't they, you know . . . ?'

'Oh, they wanted their own,' said Lorna, rejoicing in her superior knowledge. 'It just didn't happen, apparently.'

'How do you know?'

'It's a girl thing.'

'Yeah, right,' said Eliot again. He added, 'Clyde isn't so sure about her, though.'

'Oh, I think they quite like each other, really,' said Lorna, very wisely. 'It's a love-hate relationship. And it's bound to be quite traumatic for him.'

Eliot let silence suffice to show agreement. He didn't want to go into this in detail. Simba was prowling near them, purring and frantic for affection, and Eliot hadn't forgotten about that time in his life when he couldn't stop thinking of terrible things happening to Simba and whatever else. It hadn't passed his notice that the age gap between him and Clyde was the same as between Clyde and Jody. That was why, the other day, when he'd been putting up with playing Spiderman on PlayStation with Clyde, he'd said, 'You're worried about Jody, innit?'

'No,' Clyde had lied transparently.

'I can tell, you know.'

'No, you can't.'

Eliot had drummed his fingers on the coffee-table. 'That's why you're doing all that,' he'd said.

'Shu' up,' Clyde had complained.

'Jus' sayin'.'

He'd left it there – no point rubbing it in when he could tell that Clyde knew it was true.

Lorna dug Eliot in the ribs. 'So when are you going to tell me about Harriet?' she said.

'Nuffin' to tell.'

'Come on – the mad, beatnik cellist . . .'

'She's gone abroad – I told you – to New York with her parents, for ages. And she's not mad, by the way.'

'That's what you said.'

'I didn't mean, you know, *mad* . . .'

'Eccentric, then?'

'Yeah. An individual. I respect that.'

'So?'

'So what?'

'It's all right. I'm not going to ask you about . . . *intimate matters*.'

'Good,' said Eliot.

Lorna didn't want to ask him either. If she did and he answered with any candour then he might expect her to provide a tale of *intimate matters* in response. And she didn't have any. In fact, she was starting to think she might be frigid. She was worried about this, but mostly because she was not *all that* worried. It was quite interesting, though, being at a school with boys. One or two had even talked to her.

The front door opened and closed, and they heard Darren come in. He put his head round the door, saw the two of them sitting there and said, 'Where's Jody?'

'She's here,' said Lorna. 'Behind the sofa.'

Darren checked that this was true. 'OK,' he said, and left.

Eliot and Lorna swapped mystified looks.

'He's worried,' Lorna said.

'Sssh!' hissed Eliot.

Darren had run straight upstairs and Jane was calling after him. 'Hello, Daddy! We're down here! Clyde has got something to tell you.'

There was no reply from Darren.

'Darren? Are you all right up there?'

Darren did not reply.

'What's that about?' said Lorna to Eliot.

'Search me, bruv,' Eliot replied.

THE ADOPTION

* * *

The butterflies had started for Darren after he'd parked the car and finally accepted that he didn't intend to heed his doubts. He risked making himself look foolish, perhaps of being subjected to unpleasant accusations, and he was doing this without Jane's knowledge, let alone her blessing. The clinching calculation, though, was that he would be a coward to turn back. Pride, he soberly reflected, had conquered all.

He locked up and walked back along the street. The first brown leaves were falling from the handful of trees he passed and the rot of autumn touched the air. On the doorstep he rang the bell then waited, casting furtive looks to left and right. He felt bad about what he was about to do, even though he'd told himself it wasn't wrong. There were no real villains of this piece, just the flawed, the confused and the vulnerable.

The sound of slippered feet came towards him from behind the red-painted front door. It opened gradually, forebodingly maybe. Darren smiled. 'Hello, Anne!'

'Oh, hello.'

'Is this a bad time?' asked Darren, more or less telling her he didn't care.

'No, no,' insisted Anne, searching his features for clues. 'Come in,' she said, 'You'll have to take us as you find us, I'm afraid.'

Us, not me, noted Darren, as he followed her down the hall.

'Sssh,' she said, as they went past the living-room door. 'I've got a little one asleep in there.'

So she'd found a replacement quickly; a younger one by the sound of it and probably cuter.

'Take a seat,' she said.

Darren pulled back one of the chairs around the kitchen table, the one that commanded the best view of the room. She didn't sit down with him. Instead she went to the cooker where something was simmering in a large saucepan: a meaty stew, judging by the smell. Using a tea-towel to protect her hand, she lifted the lid and stirred her creation with a wooden spoon. 'I'm just stirring the dinner,' she explained unnecessarily. 'It's one of Nigella's.'

She chuckled, implying her amusement at the social gulf between disciple and mentor. Darren saw the humour in the situation too, but made a point of not showing it. He'd noticed that Anne had not even asked to what she owed the honour of his visit, as if nothing could be less remarkable than a parent to whom she'd passed one of her fostered charges dropping in out of the blue. This did not suit his purpose – he didn't want Anne to be too comfortable.

'I've got a question for you,' he said.

'Ask away.'

'About Jody.'

'Oh, yeah?' She enunciated this with a high note of surprise, as if she'd clean forgotten just who Jody was.

'I was wondering,' said Darren, 'if you have any pictures of her mother – Ashleigh. You know, from when she visited here, maybe.'

'Oh,' said Anne, keeping her eyes on the contents of the pan. 'I don't think so.'

'You don't mind me asking, do you?' said Darren, adding a pinch more northern essence to his voice to give the Londoner a false impression of sincerity. 'Only there's not one in her life-story book – you remember? It would be nice for Jody to know what Ashleigh looks like.'

'Oh, right,' said Anne. The stew seemed to need a lot of stirring.

'Do you see?' pressed Darren

'Oh, yes, I can see,' said Anne, then she said, 'Ooh, nearly forgot,' and hopped across to a wall cupboard where she rooted for something she never found, tutting and muttering, 'I wonder where that's gone, just when I'm in a hurry.'

A spasm of anger quickened Darren's pace. It lent his next words greater point and clarity. 'And the other thing is, I've a feeling somebody's been watching me.'

Anne kept on fussing and fidgeting, but she was running out of distractions. 'Watching you?' she said, laying her interest on a bit thick. 'How do you mean?'

Darren held off from replying, letting the long pause reel her in. At last, she sat down with him, bringing a cloth to the table for company. She dabbed at a sticky patch as Darren said, 'I was in a café with Jody last week, just the two of us. This young woman came in – very uncertain of herself, she seemed to me. A white woman, very pale, straight brown hair. Looked pretty wrecked . . .'

Darren broke off to scrutinise Anne's lowered forehead. That sticky stuff on the table would not budge.

'She went to the counter but left without buying anything,' continued Darren. 'And then, Anne, well it stopped being funny, because the next time I saw her she was wandering along our road. Five o'clock in the afternoon and I was coming home early from work. She didn't stay around for long . . .'

Anne's eyes rolled up slowly to meet Darren's. 'Who do you think she was?' she asked him, pretty evenly.

'Well, I don't know for certain, I suppose. But you can guess what I've been thinking, I expect.' Darren was also thinking he could hardly be less subtle than this.

But Anne kept up her shield of innocence. 'Sometimes

those social workers let things slip,' she said. 'Half asleep, that French one, I don't know.'

'Perhaps I should take it up with her, then, with the agency, whoever,' countered Darren. 'They could look into the whole thing, couldn't they?'

'They could, I suppose.' Anne interlocked her fingers and set them down in front of her, forming a defensive prow. 'It wouldn't change anything, though, would it? She'd still know what she knows – supposing it is Ashleigh, which it sounds like, I admit. I mean, you're stuck with that, I suppose – unless you move house.'

'We could tell the police.'

'I suppose so. I wouldn't know.'

Darren gazed across the room, in need of time. It seemed to be his move in this game, whatever game he was playing, something that was becoming less clear to him. He'd arrived armed with dire suspicions and a plan to see if they were justified. Now he wasn't so sure of himself. What evidence did he have that it was Ashleigh he'd seen at the café? If it was Ashleigh he'd seen walking in his road and she really had been watching the house then he was confident that Anne had leaked. But that 'if' was very big. Maybe he'd worked it all up in his head. Maybe he'd needed to to give himself a reason to feel angry enough to go round to Anne's. He did want a photograph, even though asking for one had been a pretext. Now, though, he wanted something more.

'Have you seen her lately?' Darren asked.

'Who? Ashleigh?'

'Ashleigh, yeah.'

He could see Anne calculating, then deciding. 'She's been round once, yeah,' Anne said.

'Oh, yeah?' Darren tensed. 'Any special reason why?'

'Company, I suppose. And showing off. She says she's on the wagon – on a programme to give up drinking.'

'Do you believe her?'

Anne said, 'Well, she might be. She didn't smell of it, which made a nice change, I must say.'

'What's she like?' Darren asked. 'In your opinion.'

Anne shrugged. 'A lush. What are they ever like?'

The squall of anger kicked up in Darren again. Anne's dismissal was inhumane. But maybe she thought that that was what he wanted to hear. Keeping his disquiet concealed, he asked, 'Did she say anything about Jody?'

'She asked about her, yeah.'

'What . . . what sort of thing?' He adjusted his tone when he restarted the question to sound conversational.

Anne said, 'What you were like, and everything – you and your wife. I said you were very nice, caring people and that Jody would be well looked after. I didn't tell her your names or where you lived, by the way. That must've been Giselle. Must have been.'

Darren raised a conciliatory hand. 'No, no, Anne,' he insisted, 'I'm quite sure you wouldn't do that.'

He was acting but, even so, maybe he was ready to believe her. It seemed much less important to him now, though not to Anne. At last she was looking worried. Her plea to be believed had opened her up a little and Darren saw his chance. 'Where does Ashleigh live?' he asked.

'Where?'

'Yes – where?' This was far too direct. 'I mean, how near to here?'

'Not far,' Anne replied.

'A flat? A hostel?' Darren laughed, displaying nerves. 'Just being nosy.'

Anne didn't reply. She unlaced her fingers and brought

one hand to her lips, where it settled. 'Hmm,' she said. 'You've got me thinking. Hold on a minute.'

She got up, twitchily retying the belt round her cardigan, and left the room. Darren heard her footsteps ascending stairs. He pinched his temples between a thumb and middle finger, and closed his eyes. He smelt the stew, which must have been wondering when its next stir would come.

Anne returned. She carried a clean brown A5 envelope, which she placed in front of Darren without retaking her seat. 'Have a look at that,' she said, and returned to tending the dinner.

Darren opened the envelope and reached in. His fingers touched lacquered paper. He pulled out the single snapshot and held it up by a corner to study it.

The first thing that struck him was how alike the two faces were: narrow, wan, looking at him but not looking, hoping for something and expecting nothing. In his job Darren had seen enough deprivation to log faces like these as need personified. They were quite pretty faces too, at least potentially. The mother's arms enfolded the little girl, her young cheek pressed against the child's still younger one. With the right big-name photographer, and the right fragrance to endorse, they might almost have looked chic. Darren's next observation was more clinical. The photograph was fairly recent: less than a year old, from Jody's appearance. And what about Ashleigh? Was she the girl who'd walked into the café? The girl in the road? It was possible, and yet impossible to be sure.

Still holding the photo, Darren checked to see if Anne was watching him. She wasn't. Her attention had turned to the sink, perhaps a tad studiously. He turned the photo round. On the back, in biro, was written: 'Flat 3, Asplen

House.' He turned the photograph round again. The two faces reprised their doubting appeal to him.

'You can keep that, if you like,' said Anne, tipping her washing-up bowl on its side.

Darren heard water sloshing out and draining away: cold, dirty water, he assumed. Anne seemed to be watching it as it gurgled round the plughole. 'Thanks,' he said, tucking the photo back into its envelope, then into the side pocket of his jacket. 'I'll see you again,' he said, a little brutally, and got up.

'Take care,' said Anne, looking over her shoulder but not hurrying to offer departure courtesies.

'And you,' was Darren's curt reply.

He left the kitchen and headed purposefully to the front door, resisting a passing urge to glimpse the living room and its latest short-term occupant. As he pushed the door shut behind him he spotted Anne watching him from the end of the hall, but he pretended she wasn't there.

'I shan't be coming on Friday,' said Maurice Pinder, as his Tuesday lesson reached its end.

'Oh, why's that?' asked Jane. It didn't come as a surprise, though this time she doubted it was piles. Maurice had seemed rather subdued: not his normal, irritable self.

'My mother died on Sunday and Friday is the day of her funeral. Old age. Very peaceful. Life goes on.'

That was Maurice: always to the point. By contrast Jane's automatic response – 'Oh, Maurice, I'm so sorry!' – seemed even more wishy-washy than first words uttered in response to such news usually do. The way Maurice looked at her made it even worse: extremely nervous as if about to make a large confession. Oh, God, had he *killed* his mother? Had he done it out of hatred or mercy? Was euthanasia murder? Would she keep Maurice's terrible secret or should she call the police?

'I was wondering if you'd come,' Maurice said.

'Yes, of course, Maurice,' said Jane, weak with relief. 'How . . . ?'

'I'll be needing help from someone I can trust.'

Trust? There remained, in Jane's perception, an edgy shame in Maurice's manner although there was powerful grief too, etched into the thin skin at his temples and round his eyes. 'I'll be glad to help you, Maurice. What do you need me to do?' She envisaged catering arrangements, order-of-service decisions or offering the sofa-bed to strange, buttoned-up relatives.

'Well, er, Jane,' he began. Jane was suspended between sympathy and shock. Had Maurice ever called her by her name before? It felt so *strange*. And it was agonising to watch him, hiding behind his eyelids, straining to maintain discipline over his words. 'I was hoping you'd play something,' he said.

'Oh, yes, of course I will,' she said.

'And also, well, your being there would be a help with numbers.'

'Is it a . . . small church?' asked Jane, illogically. Shut up, you idiot, she thought. Just let him talk.

Maurice closed his eyes. 'No, no,' he said. 'No, no. The problem is somewhat to the contrary. You see, apart from you and me, I'm concerned there won't be anybody there.' He blinked and leaked a tear, which he flicked away smartly as if dismissing an unwelcome do-gooder.

'No family, friends?' Jane flustered. 'Do they live abroad or—'

'Well, there aren't any to speak of, you see. It's been just Mother and me for a long time now.' Maurice produced a large, white cotton handkerchief and blew his nose loudly. His trumpeting alerted Jody, who had been happily engrossed with crayons and a colouring book on the floor. 'Ever since my father died, really,' Maurice went on. 'Thirty years ago, it was. No, thirty-two. I moved back to look after her and never moved out again.'

Maurice's father: how odd that Jane had never thought of him as having one.

'Freddie Pinder,' Maurice said, as if reading her mind. 'You won't have heard of him.'

'Might I have?' asked Jane.

'He was an entertainer,' Maurice said. 'Not a very famous one, but he got by. He sang and told jokes in pubs and theatres, I believe. My name was his idea – after Maurice Chevalier. It was an *homage* to his idol. Ridiculous, really. Of course,' he went on, 'he did it before Chevalier was accused of collaborating with the Vichy regime. Falsely, I might add.'

And, thought Jane, before the public knew he was gay. Her parents had told her and Julia all about it. 'You see, homosexuality is perfectly normal,' they'd explained. Suddenly, she could see Dorothy and Jeffrey in the garden singing 'Thank Heaven For Little Girls'. Then, bizarrely, she imagined Maurice singing it to Jody, who, in real life, was now watching him closely. In the four months since they'd first met, Maurice had still to say a single word to her.

'He left us nothing, of course,' continued Maurice, bitterly. 'Foolish man. Full of daydreams and fantasies and . . . fancy women.' He spat out the last two words. 'Thank heaven I went into accountancy. Otherwise, Mother and I would have starved.'

'What did your mother do?' Jane enquired circum-spectly.

'Oh, she was a costume designer,' he replied. 'And a housewife. Yes, she kept house while he cheated on her. She, of course, was as honest as the day is long. And the irony is, the frightful pity of it, that by the time he'd gone she was in no position to start a new life.'

'Why?' asked Jane.

'Because her health was failing – even then. Oh, yes, my dear, she'd been unwell on and off for many years. I should be grateful she lasted this long.'

It dawned on Jane what the prim phrase 'medical reasons' might have referred to – not to Maurice but to his mum. So, she thought, gallows-style, that's the end of Maurice Pinder as a figure of fun.

Maurice blew his nose again and looked a touch embarrassed. By his standards he had been free-associating, which was not his way. To spare him, Jane moved on to practicalities: the funeral's time and location; the song or songs he would like her to play. He'd said he'd telephone to tell her and that now he should be going.

'Will you be all right?' Jane asked pathetically, as she showed him down the hall.

'Oh, yes, I expect so. Plenty to do.'

On the step she thought she might peck him on the cheek, but then a question popped into her head. She asked it gently: 'You never told me – what was your mother's name?'

'Verity,' he said, sadly and surprisingly beautifully. 'Which, when you think about the lies she put up with for half her life, is really rather tragic in a way.'

Jody, in her small and cosy room, said, 'Good girl', to Dolly for eating all her dinner and doing a last wee and lying in her cot nice and quietly. Then she sat on her little bed and looked out through her open door and watched other people doing their bedtime business.

'Hello, Jody,' said the man called Daddy. He was coming from the bathroom. He was carrying Clyde. Clyde was wrapped in a big, fluffy towel.

'Hello,' Jody replied. She'd been in a big fluffy towel after her bath too. The lady called Mummy had wrapped her up and carried her, and now she was in her Pooh Bear pyjamas. They were nice.

'Hello, Jody,' said the big girl Lorna, as she came down the stairs. She was wrapped in *another* big fluffy towel and she was nearly running! She went through the bathroom door that Clyde and the man called Daddy had just come out of. She shut the door behind her.

The man called Daddy said, 'Hello, Lorna, goodbye, Lorna,' in a funny way. Then he spoke to Jody again. 'Is Dolly asleep yet?' he asked. He was whispering.

Jody nodded and at the same time saw that Clyde, who was a boy, and therefore not the same as her, was looking at her too. Jody couldn't see all of his face – it was hidden by the towel – but his eyes didn't frighten her.

'I'll come and see Dolly later,' the man called Daddy said, and he smiled and he carried Clyde into his bedroom. Jody still didn't often go in there. But sometimes she did.

'Can I see Dolly?' asked another grown-up voice. It was the lady called Mummy. Her face appeared from round the corner. Now she *looked* like the lady called Mummy. Before, she'd had all black clothes on and they were sad clothes. But now the lady called Mummy was smiling. She came into the room very, very quietly and looked at Dolly in her cot then whispered softly, 'You're a very, *very* good mummy, aren't you, Jody?'

Jody said, 'Yes.'

Then the lady called Mummy said, 'Did you have a nice time at Poppy's house while I was out?'

Jody remembered Poppy. She was all pink. 'Yes,' she said.

'I *am* glad,' said the lady called Mummy. 'And what did you do there?'

'Playin',' said Jody.

'Playing!' said the Mummy lady. This seemed to make her glad too.

'And what did you play?' she asked.

'We played babies,' Jody said.

'You played *babies*?! How fantastic! And let me think . . .' The Mummy lady pattered on her chin with her finger-tips. She had nail-paint on, and it was red. Sometimes she put it on Jody too. 'Did you play hide-and-seek?' she asked.

'Yeah,' said Jody, firmly.

'Did you hide in Poppy's house?'

Jody nodded. 'Yeah.' How happy the Mummy lady was!

'And did you count to ten?'

This time Jody just nodded, a bit uncertainly. She thought Poppy might have counted to ten. Poppy had ponies too: pretend ones. They'd done riding on them.

And now the lady called Mummy was reaching down and getting hold of her left foot. She lightly pinched each of its toes between her forefinger and thumb. 'One, two, three, four, five . . .' And then she took the other foot. 'Six, seven . . .' Jody giggled. '. . . eight, nine . . .' The Mummy lady waited. Jody thought she knew what for but wasn't sure. So she waited as well. 'Ten!' said the Mummy lady. 'Ten little Jody toes!' Then she tickled the sole of Jody's foot, which made Jody giggle such a lot that she didn't immediately hear the slightly flawed chords from the chorus of 'The Entertainer' ascending from the half-landing below.

'Ooh! What's that?' said the Mummy lady, cupping an ear.

Jody knew where the sound was coming from *and* she knew who was making it. 'Eliot,' she said.

'Yes! Eliot! Do you want to go and see him?'

Jody did. She slipped off the bed and went down the short stairs holding the banisters. She trotted past the bathroom, where Lorna's shower was thundering, and pushed at the door of Eliot's room. It opened and Jane heard Eliot say, 'Hello, Jody, have you come to listen?' and she saw Jody nod yes. Eliot said, 'Are there any monsters?' and this time Jody shook her head. And Eliot said, 'I used to get monsters, but I told them to go away and guess what?' Jody didn't do guessing yet. But she did listening. 'They're all gone!' said Eliot, answering his own question. He closed the door behind Jody and took another crack at 'The Entertainer'.

Jane listened for a minute: Eliot wasn't Scott Joplin yet but he was getting there. Then she tilted her ear away from him towards Darren and Clyde.

'Daddy, shall I tell you something?' Clyde was saying.

'Yes, please.'

'Did you know that dogs can go in space?'

'Can they?'

'There was a dog in space. In the olden days.'

'You're right,' Darren said. 'I remember it.'

'What was its name?'

'Good question . . .'

Jane leaned into the room. 'You haven't forgotten, have you, Daddy?'

Darren made a face at her. He was turning Clyde's

271

pyjama top the right way out. Clyde was lying on his bed, still wrapped in the towel.

'It isn't alive now, though, is it, Daddy?' he said.

'Isn't it? How do you know?' said Darren.

'Because it was a long, long time ago and dogs don't live as long as people.'

'That's true,' said Darren. 'Very true.'

'If I was a dog,' said Clyde, 'I'd be quite old already.'

'Yes, you would.'

'And you'd be very dead, wouldn't you?'

Darren ruffled Clyde's hair and said, 'Yep, several times over. Thanks for reminding me.'

Jane smiled and withdrew. Here was her chance to have five minutes' solitude and think of Verity Pinder, whom she had seen into the ground that afternoon. She went to her bedroom, and as she left Clyde studied his father's face. He said: 'Do cats go into space?'

'I don't think so. Ask Simba.'

'Daddy?'

'Yes, Clyde. Put your pyjamas on, please.'

'Daddy?'

'Yes, Clyde, yes?'

'Can you pretend that I'm a parcel and inside is a little sheepdog called Speedy?'

This was not an unusual request. True, it was the first time that Speedy the sheepdog had been the wonderful surprise but the parcel game had long been a favourite of Clyde's. The damp towel wrapping had most often contained a beautiful, newborn little boy called Peter or Billy and, once or twice, a little boy called Clyde. He never had any parents and the finder of the parcel knew his name by what was written on the label round his neck, which also asked that the baby boy be taken very good care of, please.

The unwrapping, though, was the essence of the thing: certain procedures had to be followed and particular rituals observed.

'OK, little sheepdog called Speedy,' Darren said.

'No, Daddy!' said Clyde. 'You're doing it wrong! You don't *know* that I'm a little sheepdog yet! You have to try to guess what's in the parcel!'

'Sorry, Clyde, sorry. I'll try again.'

Darren hadn't quite got the energy for this. Psychologically, he was still in Anne's kitchen, trying to recall exactly what she'd told him, trying to decide exactly how truthful she'd been and whether or not whatever she had said to Ashleigh had been enough for Ashleigh to track down Jody. He'd hidden the photograph in the zip-up pocket of his briefcase and looked at it ten times every day. He was unable to come to a firm conclusion as to whether he had seen Ashleigh or not. Had his imagination gone haywire? What, if anything, should he tell Jane?

'Come *on*, Daddy! You're supposed to play the game!'

Clyde was on his hands and knees with his head down. Only the bottoms of his feet were visible. Darren, recalling now the order of events, embarked on the required ritual. 'What's this on Clyde's bed? A lovely big blue parcel! I wonder what's inside it? Let me see . . .'

The parcel quivered; such gorgeous anticipation! Darren knew the feeling; he remembered it. He pinpointed the memory's source. He was inside his mother's wardrobe, concealed among long dresses and coats. She was coming to find him – 'Now, where can that little boy have gone? Is he in the wardrobe, I wonder?' – and it was thrilling to know he'd be found. Her hand would reach for him: 'What's this I can feel? I don't remember putting *this* in here . . .' and then he'd jump out, red-faced and giggling, oblivious to being in a home that would never, could never quite stop mourning.

'Come on, Daddy!' said little sheepdog Speedy.

'Sorry Clyde.'

'I'm not Clyde.'

'Sorry, sorry, sorry. Oh, look, here's a little paw. And what's this? A furry tail . . .'

An hour later Clyde and Jody were asleep. By then, Eliot and a blush-skinned Lorna had gone downstairs to immerse themselves in whatever was rude and irreverent on Channel 4.

Upstairs, looking out of their bedroom window and, surreptitiously, up and down the street, Darren said to Jane, 'This might be a dim bloke question, but why has Lorna gone to so much trouble to get sweet-smelling and clean on a Friday night when she's only staying in?'

Jane said, 'She's just practising, probably.'

'Did you used to do that?'

'Yes.'

'Is it healthy?'

Jane was busy sorting clothes, folding small items into her third drawer down. She still had an ovulation kit in there. She really ought to throw it out. When they got the adoption order, that's when she do it. Tut, tut, what a sucker for maudlin symbolism. To Darren's question, she replied, 'I think it's a positive sign.'

'She does seem much happier.'

'Yes,' Jane agreed. 'What a relief.'

Darren came away from the window. Surely he was just being paranoid. He hadn't seen Ashleigh, if it had been Ashleigh, for at least a week. But if it wasn't Ashleigh, why had he been so ready to imagine it was? It was a bit like he 'saw' his mother. But he wanted *her* to be there, didn't he?

'So how was the funeral?'

Jane had completed her task. She flopped down on to the bed. 'Not as bad as I thought it was going to be.'

'Good.'

'More importantly, not as bad as Maurice thought it was going to be.'

Indeed, measured against his expectations, the turnout had been good. The very model of conservative decorum Maurice had placed a death notice in the *Daily Telegraph*. As a result, there had been four other mourners. Verity had had a brother called Crispin, who had lost touch with her and died long ago, but he had been survived by his wife and their two daughters and all three had come down from Lancashire. The fourth attendee, who'd also seen the *Telegraph* entry, was a man called Dennis Pugh, who'd explained that he'd known Freddie Pinder 'oh, from way back, we were often on the same bill'. He'd congratulated Jane on her playing of 'Summertime' during the service, and afterwards they'd got talking. Dennis's act was animal impersonations. In the churchyard, he'd done a most impressive moo.

'How did Maurice feel about Dennis being there?' Darren asked. Jane had told him about Maurice's poor opinion of his late dad.

'He didn't seem to mind, actually. I think he secretly wishes he had a little of his father's showmanship.'

'Is that what the piano lessons are all about?'

'Could be.'

'Maybe I should take some,' Darren said.

'Why?' Jane laughed. Then she cottoned on: Darren had lost his parents too. She kissed him and let out a long, slow breath. 'Anyway,' she went on, 'he's been invited up to

Lancashire. Maybe he'll make a new life now.' Was that part of the pathos of bereavement, Jane wondered, how the death of a loved dependant can set you free?

'Laika!' Darren said, and clapped his hands.

'Pardon?' said Jane.

'Laika! That was the name of the dog! The one the Russians sent into space!' He rushed to the computer and Googled. 'Here he is,' he soon announced. 'Good God, yes. There were postage stamps of him and everything! A little pointy-nosed mongrel, stuck on letters all over the eastern bloc!' He pored over the screen. 'Yes, he died up there, of course, although the Russians denied it at first.'

'The Russians – typical!' mocked Jane.

The telephone rang next to her ear.

'That'll be the KGB,' said Darren.

Jane lifted the receiver. 'Oh, hi, Lucy,' she said.

Darren's heart missed a beat. It was partly a guilt thing, partly the fear of looking a fool. Why had he gone sneaking round to Anne's? What mad impulse had taken him there? But Lucy wasn't ringing because she'd heard he'd visited Anne. As Darren reflected later, when his mood was much more sober, why would she have been, even if she'd known he'd been there? After all, he'd done nothing wrong. Had he? And in the meantime, Jane was saying, 'Oh, *fantastic*! Oh, *fantastic*! No, no, I'm so glad you rang to tell us, no, no, no, *of course* it's not too late to call . . .'

It was the thing they had both hoped for – more so than either of them had quite known. Ashleigh had met with the court reporter. She'd understood the situation. She'd given her consent and signed over her parental rights. Jody would be theirs without a war.

After Lucy had said goodbye, they sat together for five minutes, coiled up in their embrace. Tenderness was never more tender, closeness never closer. And when the phone rang again, Jane reached for it blindly, not looking round, not wanting to let go, or be let go of. She had to, though, for now.

'Hello, Mummy . . . Oh, my God . . . Oh, my God . . . Oh, no.'

CHAPTER TEN OCTOBER

Julia was saying, 'It's incredible, Dorothy, it really is. They're on their hands and knees, these chaps, scraping away at those things so they can shove another tiny little bomb under them and blow them up. And they're doing it for nothing! I mean, I say to them, "You must be *bloody mad*," pardon my French, and they just grin at me! They say it's because they love their country. Field after field after field. I say to them, "Even if the mines don't get you you'll die of old age before you've cleared them all," and they just go on grinning. By the way, Jane, should she be doing that?'

Jane had just begun to drift away, had just started to feel the lullaby effect of her sister's waffle-yarning when the change of tack broke through her fatigue. She sat to attention. Julia added offhandedly, 'You know, safety and all that.'

In the corner of the room – Jane's parents' roomy brown bedroom – Jody was trying to climb aboard the ancestral Ransome rocking-horse, which had become a sort of *heirloom* for display. She'd flung both arms over its saddle and heaved herself up to a point where she was balanced perfectly between plunging head-first over the other side and her feet being too high for her to stretch out her toes and touch the floor.

'I'll rescue her,' said Jane.

She was glad of an excuse to move. The conversation was confining her, as was the old armchair she was sitting in. The adult company was fast becoming unendurable too. There sat Dorothy on an upright wooden chair, not so much conversing as implicitly protesting that life was going to go on in the teeth of everything and that it would be so much worse to be one of the world's starving millions. Julia was beside her, propped on the *chaise-longue*, taking the role of raconteur with almost indecent enthusiasm. And in the bed sat Jeffrey, propped against a pillow, wrapped in his dressing-gown, raising his head only occasionally. He had had a second stroke and there was only moderate hope that he'd repeat his previous good recovery.

'Jody, Jody, be careful now,' said Jane. She moved to the rocking-horse quickly. An accident, complete with crying and Julia's inevitable, unhelpful commentary, was the last thing she needed. Jody was swinging her arms from side to side. Her hair, hanging free, reached almost to the varnished floorboards below her. 'You'll fall, if you're not careful,' Jane said, striving for calm *à la* Hilary.

'No, I won't.'

'Let me help you down.'

'No!'

'Jody, *please* . . .'

'Wee!' cried Jody. 'Wee!'

'She's bored, I expect,' said Dorothy.

'Do you think we're boring, Jody?' boomed Julia, helpfully.

'How could anyone find *you* boring Julia?' said Jane.

'Oh! Well, pardon me,' said Julia, jauntily, then went into

her parody of a radio presenter smoothing over some studio guest's *faux pas*: 'And moving right along . . .' All over-compensating brightness. Then she said, 'Oh, did you want something, Daddy?'

She's all-seeing, thought Jane, bitterly, the first to notice bloody everything.

Jeffrey was moving his lips. Dorothy got up and leaned over him so that her ear was right next to his mouth. From her new, cross-legged position beside the rocking-horse, with her lap aligned to cushion Jody's head if she should fall, Jane witnessed her parents' momentary physical nearness and saw all at once the character of their remaining time together: Dorothy forever servicing; Jeffrey always needing; the last grey small-print clause of their marriage contract being honoured faithfully.

Dorothy said to him: 'Tea? You want some tea?'

Jane closed her eyes to listen. She told herself that if she could hear his reply it meant there was hope for him. Jeffrey's words limped to her across the room: 'Yes, please, Dodie. Thank you.'

'Let me make it,' said Jane. As she got up from the floor she grasped Jody under the armpits.

'No!' screamed Jody. '*No!*'

'I don't mind making it,' Julia announced.

'Please, Julia,' said Jane, beseechingly. She hoisted Jody off the rocking-horse and up over her shoulder. Jody's feet were flailing. Her toes thumped into Jane's belly. 'No!' she shouted. 'No!'

'Come on, Jody,' begged Jane. Her pretence to Julia and Dorothy was that she was giving Jody a very tight cuddle but she doubted it was fooling anyone. Her voice took on a strangled quality: 'Let's go down and find Daddy.'

'Don't *want* Daddy! Don't *want* Daddy!'

They completed their exit, wrestling. Jody was making too much noise for Jane to hear anything else as she struggled downstairs with her, yet her ears burned at the thought of what Julia would be saying: 'Bit of a challenge, that one. Little sis has got her work cut out there!'

She made it to the ground floor, Jody still resisting loudly. 'No!'

'I can tell that you are very, *very* cross,' Jane told her gamely.

'No!' shrieked Jody.

'Stupid Mummy,' murmured Jane. This 'verbal reflecting' was so much easier in theory than in reality. 'I expect you'd like to play on that rocking-horse for ever,' she persevered.

'No! No!'

'Oh, fuck it,' said Jane.

She lugged Jody out into the garden. She'd forgotten about making tea. Darren and Clyde were hunched over a shrub near the summerhouse. It was a cold, bright mid-morning and a heavy dew still shimmered on the grass. As Jane had hoped, the change of location from the stuffiness of her parents' bedroom to the chill outdoors had a distracting effect on Jody. The closer they drew to Darren and Clyde, the less conviction there was in her fury and by the time they reached them she was struggling to be put down.

'Hello, boys,' said Jane, huffing and blowing. She considered making a joke about sounding like a Wonderbra commercial but decided against it: Clyde might be embarrassed and comic self-deprecation only carried true conviction if it was anchored in solid self-esteem. She released Jody carefully. Jody curled into a ball on the damp ground and lay quite still. 'I know, I know,' said Jane, wearily, as she saw Darren observing this. 'She'll be soaking wet and cold and everything.'

Darren looked all innocence and said, 'How are things upstairs?'

'Too much,' replied Jane. 'Too much of everything. Ouch!'

Jody had kicked her, catching her sharply on the ankle. Jane stepped away, saying and doing nothing in response: ignore bad behaviour, Hilary had said.

'Too much?' enquired Darren, sympathetically.

'I'll explain later,' said Jane.

Too much painful recollection, for one thing. Before the rocking-horse incident and before Julia had got into her jolly stride, Jane had been remembering the three-day week of 1974. Coal stocks were down, the oil price had shot up; to preserve energy there were power cuts most nights and Dorothy, unusually, had taken to her bed with flu. At that time Jane had owned a battery-driven portable record-player. One blacked-out evening she'd set it up by the end of her parents' bed and, amid flickering candlelight, made all her family listen in silence to *Bridge Over Troubled Water* – both sides. By the end of that winter she could play the whole of the title track on the baby grand downstairs, minus the orchestra, of course, and even sing it when there was no one else at home. What did she think about the song now? Was it a hymn to selfless devotion or an overblown martyr's dirge?

'We're looking at spider webs,' said Clyde.

'They're fantastic in the sunlight with all this dew,' Darren explained.

'The spider who made it won't be alive for much longer, though,' Clyde added, gravely.

'Like in *Charlotte's Web*,' said Darren.

They were a double act, Jane decided. She melted at the sight of Clyde with his wellington boots on and an old coat of Eliot's that was too big for him. It would be his eighth birthday in ten days' time. Jody would be four in December. By then, she would be Jeffrey's fourth grandchild. Would he be around to celebrate?

'And then there will be new spiders, won't there?' Clyde said, and Jane could tell by the way he looked up at his father, and also at her, that although he knew this was true he still needed their confirmation.

'Yes, there will,' she said. 'We'll see them in the spring.' She considered adding, mostly for Darren's benefit, 'As long as I haven't lost it totally by then,' but she thought better of it, then jumped quickly to her left as Jody, still on the ground, kicked at her again.

That evening Jane and Darren walked through the village. It was nine thirtyish on the Sunday of a long weekend visit by the entire Grice-Ransome household, which had begun with a Friday evening rush-hour crawl and would end on Monday morning with the same thing in reverse. Back at Dorothy and Jeffrey's, Jody and Clyde were asleep. Eliot and Lorna had already gone back to London, travelling by train the previous day. Both had been invited to a party at the house of a schoolfriend whose parents were liberal and foolish enough to have said that the guests could sleep over if they wished to. Jane had received a phone call from Lorna earlier. The party, she assured her, had been 'fine'.

'Did you used to come here when you lived at home?' Darren asked, as much as anything to break into Jane's thoughts. The village pub had just come into view.

'When I was young, you mean? Yes.'

'You're still young, Jane.'

'Yes, Darren. I'm lithe, gorgeous and nineteen.'

'Like me, you mean?'

'Just like you.'

The pub was shedding a low, welcoming light into the street. Beyond it was a terrace of low, bow-fronted houses with whitewashed walls and what Darren thought of as Beatrix Potter doors. Inside the pub, he presumed, there would be shove ha'penny, snug sweaters and an open fire. He wasn't sure he could stand it. He looked down at Jane trudging by his side. She wore a big coat and a scarf, which she'd wound loosely round her throat so that she could conceal her mouth behind it in moments of need. She'd gone into her shell again, her eyes fixed firmly on the ground.

'Do we want a drink?' Darren asked.

'Not really.'

'Shall we just walk?'

'Yes, that would be nice.'

Neither spoke again until they'd passed the pub and were forging forward on the neat, narrow pavement that led towards the village green. For Jane, the pub was the repository of a piece of personal history from which she didn't feel entirely safe. Nothing terrible had happened to her there. The danger lay in dwelling on the promise she'd manifested on the premises and never been lucky or hungry enough to fulfil. There'd been a folk club in the back bar every second Friday night. Before the hired attraction took the tiny corner stage, guests were invited to perform. Jane had made her début at fifteen, Lorna's age. Long skirt, long hair, at the piano, playing 'Your Song' impeccably, but it was her friend Olivia who'd sung.

Darren knew nothing of this: Jane had never spoken of it to him. He sensed, though, that his wife was marking herself down on the scale of human worth and, as ever, it was his urgent duty to stop her.

'What are you thinking about?' he said.

'I'm remembering how it was with your mum.'

'You're pessimistic, then?'

'I'm always pessimistic, Darren, except when I'm a hopeless optimist.'

'He might make another good recovery. He's picked up a bit already, hasn't he?'

'Yes, I know, he could go on for years. I'm sorry to be such a misery.'

There was some reason to be thankful for small mercies. It was just over three weeks since the night Dorothy had called, curtailing the celebrations after Ashleigh had given consent about Jody. Jane had dropped everything, raced down to Kent in the car and met Dorothy at the hospital. They'd kept an all-night vigil there, talking and dozing in barren waiting rooms and bleach-scrubbed corridors. By the morning it was clear to Jane that her mother had saved her father's life. Dorothy explained that she had asked Jeffrey a question about the government's 'dodgy dossier' on weapons of mass destruction in Iraq and he hadn't understood what she was saying. He'd frowned and blinked as though he couldn't see. So she had rushed him to A and E immediately. 'With a stroke, time lost is brain lost,' she'd explained.

By morning it seemed that enough time had been found: enough, at least, for Jeffrey to survive. For the next fortnight Jane had shuttled back and forth, first visiting Jeffrey and keeping Dorothy company, then helping to make provision for Jeffrey's homecoming and finally supervising it, sitting in the rear of an ambulance with him while Dorothy followed in her car. He couldn't sit straight and his voice was slurred. He'd entered his home in a wheelchair.

The village green was coming into view.

'I could murder my sister,' Jane remarked.

'That bad, eh?' said Darren, slightly surprised.

'Well, maybe not murder. Perhaps a good kick in the shins would do. Or a really, really horrid Chinese burn.'

'Maybe she needs a husband.'

'Oh, you know her – she's been hinting about this chap or that chap for years. She's too bloody egotistical.'

'Perhaps you should introduce her to Maurice.'

'Now there's a really horrible idea.'

It was Julia's heartiness that got to Jane. She supposed she shouldn't let it. Coping with the sick and dying was her elder sister's vocation. Yet for all Julia's prompt return from Angola and the promise she'd made to stay in England as long as necessary, Jane was annoyed by her failure to acknowledge Jeffrey's tragedy properly: in short, to be heartbroken. The Grice-Ransomes had arrived on Friday to find Jeffrey brought downstairs for the occasion. Everyone had gathered round and gazed at him, as though meeting him for the first time. They'd listened raptly to his tiny voice. He'd gestured to them gamely from his chair. Everyone, including Jody, seemed awed by his transformation. As the hours had worn on it had appeared to dawn on the children that the grandfather they used to know had mostly gone, and in this Jane perceived a certain irony. Her father had lost his adulthood. The care he would now need to sustain him in old age would reduce him to a condition very much like infancy. For Jane, this was the truly shocking thing. Could he be like a father to her any more?

The green was small, well kept, with low-key perimeter lighting and a small war memorial in honour of the village's thirteen Glorious Dead. Remembrance Sunday was but a few weeks ahead and three poppy wreaths had already been arranged round the base. Dorothy and Jeffrey usually added their own small tribute – a pot plant or a small bouquet – at this time of year. They had never cared for war but they admired sacrifice and bravery.

Near the memorial stood a wooden bench. Darren went to it and sat. Jane perused the poppies, then joined him. She was sick of talking, even thinking, about herself – so she said nothing. And that was quite OK, because Darren understood the meaning of her silence. She hugged his arm, waiting. A single car went past. Otherwise, the young night was quiet.

Darren said, 'I wonder what Jody's making of all this.' She'd been sporadically fractious; the rocking-horse episode had been but one example of it. Darren answered his own question: 'She's quite upset about Jeffrey, I think.'

Jane couldn't know if this was true. She couldn't know if Jody remembered her previous times in Jeffrey's company – those beautiful moments in the summerhouse with the toy bricks. But she so *hated* the idea that Jody didn't that from deep inside her scarf she said, 'I think you're right.'

'That's not just wishful thinking?' Darren said.

'Oh, probably.'

'Hmm,' Darren said. He took off his glasses, blew on them and tugged out his shirt hem to clean them.

Jane had a good idea what this meant. 'Are you going to say something meaningful, O husband?'

'No.'

'Yes, you are.'

'Well, all I'm going to say is that you'll remember Jeffrey for her, won't you? Whatever has happened since and whatever happens next, you'll never forget how good he was with her, back in the summer, when she was still trying to get used to everyone.'

Jane said, 'That's true.' Indeed, she could almost hear herself reminiscing about it to Jody when she was a grown-up of, say, thirty-three and Jane was a batty old lady.

'That's why it's such a shame about her father and Ashleigh,' Darren said.

'How do you mean?'

'And the useless life-story book that tells us nothing about Jody's lost lives.'

Lost lives? That was a dramatic way of putting it. Jane took a look at Darren, who had yet to put his glasses back on. Were those his father's eyes? she wondered.

'I've got a confession,' Darren said.

'Oh? What's her name?' said Jane.

Darren faced her straight on and said, 'I've got a photograph of Ashleigh.'

'How did you manage that?'

'And I think I've found out where she lives.'

Jane's features creased with love for him, and with her own distress, 'Oh, Darren – I wish you hadn't told me that,' she said.

PART 3 ASHLEIGH

CHAPTER ELEVEN
MOTHERS

Asplen House was a nineteenth-century mansion block on a medium-sized road on the southern edge of Stepney. It had a wide wooden door but this was set back in an old stone porch that made it easy to miss amid the surrounding shops and businesses, which, in sharp contrast to the place where Jody Grice-Ransome's birth mother lived, were eager for their presence to be known. There was a panel of intercom bells on the wall of the porch but most looked broken. Jane pressed the one numbered '3' but got no reply. This foxed her until she gave the door a shove. It swung back fairly easily, despite the rucked carpet of junk mail behind it, not to mention a spent firework or two. It was approaching noon on a cold late-November Friday: a day for snuggling at home rather than venturing into the unknown. But Jane had woken early, suddenly knowing that she could no longer talk and talk with Darren about what to do with the information he had squeezed from Anne. She had to follow her impulse to act, and act alone. Once Darren had gone to work and the three older kids to school, she'd asked Maggie if she'd have Jody for a few hours.

Having to ask such a favour helped concentrate Jane's mind on the need to see through whatever she thought she was doing. She told herself, too, that having just turned forty-six, it was time she learned how to be brave.

Inside the mansion block, all was gloom. The floor was bare concrete. To Jane's right was a brown door with a tarnished metal '1' on it and before her a stone stairway with a metal rail. Expecting to be challenged or attacked at every step, she walked up the first flight and came to a landing with two more brown doors, one to either side. The photo that Darren had got from Anne was in her inside jacket pocket. For comfort she pulled it out to check the address on the back. She was aware as she did this of the deep anxiety that drove her – as if, like the image of Jody and Ashleigh, the number '3' was not indelibly stamped on her heart.

She listened at the door before knocking, but any sounds within were undetectable. It occurred to Jane that if Ashleigh was in she might be sleeping. She pictured a ruined, ghostly creature in her day clothes rising from whatever surface she had collapsed upon last night and manifesting in the doorway angrily. 'Not much in the mood for heart-to-hearts today, thank you, so why don't you piss off?' Such an outcome would be so counter-productive that contemplating it gave Jane a defensible excuse for backing out. But where else would she go except back to the realm of helpless conjecture from which she was longing to escape?

She raised the cheap metal knocker attached to the letterbox and let it go. The sound was weak so she repeated the exercise, this time slamming it down hard and then again, still harder, each time further reducing the option of retreat. The knocker was puny, yet the sound it made seemed mighty in the confined space. Then came the dire anticipation, the footsteps, the Big Brother sensation of knowing she was being watched through the spy-hole. And then, heart heading for throat, the laboured turning of the latch.

In the doorway stood the woman in the photo. She said, 'Yeah?'

Bleary-eyed, fully-dressed, suspicious.

'Hello. Are you Ashleigh?' asked Jane.

'Yeah.'

'Hello. Um, I'm Jane.'

There was no booze stink on Ashleigh, no greasy hair straggling across her face. It was, though, a face that hid from daylight. And she looked every bit as young as she was: twenty-one. Young enough, easily, for Jane to have been *her* mother as well as her daughter's.

Ashleigh worked her expression into one of helpless apology. 'Do I know you?' she said, and the question seemed genuine.

Jane was prepared for this. Ashleigh was a drunk. She might have made a new bosom buddy last night yet have no memory of it now. 'Not really,' said Jane. 'But I know your daughter Jody. I'm the one looking after her now.'

The care with which she'd selected those words! Each had been hand-picked to demonstrate her deep humility. And now she came to speak them she was in the dark about whether Ashleigh took from them the meaning she wished to convey.

Gradually, though, illumination came. 'Jane . . . Oh, yeah.' A half-laugh dropped from the side of Ashleigh's mouth. 'Yeah,' she said again. 'Yeah, I know.'

'I wanted to see you . . .' Jane had no more breath in her, no strength. For all her seniority, in age, education, status in the world, she felt at the mercy of the other woman's judgement. She had taken something from her, after all.

'Come in,' Ashleigh said.

She turned and kind of receded into a small dark living room. As Jane's eyes made out a shabby TV and some basic furniture, her memory scrabbled for reference points, cultural handholds. It found gritty English cinema, social-realist pictures made when she was a child and yet embedded in her adult consciousness: *A Taste of Honey; Cathy Come Home;* Roy Harper in *Made*. She followed Ashleigh with small, reverent steps, seeking forgiveness, feeling fear.

'Sit down,' said Ashleigh.

It was a polite suggestion but Jane was so at sea that she took it as an order, gratefully. She made out a pair of low, old-fashioned easy chairs, one of which was occupied by matted newspapers and a pile of clothes. Jane moved towards the other. Even before she had grasped its wooden arms and lowered her bottom on to its sunken seat cushion she was embarking on her apology. 'I had to see you,' she began. 'I know I'm not supposed to but I'll be the one in trouble, not you.'

'I don't mind,' Ashleigh said. She was three feet away from Jane, still standing and therefore towering over her.

Jane took in belted hipster jeans, a blue Gap sweatshirt, an ankle chain, bare feet. 'That's very nice of you,' said Jane.

Ashleigh went over to the curtains. Jane watched her open them about a foot. Daylight revealed something more of a young woman of medium height and narrow build, though with a pale inch of plumpness squeezing out round her waist. Her shoulder-length hair was dark and straight – Jody's hair – and Jane was surprised to see how clean it looked. It set her back a little. She had prepared herself for meeting a lost soul, possibly an unreachable one. The clean hair, though, hinted at someone more capable and possibly, therefore, more formidable.

'I'm sorry,' said Jane, automatically, as Ashleigh moved back towards her. Where was her hostess to sit?

But Ashleigh, paying no heed, changed direction and went into a tiny kitchen alcove. She bent to open the door of her fridge. 'Oh, shit, I've got no milk,' she said. It was her longest speech so far.

'That's all right,' said Jane. 'I wasn't—'

'I could go out and get some,' offered Ashleigh, perhaps a bit uncertainly, as though groping for the rules of mainstream hospitality.

'I'm all right, really,' said Jane. 'I just . . . I just had a few questions about Jody.'

'Yeah, yeah,' replied Ashleigh, 'How's she been?' She spoke now in a voice of sudden cheery recognition as if mention had been made of a fondly recalled cousin or an old schoolfriend. She was looking for something to sit on. There was a small round coffee-table close to them. Rather than shift the clutter from the other chair she went to it and dragged it over.

How had Jody been? The truth was complicated and Jane was inclined to keep it hidden. Ashleigh might pick up on anything, get the wrong idea, and who could tell where she might run with it? 'She's been well,' she said mildly.

Ashleigh got the coffee-table to where she wanted it, and sat down on its edge. Other sounds filled the space vacated by that of the table legs ploughing across the carpet: traffic noise from outside and an intermittent clanging from somewhere beyond the single internal door behind which, Jane presumed, must be a bathroom and bedroom. Perhaps it was an ill-fitting ventilation wheel, set rotating by the wintry wind.

'I haven't been up long,' said Ashleigh, as if in explanation. 'Can't sleep much at the minute.'

'Oh? Why?'

'Dunno,' she said, shaking back her hair. She seemed fidgety; it was the first sign Jane had seen of nerves. Awkwardness settled between the two women, or so it felt to Jane. The void between them goaded her. Jody was the only bridge.

'Listen, Ashleigh, you know, I've really got to ask you this. I'm sorry, but have you found out where we live?'

'Up Mile End way, yeah?' Ashleigh said. 'Near there anyway.'

Jane studied the other mother's face: was that a wilfully vague answer or a cheerfully general one? 'How did you find out?' asked Jane. She wanted to apologise for being so direct. And what, for God's sake, was she doing there?

Ashleigh wriggled. She said, 'Well, I was curious. You can't blame me for that.'

'So you *have* found out?' Jane saw a glimmer of defiance. 'I'm not blaming you for anything,' she said, snatching at the opportunity to be kind. 'I just need to know – would like to know, if you don't mind – how you managed to find out. Because you're not really supposed to know, are you? No one should have told you, should they? I'm just wondering if someone did, that's all.'

Here was the crunch moment. Jane wasn't ready for it. She'd expected Ashleigh to deny, deny, deny, and maybe truthfully, because Darren had told her he might have been mistaken about seeing her. Ashleigh stood up and Jane stiffened. But the other woman didn't approach her. She began feeling in her pockets. From the right one, she withdrew a ring. It took on an immediate, deep import for Jane: it had to be a wedding ring, her mother's ring, a ring inscribed with the name 'Jody'. Ashleigh slipped it on to the little finger of her left hand, then straightened all the fingers so that she could admire it. Her hands were very small. The band was of thin silver, the stone blue in a cheap, fancy setting. Ashleigh sat down again.

'I can't really say nothing about that,' she said, and from beneath her wary lashes, she surveyed Jane closely for her response.

'Why not?' asked Jane, gently, as if her tongue was pressed against a blade.

'It wouldn't be right,' Ashleigh replied.

'Would it get someone into trouble?'

'I can't say nothing else.' Her manner took on a sort of moral defensiveness.

'All right,' said Jane. 'I understand.'

Ashleigh got up again and walked to the television set. There was a packet of cigarettes on it. She returned with it, sat on the coffee-table again, took out a cigarette and tucked it under her top lip so it hung down. There was a disposable lighter on the coffee-table and a plate with biscuit crumbs on it. Ashleigh lit up, inhaled and blew the smoke over her shoulder, away from her guest.

Jane saw that she was being considerate. 'Are you missing Jody?' she asked, frantic to soften the mood.

Ashleigh wrinkled her nose. 'Yeah, I suppose.' She gave a short laugh. 'Sounds terrible, that, don't it? "I suppose".'

The strange clanging noise reached them again, this time more loudly. 'I'm not—' Jane began. She had been going to say, 'I'm not here to judge you,' but she wasn't sure she'd mean it. Instead, she said, 'What are you going to do?'

'What – now?'

'With your life.' It sounded such a drippy-hippie thing to say. It wasn't what she'd been driving at either; she'd meant, 'What are you going to do now that you've found out where we live?'

'I'm not staying round here,' said Ashleigh, quickly.

'Where are you going?' Jane's response was too eager.

Ashleigh, though, seemed unperturbed. 'Holyhead,' she said. 'I've got an auntie there. And some friends.'

'What will you – I mean, is it nice there?'

'It's all right. I'll get looked after there, you see.'

Looked after? Jane decided against asking her what she meant.

But Ashleigh answered the question anyway. 'I've got a few problems. You've probably heard.'

'Yes, yes. I have.'

The strange noise came again. It was the loudest yet and this time there was a grainy scratching too.

'What *is* that?' asked Jane. Now Ashleigh's confession had been made, it seemed all right to ask her something trivial.

'What?' asked Ashleigh.

'That scratching and rattling.'

And there it was again, right on cue.

'Oh, *that*,' said Ashleigh. 'Here, I'll show you.' She got up and walked towards the internal door, pulled it open and beckoned Jane to follow her. 'Come on,' she said. 'It's OK.'

Jane was embarrassed now. Ashleigh had clearly seen her trepidation. She followed, appalled by her readiness to do as she was bidden. Home seemed very far away.

The door opened on to a short corridor with two more doors off it, one each side. That to the right, Jane could see, led in to the bathroom. The other could only be the bedroom. Its door, too, was ajar and when the scratching sound came again, with a papery pattering, she at last worked out what was making it. This penny dropping did not settle her, though. She was sure the bedroom contained something more.

Ashleigh didn't put the light on.

'Can you see him?' she asked Jane, in a low voice, and pressed her back against the doorframe to allow Jane a better view. Jane saw a double bed, a wardrobe, clothes on the floor, more clothes draped untidily over what appeared to be a drying rack, an open suitcase and, in the furthest corner, a large birdcage hanging from an iron stand. Inside it was a parrot. It greeted them by taking one of the cage's steel bars in its beak and tugging at it, violently and fruitlessly. Having gained their attention it became still and made a small, meek cheep, which Jane took as an avian sigh of despair.

'Cute, ain't he?' whispered Ashleigh.

Jane, though, wasn't looking at the bird. She was looking to its right and lower down to where the drying clothes were hung. As her eyes adjusted she saw that they were draped not over a laundry rack but the side of a baby's cot. And then, more movement, a churning of bedclothes and a man's surface-dreaming voice saying, 'The fuck, what the fuck . . .'

Ashleigh took Jane's arm. It was the first time she'd touched her. She led her out, easing the bedroom door closed as she left, and rushed her back to the living room. They both sat down again. Ashleigh's cigarette was still going. She flicked a little ash on to the plate. 'That was Budgie,' she said.

'Budgie?' Jane wasn't sure she meant the bird.

'It shuts him up, being in there,' Ashleigh said. 'It's

darker, see? He makes so much noise. Gets on my nerves.'

'Do you let him out?' asked Jane. They were talking about parrots. Yet this was not a dream.

'Not lately,' Ashleigh said. 'He won't go back, you see. Not till he's really hungry and, well, you know birds. Not exactly toilet-trained, are they?'

'How long have you had him?'

'Four, five years. He needs a new home, actually, now I'm going.'

'Don't look at me,' said Jane, before she had realised what she was saying. For God's sake, they were suddenly small-talking like two bored strangers on a train. Then something fell into place for Jane. She saw the parrot liberated from its cage yet still confined by the flat's rooms, flapping, crashing, squawking, perching on the edge of the cot, maybe. She imagined a forgotten baby's screams.

'Can I ask you, Ashleigh,' she said kindly, 'about Jody's father? Kirk something, isn't it? Kirk Lovell?'

Ashleigh stubbed out the cigarette. This wasn't quite such a happy journey now. 'What about him?' she asked.

'Do you know where he is?'

Ashleigh shrugged: 'Nah. He fucked off back to Woking, or wherever. That's where he come from. Ain't seen him since I was expecting.'

There was no pretence at nice manners now, but Ashleigh's bile was directed beyond present company into the ether of history and betrayal. I'm not her enemy, thought Jane. I'm her listener. 'Will you see him again, do you think?'

Ashleigh scoffed: 'Shouldn't think so. I'm not looking for him and he's not looking for me. If he was he'd have come to see me, wouldn't he? I haven't gone anywhere.'

The comment served as confirmation that this had been Jody's first home, where she had spent the earliest months of her life until things had got so bad she'd had to be taken away. Eight months old: crawling and pulling herself up on the furniture – this furniture, this chair Jane was sitting on right now? – emptying cupboards and drawers. And her lone parent? Out of it, out of the house, all over the place? That was the young woman before Jane now.

'What was he like, her dad?' asked Jane, 'Look, Ashleigh, say if you mind me asking.'

'It's OK. You can ask.'

A metaphorical bad smell entered one of Ashleigh's nostrils. Jane thought about the cot again. Had Ashleigh kept it because she couldn't bear to let her daughter go or was Jane's poetic streak leading her astray? It might be that Ashleigh simply hadn't got round to moving it out. You didn't have to be a drunk to let superfluous objects become part of your furniture.

'Was he older than you?'

'Oh, yeah. Twenty-five?'

And she had been just seventeen: sixteen when he'd screwed her, maybe.

Ashleigh said, 'Why do you wanna know all this?' She was reaching for another cigarette, her fingers searching the packet without looking.

'It's important,' Jane said, 'to have a proper picture of Jody's past.'

'For who? Jody or you?'

The question was delivered with a steady stare of a type Jane wasn't used to meeting. Rather than return it, she looked inside herself for what she guiltily assumed Ashleigh was seeking: petit bourgeois self-congratulation; middle-class do-gooder vanity. Ashleigh seemed to have thought better of the second cigarette. She was listening hard for Jane's reply.

'It's going to be important for Jody when she's older,' said Jane. The stress was talking now and it had lots to say. 'Maybe not very much older, actually. You know, I'm sure, that adopted children are told they're adopted, these days, and they often want to know where they came from. They have a right to know about their birth-parents. Some of them go to incredible lengths to find out everything they can about them. Jody might be like that. I mean, she might not, but what if she is? I just want, if she asks, to be able to tell her as much about you as I can. We hardly know anything. There wasn't even a picture of you. Why was that? I know you wanted her when she was a baby. I suppose I can't understand – I mean, I'm glad, but I can't understand . . . Can you just tell me?' she implored. 'What I really want to know is how you feel about her now.'

'What I feel,' said Ashleigh, 'what I feel . . .' Without warning the effort of expressing herself contorted Ashleigh's face, stark and disabling. She started again, each word a potential bomb that might accidentally blow up in her own face: 'I know she's going to be better off with you.'

'Oh, Ashleigh, do you really think so?' The sentence just gushed out of Jane. And now she knew what she'd not known when she'd arrived – that Ashleigh's words were the ones she'd wanted to hear. Vindication. Validation. These were things that only Ashleigh could give to her and Jane had wanted them desperately.

'Do I think so?' Ashleigh asked, almost sarcastically. 'What do you think?' she looked away. It was the only crack in her wall of finality.

But Jane could no more ignore it than she could fly. 'But

how do you know, Ashleigh? Are you sure you were right to let her go?'

Ashleigh bit her bottom lip and nodded, and for a second Jane saw Jody sitting there. Then Ashleigh said, 'I saw your husband out with her one day. In a café. I saw them there.'

Jane waited. There was no need to tell Ashleigh that she knew this already and that it was the reason Darren had traced her whereabouts; no need to put it to her that she'd been spying or stalking. None of that mattered now.

'He looked like a nice man,' said Ashleigh.

'You got that feeling, did you? From seeing him?'

'He was talking to her – all the time he seemed to be. And listening.'

'He *is* a nice man,' said Jane. 'A good man.'

'You don't get too many of them,' said Ashleigh, plaintively.

'Oh, shit, look at me,' said Jane. She was dissolving into tears. She staunched the flood hurriedly with a bit of T-shirt sleeve, a bit of arm, and said, 'Oh, shit', again, to make sure Ashleigh knew she felt a fool. Compared with the beleaguered creature opposite her, what did she, Jane, have to cry about? But Ashleigh just looked on, a bit puzzled, maybe a tiny bit amused. Then there was movement in the corridor: grudging footsteps, the sound of urination from on high.

Ashleigh spotted Jane's alarm, 'It's all right,' she said.

'I can go if you want me to.'

'Just wait a minute, yeah?'

The flush went, sending out a hollow reverberation. The women waited. No one appeared.

'I'll check on him,' said Ashleigh. She went softly back to the bedroom and returned almost immediately to say, 'It's all right, he's gone back to sleep.'

Jane could see, though, that Ashleigh was fretful. 'I ought to go,' she said, getting to her feet. If there was more that she wanted to know she had forgotten it. All she was clear about was that she didn't want to meet the man in Ashleigh's bed and that she needed some quiet time to gather herself before Darren got home, when she'd have to tell him what she'd been up to.

'You're all right, no worries,' said Ashleigh. 'You can stay.'

'No, honestly. I need to get home, pick up the kids . . .' Oh dear, now she'd put her foot in it.

'You've got others, right?' said Ashleigh. 'You know, your own ones.'

'Three.'

Ashleigh had an odd look on her face. It hinted at unfinished business. 'Why did you want another?' she asked.

The candour of the question halted Jane. And her answer . . . It was all too complicated for today. 'I just did,' she said feebly. 'For, oh, all sorts of reasons.'

Ashleigh nodded acceptingly. She looked slightly secretive.

'I really must go,' said Jane.

'My home was shit, you know,' Ashleigh said, 'where I grew up. It was shit.'

Jane had no idea what to say. She stood in silence, uselessly.

'And this is shit too,' said Ashleigh, looking round her flat with disgust. 'I admit that. It's true.'

Jane's only options seemed to be to agree or disagree and neither seemed a lot of use to Ashleigh. Of course, Jane could have invited her to tell all. Some other time, maybe?

'You teach the piano, don't you?' Ashleigh said.

'Yes,' said Jane, surprised. 'How did you know?'

'Anne told me. Yeah, I did go to see her. Only once after Jody'd gone to you. I just wanted to know a bit about you, like you wanted to know about me. And Anne, what it is, she likes to talk.'

'Yes, I know.'

'She never told me anything she shouldn't,' Ashleigh said, more insistent suddenly. Perhaps she'd remembered her earlier high-minded reticence. 'She never told me your name, or anything. Not your second name or where you live,except that it wasn't very far away and I'd guessed that anyway. But how I found you . . . I just looked you up.'

Jane was puzzled. Looked her up? How, if she didn't know her surname?

'On the Internet,' said Ashleigh. 'There's an Internet place round the corner. I looked for piano teachers. There's not too many in your area. It gave your address. So I just came up one day and had a look.' She seemed to be considering saying something else, but drew back. Hilarious, thought Jane, inexplicably: she found me the same way Maurice did – the only thing they'll ever have in common. Then Ashleigh protested, 'I'm not always pissed, you know,' and it was as though she'd been wanting to tell this to someone all her life. 'And the people in the Internet place, they're all right. They'll help you.'

The explanation was an implied apology. Jane didn't want one, but it gave her an opening through which she could politely resume leaving. 'Ashleigh,' she said, 'I'm very glad we've met. Thank you for talking to me.'

Ashleigh shrugged. Her hard-girl mask shifted back into place. She led the way to the door and opened it. As Jane approached it, she said, 'I haven't had a drink for a week.'

'Oh,' said Jane. 'Is that good?'

'It is for me,' said Ashleigh. She studied Jane thoughtfully. Again she had the air of someone with a little more to say.

'When do you go to Holyhead?' Jane asked.

'Soon. Tomorrow, maybe.'

Jane nodded towards the bedroom. 'What about . . . ?'

'He knows I'm going. It's no big deal. My auntie's paying my fare. It'll be easier for me up there. Away from temptation.'

Jane had been to Holyhead once, as a student, to catch the ferry to Dublin. She recalled only drabness and queues of cars. Was there anything to do there *but* drink?

'What's your auntie like?' she asked.

'She's kind. Quite strict. She's my dad's sister. That's where my dad's from, North Wales. He lives in Tottenham now, though.'

'Do you see him?'

'Now and then. It's cos of him I'm going, really. He sorted it for me.'

'What about your mum?'

'Oh, well.' Ashleigh looked at her toes. 'She's disowned me, basically. Can't blame her, I suppose.'

'Don't say that, Ashleigh.'

She said this with great feeling and Ashleigh, responding, looked immensely sad. 'I've got to stop, you see,' she said. 'I can't go on like this again. Not like before.'

Jane stepped out on to the concrete landing but she didn't rush away. Now that she'd left the flat she could afford to allow a little space for Ashleigh to step into, should she wish to venture further from her shell. This did not happen directly. But Ashleigh detained her in another way. 'Hold on a minute, will you?' she said, and went back inside. She returned with her cigarettes. 'Could you take these?' she said. 'I ought to give them up too.'

Jane accepted the packet, and, as she pocketed it, mentally weighed the risks of asking one more question. It felt risky. But Jane was emboldened now. She had survived her foray into the unknown and nothing could prevent her escape. 'Ashleigh, are you pregnant?'

Ashleigh sniffed. She looked round the empty landing, over her shoulder, and then at Jane. 'June,' she said. 'It's due in June.'

For the first time since they'd met, something like empathy filled the space between the two mothers as they faced each other from opposite sides of the doorway.

'It's a lovely name, Jody,' said Jane.

'Oh, thanks.' Ashleigh surrendered to a tiny smile.

'Goodbye then Ashleigh,' said Jane, walking away.

'Goodbye.'

CHAPTER TWELVE
24 FEBRUARY 2004

From the kitchen came the sound of a hand whisk beating the contents of a heavy Pyrex bowl and Darren warbling snatches of 'No Woman No Cry'.

'What's Daddy doing?' Jody asked.

'He's mixing up the pancakes,' said Jane, 'and singing very badly indeed.' They were out in the garden in the last of the light. Jane was thinking of the start of spring. Jody was thinking of, well, what things meant and where they fitted in.

'What *are* pancakes?' she asked earnestly.

'They're delicious,' replied Jane and then, correcting herself, elaborated carefully: 'They are lovely things to eat. You cook them in a big frying-pan.'

'What do they look like?'

'Flat and brown. And they're yummy in your tummy.'

Jody patted her belly. 'Mmm. Yummy in my tummy!'

'Mmm!' Jane agreed. She, too, patted her belly and let her hand lie on it to check for wistfulness, as she still did occasionally. She looked down at Jody who was gazing up at her with an inquisitive expression that she had worn more and more often recently. 'How many pancakes will you eat, Jody?' Jane asked. 'Will it be one or two or three?'

Jody processed the question carefully. Which answer would make Mummy most happy? 'Three!' she shouted, and jumped in the air as best she could, given that she was wearing wellington boots.

'Three?' gasped Jane. '*Three?*'

'Yes, three!' said Jody.

'Well, goodness me!' exclaimed Jane.

'Well, goodness me!' echoed Jody, cheekily.

'Well, goodness me!' came Darren's voice from the kitchen.

'Get on with your work, Daddy,' called Jane, sternly.

Jody looked concerned.

'I'm only teasing him,' said Jane, hastily, squatting down. 'Come here. I need a squeeze.' She held her hands out. Jody stepped between them and lowered herself expertly into a pick-me-up position. Jane scooped her into her arms and nuzzled her, saying, 'Ooh, what a big potato Jody is!'

'I'm not a potato!' Jody cried.

'You're very big, though.'

'Not *very* big, Mummy.'

'What are you, then, Jody?'

'I'm a little bit big.'

'Pancakes!' called Darren, from the kitchen.

'Quick, quick, Jody!' said Jane, putting her down. 'Go inside!'

Jody did as she was bidden and soon Jane could see through the glass of the back door that all four Grice-Ransome children were gathered round the table hungrily. She would join them shortly. But first she wanted to enjoy a few more moments alone in the dusk. There was much to contemplate, not least some intangible feeling of unity because all those Jane cared for most would be settling down to the same ritual. In Kent Jeffrey might not be tossing the pancakes this year, as he had for as long as Jane could remember, but he would be eating them unaided at the table, with Dorothy and Julia for company.

Along the road, Maggie's kitchen would be swimming in children and high-calorie fillings while Nigel took cover somewhere. In Lancashire, Maurice Pinder, too, would surely be dining in the British manner and trying to decide with which pieces to entertain his hosts later. 'Jerusalem', perhaps? Or 'Any Old Iron'? Jane had taught him both. Later, she might even play them herself.

'Come on, Mummy!' shouted Clyde.

'Just a minute!' Jane replied.

Steam was gathering on the inside of the window but Jane could still see her five fellow family members and take some sneaky, voyeuristic pleasure from knowing that the more the daylight died the less they could see of her. Exploiting her deepening invisibility, she pulled a letter from the back pocket of her jeans. It was written on a single sheet of pale pink writing-paper contained in a pale pink envelope addressed simply to 'Jody' care of the adoption agency. Jane unfolded the letter and squinted at the page.

Dear Jody,
I am sending you this letter because I am your birth mummy and I want you to know some things about me. My name is Ashleigh Jones. I am 21 years old. At the moment I live far away from you. But that doesn't mean I don't think about you, because I do. Maybe when you're much older you would like to meet me. I think I would like to meet you. Until then I hope you like the picture of me.

With Love From Ashleigh.

Jane slipped the letter back into her pocket. Later she would put it in the same safe place as the photo, a posed snapshot of Ashleigh looking a little less haunted than in the one taken by Anne and a little fuller in the cheeks. For the time being she and Darren were going to keep these things from their new daughter, maybe until late summer after Ashleigh's baby was born, maybe later, depending on Jody, depending on Ashleigh, depending on what tomorrow might bring. It was still a case of taking one day at a time. But Jody's recent yesterdays had given good cause for optimism: her fourth birthday; her first Grice-Ransome Christmas; her tentative interest in Darren's bird box; each little piece of progress she had made. Jane was full of expectation. And as she started for the kitchen she noticed in a flowerbed the year's first crocuses venturing overground. It was, of course, extremely corny to interpret this as an omen for the future. But Jane decided she would anyway.

You can buy any of these other bestselling
Headline books from your bookshop
or *direct from the publisher*.

FREE P&P AND UK DELIVERY
(Overseas and Ireland £3.50 per book)

Single Men	Dave Hill	£6.99
Getting Out Of The House	Isla Dewar	£7.99
Two Of A Kind	Mina Ford	£6.99
Eleven on Top	Janet Evanovich	£6.99
The Eternal City	Domenica de Rosa	£7.99
The Lost Garden	Mary Stanley	£6.99
How Will I Know	Sheila O'Flanagan	£6.99
Olivia's Luck	Catherine Alliott	£7.99
Dad's Life	Dave Hill	£6.99
The Chase	Candida Clark	£7.99

TO ORDER SIMPLY CALL THIS NUMBER

01235 400 414

or visit our website: www.madaboutbooks.com

Prices and availability subject to change without notice.